PRAISE FOR THE NOVELS OF

MAYA BANKS

"Heated investigative romantic suspense . . . Intense, transfixing."
—*Midwest Book Review*

"Definitely a recommended read . . . filled with friendship, passion, and most of all, a love that grows beyond just being friends."
—*Fallen Angel Reviews*

"Grabbed me from page one and refused to let go until I read the last word . . . When a book still affects me hours after reading it, I can't help but Joyfully Recommend it!"
—*Joyfully Reviewed*

"I guarantee I will reread this book many times over, and will derive as much pleasure as I did in the first reading each and every subsequent time."
—*Novelspot*

"An excellent read that I simply did not put down . . . A fantastic adventure . . . covers all the emotional range."
—*The Road to Romance*

"Searingly sexy and highly believable."
—*Romantic Times*

sweet temptation

MAYA BANKS

Berkley Books / New York

THE BERKLEY PUBLISHING GROUP
Published by the Penguin Group
Penguin Group (USA) Inc.
375 Hudson Street, New York, New York 10014, USA

Penguin Group (Canada), 90 Eglinton Avenue East, Suite 700, Toronto, Ontario M4P 2Y3, Canada
(a division of Pearson Penguin Canada Inc.) • Penguin Books Ltd, 80 Strand, London WC2R 0RL,
England • Penguin Ireland, 25 St Stephen's Green, Dublin 2, Ireland (a division of Penguin
Books Ltd) • Penguin Group (Australia), 707 Collins Street, Melbourne, Victoria 3008, Australia
(a division of Pearson Australia Group Pty Ltd) • Penguin Books India Pvt Ltd, 11 Community
Centre, Panchsheel Park, New Delhi–110 017, India • Penguin Group (NZ), 67 Apollo Drive,
Rosedale, Auckland 0632, New Zealand (a division of Pearson New Zealand Ltd) • Penguin Books,
Rosebank Office Park, 181 Jan Smuts Avenue, Parktown North 2193, South Africa • Penguin China,
B7 Jiaming Center, 27 East Third Ring Road North, Chaoyang District, Beijing 100020, China

Penguin Books Ltd., Registered Offices: 80 Strand, London WC2R 0RL, England

This book is an original publication of The Berkley Publishing Group.

This is a work of fiction. Names, characters, places, and incidents either are the product of the author's
imagination or are used fictitiously, and any resemblance to actual persons, living or dead, business
establishments, events, or locales is entirely coincidental. The publisher does not have any control over
and does not assume any responsibility for author or third-party websites or their content.

PUBLISHING HISTORY
Heat trade paperback edition / April 2010
Berkley trade paperback edition / January 2013

Berkley trade paperback ISBN: 978-0-425-26698-4

The Library of Congress has catalogued the Heat trade paperback edition of this book as follows:

Banks, Maya.
Sweet temptation / Maya Banks.—Heat trade pbk. ed.
p.   cm.
ISBN: 978-0-425-23258-3
I. Title
PS3602.A643S85   2010
813'.6—dc22
2009041105

PRINTED IN THE UNITED STATES OF AMERICA

10   9   8   7   6   5   4   3   2   1

sweet temptation

PROLOGUE

Angelina Moyano watched from a distance as Micah Hudson stood over the two headstones in the small graveyard. She studied him from behind a large oak tree, her small hands gripping the rough bark. It was always like this. At dawn he'd come to honor their memories. Just as he did every year.

The sun's rays were barely peeking over the horizon, but the Florida humidity was already thick and heavy, each breath a struggle in the cloying heat. She chanced a look over her shoulder, damning her paranoia that she'd been followed, but she couldn't afford to take chances. Seeing nothing, she turned her attention back to Micah.

He knelt at Hannah's grave and carefully laid a single yellow rose, her favorite, just below the marble slab that marked her death. He kissed his thumb and the ridge of his forefinger then laid his hand over the flat ground.

Angelina sucked in her breath. It was different this year. Before he'd always stood there looking so haunted, his eyes filled with grief and regret. This year . . . this year he seemed to be saying good-bye.

Her eyes filled with tears when he turned to David's grave and drew a simple rosary from his pocket. He kissed the beads and then laid them at her brother's headstone.

Sadness knotted her throat. She missed them too. She missed Micah, but he was as lost to her as David and Hannah. Maybe now he was ready. Ready to let go. He had grieved long enough. *She* had grieved long enough.

He rose, shoving his hands into his pockets. For a long moment he simply stood there as the early morning light grew a little brighter.

Warmth flooded the place where Micah stood, and Angelina took it as a sign that it was time.

"I love you," she whispered, letting the wind carry her words away.

When he finally turned and walked back toward his truck, she waited only long enough that she wouldn't be seen, before she darted back to her car. She would have to hurry if she was going to get to Twilight before he did.

It was where he always went after he paid his homage to his former wife and David, his best friend. Only Angelina understood the need that drove him. Only she understood his pain, knew his private demons. She would help him because she could do nothing else. She'd loved him far too long. Maybe now he could finally love her in return.

She took the shortest route to the club and whipped into the back parking lot ten minutes later. Though it operated twenty-four hours a day, at this time of the morning it was usually empty, and she knew that was one of the reasons Micah always chose this time to come.

Grabbing her bag, she hurried inside the employee entrance and checked with Rose, who manned the front door.

"I'm here, Rose. Just give me a minute to change. If he gets here, put him in room one."

"Hey, baby. I see him walking up now, so scoot on back so he doesn't see you."

"Thanks, Mama Rose." She blew a kiss to the older woman and ran for the dressing room.

She didn't go for garish dress-up. No leather, no high-heeled boots. No, save for the mask that protected her identity, she went with black jeans and a long-sleeved black shirt. Her long, dark hair was drawn into a braid and tucked down her shirt. She was as nondescript as they came.

The last item was the leather mask that covered her from the neck up. Only her eyes were visible, and they blended with the dark leather, dark, almost black.

David would have killed her if he were alive. He and Hannah would both be horrified that David's little sister was for all practical purposes a surrogate daughter to a woman who owned one of Miami's most successful bondage clubs.

Micah would look at her with those dark eyes and ask her what the hell a little girl like her was doing in a place like this.

And it was all because of him.

A soft knock at her door had her whirling around as Mama Rose stuck her head in.

"He's ready for you."

Angelina nodded and walked out the door and down the hall to one of the flogging rooms. When she entered, she sucked in her breath so hard her chest hurt.

Her reaction to him never dimmed. The sight of such a powerful, proud man standing in the middle of the room, bared to the waist, his hands high above him, tied to a spreader. He was utterly magnificent.

On another man, his pose might seem submissive. Weak. Only she knew better. Underneath the seemingly calm surface was a man who seethed with emotion. Dark and boiling. And she would call it to the surface.

His head rose when he heard her footsteps. There was a vulnerability to his eyes she hadn't seen in the past. As if the emotion bubbled that much closer to the surface. Before he'd buried it, only releasing it with his pain.

Not everyone would understand his needs. But she did. Oh, how she did. She would set him free. She would give him what he needed.

"I need . . . Don't go easy," he said in a low voice.

She nodded her acceptance of his request. She alone understood his need for this kind of pain. They were more alike than he would ever know.

She uncoiled the whip and let the end fall to the floor as she circled behind him. Such beauty. His back was broad, his waist lean and narrow. The muscles tensed and bunched between his shoulder blades as he readied himself for her strike.

How long she had practiced, relentlessly perfecting her method, so she would never disappoint him. He was safe in her hands.

The first lash landed against his skin with a deafening crack. He jerked but quickly righted himself and went still, awaiting the next. She flicked her wrist again, exerting just the right amount of force, and placed an identical stripe across from the first.

She forced herself to relax, to not allow the welling emotion to bubble up. Calmly and methodically she kissed his back with the lash, watching as he jumped and bowed under the whip.

Sweat glistened on his back, dampened his hair until it fell in limp curls past his neck. Still she continued, sensing he needed more. She striped one side then the other, working a path down to his waist.

As she worked her way back up, blood beaded and shone in the low light. Finally. Release. Lightly, like a lover's kiss, she whispered the whip across his shoulders until they were slick with blood.

It was like making a cut in a festering wound. The relief was profound, as pressure—and pain—escaped the seething cauldron. His hands clenched in their bonds, his wrists flexing as he raised his head, looking upward as if he was seeking redemption.

With every stroke, she lavished him with her love. It would have seemed bizarre to someone who didn't understand. An unacceptable outlet for many. But this was his way. She accepted it, as she did him.

A heavy sigh escaped him, the only sound he made the entire time. His shoulders drooped, and she knew it was enough. She let the whip fall and walked around to face him.

His eyes were closed, but his cheeks were streaked with tears. Her own eyes clouded with moisture. He'd never cried for them. Not at the funeral. Not at the graves. Not afterward when he'd driven her home. And then he'd simply disappeared, dealing with his grief as he did everything else. Alone.

She ached to hold him, to tell him it was all right, that Hannah and David loved him too. That *she* loved him. That he didn't have to be alone any longer.

Instead she stepped forward and cupped his face lovingly in her hands. She pressed a kiss to his forehead and whispered in a husky voice he'd never recognize, "*Vaya en paz.*"

Go in peace.

As she stepped away, he looked up at her with glazed, unfocused eyes. Another tear slipped down his cheek, marking a raw trail on his face.

"Thank you," he said in a husky voice.

She simply nodded, knowing that even if she dared, she wouldn't have been able to speak around the knot in her throat. She kissed the shaft of the whip and laid it carefully at his feet.

She left the room on shaky legs, knowing Mama Rose waited to free Micah and to attend him in whatever way necessary. She also knew he'd refuse the older woman's attentions and would be gone within minutes.

She shed her mask, for the last time. It was all she could do not to run back down the hall and throw her arms around him, beg him to take her with him. Letting him go instilled in her a fierce ache. Because this time he wouldn't be back. With that realization, she knew that it was now or never for her. She'd given Micah the time he needed to heal. Now it was up to her to go to him. Show him it was okay to love again.

He might not be coming back to Miami, but there was nothing to stop her from going to Houston. She had to go. She couldn't stay here. It wasn't safe, and Micah was all she had to run to.

CHAPTER 1

HOUSTON, TEXAS

He didn't see her right away. His view of her was obscured by the typical eclectic mix of sexcapades. Business as usual on a Saturday night at The House. The common room where people met to play and act on their fantasies was alive with the sounds and smells of sex.

Micah Hudson sauntered farther into the room, his gaze scanning the erotic mix of flesh. It struck him—as he paused to stare at a beautiful woman being pleasured by an equally beautiful woman—that he was bored. Restless. Cagey even.

His concentration left the pair when he heard the unmistakable slap of leather against skin and a breathless sound of pleasure that rose and quivered around his ears. Beckoning him. Where?

And then he saw her. Small, curvy and striking. Her nude body glowed in the soft lighting, her skin a light creamy brown, hinting at Hispanic heritage. Her hair slid like a waterfall over her shoulders, parted down her spine by the slither of a whip as it met her flesh again.

He couldn't see her face, and suddenly he wanted to very much. Were her eyes closed in ecstasy, her face soft and warm with pleasure?

Her rounded buttocks shook slightly as her body swayed in the grip of the whip. Her feet moved, arched and then replanted as she braced herself. It was much like a dance, her rhythm intoxicating and erotic.

High above her head, her hands flexed and tightened against the rope that held her wrists captive. Her skin rippled over her shoulder blades as they dipped and caused a slight hollow. Then she relaxed again, and her low moan drifted to him once again.

Beautiful. She was fucking beautiful.

Desire whispered through his veins, gathering momentum, moving faster, surging through his groin. His dick tightened painfully, and he shifted to alleviate the uncomfortable tension.

No longer able to stand watching from afar, he moved forward, working his way through the crowd. Around the people watching the flogging. He circled so that he could see her profile.

Disappointment settled into his chest when he saw the half mask covering her eyes.

His gaze traveled over her luscious, plump lips that were perfectly bowed and untarnished by lipstick. They parted again as another sensuous gasp escaped from her throat.

He could no longer hear the slap of leather or the conversation around him. The sounds of the other occupants fell away, and all he could hear was *her*.

Her breasts, high and firm, smaller than he usually liked, jiggled when she endured another blow. The nipples, brown, darker than her skin, erect and puckered, soft looking . . . What would they taste like? How would they feel in his mouth? Between his fingers?

His fingers curled. He could feel the slight weight of the globes in his palms as surely as if he were standing in front of her, measuring their size with his hands.

She was a perfect hourglass, her hips slightly wider than her waist, her belly flat and drawing attention to the soft curls between her thighs. They were dark like the fall of hair spilling over her shoulders, and they shielded her femininity, revealing nothing of what lay beneath.

But he could imagine. Oh yes, he could feel her damp heat as he parted the tender folds and delved beyond the silky curls. He'd stroke a finger over her clit and then trail lower to her center, stroking inward, feeling the clasp of her pussy sucking him deeper.

Jesus. Sweat beaded his brow, and his cock swelled and strained against his fly.

What about her did it for him? It wasn't as if he didn't see women like this in The House all the time. Was it the mystery? Was it her arresting beauty? Or maybe it was the way she arched and bowed her body, seeking the kiss of the whip even as she flinched away.

She was into it in a big way. Deep. Her eyes were closed, but he was sure they were dark like the rest of her. Those sumptuous lips puckered and parted, opened and closed. She made the most delicious, arousing noises, and he wasn't the only one affected.

Other men watched, as transfixed by the sight as Micah was. Lust blazed in their eyes. They wanted her, but so did he.

Oh yeah, so did he.

He started forward again, his entire concentration on her, on the man making her writhe beneath the whip.

Cole looked up as Micah neared, and he paused, whip held high in the air. And then as if sensing his approach, the woman turned her head and opened her eyes.

Liquid heat exploded through his body. Her eyes were so expressive, so bright with passion, and she didn't look away once their gazes collided. He could drown in those dark pools.

Her lips trembled, and for a moment he sensed deep vulnerability, a fact that made him suddenly fiercely possessive.

No, he couldn't look away any more than she could, and he waited for what he wanted. Acceptance.

Her small, pink tongue flicked out, licking over her lips in a sudden, almost nervous motion, and then she nodded, need firing in her eyes.

Cole reached out to touch her shoulder, and it was all Micah could do not to react violently. He didn't want Cole—or anyone else—touching her. She was his for this moment.

"Are you sure?" Cole said in a low voice only she and Micah could hear.

Her gaze flickered, and she turned briefly to look at Cole. Again she nodded, and her eyes flashed as she refocused her attention on Micah.

Those lips. God, those lips. He was dying to taste them, and suddenly he knew he had to. Even as he took the whip Cole extended and stepped forward, his movements were jerky and urgent.

He cupped her jaw in one hand, slid his fingers over the softness of her cheek, then slanted his lips over hers and took them hungrily.

He swallowed her gasp. Her taste exploded onto his tongue as he swept it over her mouth, inward, stroking deep. Sweet. Warm. Soft like a woman should taste.

Her tongue met his, boldly tasting him in return. Hot and wet, they dueled, neither backing down. An electric current raced up his spine, ricocheted off the base of his skull and sizzled over his nerve endings like a bolt of lightning.

Starved for air, he yanked himself away, his breaths coming in quick, jerky pants. She stared at him in wonder and swayed against the bonds holding her hands.

He took one step back and slowly circled until he stared at the slim column of her spine.

"Dance for me."

The whip uncoiled and then came alive, arcing and then landing with a sharp crack. A glow rose on her skin, and her erotic moan hovered, sweet and arousing.

The room quieted, and her soft cries grew louder, more frequent. Moans. Sighs. A woman on the verge of climax.

She captivated him. Mesmerized by the sight of her reacting to his whip, his touch, his command, she excited him on a primitive level. She touched him in places that hadn't felt warmth in a long time.

He didn't understand it, but he latched on to it like a man starving.

The whip coiled and snapped, hissing and then landing, the welt rising on her skin. She rose up on tiptoe, her body straining even as she arched her back, waiting, wanting another lash.

The muscles in her slender arms rippled, and her fingers splayed out, stretching and then curling into her fists again. Faster, she moved in time with the lashes, dancing an erotic rhythm that held the room in her thrall. Race to release. Micah watched in fascination as he worked her into a heated frenzy.

The last lash fell just as a cry of sweet ecstasy burst from deep inside her. The sound was primal and beautiful, and it instilled an ache in his gut that extended to his balls. He was painfully erect, his cock bulging against the zipper of his jeans. He wanted nothing more than to shove his pants down and bury his cock between her ass cheeks. He wanted her ass, her pussy, her mouth. He wanted this woman.

No longer able to keep from touching her, he ran his fingers over the thin welts crisscrossing her back. She moaned softly, leaning into his caress. He smoothed his palms up her back and then under her arms and down her sides.

Wanting to look into her eyes, to see her again, he walked around her, letting his hand trail over her skin until his fingers rested on her belly and he stood over her.

"Look at me," he said huskily.

He lifted his hand to her chin, tilted it up so her gaze met his. "You're so beautiful."

Her lips curved upward in a tremulous smile, and he traced the fullness of her bottom lip with his thumb.

He dropped his head to hers, their mouths touching. He paused, taking it slower this time, wanting to savor her sweetness.

"I want you. I want you so much it's killing me."

His voice was hoarse and needy, but he didn't care. He only knew if he didn't have this woman, he'd go crazy.

He reached up to untie her hands, and when they were free, she faltered, her knees buckling. He caught her to him, her body melting into his. She felt so damn good, and his zipper was trying to brand a permanent tattoo on his dick.

Wanting to feel the silk of her hair, he dragged his hand through it, enjoying the sensation of it sliding through his fingers.

"Will you come home with me?" he murmured.

His lips were just centimeters from hers. Her breath blew over his face, and he inhaled.

She stared back at him, desire warming her eyes.

He tucked a long strand of her hair behind her ear, and his thumb snagged on the mask. He wanted to see her, wanted to know more about this woman he was determined to possess tonight.

She uttered a sharp protest and raised her hands to grip his, all the while shaking her head in mute denial. She tried to turn away, but the mask slipped and caught in her hair.

A strangled sound erupted from her throat and she hastily backed away, but not before he saw her features.

Shock hit him square in the balls.

He was going to be sick.

Angel. David's sister.

Dear God, what had he done?

She stared back at him, frozen, her eyes wide and almost frightened. The beautiful naked woman standing in front of him was quickly replaced by images of Angelina at sixteen. Innocent, with a dazzling, flirtatious smile, the kind that a kid wore when she thought the world was hers on a silver platter. He couldn't conjure an image of her older. She was stuck as that sixteen-year-old kid. How old was she now anyway?

David's sister. Goddamn it.

Fury quickly replaced his utter disbelief. "Angelina, what the *fuck?*"

CHAPTER 2

$\mathcal{M}$icah grabbed Angelina's shoulders and pulled her close to him to shield her from view, but that was damn near impossible with a room full of people and her bare-assed naked.

He yanked his head around, looking for something—anything—to cover her with.

"Where are your goddamn clothes?"

"Micah, stop," she protested.

The shock of hearing her speak momentarily halted him. The slightly accented speech reminded him so damn much of David. Her voice was huskier than it was when she was younger. Sexier. Fuck!

He shook his head and resumed his search, his gaze lighting on a discarded sheet from one of the beds. It would do.

Dragging her with him, he strode over to snatch the sheet from the floor. He draped it over her shoulders and then wrapped it completely around her, holding the ends as he looked for an escape route.

"Micah, stop! What are you doing?"

There was a spark of anger in her brown eyes, but he ignored that. She could be pissed all she wanted, but he was getting her the hell out of here.

Now that she was at least covered, he herded her along the edge of the room toward the door. They entered the hallway that led to the stairs, and he all but dragged her down the staircase and into the hall leading to the front entrance.

"Where are you taking me?" she asked.

There was trust in her tone, and it pissed him off more than finding her here. He'd just flogged her, seen her naked, lusted over . . . touched her. For God's sake. This never should have happened. He hated himself, but he was angrier with her. She shouldn't be here. She shouldn't even know places like this existed.

"Out of here," he said gruffly. "Not another word until I get you home. I swear, Angelina, I don't know what the hell you thought you were doing, but it ends right here, right now."

One of Damon's burly security men stepped in front of the door and folded his beefy arms over his chest as he stared belligerently at Micah.

"Goddamn it, Mav, get out of the way," Micah swore.

"Micah, what the fuck are you doing?"

Micah turned around to see his good friend and the owner of The House, Damon Roche, striding down the hall from his office. He sighed, irritated with the interruption. He kept a firm grip on Angelina's arm while he waited for Damon to say his piece.

"Well?" Damon asked when he stopped a few feet away. His eyes were narrowed, the classic Damon annoyed expression, but he didn't say anything further. He merely pinned Micah with an expectant stare and waited.

"Well fucking what?"

Damon made a move toward Angelina, and Micah pulled her back. The sheet slid down over her shoulders, but she held the ends tightly around her breasts. Her hair was pulled around and hung down one side, and Micah could see the marks—his marks—on her back, and the knot grew bigger in his gut.

He yanked the sheet back up, covering the bare expanse of her skin as if that would somehow erase what had happened just minutes before.

"You want to tell me what the hell you're doing?" Damon demanded. "Jesus Christ, Micah, have you lost your mind? Let her go. Now."

Micah scowled at the challenge in Damon's voice. Mav took a step forward and reached for Angelina. It didn't matter that Damon and Mav were obviously trying to protect Angelina.

"Don't you fucking touch her."

Mav looked to Damon for guidance, and Damon held his hand up to stay his security man.

"You can't come in here, grab one of my club members—hell, you can't pull this shit here with anyone, member or not—and drag her out of here against her will. What's come over you, Micah?"

Micah glanced at Angelina and wondered why the hell she was being so quiet. She hadn't said much more than a few words. He couldn't even conjure guilt over the notion that she was unwilling. She sure as hell hadn't been unwilling when she'd given him that sultry invitation with those deep brown eyes. Christ, she'd had him whip her. He wanted to puke.

"This is a private matter between me and Angelina," Micah said.

"I'm not letting you leave here with her," Damon said calmly.

Angelina put her hand on Damon's arm. It looked small and

dainty in comparison, and all Micah could think was that those hands had been tied together while he marked her naked body.

"It's all right, Damon," she said in a low voice.

She trembled in Micah's grip, and he loosened his hold. His gaze dropped over her arm to make sure there were no marks from his fingers. He'd done enough damage for one night. Now he just wanted to get her out of this place as fast as humanly possible.

"Do you know Micah, Angelina?" Damon asked, his expression skeptical. "You don't have to go with him, friend of mine or not. My first responsibility is to my members here. I wouldn't allow any woman to be manhandled as Micah has done you."

"Member?" Micah bit out. "Are you telling me Angelina is a god-damn member?"

He looked to her for confirmation, but she wouldn't look at him. She was staring at Damon, her expression calm.

"I know him," she said simply. "He won't hurt me. He's angry because he doesn't understand."

"Understand?" His head was going to explode. "I understand that I'm getting you the hell out of this place, and under no circumstances are you to ever set foot in here again." He glared at Damon as he said the last. "And I expect you to see to it."

"What's going on here?" Damon demanded. "This isn't like you, Micah. I won't let you walk out of here until one of you provides me with an acceptable explanation."

"She's David's *sister*!"

Damon's eyes flickered as understanding dawned. "I see."

Micah made a sound of disgust. "No, you don't see. Christ, Damon, you're letting teenagers in here now?"

Angelina turned to him, one finely arched eyebrow creeping upward. "I'm twenty-three years old, Micah. Hardly a teenager.

Certainly not in need of a babysitter, though you seem keen to sign up for the job."

He stared back at her in disbelief. Confusion jacked through his mind like a buzz saw. Twenty-three? How had she gotten from a sixteen-year-old to a woman of twenty-three? Had it really been so long? How could he have lost so many years?

"At least let her dress," Damon said quietly. "There's no need to take her out like this. I'll send Maverick up for her clothing." Then he glanced at Angelina. "Do you want to leave with him, Angelina? I'll be more than happy to provide a ride home for you. I can arrange for one of my men to take your car home."

"She's leaving with me," Micah growled. "Now, if we can dispense with the chitchat, I'd like us to be on our way."

Damon motioned for Maverick to go upstairs to retrieve her clothes, and then he reached for Angelina's hand.

"You can change in there," he said, pointing to one of the rooms a few feet away.

She looked expectantly toward Micah and then dropped her gaze pointedly to his hand on her arm. Grudgingly he let it fall away.

As Damon opened the door, Maverick appeared holding Angelina's clothes. Clutching the sheet tightly around her with one hand, she took the jeans, shirt and shoes and disappeared into the room.

Damon immediately rounded on Micah. "I don't care what your problems are in the future, don't ever let something like this happen again."

Micah ground his lips together and tried to hold his temper in check.

"I'm going to assume you had no idea who Angelina was when you gave her membership."

Damon's eyebrow went up. "There are a few things you need to remember, Micah. This is my club. You don't vet my members. You don't make the decisions. And you sure as hell don't take advantage of your membership here. Angelina is an adult. She was reviewed just like any other person applying for membership here."

"Did. You. Know. Who. She. Was?"

Damon sighed. "Of course not, Micah. How the hell would I? You've only told me cursory details of your friendship with David and the unique relationship you and David both shared with Hannah. I'm not even sure you ever told me what David's last name was, so how on earth would I associate a beautiful young woman named Angelina Moyano with your past?"

Micah sighed. "You're right. I'm sorry, man."

He dragged a hand through his hair and shook his head in disbelief. He was still reeling from the shock of the whole fucking night.

Damon looked skeptically at him. "Can I trust you to see her home or do I need to take care of it?"

Micah scowled. "When the hell have I ever been a threat to a woman? She's coming with me because she and I have a hell of a lot to discuss. Namely what she's doing here in Houston, why she didn't come to me before now, and what the *fuck* she's doing here allowing men to see her naked, to touch her and mark her."

He shook his head again, too furious to continue.

"Goddamn it, Damon. I was the one who flogged her. I lusted over her from the time I walked into that room. I kissed her, I touched her and then I marked her. I asked her to come home with me because I wanted to fuck her. And then the damn mask came off and I'm staring at David's kid sister. David would roll over in his grave if he had any idea what I did."

Damon's mouth twisted in sympathy. "Try to remember she's not the teenager you have set in your mind. She's a woman now. A stunning woman who's obviously in charge of her sexuality."

Micah made a strangled sound that got stuck in his throat. It was all he could do not to childishly cover his ears and eyes.

"Fuck me."

Damon laughed then clapped a hand on Micah's shoulder.

The door opened and Angelina stepped into the hallway, her eyes hooded and wary as she stared back at Micah. As beautiful as she was naked, she looked just as gorgeous fully clothed. Her jeans rode low on her hips, hugging every curve all the way down. She wore a simple sleeveless tank that showed a hint of the outline of her nipples and fit her slim waist like a glove.

"So where are you taking me?" she asked.

The question was asked innocently enough, but there was still enough reserve in her expression that he knew she was uneasy.

He worked to remove his scowl, but he finally gave up. She needed to know just how stupid she'd been for coming in here, and he wasn't in the mood to soothe any feathers he may have ruffled.

He grabbed her hand, irritated with the way her slight fingers curled trustingly around his.

"Where I'm taking you is home. My place. You and I are going to have a long talk."

CHAPTER 3

$\mathcal{A}$ngelina glanced over at Micah as he roared into the parking lot of his apartment complex. Of course it wouldn't have occurred to him to take her to where she was staying. He wanted to bawl her out on his turf.

She had to suppress a smile as he turned to her, his scowl still in place. It wasn't as if she hadn't expected stiff resistance. He was Micah after all, and it would take more than one night to make him see her as anything other than David's little sister.

"Inside," he directed as he opened his door.

Angelina reached for the handle and hopped out of his truck before he could come around to collect her. She met his gaze evenly, and his scowl deepened as he clasped her elbow and guided her toward the building.

At the door, he fumbled with the keys, shoved it open and herded her inside. He flipped the lights on, and she blinked as she glanced around.

The place looked so sterile and uninviting, as if no one really lived here. It reminded her of her own hotel room, where she lived out of a suitcase and never made herself at home.

It wasn't the Micah she was used to. She'd spent a lot of happy hours at his, David's and Hannah's house. But then Hannah had made it that way.

Her mouth drooped, and she wiped at it in an attempt to remove the unhappiness that arose when she thought of David and Hannah.

Micah dropped his keys on the coffee table then spun her around to meet his gaze.

"Now suppose you tell me what the fuck is going on here, Angel."

She smiled at his use of the nickname he'd given her. Butterflies danced in her stomach until she was left with a queasy sensation. How much to tell him? What was she supposed to say?

I'm running, Micah. To you. I need you. I love you. I'm scared. I love you. I want you to love me too.

None of it seemed like a good idea. She sounded desperate and not in control, and the last thing she wanted to do was face Micah with any disadvantage.

"Why are you so angry?" she asked in an effort to diffuse some of the explosive tension.

His jaw twitched suspiciously. "Okay, let me start with the basics here." He dropped his hand from her elbow and began counting off on his fingers. "One, what the hell were you doing in The House? Two, why didn't you immediately divulge your identity when I walked up? Three, what are you doing in Houston? Four, why didn't you tell me you were in town? Five, the coincidence of you showing up at the same club I frequent is staggering. I don't believe for a moment you didn't know you'd see me which brings me back to number one."

"Wow. Just wow, Micah."

She trembled with anger. Her fingers curled into fists at her sides as hurt and an old sense of betrayal washed through her all over again.

No longer able to keep eye contact with him, she turned sharply, her chest heaving. It was more difficult than she'd thought. She wanted to lash out at him, ask him why he'd left her.

He turned her around again, cupped her chin in his hand and forced her to look at him. "This can't come as a surprise to you, Angel. How did you *think* I'd react? Don't look at me with those hurt eyes and play the victim here."

She tried to step away, but he held her firm.

"Tell me something, Micah. If the mask had stayed on, would you have taken me home and had sex with me?" she taunted. "You wanted me. You can't deny it."

His eyes blazed with a mixture of heat and anger, as though he remembered all too well his reaction.

They were interrupted by a knock on the door. Micah scowled and then shot her a warning stare. "Don't move."

She shrugged and watched him walk away. A sigh escaped, and her shoulders slumped downward. Damn it, none of this had gone the way she'd planned. She hadn't intended him to find out her identity the way he had. Maybe the entire idea had been stupid, but she'd wanted to make him see the woman she was before she revealed her identity.

A moment later, he returned, her keys jingling in his hand. He slapped them down on the coffee table next to his.

"Damon had your car brought here."

She nodded.

He stared at her for a long moment, and then he closed the distance between them, this time turning her away from him. His fingers trailed over her back and pulled at her shirt.

"Are you all right?" he asked quietly. "Did I hurt you badly?"

She sucked in her breath when his palm met her bare flesh and soothed over the welts that still heated her back.

"No, you didn't hurt me," she said huskily.

His hand stilled on her back, and he hastily arranged her shirt. There was too much tension emanating from him. It was thick and unwieldy between them.

She turned and without giving him any warning pushed into his arms, hugging him tight. He tensed even more but didn't push her away.

"I missed you so much," she choked out.

"Hell," he muttered as he wrapped his arms around her.

"Why did you leave?"

It burst from her before she could call it back. She rested her forehead on his shoulder thinking how badly she'd screwed up this entire reunion.

He grasped her shoulders and gently pulled her away from him. "Listen to me, honey. You and I have a hell of a lot to discuss. I want you to sit down and talk to me, okay?"

She allowed him to guide her down onto the couch.

"Are you hungry? Thirsty?"

She shook her head.

He retreated to an armchair diagonal to the couch and sank down with a heavy sigh. His unruly hair dangled below his ears, and he dragged a hand through the slight curls until it pulled them away from his face. The diamond in his left ear glinted in the light, an earring she'd given him for Christmas. Would he even remember that fact?

"I couldn't stay, Angel. You of all people should know that."

"No, I don't know that. Or maybe I do and I'm still angry," she admitted. "I had no one, Micah. You, David and Hannah were my only family. They died and you left. Can you even try to understand how that made me feel? I was alone, scared to death, and my world had been turned upside down."

"You had the force," Micah said gruffly. "They never turned their back on family. They would have done anything you needed."

Anger heated her veins, and her pulse thrummed fiercely. "Would they? They all thought David betrayed you, that he was leaving with *your* wife when they had their accident. They weren't lining up to offer me anything. To them I was the sister of the cop who betrayed another cop, and I couldn't tell them any different. I couldn't tell them the truth about what Hannah was to both of you because then I would have been betraying *you*."

He stared at her, his eyes raw with regret. "God, Angel, I'm sorry. I won't lie. I wasn't even thinking about you or how it must have looked when David and Hannah died together. I just had to go or go crazy. I couldn't stay there after losing them both. I never thought . . ."

He closed his eyes. "I never meant to hurt you, Angel. You're David's sister. I should have taken care of you, protected you. How did you—?" His voice cracked. "How did you make it? What did you do?"

She blew out her breath. "I didn't intend to make this a guilt fest, Micah. What's done is done. I survived. I was angry and hurt, maybe more than I thought. Seeing you again brought it all back. I'm sorry. I shouldn't have blurted it out like that."

She stood, rubbing her hands down her pant legs. "I should go. It's late."

He rose abruptly, his eyes flashing ominously. "We aren't finished, Angel. Not by a long shot. You still haven't told me what you're doing here, why you were at The House, and what the hell you were doing naked in front of all those damn people."

She smiled faintly as she watched the tension creep back into his face. Despite the fact that he'd abdicated any responsibility toward her, he seemed suddenly gripped by the urge to protect her from all the big bad wolves out there. Only he was the biggest, baddest wolf, and she didn't want to be protected from him.

"I think it's best if we don't discuss that," she said in an even tone.

His mouth gaped open and then his lips snapped together in anger. "You don't get to decide what we do and don't discuss. You're not going anywhere until you give me some answers, baby doll."

It made her positively quivery when he got authoritative. She'd always loved that about him, his alpha take-charge attitude. She craved him and that power, had been drawn to it since before she understood what exactly it was that attracted her to him.

Part of her wanted to acquiesce, to offer her submission and give herself over to his keeping, only she knew better than to think it was what he wanted from her. Oh, she knew he wanted her obedience, but he wanted the obedience of a child, not of the woman she was. He was bent on seeing her as the teenage sister of his best friend—a friend he'd shared the woman he'd married with.

"I'm well aware that you're a man used to getting your way. But this time, I'm afraid you're destined for disappointment. You wouldn't like my answer anyway, so it's better to end tonight on a more positive note."

He stared at her in utter disbelief. When she started to move toward the door, he stepped in front of her, his eyes narrowed to slits.

"Oh hell no, Angel girl. That isn't the way things are going to work. You have a hell of a lot to answer for."

"I don't answer to you, Micah," she said evenly. "You don't want anything from me. You're not ready to offer me anything. When that changes, we'll talk."

She glimpsed his astonishment as she scooped up her keys and headed for the door.

"Angel, damn it!"

She opened the door and hurried into the night, ignoring his command for her to get her ass back inside. She didn't stop until she got to her car, and she refused to look up, knowing she'd see Micah standing there.

Doors locked, she cranked the engine and backed from the parking spot as Micah pounded on her window. With a quick glance in his direction to make sure she wasn't going to hit him, she accelerated out of the lot and left him standing in the dark, staring after her.

CHAPTER 4

Angelina let herself into her hotel room and tossed her keys onto the bed. The interior was dark and somewhat gloomy, with only a dully lit lamp to offer illumination. It certainly wasn't the best of accommodations, but this would be the last place someone would look for her. At least she hoped.

She trudged into the bathroom and turned the hot water on in the sink. A shower would feel good, but she didn't want to erase Micah's touch or to relieve the slight heat that was still present from his whip.

She washed her face, brushed her hair and pulled it back into a ponytail. A glance in the mirror told her she looked tired. Hollow-eyed and worried.

She stripped out of her clothes, left them on the floor of the bathroom, and walked nude back to where her suitcase lay on the bed. She shoved it off, not bothering to pull on a shirt. Bed was calling her name, and she didn't waste any time answering.

She lay on her belly, letting the draft from the rattling air conditioner blow over her back. Dreamily, she closed her eyes and relived those moments before Micah discovered who she was, when for a while she'd been his to command.

He'd wanted her, wanted her desperately. She'd seen the lust in his eyes, felt the tremble of his hands on her flesh. The barely restrained power she'd sensed boiling within him had been like a drug to her. Addictive, alluring. Intoxicating.

She'd always known how it would be with Micah, and it seemed she'd spent most of her life waiting and wanting. She'd entertained herself with vivid fantasies of him capturing her, of him forcing her to his will. His possession.

She shivered, her belly clenching as she remembered every single sound he'd made, his breathing, his words. His lips on hers, his taste. How he felt.

Longing didn't begin to cover the magnitude of her feelings. She needed him as she'd never needed anyone else. David and Hannah were family. David was her brother, and Hannah was as much a sister to her as she could be. But Micah? From the beginning, she'd separated Micah into a whole different category. One forbidden to her but no less tempting.

If it would bring David and Hannah back, she'd give up any hope of having Micah. Micah had loved Hannah deeply, and as much as Angelina herself loved Micah, she'd stand on the outside looking in forever if it meant having her family again.

But they were gone. She and Micah were left. She knew him like no one else did. She knew his secrets, his desires, the man behind the easygoing façade. She could give him what he needed, but would he ever decide she was what he wanted?

"No guarantees in life, Angel baby," she whispered, smiling sadly as David's words floated from her lips.

A sound at her window made her freeze. Then she laughed and buried her face in her pillow. What a jumpy moron she was. She was on the fourth floor of a shabby hotel. Who'd be at her window? Spider-Man?

She had to quit flinching at shadows and looking over her shoulder at every turn. Okay, so maybe continuing to look over her shoulder was a good idea. She couldn't afford to be too careless, even though she knew she'd covered her tracks well. She hadn't lived in a cop household for years not to learn anything about stealth and evading.

There was no reason for anyone to know she was here. She'd ditched her car, bought another under an assumed name, used cash, and no one in Houston apart from Damon Roche and Micah Hudson knew what her real name was.

Tomorrow she'd start her job search. Thanks to her Hispanic heritage, she could pose as an illegal immigrant and get a job that paid under the table. She had funds stashed, but she couldn't afford to lean on those unless absolutely necessary.

And God willing, it wouldn't be necessary. She could start a new life here. Nothing was left for her in Miami. Micah never needed to know about her problems. She didn't want him to be with her for any other reason than she was what he wanted.

CHAPTER 5

*A*ngelina woke with a strong sense of purpose. She dressed and was out of the hotel early, just as the sun crept over the horizon. Determined to get her job situation squared away as soon as possible, she hit the cafés in walking distance of the hotel, and at the third she scored a job as a waitress. The manager *generously* offered to let her work for tips only, and she could take what she earned home in cash each night.

It wasn't ideal, but it could be a lot worse. She was friendly and outgoing, and she wasn't afraid of hard work. After arranging her schedule, she went back to the hotel and dialed Damon Roche's number at The House. One of his employees said he wasn't in but he was expected within the hour. She hung up and collected her keys. By the time she got over there, she wouldn't have long to wait.

She took her time, stopping at a drive-thru for breakfast. When she drove up the winding paved drive of The House, an hour had passed. Hopefully Damon would be in by now. She wanted to smooth any ruffled feathers and figure out where she stood.

While her cursory investigation into Micah's life in Houston had revealed his membership at The House, she hadn't realized he and Damon were friends. She'd be lucky if she was ever allowed back in again. Micah had probably already screeched at Damon beyond his explosion the night before.

She parked close to the entrance, noting that there were only two other cars in the designated parking area, one of which was a slick-looking BMW. Damon's? She hoped so.

She got out and strode to the door to ring the bell. Within a few seconds, the door opened, and she was greeted by a plain-faced gentleman who peered inquisitively at her.

"I'm here to see Damon Roche," she said

"Do you have an appointment?"

She blinked. "Um, well, no. I called earlier and was told he'd be in. Can you tell him Angelina Moyano would like to talk to him?"

He gestured for her to come inside, and she followed him into a luxurious sitting room.

"I'll see if Mr. Roche is willing to meet with you," he said politely.

She nodded and sank onto the sumptuous leather couch. She studied the room while he was gone, taking in the tasteful décor. Everything about The House spoke of refinement and elegance. No matter what went on behind closed doors, there was a distinct air of class. It was hard to feel cheap or tawdry in such a place, and maybe that was the point.

"Angelina," Damon said as he strode through the doorway. He stopped in front of her, his expression inquiring. "You wished to speak with me?"

She rose to stand before him, warming to the spark of authority in his voice. This too was a man well used to being in charge.

"Yes, please," she said, trying to keep the uncertainty from her voice.

He held a hand out to touch her arm. "Come into my office. Would you like coffee or juice?"

She shook her head and followed him down the hall and into a spacious office that oozed raw masculinity.

"Have a seat," he said as he walked around the desk to his chair. He sat and leaned back, studying her with his deep brown eyes. A wide, gold band circled his ring finger, surprising her. Why, she wasn't sure, but the idea that he had a wife seemed odd. Did she mind his ownership of a place where sex was as common as drinking water?

"What can I do for you, Angelina?"

She grimaced, twisting her mouth into a rueful smile. "I wanted to know if my membership was still valid."

His fingers formed a triangle, the tips coming together to rest against his bottom lip as he continued to stare levelly at her. "Is there any reason it shouldn't be?"

"Let's not pretend you aren't friends with Micah. Guy's code and all that. I've witnessed the biggest boys club in the world when my brother and Micah were on the police force."

"Yes, we're friends."

"Are you pissed that I withheld that I knew him during my application process?"

Damon sighed. "What are you really asking, Angelina? If you

want to know if Micah has demanded I bar you from the premises—
one, he doesn't have the right to demand anything, friendship not-
withstanding. And two, I haven't heard a word from him since last
night."

"Then I'm welcome here?"

Damon nodded.

She started to rise, but something in his expression stopped her.

"Can I ask you something, Angelina? It's strictly personal, and
you shouldn't feel obligated to answer. It won't affect your standing
here. But as I stated, Micah and I are friends. He's told me about
David and Hannah."

Her eyes widened in surprise.

"Yes, I know," he said quietly. "Why are you here? I've never seen
Micah anything but in control, and last night you managed to completely unhinge him. I can't help but think it was intentional on
your part."

Slowly she nodded.

His eyes narrowed angrily. "What game are you playing? I don't
want him hurt."

"Neither do I," she said evenly. "I'm the last person who would
ever hurt him."

One eyebrow rose, and understanding fired in his eyes. "Are you
sure you know what you're doing?"

She raised her hands palms up. "That's the million-dollar question," she murmured. "I can give Micah what he needs. I understand
him better than anyone else."

"But does he understand *you*?" he asked gently.

Her lips tightened. "He doesn't see me. He doesn't *know* me. But
he will. He will."

Damon studied her another moment. "Are you okay, Angelina?

Is there anything you need? Are you here in Houston permanently or will you be going back to Miami?"

"I'm fine," she said quietly. "And there's nothing left in Miami for me. Everything I want, I need, is here."

"I see. Then I wish you well, and I'd ask that if there's something you need, to come to me. Micah can be hard, as I'm sure you well know. You have a difficult task in front of you. I don't want to see you—or him—hurt."

She held on to her smile, willing it not to fall as she rose. She hadn't allowed any doubt to creep in and take hold, and by God she wouldn't do it now.

"Thank you," she said sincerely. "It's always nice to know there are people I can count on. You can never have enough of those."

Micah stalked into Malone and Sons Security and grunted an acknowledgment at Connor as he passed him in the hallway. Usually he'd amble into Faith's office, where everyone gathered for coffee in the mornings, but today he wasn't fit company for a viper, much less people he cared about.

Once in his office, he closed the door and paced back and forth in front of the window. He stopped to stare broodingly out the blinds, his mind about to blow.

Where the fuck was she? Where had she come from? And why the hell had he let her just walk out of his apartment? Of all the stupid stunts he'd pulled, this one had to take the cake.

She'd knocked him so hard on his ass that he hadn't found out even the most basic information. Like where she was staying. Was she here visiting? Was she thinking of moving? Whoa. And then there was the fact that she'd come on to him like a tornado.

Okay, so maybe she hadn't exactly come on to him. Technically he'd made the moves, but she damn sure hadn't done anything to stop him. And that was what was burning a hole in his head this morning.

Why?

He hadn't mistaken her responsiveness. She'd given herself to him as sweetly as any woman ever had. She'd gone quiet and supple underneath his touch. She'd taken everything he'd given and would have given him more. A whole lot more.

Seeing her had been a big enough surprise. Seeing her naked with his marks on her body had been a huge *what-the-fuck* moment.

He wearily ran a hand through his hair and closed his eyes. He hadn't slept—how could he? Angelina was here. With her she'd brought back a lot of memories that he'd purposely left behind in Miami. Even though he went back each year, every time he left it all behind and took none of his baggage back to Houston. He liked it that way. It was how he dealt with it all.

Only now his past was staring him straight in the face in the form of a challenge he had no inkling of. What did she want from him?

The idea of her being in Houston—young and alone—burned a hole in his gut. David had always been hugely protective of her. They'd lost their parents when Angelina was a kid and David was barely out of high school. David had been brother, mother and father to her, and later Hannah had taken on the role of mother figure even though only five years separated the girls in age.

Girl. Hell. Angelina was no girl now. He only wished he didn't have firsthand knowledge of that fact.

He frowned. David and Hannah had taken an almost parental view of Angelina. Well, maybe not parental as much as they both viewed her as a younger sibling. How had *he* seen her? It had appalled him that he was seeing David's sister. Naked. Touching her. Kissing her. But he'd never looked at her as his sister.

Beautiful young girl. Yes. Too young for him. At the time. Sixteen to his twenty-eight. But now she was twenty-three and the age difference didn't seem as vast.

"Jesus Christ, are you actually trying to rationalize this?"

Now he was talking to himself. Just great.

First things first. He had to put aside the dissection of what had happened. He needed to *forget* it had happened and focus on the important details. Like where she was and if she needed help.

His door opened, and he turned to see Nathan Tucker stick his head in.

"Hey man, Pop is here and is ready to start the morning meeting. You in?"

Nathan looked curiously at him, and Micah didn't blame him. Usually Micah was the first one to saunter into Faith's office, offer a kiss, snag some coffee and preferably the first donut.

He gave a short nod. "I'm coming."

Nathan retreated but left the door open. Thinking he might as well get it over with, Micah followed him down to Faith's office.

He didn't miss the curious stares thrown his way as he walked in and took a position against the wall beside Faith's desk.

"Morning," Faith said with a smile.

He softened, despite his dour mood, and returned her smile. "Morning, baby doll."

Though her gaze was inquisitive, she didn't say anything. He shot her a look of gratitude.

"Well if we're all here now, can we get this show on the road?" Pop's grizzled voice rose in the otherwise quiet room, and he stared pointedly at Micah as he spoke.

Micah listened halfheartedly to the division of jobs and duties. He was too busy thinking about Angelina and how the fuck he was going to find her. How stupid of him was it to just let her go without knowing a thing about her circumstances?

He almost raised his fingers and snapped them as it occurred to him that Damon might know. Of course. She had to have undergone a rigorous screening before she was given membership to The House.

"Don't let us keep you," Pop said dryly.

Micah blinked and snapped his attention back to the older man. Connor, Gray and Nathan were all staring at him with open curiosity. Faith's look was more sympathetic, while Pop's eyes were full of amusement.

"Late night, son?" Pop asked.

Micah grunted. "No. Yes. Sorta."

"Well hell, make up your mind. Preferably on the way to the job." Pop thrust an invoice toward Micah. "You're on your own today and it looks like that's probably a good thing. Don't look much like decent company if you ask me."

Micah bit back the obscenities he wanted to blister the world with and took the paper. With a glance in Faith's direction and a quick wave, he started after the others.

In the hallway, Nathan hung back until Micah caught up with him.

"Hey, man, everything okay with you?"

"Yeah. Fine."

Nathan shrugged, and the two exited the office building into the parking lot.

"Want me to ride along with you?" Nathan offered. "I've finished up my job, so I'm pretty free this morning."

Micah paused at his truck. "I appreciate the offer, but as Pop said, I'm not decent company."

He glanced down at the invoice. Simple installation. Shouldn't take but two hours tops, and Nathan would still have time to spend the rest of the day with his girl Julie if he wanted.

"Hey, would you do me a favor and take this job? There's something I need to do."

Nathan's eyebrow went up in surprise. "Uh, well, okay. I can do that."

"Thanks. I wouldn't ask, but it's important."

Nathan took the piece of paper Micah extended toward him and hesitated. "Everything okay with you?"

"Yeah. Fine. Just something I have to take care of."

Nathan nodded, folded the sheet and headed toward his truck.

Micah climbed into his own truck and pulled out his cell. It was nice to have friends. Good friends who'd do anything for you and not ask questions. He'd had that kind of friendship with David, and he'd been lucky enough to find it again with the guys he worked with at Malone and Sons.

As he drove out of the parking lot, he hit Damon's private number on speed dial.

"Where are you?" he asked bluntly when Damon answered.

"I'm heading to my downtown office," Damon replied. "Is something wrong?"

"I'll meet you there in half an hour," Micah said and closed his phone.

He navigated the midmorning traffic and parked outside the downtown high-rise twenty-five minutes later. On the elevator ride to the top floor, he tapped his foot impatiently. Of course Damon would have the best of everything. Best offices, best view, expensive-ass furnishings. And he'd probably be waiting with some refined, high-brow alcohol.

Micah ignored Damon's secretary and headed into Damon's office. He gave one polite knock but didn't wait for a response.

Damon didn't bother to rise, though just as Micah had predicted, there was a glass filled with amber stuff waiting on the edge of the polished desk. Micah sat but didn't reach for the drink.

Damon surveyed him calmly and waited. Micah wasn't used to this uncertainty, to second-guessing his decisions. To the absolute knowledge that he'd royally fucked up.

"Christ," Micah muttered. "I fucked up, Damon."

Still, Damon waited, only responding with the lift of one eyebrow.

"I need any info you have on Angelina."

"I think you know I can't do that."

"Let me rephrase. I don't need personal information. I need to know where I can find her. It's important. I don't like the idea of her being in Houston alone, staying God knows where. I let her walk out of my apartment last night, and now I don't know where to find her. I don't know if she's okay, if she needs anything."

"She seemed well this morning when I saw her," Damon said.

Micah surged forward. "Where did you see her?"

"She came to see me at The House early."

"What the hell was she seeing you about?"

Damon just stared back, his expression unreadable.

Micah cursed again. "Okay, so you won't tell me that. At least tell me where I can find her. Damn it, Damon, I'm worried about her. I just need to make sure she's taken care of. I owe David that much."

"Interesting that you feel you owe David but not Angelina herself."

"Don't fucking play psychologist with me, man. Pisses me off."

"Only because I make a valid point," Damon said in an amused tone.

"Look, she's David's little sister. Hannah mothered her."

"And you?" Damon asked.

"She was David's *sister*," he said as if that explained all things. And didn't it?

Damon chuckled. "In other words you never saw her, and now suddenly you do."

"No, the hell I *don't* see her," he answered fiercely.

It was a stone-cold lie, and they both knew it. Micah closed his eyes and shook his head.

"How did she know, Damon? How the hell did she know that I'd respond to her bound and naked, begging for the kiss of the whip?"

"I'd say she knows a lot more about you than you do about her."

"No shit," he muttered. "Tell me where I can find her, Damon. You sure as hell wouldn't let me get away with not telling you something where Serena is concerned."

Damon scowled, and Micah knew he'd scored a hit.

"Hell," Damon bit out.

"Tell me," Micah persisted.

Damon sighed and opened his laptop. "I can only give you whatever she put on her application. Don't ask for anything else. I won't give it."

Micah shrugged. As long as he found her, she could damn well tell him the rest.

After a few moments of clicking, Damon raised his head. "She's staying at the Starlight Motel. No address given."

"Never heard of it," Micah said with a frown as he rose. "Thanks, though. I'll call 411 to get the address on my way out."

"Hey, Micah," Damon said when Micah was almost to the door. Micah paused and turned around.

"Take it easy. Don't go in with both barrels blazing, okay?"

Micah gave a dry chuckle. "Yeah, I'll try."

CHAPTER 6

*J*ust when he thought he couldn't get any more pissed off, Micah pulled into the parking lot of the Starlight Motel and stared in disgust at the run-down four-story building. He'd thought the directions were bogus when he entered the seedy, dangerous-looking area. Or at least he'd hoped they were.

He slammed the truck door shut and stalked toward the motel office, noting more than one broken pane on the windows of the rooms. What the hell did she think she was doing staying in a place like this?

The clerk at the desk gave him a bored look when Micah entered.

"Angelina Moyano," Micah said tersely. "Which room?"

The clerk didn't so much as blink or attempt to move from his slouched position in his chair.

"Don't have anyone here by that name."

"How the hell would you know?" Micah demanded. "You haven't even looked."

The clerk raised a paper cup and spit a stream of tobacco into it. "Hotel ain't full. I'd know if someone by that name was booked in here."

Micah held his temper in check. Barely. "Curvy Hispanic girl. Long, dark hair. Very pretty. Brown eyes. About this tall." He held out a hand and indicated a height that came to his shoulder.

"Room 417."

Micah couldn't decide whether to be glad the punk had offered up the information so readily, or to reach across the counter, yank him up by his shirt and beat the living hell out of him.

But since Angelina wasn't spending another minute in this dump, he wouldn't worry about the potential danger she faced.

Not surprisingly, there was an out-of-service sign on the elevator. Muttering under his breath, he climbed four flights of stairs. Finally at Angelina's door, he paused and stared at the flimsy frame. A good stiff wind would blow it down.

He knocked and waited, shoving his hands into his jeans pockets. Several long seconds passed. He couldn't fault her for not answering; in fact, if she'd blindly answered the door, he'd have tanned her little ass.

He stepped forward and knocked again. "Angelina, open the door," he called.

He relaxed when he heard the dead bolt flip. The door creaked open, and he was met with a pair of dark eyes peering out of the two-inch crack.

"Micah?"

"Yeah, Angel, it's me."

Relief flashed in her eyes as she opened the door wider. "What are you doing here? How did you know where to find me?"

He shoved in past her, taking in the tiny room. "Don't act so surprised. You had to know I'd find you after your disappearing act last night."

She closed the door and turned around to face him. "By all means, come on in."

Against his better judgment, he let his gaze drop down her body. Damn it all to hell, when had she developed such a killer body? He shook his head and focused somewhere else. Anywhere but on her.

"What the hell are you doing here?" he demanded. "This place isn't fit for rats, for God's sake."

She shrugged, a tiny, delicate motion that drew attention to the slim column of her neck. "It was what I could afford."

"Pack your things. We're getting out of here."

When she didn't move to comply with his order, he went to the bed where her suitcase was opened and things were lying in neat little piles to the side. He tossed everything in the suitcase then looked around to see if there was anything else he'd missed.

Angelina was watching him through narrowed lids, her arms crossed over her chest.

"Not that I don't love having the busywork done for me, but would you mind telling me what the hell you're doing?"

"I'd think it was obvious. Getting you the hell out of here."

She dropped her arms and took a step toward him, which had him hastily backing up. God, he was acting like a first-rate pussy, but if she touched him, he couldn't be responsible for what happened.

His skin tingled in sharp awareness, and hunger, raw and volatile, rose inside his gut. For a moment he saw her as she was the previous night. Naked, her skin glowing, her hair sliding like silk over her back.

Christ but he was going to need to pour bleach in his eyes to rid himself of that image.

"I've seen you twice in the last twenty-four hours and each time you seem determined to relocate me. Why is that, Micah?"

He snorted. "That's a dumb-ass question. I find you in a place devoted to public sex acts. Like I'm not going to have anything to say about that? And now you're in some seedy-ass motel. You'll be lucky if you aren't raped or killed or both in this joint."

"I see. And what is your proposed solution, send me back to Miami?"

That thought had occurred to him, and he would have certainly suggested it already if he knew why she was here in the first place.

"Why are you here?" he asked as he sat down on the bed.

She lifted one shoulder and glanced away, her eyes flickering with emotion. "There's nothing left for me in Miami. I thought Houston would make a nice change. I don't know anyone anywhere else. It seemed logical enough to come here."

Where he was.

Though it was left unsaid, it was certainly implied.

"Are you in some kind of trouble, Angel girl?" he asked gently.

She gave him a startled look. "Why would you ask that?"

"Seems like a logical question given your sudden appearance and your reluctance to return to Miami."

She looked pointedly at him. "You never went back."

He ignored that statement. It made it seem too much like he'd been running from his past. Hadn't he been, though?

"You can stay with me until you find a decent place."

He nearly groaned when he realized what he'd said. So there wasn't another alternative, none that would assure him of her well-being anyway, but the idea that she'd be under his roof, sharing his space, and be a constant reminder of last night . . . He was fucked.

She frowned slightly as she studied him. "You seem less than thrilled at the idea of having me in your place."

"Of course you're going to stay with me. It's not like we haven't lived together before," he said with a half smile.

Angelina had lived with him, David and Hannah for nearly a year until she graduated high school. Truth was he hadn't seen much of her during that year, or maybe he just hadn't been paying attention. She and Hannah had been close, and David had been extremely protective of her. With that many guardians, she sure hadn't needed him to sign on for the job.

You didn't see her.

Damon's words floated back to him. No, he hadn't seen her then, but he sure as hell wasn't suffering that problem now.

She stared at him mockingly. "Do you really think me staying with you is such a good idea when I have no intention of keeping my hands to myself?"

He did a double take, sure he hadn't heard her correctly. She looked cool as a cucumber, her stance relaxed and a mischievous twinkle in her eyes that warmed him to the bone.

Hell, what could he say to that?

Deciding to go with option B, which was to ignore—he loved option B—he finished zipping up her suitcase then turned back to her as if she'd never said a word about her hands—or not keeping them to herself.

"Is this everything?"

She nodded.

"Then let's get the hell out of here. I need a drink."

Or maybe the whole damn bar.

CHAPTER 7

ngelina was glad to see the last of her hotel. The idea of staying with Micah comforted her way more than she would have liked
to admit, but the truth was he made her feel safe. He'd always made
her feel safe.

Plus she intended to see him often, and if she was staying with him,
she wasn't exactly going to have to work hard at that goal any longer.

Now she wouldn't worry about her paranoia about being followed
from Miami. She'd no longer be alone.

She leaned back against the couch in Micah's living room and
let out a small sigh of contentment.

Micah eyed her from his perch in the recliner as he pointed the
remote at the TV and changed the channel for the thirtieth time in
the last half hour.

"What are you looking so happy for?"

She raised an eyebrow in his direction. "Suspicious much? I was
just thinking that it's nice not to be alone."

For a moment it looked like he was going to say something, but then his lips closed into a firm line. Finally he lowered the remote and turned his head in her direction.

"You aren't alone, Angel," he said gruffly. "We'll work it out for you here. You can stay with me until you're on your feet and then we can find you a good place to live. Have you thought about what you're going to do yet?"

"Oh, I've got a job already," she said cheerfully.

"You do?"

She would have thought he'd look more enthused, given that she was going to be living in his apartment. He looked warily at her as he waited for her to expound.

"I picked up a waitressing job that was within walking distance of the hotel. Of course now I'll have to drive."

Micah was shaking his head before she ever finished.

"No. Not no, but *hell* no."

"Excuse me?"

"You heard me. You aren't working in that neighborhood. Christ, Angel, use your head. A gorgeous young girl walking to work in that area? I don't even want you driving. You're just asking for trouble."

She smiled. "Am I?"

He looked thoroughly confused. "Are you what?"

"Gorgeous."

Micah swore and closed his eyes.

"Why do you fight your attraction to me so hard?"

"I am not attracted to you," he muttered.

"Liar," she mocked. "You may not want to want me. But you do."

"Why are you doing this?" he demanded.

"Don't ask questions you don't want the answer to, Micah."

He opened his mouth then snapped it shut again. He looked frustrated enough to strangle her.

"You're right. This isn't something we should be discussing."

"Oh, but I'd love to discuss it," she persisted. "Even better, I'd love to dispense with conversation altogether and let our bodies do the talking."

"You're incorrigible." Disbelief shadowed his voice, and he looked almost bewildered.

She smiled. "Don't forget it."

"You sidetracked me on purpose," he accused.

She gave him an innocent look.

"I don't want you taking that job, Angel. You could find another one close by here. Even if it took you a few weeks. You know I'll help you."

"I have no doubt you would," she said calmly. "I can find a job here if it'll make you feel better."

Relief shone stark on his face. He really had been worried.

"I'll start looking tomorrow while you're at work."

He looked disgruntled for a moment, and she laughed.

"Tell me you didn't think you were going to babysit me twenty-four seven."

He glared at her and turned back to the TV.

"I think I'll go to bed," she said as she stood.

She stretched lazily, forcing Micah's attention back to her. His gaze was warm on her skin. She walked over to the recliner, and before he could react, she slid onto his lap, dangling her legs over the side of the chair. She wrapped her arms around his neck and pulled him forward to meet her lips.

He was as stiff and unyielding as cement. Her tongue flitted out to playfully lave over his closed lips. The nearly violent thud of his pulse signaled that he was definitely not immune to her.

"Kiss me," she whispered. "Forget everything but the fact that there's you and me. Kiss me."

With a tortured groan, he gave in, opening his mouth to take control of the kiss. She melted against him with a deep sigh. Their tongues met in a heated rush. Like chocolate melting in the sunshine. Sweet. Strong. A little wild.

Her fingers rolled and twisted the hair at his nape while his hands rested at the small of her back, his arms across the tops of her thighs.

She wanted them to move. Wanted him to touch her, to take an active part beyond returning her kiss. But she knew he wouldn't, just as she knew the instant that the moment was over.

He yanked away, his breath coming in a ragged gasp. His eyes were wild-looking, the pupils dilated, making his brown eyes appear black.

"No. *No*," he ground out. "We can't do this, Angel."

Silently, she slid from his lap, gaining her footing with trembling legs. She wouldn't look at him, refused to acknowledge the regret she knew she'd see in his eyes.

Never once looking back, she walked stiffly toward her bedroom, her hands fisted at her sides.

"Angel," he said in a hoarse, needy voice.

She froze and waited, but he didn't call her back. Her shoulders slowly drooping downward, she continued her path to the bedroom. When she was inside, she quietly closed the door behind her.

With a dry laugh, she dropped onto the bed. She was probably the first woman Micah had ever said no to. He was a complete and utter pushover when it came to females. He loved them, protected them and didn't care who knew it.

So why couldn't he see her? Why couldn't he love her, desire her, get past the fact that she was David's sister?

What she needed was a sledgehammer and then she could beat some sense into his thick head.

There were different kinds of sledgehammers, and she'd have to make do with the metaphorical kind. Micah might not see her, might not want to see her, but he wasn't blind nor was he immune to her as a woman.

She had an edge over most females because she knew what made him tick. Now she just had to use that knowledge to her advantage.

CHAPTER 8

"*S*o what bug's been up your ass lately, Hudson?" Gray Montgomery asked.

Micah scowled as he handed the menu back to the waitress. He and the other guys from work, Gray Montgomery, Nathan Tucker and Connor Malone, were at their regular lunch haunt, Cattleman's, only they weren't usually discussing one another's personal business.

"You have been unusually cranky. Not get laid lately?" Connor drawled.

At that Nathan scowled, since he was still a little touchy about the fact that his current girlfriend was the last woman Micah would have been with.

"The world doesn't revolve around when I got laid last," Micah said dryly.

Gray blinked. "It doesn't? I thought that was the standard male milestone for keeping time."

Nathan laughed. "It is, or at least it's what the women would have you believe."

"I told Faith I had a headache last night," Gray said with a straight face. "There's only so much I can take. She's an animal!"

Micah hooted with laughter, relaxing now that the focus was momentarily off him.

Connor groaned and covered his ears. "Not cool, man. Not cool at all. I don't need that kind of information about my sister."

"Your sister's hot," Micah pointed out.

Nathan grimaced. "I'm going to have to go with Connor on this one. I see Faith too much as a little sister to want to imagine her as an animal in bed."

Gray snorted. "It wouldn't matter anyway because if you so much as breathed wrong at another woman, Julie would have your nuts."

Everyone laughed as Nathan turned a dull red.

"The man is completely whipped," Connor snickered.

Nathan smiled. "I don't have any problem admitting she's got me completely wrapped around her finger."

"There are worse things than having the love of a good woman," Micah said sincerely, while Gray and Nathan both nodded in agreement.

Connor just studied him curiously. "So is that what has you in a tailspin? A woman?"

Micah let out a grunt. "In a manner of speaking, though it's not what you dickheads are thinking."

"Ahh," Gray said.

Micah flipped him the bird. "The sister of an old friend of mine is in town, and I've got my hands full trying to keep her out of trouble."

Gray frowned. "Trouble? What kind of trouble?"

Trust Gray's cop instincts to get all riled.

"She's a good girl," Micah said with a note of defensiveness even he could hear. "And that's the problem. She's a good girl with no idea of what can happen to a good girl in a big, strange city."

Connor scowled. "Then why the hell is she here and where is her brother?"

"David died a few years ago," Micah said quietly.

Even now, after so long, it hurt to say out loud that David was gone.

"He was the only family Angelina had."

"So you feel obligated to look after her," Connor said.

The others nodded in understanding.

"Well, yeah," Micah said.

Nathan raised an eyebrow. "Not going well?"

"It's going just fine. Or it will be as soon as we get a few rules straight."

Gray choked on his drink and commenced to coughing. "Yeah, good luck with that," he wheezed.

"How old is she anyway?" Connor asked.

"Twenty-three," Micah muttered.

"Is she hot?"

"Very," he said before he could think better of it. Then he swore. "No, she damn well isn't hot. And I don't want you to even so much as look in her direction. You got me?"

Connor held up his hands in surrender. "Whatever you say, man. I swear you guys do your best to keep me away from all the good ones. I should be dating Julie. Not bonehead over here," he said as he jerked a thumb in Nathan's direction.

Nathan snorted. "You're not man enough for her."

Connor scowled. "And I suppose you are?"

"She's with me, isn't she?" Nathan returned smugly.

Gray leaned forward, ignoring the bickering between Connor and Nathan. "So you're spending your evenings babysitting her at her place or what? And what about during the day? Not like you can keep an eye on her all the time."

"She's staying with me until we can find her a decent place. She's going to be looking for a job."

For once they fell completely silent as they stared back at him. Gray coughed discreetly and Nathan made a show of clearing his throat. Connor's eyes gleamed with unholy amusement.

"So you have a young, hot girl living with you, and you're in a bad mood?" Connor asked.

"Shut the fuck up," Micah growled.

"Blue balls," Gray said with a sage nod. "What our man has is a case of the blue balls."

"Fuck you," Micah said crudely. "Fuck all of you."

They laughed uproariously while Micah just shook his head.

Gray pointed a finger in Micah's direction. "Mark my words, Hudson. Your ass is toast."

After an afternoon of ribbing, Micah was ready to get home, crack open a cold beer and watch some TV. Then he remembered he had no food in the house, and while he had nothing against two-day-old pizza, he didn't see Angelina sharing his appreciation for it.

He stopped at the local grocery store, piled a bunch of stuff he thought she'd like in the buggy and headed to the checkout. Half an hour later, he pulled into his apartment complex and frowned when he didn't see Angelina's little tin can in the parking spot next to his.

Maybe she was still out job hunting.

He made two trips to get the groceries in, and it wasn't until he started to put them away that he saw the piece of paper propped against the canisters.

He picked it up and unfolded it, his gaze scanning the neat handwriting.

Micah,

Gone to The House to play. ☺ Don't wait up for me.

Love, Angelina

Micah dropped the paper and was immediately assaulted by a pounding headache. Fuck a goddamn duck. What the *hell* did she think she was doing? Besides driving him out of his damn mind.

He pinched the bridge of his nose between two fingers and closed his eyes to assuage the sensation of someone stabbing him in the eyeball.

He was haunted by the images of Angelina the first time he'd seen her at The House. What the hell would he find her doing this time?

Damon wouldn't be there, so he couldn't call him and demand he throw her out, not that he would anyway, but at least he could have made sure Damon watched over her. Cole was a good guy, but shit, he was the one flogging her the first night. And what guy with a working set of balls wouldn't leap at the opportunity to bend a gorgeous woman to his will?

Leaving the groceries in the sacks, he made a grab for his keys and headed for the door. He and Angelina were definitely going to come to an understanding. Right after his hand warmed her

little ass. And he'd make damn sure the little brat didn't enjoy it
either.

Unfortunately for him, his dick stood up and paid attention at
the idea of having her over his knee. Yeah, she might not like it—or
maybe she would—but he damn sure would.

The drive to The House seemed interminable. It was almost
completely dark when he pulled up the drive, and it irritated the hell
out of him to see Angelina's car in one of the spots closest to the
door. Little hellcat had been here awhile.

He strode inside, and while he did a cursory check of the downstairs social rooms, he knew in his gut he'd find her upstairs where
all the action took place. He just hoped like hell he didn't have to
barge into one of the private rooms and drag her out. Damon would
have his ass in a sling, and he'd probably be barred from the premises
for life.

When he got to the top of the stairs, he made a beeline for the
common room. He hit the doorway and to his relief didn't see Angelina as the star attraction again. But that begged the question of
where exactly she was.

There, in the far corner of the room, he saw her. All the breath
left him in a painful rush. It was as if someone punched him squarely
in the diaphragm.

Lust and rage vied for equal airtime. Angelina. Nude but for the
ropes intricately wrapped around her upper body, under and above
her breasts so that the small globes were displayed to their best advantage. The nipples—lush and erect—dark brown, like velvet. She
was kneeling, her long hair sliding forward over her shoulders. Her
arms were bound behind her, her knees spread, her pose one of complete supplication.

God, how he longed to answer her plea for domination.

Three men surrounded her, their hands touching her, slid-

ing through her hair, reaching to finger her nipples. Then they
hoisted her to her feet and one cupped her chin, tilted her lips to
meet his.

He plundered her mouth. Ravaged it until she gasped for air. He
wasn't gentle with her, a fact that enraged Micah. His reaction per-
plexed him. He knew he wouldn't be gentle with her, but another
man treating her so roughly provoked a deep rage inside him.

When the man pulled away from Angelina, her lips were swollen
and bruised looking. Her eyes glittered, and Micah saw a need that
wasn't being fulfilled. She looked hungry. Like a woman seeking but
not finding.

The other two men dropped down, and then their lips closed
over her protruding nipples. She gave a small cry that seemed to
satisfy them. They nursed like two starving men.

The picture was provocative and erotic as hell.

Would she allow them to fuck her? Is that what she wanted? To
be dominated and possessed by multiple men?

Part of him wanted nothing more than to watch while they took
her, but another part of him was outraged that David's sister was
here, being pawed by strange men.

Another voice whispered deep, dark—and sensual, sliding seduc-
tively through his veins.

*You want her. You want to be the one who owns her. You're jealous.
You're crazy jealous.*

Angelina was lifted by the two men who had suckled at her
breasts. They each hooked an arm under the crook of one of her
knees and spread her until she was open and vulnerable to the
other man.

Adrenaline pumped like thunder through Micah's veins. He was
riveted to the sight of the lush, feminine flesh, spread, open to inva-
sion. She was excited. Her pussy was wet and swollen, and he broke

into a sweat as he imagined guiding his cock through her folds and ruthlessly opening her with his thrusts.

His balls ached fiercely. His dick was impossibly hard and screaming for relief.

A feminine hand slid over his arm and over his middle, snaking down to his crotch. Surprised and irritated by the interruption, he turned to see a woman next to him, her eyes glittering with lust.

"Let me take care of this for you," she murmured as she cupped the bulge between his legs. "While you watch her."

It was tempting to push her to her knees, free his cock and shove it into her mouth while he watched Angelina. But he wanted nothing to distract him.

Gently, he pushed her hand away and returned his gaze to Angelina. As the two men held her open, the first man lowered his head and swept his tongue over her swollen flesh.

Her belly arched, and she nearly bowed out of the two men's hands. The first man followed her with his mouth, delving his tongue deep, sucking and feasting on her pussy.

Micah was in danger of doing something he hadn't done since he was a teenager. If he so much as moved he was going to come in his pants.

What did she taste like? Was she sweet like she looked or was she all spicy heat like the mischief that gleamed in her eyes?

Why aren't you putting a stop to this? Why are you about to jack off while you watch Angelina being fucked by a crowd of horny men?

The man eating her pussy pulled away, licking his lips like a satisfied cat. While the other two men held her, he reached for a dildo from one of the nearby tables. He tore the wrapping from it and it gleamed obscenely in the light.

He moved back to Angelina and slipped between her thighs. His long fingers probed at her entrance, stroking up and down and then inside, burying his finger to the knuckle.

Angelina whimpered and bucked until he issued a sharp slap to her clit. Before she could react, he positioned the dildo and thrust deep.

Her cry echoed over the room. The man stepped away, leaving the fake dick lodged to the hilt in her pussy. He motioned for the other two men to lower her.

They forced her to her knees and nudged her thighs apart.

"Hold it in," the man ordered her as he nudged the base of the dildo with his foot.

She nodded her acceptance, her eyes wide and so damn innocent looking that it nearly slew Micah on the spot.

The man reached for a pair of nipple clamps then pinched one nipple between his fingers before attaching a clamp to the velvety soft point.

Angelina bit her lip, and Micah almost nodded his approval.

He swallowed rapidly. She wasn't his, and yet he was standing here casting himself as her master, silently offering approval when she performed well.

Move. Go to her.

His feet were encased in cement. All the blood in his body was pooled in his groin. He needed relief so badly that he was about crazy.

He was riveted by her beauty. By the sheer eroticism of the scene playing out before him.

The clamps now attached, the man stepped away and methodically unfastened his jeans. Not bothering to remove them, he reached in and pulled out his cock. With it fisted in one hand, he moved forward again.

He slid his free hand over the top of her head, his fingers tangling in her hair. Roughly, he forced her head back and guided his dick into her mouth.

The other two men also freed their cocks from their pants, but they stood to the side, stroking their erections with impatient hands.

Micah watched in fascination as the first man fed his dick deep into Angelina's mouth. Her neck muscles bulged with the strain as the man pushed his way forward. When she closed her eyes, he yanked at her head.

"Look at me," he ordered.

Her eyes flew open and stared pleadingly at him. He backed out, allowing her a quick breath before he thrust again. His balls bulged against her chin, and Micah could hear the sucking sounds she made.

Then her gaze found him. She looked past the man thrusting into her mouth and connected with Micah. He froze, unsure of what to do.

Calm entered her eyes, as if she felt safer and more secure now that she knew he was here. Her entire body relaxed, and she let her temporary master fuck her mouth with abandon.

And fuck it he did. Over and over he forced himself into her mouth with a brutality that made Micah wince, and yet he did nothing to stop it.

Her gaze never left Micah as she gave herself over to the man fucking her mouth.

Suddenly the man at her mouth yanked his cock away. The three men jerked frantically at their straining erections. Semen hit her lips, her cheeks, her breasts, her shoulders and her slim back. It ran down her body in hot, thick streams.

Finally they milked the last of their releases, moving closer so that it all dripped onto her skin.

And still she stared at Micah with her dark, trusting eyes. Micah felt sick, and yet he was so unbelievably turned on that he hurt.

Angelina was pulled to her feet as the men wiped the semen from her body, but she uttered something to them, and with a quick glance in Micah's direction, they moved away.

She stood, staring at him. Her arms tied behind her back, the dildo still lodged in her pussy.

"You know you want me," she said in a quiet, taunting voice. "Tell me, Micah, did they do it right? Were they too gentle? Would you have whipped me for the slightest infraction? Did you want it to be your cock in my mouth?

"Come to me. Free me," she whispered. "Take me."

A red-hot haze of need exploded over him. He closed the distance between them, his pulse pounding so hard in his ears it deafened him.

He grasped her shoulders, lust overtaking him, ruling him, whispering to him to take what was his.

With quick, jerky motions he spun her around and threw her over the arm of one of the plush couches. Even as he reached for the fly of his jeans with one hand, he reached between her legs to pull the dildo from the clasp of her pussy.

It came slowly, her swollen tissues reluctant to release the fake cock. It came out with a slight sucking noise, glistening with her fluids.

He tossed it aside as his fingers finally pulled his cock free of his pants. He was on her in an instant, mounting her from behind like a rutting animal.

He spread her, positioned himself and thrust savagely into her.

Pleasure exploded through him, the relief so intense he was dizzy. She unhinged him. He was mindless, stroking, thrusting, seeking to punish her only because it pleased him to do so.

He strained forward, determined she would take all of him. Her slender fingers were balled into fists at the small of her back as her wrists strained against her bonds.

Her body shook with the force of his thrusts, and he grasped her hips, pulling her back to meet each one.

Too soon, only seconds, his release raced with the fury of a firestorm, through his balls, up his cock. He closed his eyes and bit back the cry of triumph as he spurted deep inside her body.

Never had anything felt so primitive, so right, so absolutely satisfying.

His legs trembled and threatened to buckle. He leaned into her body, gasping for breath. Slowly he regained awareness. Her warm, sweet body quivered below his, her pussy softly contracting around his still-hard cock.

Oh God. Oh God. What had he done?

He'd abused her, taken her. He'd come inside her, for God's sake. No condom. Fuck. Fuck. *Fuck.* He'd *raped* her.

His hands shaking uncontrollably, he grasped her hips and carefully pulled out, wincing at the warm rush of semen that seeped from her swollen pussy.

"Oh God. Angel," he whispered. "Angel girl. Baby girl, I'm sorry. Oh my God, I'm so sorry."

He yanked at the ropes binding her hands and then gently picked her up from the couch so he could unwind the rest of the rope.

He couldn't—wouldn't—meet her eyes. He was too afraid of what he'd see. He'd used her. He'd hurt her. He wanted to die.

When the last of the rope fell away, he hastily arranged his pants and then pulled her into his arms. Her heart beat against his body like a little baby bird trying to fly for the first time. Erratic. A little frantic.

He smoothed a hand over her hair and pressed a kiss to the top of her head.

"I'm so sorry, Angel girl. I never meant to hurt you. I'm so damn sorry. Are you all right? Did I . . ." He swallowed hard. "Did I do any damage? Jesus, I didn't even use a condom. Maybe I should take you to the hospital."

No words had ever hurt him more, but he owed it to her not to shy away from what he'd done. He deserved to have his ass kicked and thrown in jail.

Angelina stirred in his arms and pulled away so she could look up at him. What he saw shattered him. Trust. Still shining in her soft eyes. His gut twisted into a huge knot that threatened to suffocate him.

"You didn't hurt me," she said gently. "I've never orgasmed so hard in my life."

She'd come? It shamed him to admit that he hadn't given a moment's thought to her pleasure or care. He'd been a mindless fucking machine only intent on gaining relief from his torment.

She reached up to touch his face, her fingers trailing over his cheekbone until finally she cupped his jaw.

"You only did what I asked you to do, Micah. How is that wrong?"

"You're too sweet, too generous and too damned naïve," he growled. "Where are your clothes?"

She pointed to a chair a few feet away where her jeans, underwear, shirt and shoes were. He stalked over and then returned with everything.

As gently and as patiently as he knew how, he dressed her, taking care not to abrade the bruised parts of her body. Every time he saw a fingerprint, or the red area where the ropes had dug into her skin, he felt sick.

Finally he handed her the shoes, and she slipped them on.

"Let's go home, Angel. You need someone to take care of you tonight."

She smiled faintly. "I love the way that sounds coming from you."

CHAPTER 9

$\mathcal{A}$ngelina barely had time to park her car before Micah opened her door and urged her out. To her utter shock, he swept her up into his arms and started carrying her toward the door to his apartment.

"Micah, I can walk," she said with a laugh.

He ignored her and kept walking. Not really wanting to argue the point, because she was in his arms after all, she sighed and snuggled into his chest.

Exhaustion beat at her temples, and her limbs felt heavy and laden. She wanted to sleep for about twelve hours, preferably in Micah's arms, but she wasn't fooling herself over that possibility.

He was horrified over what happened. The guilt in his eyes made her gut clench. For a guy who prided himself on his iron control, what had happened wasn't just a presumed betrayal of her but also of himself.

She couldn't feel bad, though. She'd never reach him as long as that control was in place. And she still shivered over the raw power he exhibited when he'd taken her.

Taken her. It seemed so tame a term to describe it. He'd owned her. Possessed her. She'd been completely and utterly his, his possession to do what he wanted with.

Desire and lust simmered and burned low in her abdomen despite her thinking she couldn't possibly be aroused again.

She'd loved his touch. His power. The way he hadn't asked. He'd simply taken what he deemed his.

She shivered again as he elbowed his way into the apartment.

"Are you cold?" he asked in concern.

She shook her head. "No, just remembering."

He stiffened, and the tortured look returned to his face. She started to correct his assumption that it was a bad remembrance for her, but he set her down on the couch and immediately went about removing her shoes.

"I'm going to go start a hot shower for you," he said in a low voice. "It'll make you feel better. Take your time. Are you hungry? Do you want me to fix you something to eat?"

She smiled. "The shower sounds heavenly, and no, I'm not hungry."

"Okay, I'll be right back."

She watched him stride away, his face creased into lines of worry. With a sigh, she sank against the back of the couch and closed her eyes. Always, *always* she'd known that sex with Micah would be nothing short of amazing.

She craved that darker edge, the thin line between right and wrong. He was all she wanted, and she wanted him as he was—dark, brooding, unapologetic—not as he thought he should be. She wanted to be his.

"Angel?"

She opened her eyes to see Micah standing over her, concern bright in his eyes.

"Are you sure you're okay? I can still take you to the hospital. Are you hurting anywhere?"

Boy, were they going to have a long talk when she got out of the shower. This guilt complex was quickly fraying her nerves.

She reached out so he could help her up, and he quickly took her hand and gently pulled her to a standing position. Ignoring his question entirely, she went toward the bathroom, her need for gallons and gallons of hot water outweighing her desire to kick Micah's ass.

The bathroom mirrors were already fogged up, and she let out a blissful sigh as she stripped down and stepped into the shower. For a long moment she stood in the spray, eyes closed as she relieved the sensation of Micah's hands on her, his cock inside her and the most intense orgasm of her life. She'd lit up like a firecracker the moment he thrust into her. She'd started coming and hadn't stopped until he'd found his own quick release.

Realizing she'd spent a long time in the shower and Micah was probably wearing a hole in the carpet in the living room, she turned off the water and stepped out to dry off. She'd just gotten the towel wrapped around her when the door opened and Micah stuck his head in.

After a quick glance, presumably to see if she was halfway decent, he shoved into the small bathroom.

"You were taking a long time. I wanted to make sure you were okay," he said gruffly.

With a sigh she let the towel drop so that she stood nude before him. He took a hasty step backward, and she almost rolled her eyes. It wasn't as though she was going to jump him.

"I'm fine. See?"

She turned in a circle so he could see her body for himself.

She couldn't control the quiver when his fingers brushed across a faint bruise on her hip.

"I bruised you," he said, his voice heavy with regret.

"I bruise very easily, Micah. You didn't hurt me."

When she'd turned back around fully, he took her hands and turned her wrists over. His thumb rubbed across the red lines left by the ropes, and his expression grew stormy.

"They tied them too tight. There was no need for them to hurt you. I should have stepped in and put a stop to it all."

"Why didn't you?" she asked curiously.

He swallowed and looked away. Then he reached for the towel and carefully wrapped it around her.

"Go get something on. You can borrow my robe if you want. There's a lot we need to talk about, and it can't wait."

She frowned at the urgency in his voice and reached for the robe hanging on the towel rack.

"I'll be in the living room. Are you sure you don't want something to eat?"

"Go," she said, shooing him with her hands.

He backed out of the bathroom, and Angelina dropped the towel to put her robe on, shaking her head the entire time. She gave her hair a thorough rub before she did a quick comb-through to rid it of tangles.

Fingering the strands from her face, she left the bathroom and returned to the living room, where Micah sat on the sofa, his elbows on his knees, his head down.

When he heard her, he looked up then stood.

"Sit down," he urged.

She plopped onto the couch, careful to keep the robe gathered around her.

"Angel, I think we should take you to the ER."

"But I'm not hurt!"

"I didn't use a condom."

"Yes, I know."

Micah ran a hand through his hair. "Aren't there shots they can give you? You know, so you don't get pregnant? Or at least a pill you can take?"

She leaned forward, wishing he'd at least sit down instead of hulking over her so tense he looked like he'd implode at any moment.

"Micah, come sit down. Please."

She patted the space beside her, and he hesitated before finally walking around to sit where she motioned.

"I get that you're feeling guilty. I get that this whole night didn't go at all like you thought it would or even wanted it to. But you're making a lot of assumptions and you're taking credit for sins you didn't commit."

"What the hell is that supposed to mean?" he muttered.

"I'm on birth control. I'm not an idiot. I wouldn't take chances like that. I also made damn sure those men I was playing with weren't going to go too far. With or without a condom."

"I didn't give you the choice," he said painfully.

She gave him a patient look. "I asked for what you gave me. I pushed you. I provoked you and got exactly the response I wanted. Despite what you might think, I'm not too young. I'm responsible, or mostly responsible," she added with a slight twist of her lips.

"It's not just about pregnancy. I didn't protect you. I didn't protect myself," he added. "Goddamn it, Angel, I've never not worn a condom in my life. Even when I lost my virginity a lifetime ago, I wore protection."

"I understand why you're upset. I'm safe. I'll understand if you don't want to take my word for it. I can have whatever test you want. I've had unprotected sex once. I was a teenager. It was my first time. We both knew better, because God knows David drummed the concept of safe sex through my head often enough." She smiled sadly. "He was always so much more of a father to me than our real father ever was. Anyway, I told him what happened. He was disappointed, but he immediately took me to the doctor so I could get a prescription for birth control, and he also bought me enough condoms to last a lifetime and told me I no longer had an excuse for not carrying them with me at all times."

Micah smiled. "That's David. Mr. Prepared."

"I miss him."

"Yeah, so do I."

"Micah?"

"Yes, Angel girl."

"About tonight."

Micah reached over and squeezed her hand. "I'm sorrier for tonight than you'll ever know. I'd cut off my right arm before I'd ever hurt you. We need to come to an understanding. I want you here. I want to help you. I don't want you out there alone. But I need to know you're safe, and I'd rather you not go back to places like The House."

She blew out her breath, her cheeks puffing in frustration. There was so much in his statement she wanted to deny, to refuse, but now wasn't the time. She didn't want him to be sorry, and she damn sure wanted to make certain what happened tonight happened again. And again.

All she wanted was to curl into his arms and rest. Just for a little while she wanted to feel his strength and the tenderness she knew he was capable of. Yes, she wanted his power, his control, his dominance, but she wanted it all, his complete care. His regard. His love.

"Hold me," she whispered as she leaned toward him. "Please?"

He hesitated as if wavering on the brink of indecision. She didn't give him a chance to deny her. She moved into his space, cuddled against his chest and wrapped her arms around his waist. She rested her cheek against his collarbone and nestled her head just below his chin.

Nothing was going to ruin this moment for her. She would savor every sweet second.

Gingerly his arms curled around her, and he leaned back, taking her with him as he reclined against the back of the sofa. They sat in silence as he absently rubbed his palm up and down her back. The heat of his touch scorched her even through the thick material of the robe.

"I don't want you to be sorry, Micah," she said softly. "I'm not. Don't you understand? I know you. I can give you what you need."

His entire body went stiff. For a long moment he sat there, his hand still against her back. And when he finally spoke, the absolute certainty in his voice made her heart sink.

"But I can't give you what you need, Angel girl."

CHAPTER 10

Angelina trudged into the kitchen in a pair of pajama shorts and a muscle shirt, yawning broadly as she rubbed her eyes.

"Want something to eat?" Micah asked. "I'm doing toast and juice."

She stood by the counter and looked around like she was having a hard time getting her bearings. Guilt crushed him. She looked tired and vulnerable, and he still wasn't convinced he hadn't hurt her. She was a small woman, and he was *not* a small man.

His entire gut clenched as he remembered the way her pussy had gripped him. So tight that he'd had to force his way in, pushing against her body's natural resistance.

Jesus, he had to stop thinking about her. This was insane. She was David's little sister. She trusted him, and he'd used her in an unforgivable manner to slake his lust when any of the other women in that room would have been more than willing to take whatever he wanted to dish out.

But no one had fired his senses like sweet, innocent-looking Angelina, a woman who knew everything he'd tried so hard to forget.

His head jerked up when the doorbell rang. What the hell? It was six in the morning.

"I'll get it," Angelina said as she started forward.

"I don't think—"

But she'd already disappeared into the hallway.

Angelina opened the door and peered out at the two men standing just a few feet away. They were both tall. One was solidly muscled and looked intimidating with his bald head and goatee. A small gold hoop hung from his left ear. He wasn't someone she'd want to meet on a dark street.

The other man was leaner but no less muscled, and he wore his muddy blond hair in a short military style. Both had on faded jeans and casual T-shirts, and both looked at her with open curiosity.

"You must be David's sister," the guy with the muddy blond hair said.

"Uh, yeah," she said cautiously.

"What are you two boneheads doing here at this hour?" Micah growled from behind her.

She jerked around just as Micah pulled her back and stepped toward the two men.

"Not going to introduce us?" she murmured.

Micah scowled. "Guys this is Angelina Moyano. Angel this is Connor Malone and Nathan Tucker."

"And which is which?" she asked in amusement.

The bald guy grinned, transforming his badass looks into boyish charm. "I'm Nathan." He jerked his thumb to the side. "This is Connor. We work with Micah."

"That doesn't explain what the hell you're doing here," Micah said darkly.

"Ah, well, you're usually gone by now, so we were just checking to see if you were coming in," Connor said.

Micah shot them both murderous glances that suggested he didn't believe a word they said. Angelina cleared her throat to disguise her laugh. "Well, it was nice meeting you two, but I really need to get dressed and ready for work."

At that Micah seemed to forget all about his two friends.

"You found a job already?" he demanded. "Where? Doing what?"

"A little café two blocks from here."

"Waitressing? Why the hell are you waitressing? I know damn well David would be spinning in his grave. He made sure you were able to go to college. You did graduate, didn't you?"

"You'd know if you'd bothered to be there," she said lightly to disguise the quick flash of hurt. "You couldn't leave fast enough after David and Hannah died."

Immediately Micah's face became a stone wall. "That's enough."

She glanced between him and his friends' confused expressions. "They don't know about Hannah?"

"I'll see you two at work," Micah said to Connor and Nathan right before he slammed the door in their faces.

She stared at Micah. "They don't, do they?"

"I don't talk about Hannah," he said in a tight voice. "I never talked about David either until you arrived and I had to explain who you were."

She turned away and walked down the hallway toward her bedroom.

"Angel," he called.

But she ignored him and shut the door to sever the connection.

She sank onto the bed then flopped back to stare at the ceiling. Maybe he hadn't let go of Hannah after all. Was he still deeply in love with her? Is that why he was convinced he couldn't give Angelina what she needed? Was he still mourning his dead wife?

When he'd come to Miami that last time, just before Angelina left to come here to Houston, she'd been convinced he'd let go. She'd watched from a distance as he'd visited David's and Hannah's graves and wondered why she wasn't important enough for him to even check in on. There had been such a finality to his actions, and she'd known then he wouldn't be back again. It was what prompted her to finally act on her long-held feelings for him. Three years was a long time to mourn a lost love.

"Oh, Micah," she whispered. "Have you been running from your past all this time? Have you tried to forget us? Is that why you left me too? Was I a reminder of everything you lost?"

She'd been so certain that Micah was ready to love again, but now . . . Now she wasn't so sure.

Emotion knotted her stomach. And fear. Fear of being alone again. Because she knew without a doubt that she couldn't stay here. She couldn't pretend to have a platonic relationship with Micah. She wouldn't hide her feelings, not that she could. Not after hiding them for so long.

She'd thought the best approach was a direct one, but now she realized she'd pushed him too hard, too fast. She'd seen the haunted, pained look come over his face when she'd said Hannah's name. No man looked like that over a mere mention of someone's name if he'd moved past his grief.

And she couldn't stay if she had no chance of winning his heart.

Micah hadn't planned to go in to work that morning at all. How could he and leave Angelina after what he'd done? He had already called Pop before Nathan and Connor barged in all curious about Angelina and wanting a glimpse. Nosy bastards.

He'd fully intended to spend the morning with Angelina, if for no other reason than to establish some ground rules regarding their relationship.

Relationship. Jesus. He wasn't sure what they had, but him leaving her to fend for herself after David died was hardly the foundation of a relationship.

Before he could make Nathan and Connor leave, or tell them he *wasn't* coming into work, Angelina had dropped all that crap about her job, then Hannah had been brought up and Angelina had high-tailed it to her room.

He'd left only because the idea of staying in his apartment was enough to drive him insane. And so here he was, out driving. No clear destination. A brand-new pack of smokes lying on the seat beside him—already half gone.

So much for his resolve to quit.

His lungs would feel like shit later, but for now each inhale was about all that was keeping what little sanity he had intact.

He slowed when he arrived at Damon's huge-ass house, and for a long moment he sat in his truck, staring up the driveway. He hadn't intended to end up here, but maybe he'd known that he needed to clear the air with Damon. He wanted for Damon to hear about it from him, not get it secondhand from someone who'd seen everything at The House.

After tossing the cigarette butt out his window, he pulled into the driveway and drove up to the house. Damon might not even be home, although he did spend a lot of time working from the house now that he and Serena were married. She'd moved her own offices into his house and had continued running her business, Fantasy Incorporated, after encouragement from Damon.

Micah liked Serena. He'd had his doubts in the beginning that she could be the kind of woman who would make Damon happy. A submissive woman. Not just in bed, but in all aspects. But the two were happy, and though Serena herself had doubts at the onset of their relationship, she hadn't given up, and for that she had Micah's utmost respect and affection.

Apart from David, Damon was the closest Micah had allowed anyone. Oh, the guys at work were his buddies. There was no doubt about that. Great friends. He liked them all. But he'd never confided in them anything of his life before his arrival in Houston. Only Damon knew of his relationship with Hannah and that he and David had . . . shared her.

Before he was fully out of the truck, he looked up to see Damon standing in the open doorway of his home. He was leaned against the door frame, watching Micah as he walked toward him.

When he was a foot away, Micah stopped and shoved his hands into his jeans pockets. "I need to talk to you, Damon."

Damon nodded. "Come in. We can go onto the terrace. I hope you won't mind that Serena will join us in a moment. This is our day together, and I don't like to be away from her."

"I don't want to interrupt," Micah began.

But Damon ignored him and merely gestured for him to follow. Micah sighed. Damon was a smooth bastard. It surprised Micah that as alike as they were they got along so well. Neither liked to budge, and both were accustomed to doing things their own way.

"Want some coffee to go with all those cigarettes you've smoked?" Damon asked as they stepped outside the back.

Micah grimaced. "Smell that bad, huh."

Damon smiled. "Thought you'd quit? Or was that last week."

"Fuck you," Micah grumbled. "I hadn't had a smoke in three

weeks until today, and before that I'd narrowed it down to one or two a day max."

"So what prompted today's black lung?"

Damon sat and motioned for Micah to do the same. Micah sank into one of the patio chairs and briefly closed his eyes.

"Have you ever done something that you knew in your bones was unforgivably wrong? Not just a mistake, but something that went against every one of your principles?"

Damon's expression grew pensive. "I can't say that I have."

"It sucks," Micah said bleakly.

There was a brief hesitation. "What happened?"

Micah struggled with what to say, how to say it. And then he figured there was no pretty way to put it.

"I pretty much raped Angelina at The House last night."

To Damon's credit, he didn't react. He didn't say anything, nor did his expression change. He just waited.

Micah related the entire episode, from the time he walked in to see the three men with Angelina to the time he tossed her over the end of the couch and fucked her. Without a condom.

"You lost control."

"I raped her."

Damon shook his head. "Even Angelina refutes that. You said so yourself. She wanted what happened."

"I didn't give her a *choice*. Goddamn it, Damon. What we do is all about choice. We take, we take a hell of a lot from a woman, but it's because she chooses to give it. I'm demanding. I like submissive women. Completely and utterly submissive. But never, *never* have I ever lost control like that. Never have I hurt a woman."

"Have you spoken to Angelina? Told her all this?" Damon asked.

Micah sighed. "It's complicated. I get the feeling . . . I get that she wants more from me. What I mean is that she wants something I can't give her. And I won't use her as some sexual toy. She deserves better than that. I don't understand my reaction to her. I've had women since Hannah. I've enjoyed women. But with Angelina there is something that I just can't explain. It's not fun and laid back with her. It's not sexy and casual. I can't be around her and not want to take her over. I have such dark thoughts. And goddamn it, Damon, she's David's sister. Of all the women in the world, she is off-limits."

"Why?"

Micah stared at him like he'd lost his mind. "What the hell do you mean, 'why'? It's self-explanatory. Hell, she lived with me and David and Hannah for a year. She's . . . family."

"She's not family, Micah. She's your best friend's sister. Big difference."

"I can't believe you're being so calm about this," Micah muttered. "For God's sake, Damon, I raped a woman in your damn club."

"Is that why you came? You want me to punish you? Want me to kick you out and tell you never to come back? I'd say you're doing a good enough job of beating up yourself. You don't need my help."

Micah let out a sound of frustration.

"Go home and talk to Angelina, Micah. I get that this has knocked you for a loop, but what you did wasn't rape. She was willing. Very willing, I'd say. Are you going to sit there and tell me you've never fucked a woman when she was tied up and helpless under your hands?"

"Uh maybe I should come back," Serena whispered from behind them.

Both men turned to see her standing there, her expression unsure as if she was afraid of intruding. Micah gentled his expression, not wanting to put her off.

She glanced down self-consciously at her silk robe that fell to mid-calf, and Micah knew that was all she had on. Her feet were bare, but Damon always teased her about her love of being barefooted.

Damon simply held out a hand to her, and she walked over to kneel beside him. She laid her head on his lap and rubbed her cheek lovingly over his thigh.

"Serena mine, what have I told you? Your poor knees."

He pulled her into his lap and wrapped his arms possessively around her waist, letting his hand rest on the curve of her hip.

"Hello, Serena," Micah said with a smile.

She smiled back. "Am I interrupting? You both sounded so serious."

Micah felt his chest cave just a little. He did love this woman. He loved all the women his friends had hooked up with.

"Damon was just kicking my ass. You probably saved what little was left of it."

Serena arched a disbelieving eyebrow. Damon nuzzled her neck, nipping lightly at the curve of her shoulder.

"Micah is having woman trouble," Damon said by way of explanation.

"Nice, Damon. Real fucking nice. Sorry, Serena."

She laughed and waved a hand. "Are you really having woman trouble? I never thought to see the day. Don't women generally throw themselves at you in all directions?"

"It's complicated, and I'd appreciate it if you didn't tell the girls. They'd just tell Nathan and Gray, who'd use every opportunity to make my life hell."

Serena smiled gently. "I won't tell Julie and Faith. They love you to pieces, you know. They'd help you without any questions if you ever needed it. So if you ever want to talk . . ."

"Thanks, sweetness," he said with genuine affection. "I love all of you to pieces too. But this is . . . this is something I'm going to have to work out on my own. I'd hoped . . . I'd hoped that when I moved here I'd leave my past behind. It was a mistake, one I'm paying for now. I made some bad choices and hurt someone in the process. Now I've got to figure out how to make it up to her."

Serena reached out and touched his hand. "If there's anything I can do to help . . ."

He blew her a soundless kiss. "I appreciate it. Both of you."

She wrinkled her nose. "I didn't, however, promise not to tell Faith that you're smoking again."

Micah closed his eyes and groaned. "What is it with you people? For the love of God, don't sic Faith on me. At least Julie will light up with me every once in a while when Nathan isn't looking. But Faith is like a frickin' pit bull. Nag, nag, nag. I don't know how Gray puts up with her."

"Micah, about your . . . woman . . . Is there anything I can do? I mean, is she new here? I heard enough of your conversation to get the impression she wasn't from here and that she was someone you knew in the past. The girls and I could introduce ourselves, maybe go out and have some girly fun."

Both he and Damon groaned.

"Hell, woman, the last time you all went out for girly fun, you ended up nearly passed out on the floor at Cattleman's, and Nathan had to call me and Gray to come get you."

Micah sighed. He wanted to be able to trust Serena, but she was close to Faith and Julie, two women he'd been intimate with. It would be awkward as hell for Angelina to be exposed to them and vice versa.

"What is it?" Serena asked. "You look so . . . torn."

Damon squeezed her hand lovingly. "Don't pressure him, love."

"No, it's okay," Micah said. "It's just complicated. I swear I keep saying that, but there's no better way to explain it."

He looked at Serena and swallowed. "Angelina is, was, my best friend's younger sister. I was . . . married." The words nearly strangled him, but at least he hadn't had to say Hannah's name.

Serena looked at him in shock. "Married? Why does no one know this? I mean why is it such a secret?"

"Damon knows, and again—complicated. David and I . . . we both loved the same woman. David was my partner on the force. We shared everything. Including the woman I married."

Serena's mouth formed an O of surprise.

"The thing is, I love Faith and Julie, and you know that I've been with them both. I've had threesomes with them. Casual. Fun. Meaningless. But the last thing I ever want them to know or suspect is that the entire time I was making love to them I was pretending they were another woman. They don't deserve that and I'd never hurt them that way."

Serena's lips turned down into an unhappy frown. "Oh, Micah. I'm so sorry. What happened?"

Micah shifted uncomfortably at the idea of spilling his guts for only the second time since Hannah died. In for a penny and all that crap. He'd already gone this far, and Damon would probably tell her later anyway.

"David and Hannah died in a car accident."

Tears filled Serena's eyes. "How awful for you to lose your best friend and the woman you loved at the same time."

"Everyone thought they were cheating on me," Micah said bitterly. "That they were skipping town together. We didn't advertise our relationship. Hannah married me, but David was an equal in the relationship. I didn't have my head in the job anymore after they died. Everyone pitied me. Stared and talked behind my back. I made a stupid mistake, got injured. It was easier for me to use that as an excuse and just leave. Only I left Angelina, and, God help me, I never gave her another thought. I'm a selfish bastard and my sins don't end there."

"But she's here now," Damon pointed out. "A good opportunity to atone for those sins, don't you think?"

"It would've been if I hadn't compounded them," Micah said painfully.

"Quit being so hard on yourself. Angelina strikes me as a very resilient, intelligent woman who knows precisely what she wants and isn't afraid to go after it."

"If I only knew what she wanted," Micah said with a sigh.

Damon raised an eyebrow. "I thought that much was obvious, Micah. Clearly, she wants you."

CHAPTER 11

$\mathcal{A}$ngelina dodged a customer not looking where he was going and continued to the table with the tray she was carrying. Her first day hadn't been a cakewalk by any means, but she caught on quickly, and her trainer had already turned her loose on her own small section of tables.

She distributed the plates with a smile and started back toward the kitchen when the manager motioned her to stop.

"Table six is yours."

She nodded and turned in that direction then stopped in her tracks. Micah's friends Nathan and Connor sat in the booth with another man. With a roll of her eyes, she took her order pad out of her apron and approached the table.

At least they didn't act surprised to see her.

"Let me guess. You just happened to be in the neighborhood," she drawled.

Connor grinned. "Hell no. We hit two other cafés before we found the right one."

"Uh-huh. Any particular reason or did you not get enough of an eyeful this morning?"

"Chalk it up to curiosity," Nathan said. "It's not every day we get to see Micah's nuts twisting in the wind. Wanted to see the woman responsible."

The other man cleared his throat. "Since these morons aren't going to introduce use, I'm Gray Montgomery, Connor's brother-in-law."

She stuck out her hand. "I'm Angelina Moyano."

"Very pretty name," Gray said as he took her hand in his firm grip.

"What can I get you?" she asked when she'd retracted her hand.

"Ah hell, we weren't really going to eat," Nathan said.

"Speak for yourself," Connor protested. "I'll have the special with gravy. Oh, and bring me a cheeseburger, the large one, and some fries with that too."

Angelina gaped at him.

Gray just shook his head. "He has a hollow leg."

Angelina let her gaze wander down Connor's very fit body. Wherever he put it all, it certainly didn't hang around.

"Just coffee for me," Gray added.

"I'll take a chocolate shake," Nathan said.

"Coming right up."

She turned and hit her other tables on her way to the kitchen, refilling drinks before she placed Connor's order. She shook her head as she entered the information into the ordering system. How could he possibly eat that much and still be as buff as he was? He

must get a lot of exercise, either that or he was one of those disgust-
ing people blessed with really good genes.

Next she got their drinks and brought them to the table.

"So, are you staying here?" Connor asked casually. "I mean in
Houston. Permanently. Or are you just visiting?"

"Yep."

They all looked chagrined when she didn't offer anything
more.

"Was that a yep, you're staying or a yep, you're just visiting?"
Nathan asked.

She smiled. They were cute in an obvious sort of way.

"Maybe y'all can help me out with something."

They looked curiously at her.

"I need a cheap place to stay, and preferably somewhere that
doesn't need to know my life history."

Gray frowned at that statement. Nathan's brow furrowed and
Connor just studied her with an inscrutable expression. They made
her uncomfortable, and in that moment she realized she'd underes-
timated their playful charm.

"Shouldn't you be talking about this with Micah?" Nathan asked
carefully.

She twisted her lips. "Let's just say Micah and I don't see eye to
eye on everything."

"You need to be careful," Gray cautioned. "There are a lot of
places that a girl like you has no business being in."

It was on the tip of her tongue to ask him what exactly a girl like
her was, but she let it go. She knew what he was trying to say.

"That's why I asked you for help," she said patiently. "You know
the city, right? You could point me away from the not so great
places." She glanced over her shoulder. "Shoot. Never mind, okay?
I'll figure something out. I gotta see about my customers."

She left them, knowing they were still staring at her. Micah would probably know what she was planning before they ever left the café.

When Connor's order was up, she balanced the tray and took it to the table. She set the mound of food in front of Connor while Nathan and Gray looked at him in disbelief.

"Anything else?" she asked.

"God, I hope not," Gray muttered.

"Okay, well here's your check. Just pay the cashier on your way out," she said cheerfully. "Nice meeting you, Gray."

She started to walk away when Connor caught her arm.

"Angelina, wait. If you were serious about looking for a place to stay, there's actually an apartment in Micah's complex. We all sort of live there actually. Well, Faith and Gray moved out, but Nathan, Micah and I still live there."

She shook her head. "Oh, I couldn't possibly afford an apartment there."

"How do you know?" Connor asked. "I haven't told you what the rent is."

"I know," she said firmly. "They're way too nice to be in my price range. I need something along the lines of an efficiency. Preferably furnished, because I don't have the cash to be furniture shopping right now."

All three men frowned, and she shifted impatiently, suddenly eager to escape their scrutiny. At least now she knew why Micah was friends with them. They were all alike. Overbearing and very male.

"I happen to know the owner of the complex," Connor said. "I'll talk to him and see what I can do."

Nathan and Gray both snorted, and she frowned at them, wondering what private joke she was missing out on.

"Look, I appreciate it, Connor, but I really can't afford that kind of apartment, and, well, Micah probably won't want me living that close to him anyway."

"Now hold on," Gray said. "You don't think he'd want you where he could at least be assured of your safety? No better place than right there at his own complex."

She smiled a little sadly. "Micah will be very glad to see the back of me."

Nathan cursed softly, and Connor frowned even harder.

"What time do you get off?" Connor asked.

Startled by the abrupt change in topic, she shot him a questioning stare. "Two."

"Did you drive or do you need a ride?"

"Uh, I drove."

"I'll meet you at Micah's apartment at two fifteen then."

"Whatever for?"

"To show you your apartment. It's not furnished yet, but I'm sure we can work something out."

She stared at him in complete befuddlement. "What, do you own the place or something?"

"Not exactly," Connor replied. "My dad does."

"Oh, I couldn't let you do that. You don't even know me."

He put a firm finger over her lips. "Two fifteen. Micah's place. You're Micah's. That's all any of us need to know. We tend to look after our own around here."

Gray nodded his agreement, and even Nathan had donned a fierce look at her resistance.

"But I'm not Micah's anything!" she protested.

Her announcement was met with uncomfortable silence.

"He running hard?" Gray asked softly.

God, how the hell had she gotten into such a conversation with complete strangers? And friends of Micah's at that. Like she wanted her feelings bandied about in some amused male conversation later?

She clamped her lips shut and stared mutinously at them. "I need to go now."

"Two fifteen, sweetie," Connor said gently. "Don't be late. I hate to be kept waiting."

Nathan and Gray cracked up, laughing so hard that Nathan started wheezing. She just looked at them in bewilderment.

"He's never on time for anything," Nathan explained between bouts of laughter. "If he says two fifteen, be ready around three."

Connor shot him a dirty look. "I do not keep a woman waiting. Ever. It's bad for my sex life."

Angelina chuckled. She could see why they irritated Micah so, but then when Micah wasn't being so damn serious around her, he was the king of practical jokes. She wanted to see and enjoy that lighter side of him again. Obviously he shared it with his friends, but with her, he was strung as tight as a rubber band.

Connor turned back to Angelina. "Seriously. Two fifteen. I'll be on time and waiting." He held up two fingers. "Scout's honor."

She rolled her eyes. "Okay. I won't turn down that offer. After last night, I have a feeling Micah is going to kick me out anyway."

They looked at her with a mixture of disbelief and questioning, as if they couldn't quite tell whether or not she was teasing, and were about to burst with wanting to ask her what she meant.

Before they could, she headed toward the next table to refill more drinks.

"What do you make of this?" Nathan murmured after she'd gone.

Connor stared at her for a long time as she smiled and served the other customers. "I don't know. I know Micah's been acting pretty damn weird. It's not like him to be so . . . serious around a woman. Or so grumpy."

"I'm more curious what her story is," Gray said. "What's with wanting an apartment where no one checks her background?"

"Leave it to you to pick up on that," Nathan said. "Think she could be in some kind of trouble? Maybe that's what's setting Micah off?"

Connor frowned. "I dunno. She seems so . . . innocent."

Gray snorted. "Some of the best criminals are."

"Oh come on," Nathan scoffed. "Criminal my ass. If that girl's a criminal, I'm Martha Fucking Stewart."

"I knew going out with Julie was going to turn you into a fucking pansy," Connor said in disgust.

"Want to take it out to the parking lot and see this pansy kick your scrawny ass?" Nathan challenged.

"Boys, boys," Gray said.

"I wonder why Micah would have kicked her out," Connor said, turning the conversation back to the matter at hand. "Or do you think she was kidding about that?"

"I think she was only half kidding," Nathan said.

Gray nodded. "You should probably stay out of it, Connor. Micah won't like you interfering."

Connor studied Angelina, looking at the fatigue and sadness behind the bright smile. Fuck Micah. Micah might be the softy when it came to women, but for whatever reason, he wasn't treating this one very well, and while Connor liked to tease Micah about being such a pushover, Connor didn't like to see an unprotected woman either.

True, it wasn't any of his business why Micah had his head up his ass when it came to Angelina, but it didn't mean Connor was going to turn a blind eye and let her rent a place where she was going to get mugged, raped or killed.

The guys liked to give him a hard time because he was so protective of his sister Faith. Well they could just give him shit for taking Angelina under his wing as well. Because he damn sure wasn't going to direct a young woman out into the city unprotected.

CHAPTER 12

*A*ngelina left the café at five minutes to two and slid into her car. It was actually a decent temperature for this early in the fall, and she started to roll down her window after she inserted her key.

She stopped and stared around the interior, a frown pulling at her brows. Something was weird. She glanced down at the console and the miscellaneous items she had housed there. A few pens, a pack of gum, a tube of lipstick, dental floss, two envelopes . . . Her pictures were gone.

She rummaged through the stuff looking for the two snapshots of her and David that she always kept in her car. Where the hell could they be?

A prickle of unease snaked up her spine. Had someone been in her car?

She closed her eyes, shook her head and then leaned back against the head rest. A rueful laugh escaped. She was being ridiculous. No one had been in her car. It had been locked and there was no sign that anyone had broken in. Plus she was no longer in Miami, and she'd been careful. There was no reason to believe she could possibly have been followed to Houston, and moreover, why would someone make the effort?

The pictures must be with her other stuff. Maybe in her suitcase or one of her purses. Her wallet maybe. She'd find it all when she unpacked eventually.

She cranked the engine and rolled her shoulder in an effort to shake off the sense of foreboding. Scaring herself to death wasn't high on her list of priorities for the day. Finding a place to live, however, was.

On the way to Micah's apartment, she took mental stock of her finances. She still had cash socked away in her bank account, but she'd be an idiot to access it right now. Maybe later, when she had a few paychecks under her belt, she could take a weekend trip, drive a few states north and withdraw a large amount from the ATM or just arrange for a wire transfer. She'd research her options when the time came.

For now, she had what cash she'd dared bring with her and today's wages. As great as it would be to have a nice, safe apartment close to Micah, she doubted it was in the cards. The money just wasn't there, and she doubted people like Connor understood just what it was to have a hand-to-mouth existence.

Her plan to convince Micah that he needed her seemed pretty silly and more than a little naïve. It wasn't something that could happen overnight, and it damn sure couldn't be forced by living in close proximity.

If it was going to happen, she'd have to give him time.

A few minutes later, she pulled into her parking spot and looked over to see Connor standing against his truck waiting for her. She honestly hadn't been sure he was serious.

He certainly seemed serious now, with the way he was striding toward her car. Any playfulness from lunch had disappeared and been replaced by a stern somberness.

She almost groaned. Yet another male determined to play big brother. Yeah, she appreciated it, but did no one ever look at her and see a hot-blooded attractive woman?

When Micah could actually forget she was David's sister, he certainly didn't have a problem with lusting after her. Too bad he had to come to his senses on a regular basis.

"Hey," she said in greeting when Connor walked up.

"Hey, Angelina, you ready to look at the apartment? I figured Faith's old one would be best because it's situated in the middle of mine, Nathan's and Micah's. We sorta put her there on purpose, but that was before Gray came along."

Angelina cocked her head. "Do all of you have bizarrely over-developed protective tendencies when it comes to women?"

He blinked as if that were the dumbest question he'd ever heard.

"Well no, not all women. Just the ones who belong to us."

She shook her head at him. "I don't belong to Micah, Connor. He doesn't claim me at all. I'm just David's sister, and believe me, he hasn't spared me a thought over the last few years."

Connor shrugged. "Just because he's a dumbass doesn't mean the rest of us are. You're here now, and by virtue of your relationship with Micah, whatever that may or may not be, you belong to us and we look out for our own."

She couldn't contain the smile as she stared up at him. It was nice to have . . . people. People she could count on. She hadn't had that in so long, and God she'd missed having that connection. Friends. People she in turn could care about.

"Aw now don't go and cry on me." A look of sheer male panic crossed his face.

She blinked away the threatening moisture and impulsively reached out to squeeze his hand. "Thank you."

He smiled and chucked her gently on the cheek. "You looked like you could use a friend. I guess I'm volunteering."

For the first time in a long while, she felt lighter and a little more optimistic.

"Now come on. Let's go see that apartment."

"Serena, swear to God, if you don't spill, I'm going to hurt you."

"Ow, ow! For God's sake, Julie, lighten up on the hands," Serena yelped. "I'm going to have bruises."

"Don't look at me for sympathy," Faith said from the other massage table.

Serena glared over at Faith, who innocently studied her nails while Julie mauled Serena's back.

"I can't believe I cut out on Damon on our day together to come here and be abused," Serena sniffed.

"What you should have done is cut out on Damon to come here and give us the dirt," Julie said as she forcefully kneaded Serena's shoulders.

"What dirt?" Serena asked.

Faith groaned. "Come on. Micah? Bug up his ass? He didn't show up for work today. Totally not like him. Then he shows up at your house to talk to Damon?"

Serena frowned. "I can't tell you guys. Seriously."

Julie's hands stilled. "What do you mean you can't tell us? It's us. Who else would you tell? I mean I tell you guys everything. And I mean everything. Things I totally shouldn't. Like all those details about my supposedly anonymous threesome that wasn't so anonymous after all?"

"Not to mention all the details on my sex life," Faith muttered. "I could have remained little miss innocent in your eyes if it weren't for that."

Serena and Julie both snorted with laughter.

"Seriously, Serena, what's wrong with Micah?" Faith asked. "I'm really worried about him."

Serena saw the very real concern in Faith's eyes. Faith and Micah were certainly close, which made it all the more strange that Micah had never shared any of the details of his past with anyone here.

She sighed and rolled over, reaching for the robe to cover herself. She sat up and let her legs hang over the side of the table while Julie and Faith eyeballed her in expectation.

"I really can't. I mean he was speaking in confidence to Damon."

The peal of a cell phone split the air. Faith hopped down from her table and snagged her purse. After a few minutes of fumbling, she dragged the phone out and hastily slapped it to her ear.

"Hello? Oh hi, Connor, what's up? Um well yeah I have some stuff we didn't move to the house. Why do you ask? Sure, you can have it, but didn't you just buy your 'guy' furniture for your apartment? Surely you can't be interested in my girly stuff."

Serena and Julie snickered.

A bemused expression spread across Faith's face. Then confusion followed by speculation. Julie looked at Serena and whispered, "This has to be good whatever it is. She looks like she swallowed a fly over there."

"It's in the storage building, the one a block over from the complex. Gray has the key, and he should be home. Well how would I know if he'd help you move? Call him. You're interrupting something important here, brother dear. Uh huh, okay whatever. I'll talk to you later and don't think I won't want every little detail."

She closed the phone and eyed Serena and Julie with a peculiar glint in her eye. "Well that was interesting."

"Do tell. We're dying of curiosity over here," Julie drawled.

"He wanted to know if he could have some of my old furniture that's in storage. Apparently he's moving someone into my old apartment. He broke off and was talking to her for a minute, and he called her sweetie."

Julie's mouth dropped. "Sweetie? Mr. Gruff called a chick sweetie? I mean he's usually so straitlaced."

"Oh, he is not," Faith huffed. "He can be serious, yes, but he jokes around with the guys with the best of them, and you try being his sister."

"Maybe he's seeing someone?" Serena offered. "I mean he's a good-looking guy. Drool-worthy. It shouldn't be a shock to hear him with a woman."

Faith shrugged. "No, but you have to understand. Connor keeps his distance. He's a strictly casual guy, and suddenly he's moving her into my apartment and getting her furniture and stuff."

"Wonder who she is," Julie murmured.

"I think he called her Angelina. Well, when he wasn't calling her sweetie," Faith said with a laugh.

Serena's mouth went slack. She was pretty sure she looked like a guppy gasping for air.

"What?" Julie demanded before Serena could regain her composure.

"Shit," Serena whispered. "I don't believe in coincidences that huge. Micah's woman's name is Angelina."

"Whoa, back up. Micah has what?" Faith asked.

Serena sighed. "Hell. I'm not supposed to be sharing any of this crap with you guys. It's deeply personal to Micah."

Julie sniffed. "Does anyone else find it ironic that the only one here who hasn't slept with Micah is the one with the personal information?"

Faith rolled her eyes but laughed. "We're not letting you out of here until you tell us everything, Serena. It's not like we're going to run out and tell the world."

With a resigned shrug, Serena related the morning's conversation between Damon and Micah. By the time she'd finished, Faith's eyes were round with shock.

"Wow, I had no idea," Faith whispered. "Married. I can't even get my head around it."

"Okay, so what's this chick doing with Connor if she's with Micah?" Julie asked with a scowl.

"From what I gathered there isn't a relationship between Micah and Angelina, though it seems Angelina wants one," Serena said.

"Again, so what the hell is she doing with Connor?" Julie persisted.

"Maybe he's just helping her," Faith pointed out. "It certainly sounds like she could use it."

"And calling her sweetie all the while, huh?" Julie said snidely.

"Sheathe the claws, girlfriend," Serena admonished Julie. "Micah is a big boy. I sincerely doubt Angelina is doing him any harm, and like Faith said, I'd say she needs the help and friendship. I gathered from Micah's conversation that he pretty much walked out and never looked back. That had to be hard for her."

A calculating light glinted in Julie's eyes. "Then maybe we should drop in and see if there's anything we can do."

CHAPTER 13

"Okay, sweetie, all done for now."

Angelina stared in disbelief at the now furnished apartment. She couldn't even begin to comprehend that it was hers. She had a bed, furniture, dishes even.

Tears gathered in her eyes, and she hastily blinked them away. "I don't know how to thank you," she said huskily.

Connor smiled. "You'll thank me by not crying."

"It's generally known men are worthless human beings around female tears," Gray said from across the room.

Angelina laughed. An ache bloomed in her chest until it threatened to crush her. Was it any wonder Micah hadn't come back to Miami? He had a life here. Wonderful friends.

"Hey, why the sad look all of a sudden?" Connor asked.

She glanced up and grimaced. "Just thinking."

"About?"

"That I could understand why Micah never went back to Miami," she said softly. "He has a good life here. Wonderful friends."

"You have us now too," Connor said.

She looked at him in disbelief. "Just like that?"

Gray moved closer and threw one arm over her shoulders. "Not so long ago, I was the outsider here. This is a great group of people. I wouldn't trade them for anything even when they're royal pains in my ass, and believe me, they are."

Connor flipped Gray off. "The only reason I tolerate you is because you took a bullet for my sister."

Angelina's eyes widened, and Gray just shook his head.

"So you like it?" Connor asked.

"Like it? I love it! It's more than I dared hope for. I was just wanting something that was mine. It didn't have to be big or gorgeous."

"Well, it's yours for as long as you want it," Connor said with an easy grin. "I should warn you now that Pop will probably happen by. I've told him all about you of course, but he's like a mother hen with his chicks. He'll want to come by and cluck over you."

"Just don't mind his bluster," Gray warned. "He's all gravelly and full of shit, but underneath he's a complete and utter pussycat."

"He sounds wonderful," Angelina said with a sigh. "You're lucky to have such a great dad," she told Connor.

"Your dad not alive?" Connor asked.

"No. He died when I was young. David always took care of me."

Connor exchanged quick glances with Gray, and she hastened to change the subject.

"Hey, you guys should probably get on out of here. Your wives will be wondering where you are."

Connor scowled. "I'm not married."

"No, but I am, and she's right. Faith will be wondering where I am," Gray said.

"Thank you again so much," Angelina said feelingly. Impulsively she reached out and hugged Gray. "Micah is lucky to have all of you."

Gray squeezed back and ruffled her hair affectionately as he pulled away. "As Connor keeps trying to tell you, you have us now too, like it or not. Just let me know if there's something you need, okay?"

She smiled and nodded.

"Someone want to tell me what the fuck is going on?"

Everyone turned to see Micah glowering in the door, his gaze fixed on Angelina.

"Hey, man, chill," Gray said in an easy tone as he started toward the door. "We're just helping Angelina get moved in."

"I see." His gaze never left Angelina, and she felt her skin peel back under the force of his scrutiny. "And when were you going to tell me you were moving?"

She sighed. "I need to go over to your place to get my bag if that's okay. We can talk on the way."

"You want me to stick around?" Connor asked with a cautious glance in Micah's direction.

Startled, she shook her head. Whatever Micah's dark mood, he certainly wouldn't hurt her. Maybe peel an inch or two of her skin off, but that would be it.

"Beat it," Micah growled in Connor's direction.

Connor stiffened and walked casually over to where Micah stood. "You know I've about had all I can take of your surly-ass attitude," he said softly. "Whatever your problem is, don't take it out on us and sure as hell don't take it out on Angelina."

Micah closed his eyes for a moment then looked back at Connor. "I'll talk to you later, okay, man? Just . . . just let me speak to Angelina."

Connor glanced back again at Angelina and she nodded, encouraging him to go.

"Thank you," she said quietly.

"I'll swing by to check on you tomorrow," Connor promised as he and Gray headed for the door.

As soon as the door closed, Micah closed the distance between them, his eyes so serious. He reached out to frame her shoulders, his fingers shaking a bit against her skin.

"Angel, what's going on?"

She swallowed and prayed not to lose her composure. She had to handle this just right.

"This apartment sort of fell into my lap. It seemed perfect. I know you don't want me at your place, and there is no way I could afford this without Connor's help. I couldn't pass it up. He and Gray gave me some of Gray's wife's old stuff and voilà, here I am in my own place."

"What kind of help is Connor giving you?" Micah asked darkly. "How the hell did you get hooked up with him or Gray? And why the hell didn't you come to me about moving? I would have helped you, Angel. If you need money or furniture, whatever it is, you can come to me."

She shifted uncomfortably. "I didn't plan this. Connor, Nathan and Gray ate lunch in the café where I work today. I asked them if they knew of any places I could rent. Connor said I could have this place. It was too good of an opportunity to pass up. He and Gray offered to move Faith's stuff here. No reason I shouldn't go ahead and move in."

She lifted her chin and stared him directly in the eyes. "It's better this way. You won't be tripping over me, and you can go back to doing what you do best. Avoiding me and your past."

He sucked in his breath, quick pain flashing across his face.

"I can't seem to do anything but hurt you, Angel girl."

She reached out and touched his cheek. "It's my fault. I barged into your life. I was wrong to expect things to be different. I assumed . . . after three years . . . I guess I thought you might have put it all behind you now."

His Adam's apple worked up and down. "I won't leave you this time. If you need me, if you ever need anything, promise you'll come to me immediately."

She nodded.

He pulled her into his arms, hugging her tightly against his chest. For a long moment they stood there, her cheek resting against his shoulder.

"Are you sure this is what you want?" he finally asked. "You're welcome to stay with me for as long as you need."

She extricated herself from his grasp and smiled faintly. "I think you and I both know it wouldn't work for me to stay with you. I can't resist you, Micah, any more than you seem to not be able to resist me. Only I don't want to resist you, and you want anything but to give in to the attraction between us. Until that changes, I don't see that we can possibly live in the same apartment."

His eyes were haunted, so dark and emotion-filled. "I can't give you what you want, Angel girl. What you need."

"How do you know what I want?" she challenged. "You've never asked."

He shook his head and turned away, the wall slowly sliding back into place between them. "Let's go over to my place and I'll help you get the rest of your things to bring here, unless you'd rather stay the night over at my place, until you get more settled in."

"No. I'll stay here. No sense putting it off."

"I'm sorry," he said in a quiet, almost dead voice.

"Don't be," she said with forced cheerfulness. "I'll survive. I've done it before."

He cursed softly and started toward the door, leaving her to follow behind.

CHAPTER 14

Angelina surveyed her handiwork and flopped on the sofa with a tired sigh. Her days in her apartment had been quiet but satisfying. She'd gone shopping at a local thrift shop for some of the essentials like linens for the bed and towels and washcloths. Then she'd hit a few garage sales, and though the pickings were slim due to the lateness of the hour, she'd found a few items and returned to arrange everything.

Now to figure out what to have for dinner in her new home now that she had groceries. As celebratory meals went, it would be lean. She had a choice between canned soup or a sandwich. No reason not to splurge and have both.

With a gleeful smile, she got up and headed into the kitchen. No sooner had she dragged out the sandwich fixings than her doorbell rang. Frowning, she went to the door, rising on tiptoe to see out the peephole. There were only a handful of people it could possibly be, and yet when she got a good look, it was none of them.

Three women stood outside. Three really beautiful women. Maybe they were Avon ladies? They looked harmless enough, though David and Micah had drummed into her head that criminals didn't have a neon sign on their foreheads advertising the fact. Some of the most heinous were in fact very normal, everyday-looking people.

They probably had the wrong apartment.

She cracked open the door, leaving the chain clasped. "Can I help you?"

The woman in the middle, a brunette with some pretty spectacular cleavage leaned forward. "Angelina?"

So much for them having the wrong apartment.

"Who wants to know?" Angelina asked suspiciously.

David had always said, when in doubt, go on the offensive.

The blonde slipped forward, a sweet smile curving her lips. "I'm Faith Montgomery, Gray's wife?"

Angelina relaxed. She shut the door, fumbled with the chain and then reopened the door.

"Sorry. It's just that I don't know anyone here, and I wasn't expecting you. Cop's sister," she said with a slight shrug.

Faith smiled warmly at her and then looked down at the covered dish she was holding. It was then that Angelina saw that the other two women also carried stuff, including a gallon container of what looked like tea.

"We brought dinner. Hope you don't mind us barging in on you. We didn't figure you'd had time to grocery shop or anything yet," Faith said.

Remembering her manners and that she was clutching the door like a lifeline, Angelina hastily stepped back.

"Come in please. Forgive my rudeness. I just didn't expect . . . You shouldn't have gone to so much trouble."

The voluptuous brunette sailed past followed by a taller woman with long black hair and exotic blue eyes. Sleek. Like a cat. It was the first thought that popped into Angelina's mind.

"Oh, it was no trouble," the shorter brunette said. "Faith did all the cooking. She's Miss Domestic. Serena and I are rather hopeless in that area."

"Forgive our manners," the woman Angelina guessed had to be Serena said. "We haven't even introduced ourselves. The rather loud obnoxious one over there is Julie Stanford."

Angelina raised an eyebrow, but Julie didn't seem offended by the introduction. Her eyes twinkled with amusement and her teeth flashed as she grinned.

"Faith has already introduced herself, which leaves me. I'm Serena Roche."

Angelina's eyes widened. "You're Damon's wife?"

The other women's expressions turned inquisitive. Serena smiled. "Yes, I am. I didn't realize you'd met."

Angelina flushed, realizing that she'd opened a door she'd rather have not, especially in front of women she'd just met.

"That blush certainly tells me she has," Julie drawled. "First Connor, now Damon. Next she'll be telling us she's hooked up with Nathan."

Angelina eyed her uneasily but some devil prompted her to ask anyway. "Nathan Tucker?"

Julie's eyes narrowed. "You do get around for someone who just came to town."

Angelina sighed. So this wasn't a social visit or a friendly welcome-to-the-neighborhood type thing. It was a fact-finding mission.

"Ask what you want to know," Angelina said wearily. "I never was any good at catty/bitchy games. I haven't flirted with, spoken inappropriately to, looked at wrong or otherwise propositioned Connor, Nathan, Gray or Damon. I met them through Micah. End of story."

Julie studied her with grudging admiration. "I like bluntness."

Serena and Faith both snorted.

Serena stepped between Julie and Angelina and laid a hand on Angelina's arm. "Ignore Julie. She gets grumpy and possessive when it comes to Nathan. Are you hungry? The food we brought is still warm, and Gray makes the best sun tea. We could sit down and relax. Contrary to what Julie might think, we didn't come to interrogate you."

"You'll forgive me if I don't quite believe that," Angelina said as she motioned them toward the kitchen.

"Okay, well maybe our motives aren't entirely innocent," Faith said as she took plates down. She glanced around. "You don't have a table or chairs yet. I thought I still had one in storage. Guess we can eat in the living room."

"We actually came about Micah," Julie said with a gleam in her eyes. "We didn't realize you were so well acquainted with the rest of the guys."

Try as she might, Angelina couldn't control the wash of hurt at the mention of Micah. The women went silent, and to cover the awkwardness Faith poured a glass of tea and shoved it toward Angelina.

Faith took the cover off the casserole dish to reveal lasagna.

"Faith makes the most awesome lasagna," Serena said with a sign.

"Everything Faith cooks is awesome," Julie said.

They all filled their plates and headed into the living room. Julie flopped onto the couch, next to Angelina, while Faith and Serena sat cross-legged on the floor in front of them.

"You may as well ask," Angelina said in resignation. "I can practically see the questions rolling around in your heads."

"What's the deal with you and Connor?" Julie asked bluntly.

Angelina looked up in confusion. That wasn't a question she'd expected.

"I'm not sure I understand."

"Julie, chill," Serena reproached. "We're nosy, yes, but it's none of our business."

"Yeah, and if you have a prayer of making her talk, you probably shouldn't piss her off," Faith pointed out.

Angelina burst out laughing. "Are you people for real?"

Serena smiled. "We're really not total bitches."

"Speak for yourself," Julie said cheekily.

Serena shot her a dark glance.

"Anyway, as I was saying we're just really curious about you," Julie continued. "Micah is special to us all . . ."

Sudden understanding came to Angelina. If it hadn't been so patently absurd, she'd have laughed. But what she wanted to do more was cry.

"I think I understand," Angelina said as she set her plate aside. "You're worried I'm going to hurt Micah." She had to swallow back the bitter laugh. "You think I'm fucking with him and encouraging Connor or one of the other guys."

Faith winced. "Well when you put it that way, it sounds pretty bad."

It wasn't as if Angelina didn't already have her heart on the line. When it came to Micah, she had no pride. And really why should she be ashamed to let it out? She hadn't done anything wrong, not unless throwing yourself at an unwilling guy was a crime.

"First, there is nothing going on between me and Connor. I just met the man a few days ago when he and Nathan came by Micah's apartment. Then at lunch Connor, Nathan and Gray came by the café where I work."

"And they say women are nosy," Julie said dryly. "I'll have to give Nathan shit over this."

"I asked if they knew of any cheap places to rent. I can't—couldn't stay with Micah. Connor told me about this place and then he and Gray moved the stuff in." She glanced over at Faith. "Thank you by the way for the furniture. I can't tell you how much I appreciate it."

Faith smiled. "Was glad to help."

"So that's it?" Julie asked, a confused look on her face. "I mean Connor's calling you sweetie and shit. It's not like the man to get all soft like that."

Angelina sighed, knowing this tale was only going to get more involved and more humiliating for her. Part of her wondered why she didn't just tell them to mind their own damn business and get the hell out. The other part of her latched on to the possibility of understanding and friendship. Even if that was a naïve notion.

"If I had to guess, Connor feels sorry for me," she said carefully. "They all feel sorry for me."

The three women exchanged puzzled glances.

"Why would they feel sorry for you?" Serena asked gently.

"Because Micah couldn't be more obvious in his disinterest in me. And apparently I'm too obvious with the fact that I want *him*."

Faith's mouth formed an O, and Julie frowned, sympathy and understanding flashing in her eyes.

"What the hell's wrong with Micah?" Julie demanded. "You're flipping gorgeous."

Angelina smiled wanly. "Thank you. I should correct my statement. He's attracted to me. There's plenty of chemistry, but he doesn't want to want me. He's quite adamant about it. And the thing is, he's still living in the past. There's a lot you guys don't know about him from before he came to Houston. I hadn't realized how much he's kept buried."

The others exchanged glances again, and Serena looked decidedly guilty. "Well we know about his past. Now, I mean. We didn't before." She looked unhappily at the others. "You see? I should have never let you guys pry that information out of me. It wasn't mine to share, and now it's going to get back to both Damon and Micah, I know it."

"Micah won't hear it from me," Angelina muttered. "We aren't exactly speaking very much."

"He feels so guilty over what happened," Serena said gently.

Angelina flushed and wished the floor could open up and swallow her.

"What does he feel guilty for?" Julie demanded. "Clearly you didn't tell us everything."

Serena shook her head at Julie.

"He shouldn't feel guilty," Angelina said softly. "Everything that happened was at my instigation. I know Micah. So much better than he knows me," she added wistfully.

"You know about his, um, proclivities then, huh," Julie hedged.

Angelina smiled. "I believe the question here is how *you* know about them."

Julie had the grace to flush.

"There's nothing about Micah I don't accept," Angelina said. "We're the same, he and I, but he'll never see that as long as he refuses to see me as anything more than David's little sister."

"So you're giving up?" Julie challenged.

Serena and Faith shot her sharp glances, but Julie barged ahead.

"Believe me when I say I know all about pursuing an oblivious, hardheaded man. God knows I should have given up on Nathan eons ago. The man's as thick as a brick."

Angelina couldn't help but giggle as she imagined big, badass-looking Nathan with brash, outspoken Julie. He probably cowered in terror.

"I'm not giving up on Micah," Angelina said. "It's complicated. Just have to give him space. He hasn't let go of Hannah, and until he does, there's no room for me in the equation. That's assuming he can ever feel anything for me beyond raging lust."

"Lust is good. Nothing wrong with lust," Julie said.

Serena laughed. "Shut up, Julie."

"So what are you going to do?" Faith asked.

"I wait," Angelina said.

"Fuck that," Julie said rudely. "I'm making it my self-appointed mission to make damn sure you don't sit around pining for his ass. It's not like he's been celibate while he mourns his dead wife."

Faith winced. "Damn, Julie, could you try to be a little tactful?"

Julie shot them both a look of bewilderment. "What? It's the truth. Besides, a man takes a woman who sits around totally for granted. She needs to get out, meet people. Have some fun. It can't be fun moving to a new city where the only person you know has decided to ignore you."

Angelina's lips twisted into a rueful smile. "You certainly have a way with words. No wonder Nathan is so smitten."

Serena and Faith burst out laughing.

"Oh my God we have another Julie on our hands," Faith exclaimed.

Julie grinned. "I knew I was going to like her."

Serena rolled her eyes. "Oh please. You were ready to scratch her eyes out when you thought she was Micah's woman and she was having a thing with Connor."

"Seriously?" Angelina asked with a laugh.

Julie slanted a sideways glare at Serena. "Yeah well, at the time my info wasn't up-to-date. And now that it is we need to discuss jazzing up your social life, which means I will be the one who has to save you, because these two are boring old maids now that they've married."

"Oh Lord," Faith groaned. "Be afraid, Angelina. Be very afraid."

"What are you doing next Friday night?" Julie asked.

"I think you know I'm not doing anything," Angelina said dryly.

"Okay, well I'm dragging Nathan to this really great club for some dancing. Why don't you go with us?"

Serena's mouth fell open while Faith looked a cross between horrified and hysterically amused.

"You're taking Nathan where?" Faith asked.

"You heard me," Julie said.

"Poor Nathan," Serena murmured. "What did he do to you to deserve this? Are you still punishing that poor boy?"

Julie uttered a *hmmph* as she glared at Serena and Faith. "It's part of our deal. One weekend he chooses what we do and I get to choose the next. And if I have to endure a monster truck rally then he can damn sure go shake his ass with me."

Angelina covered her mouth to prevent the laughter, but it spilled out anyway.

"I know I've just met him, but I can't see him at some club unless maybe it was a biker bar."

Julie grinned. "He would look good on a Harley, wouldn't he?"

Angelina nodded.

"So you want to go? Nathan won't mind so much if he gets to escort two hot women around."

"Thank you," Angelina said with a smile. "I'd love to go. I love to dance. Miami has some fantastic clubs."

"Okay, great. We'll pick you up Friday then. Just don't wear something too sexy. I don't want to kick your ass if Nathan starts gawking."

"Uh, Julie, don't you have that bass-ackward?" Faith asked. "If your man is gawking, you should be kicking his ass not hers."

"Oh, don't worry," Julie said sweetly. "I won't kick her ass until after I've removed his nuts."

CHAPTER 15

If Micah thought that not seeing Angelina or being near her would somehow remove the searing lust that raged through his veins, he was wrong. If anything, he wanted her even more. His craving was dark and ran deep, and in his darkest fantasies it shamed him the things he longed to do to her.

His friends and coworkers watched him suspiciously, seemingly weighing his mood. He could see the judgment in their eyes, knew they condemned him for crimes committed. Only Faith seemed to try and make the effort to talk to him, and it pained him to rebuff her attempts, but what was he going to tell her? That he dreamed of completely dominating his best friend's little sister to the point of tying her to him day and night, slaking his lust and desires and rousing the simmering passion in her dark eyes?

He had to stop thinking about her. How was it that he'd been able to turn off thoughts of Hannah and David, and yet he couldn't block one sensual angel from his mind? She haunted his dreams and she haunted his days.

But with her came memories that he had no interest in reliving. Happier times when he, David, Hannah and Angelina had been a family.

"Micah?"

Faith's soft voice carried through his bleak thoughts. He looked up from his desk to see her standing at his office door, a cup of coffee in hand.

"Hey, doll, come in," he said with what he hoped was a welcoming smile.

"You missed the morning coffee-and-donut session, but I saved you a cup and the last donut."

She set the steaming cup in front of him, and he sniffed appreciatively at the aroma.

"Thanks," he said sincerely.

"You're welcome," she said and smiled sweetly at him.

"Everyone ready to lynch me yet?"

She laughed. "Oh, come on. They're guys. Their sole comments amount to something about a stick up your ass and they're taking bets on how long it'll take you to correct the problem."

He snorted. "Amazing how fast shit gets around."

She hesitated for a moment, biting her bottom lip as if deciding whether she wanted to say something.

He sighed. "Just say it, doll. I'm not going to bite your head off."

She smiled faintly. "We're family. You know that, right?"

A peculiar curl unsettled his stomach.

"I guess what I'm trying to say is that we're all here for you. I can't speak for the guys, but I love you a lot you know."

They both chuckled at that.

Micah reached out and touched her hand. "I love you too, doll. You're one of my favorite people."

"So you know you can always talk to me about anything. After all, we've been far more intimate than most friends."

He laughed outright at the devilish gleam in her eyes. Though there certainly hadn't been any residual awkwardness after their threesome with Gray, neither had they ever talked about it.

"I know, I know," he said. Then he hesitated. "I hope me not ever saying anything about my past . . . about Hannah . . . didn't hurt your feelings. It's not like I didn't trust you or anything. I just never talked about it to anyone."

"I understand." She cocked her head to the side and stared at him with those wide green eyes. "I like her, you know."

"Like who?" he asked.

"Angelina."

That sinking sensation in his gut intensified. "I take it you've met," he said stiffly.

She studied him with a hint of confusion. "Sure. Connor gave her some of my old furniture. Serena, Julie and I went over the other night to bring her dinner and see if she needed anything else."

It had happened despite his best efforts. His past and present were colliding, and there wasn't a damn thing he could do about it.

He hadn't wanted Angelina to meet his friends. He hadn't wanted them to know about Hannah or David or any part of his life in Miami. He wanted to resent Angelina, but he couldn't look past his own guilt to be angry with her.

"She's a good girl," he said in response to Faith's statement.

Faith snorted, surprising him. "I get the distinct impression she's not a good girl at all. In fact, I'd be willing to bet she's very, very bad."

"Enough," Micah bit out. "I don't want to discuss Angelina."

Faith held her hands up. "Sorry."

She moved back toward the door, but when she got there, she paused and turned around to look at him.

"Tell me something, Micah. Do you think because you lost someone you loved that you don't ever deserve another chance at happiness?"

When he didn't answer, she turned and walked away.

Angelina's week had been busy at the café, and when she got off, she'd spent her time decorating the apartment with inexpensive items she picked up at the thrift shop.

Thanks to Hannah, Angelina had developed a few crafting notions and was handy with fabric. Unfortunately, Hannah had given up trying to teach Angelina any culinary skills. Which was a shame because Hannah was fantastic in the kitchen.

At night in her apartment, Angelina listened to the smooth sounds of her favorite Cuban band and dreamed of lying in Micah's arms and making love to the beat of the music.

She had to admit that Julie was right about one thing. Sitting around mooning over Micah would make her crazy. She was glad Julie had talked her into going out with her and Nathan tonight.

Excitement thrummed in her blood at the prospect of dressing up, looking good and spending the night on the dance floor. She brushed her hair until it shone and spilled over her shoulders in soft waves. All the makeup she bothered with was eyeliner and a pale lip gloss.

As for clothing, she opted for hip-hugging, low-slung jeans and a tank top that bared a narrow strip of her belly. Satisfied that she looked her best, she went in search of the sandals she wanted to wear. When the doorbell rang, she hurried to answer and found Nathan and Julie waiting for her.

"Hey, girl," Nathan said with a grin. "Julie tells me you're going along to witness my torment."

Angelina laughed. "It won't be that bad, surely."

"You've never seen me dance."

She followed them out to Nathan's truck and laughed when Nathan had to hoist both her and Julie into the cab.

"We're swimming in testosterone," Julie said with a groan.

"Stop giving me shit about my truck," Nathan said good-naturedly.

Twenty minutes later they arrived at a brightly lit club, and as soon as they opened the truck doors, the music belted over their ears.

"Hell, we haven't even gotten inside yet," Nathan muttered.

Julie grabbed his hand and started pulling him toward the entrance. "Stop being such a baby and come on."

Angelina let the rhythm invade her body before they ever got through the doors. Her skin rippled and rolled with her movements.

"It's all that Latin blood," she hollered over the music when Julie grinned at her.

"Knock yourself out," Julie called. "Nathan and I will be around."

Her hips rolling and her arms up, Angelina moved into the crowd. Plenty of men danced around her, and with her, but she was careful to keep moving and not give anyone her attention for too long.

After six consecutive songs, she was breathing hard, but she hadn't felt so energized or alive in a long time. A tap on her shoulder had her turning, and she saw Julie's laughing face and Nathan's resigned one.

"Come on, Angelina, let's give Nathan a show," Julie yelled.

"Oh hell," Nathan said as he backed up.

Julie pulled him to her, doing a sexy shimmy down the front of his body. Angelina moved in from behind until they had him sandwiched between them.

"They're all going to be jealous bastards," Nathan said over the boom of the music.

"That's the idea," Julie yelled back with a cheeky grin.

While Angelina and Julie shook and gyrated in time with the music, Nathan sort of rotated at intervals and tried to make it look like he was dancing. Angelina grinned. He was definitely enjoying the view of Julie's cleavage. His eyes hadn't left her all night.

They made a striking picture, the two women moving up and down Nathan's body in sexy, sensuous movements. More than a few people stopped and stared. After a while Nathan relaxed and got into the spirit of things. He took turns wrapping an arm around each woman's waist, undulating his body in time with theirs.

When the music segued into the next song, Julie leaned in. "Let's take a break."

Angelina followed them over to one of the tall tables to the side.

"Do you ladies want a drink?" Nathan asked.

"Definitely," Julie said.

Nathan held up a hand to motion to the waitress making her rounds.

"Order up," he told them when the waitress came around. "My tab."

Angelina ordered a club soda, and she couldn't hear what Julie yelled to the waitress. Nathan ordered a beer, and they stood back to wait.

Within a few minutes, the waitress was back with their drinks, and Angelina sipped at her water while dancing in place as the music swelled around them.

They stood through two songs and then Julie hollered across the table. "Wanna go back out?"

Angelina waved them on. "You two go ahead. I'm fine here for a while."

Julie dragged a laughing Nathan back onto the dance floor and proceeded to wrap herself around him. They were so cute together. Angelina wistfully noted the tenderness in Nathan's eyes—eyes that never left Julie even for a moment. It was obvious he was crazy about her.

She downed the last of her drink and set the glass on the table. After checking to make sure Nathan's and Julie's drinks were empty so nobody would mess with them, she shoved them over to the side and started for the bathroom. Others might be amused at her paranoia, but you could never be too careful. David had certainly drummed that into her head.

A peculiar sensation assailed her when she got to the doorway leading into the restrooms. She grabbed the frame to steady herself and raised her other hand to her temple. It was hot as hell with so many people packed in as they were.

She went into one of the stalls and frowned at how weak she felt when she'd completed her business. Stumbling out of the stall, she went to the sink to splash cold water on her face. Something didn't feel right. Was she sick?

She lurched out of the bathroom, intent on getting back to Nathan and Julie. The room swarmed around her. Faces yawned and stretched into ghoulish masks. The cascading lights blinded her, overwhelmed her, and the music pulsed so loudly in her ears that she clamped her hands to them in an effort to make it all go away.

She took a step and nearly went down. Oh God. Someone had drugged her. As careful as she was—she hadn't left her drink unattended even for a moment—someone had slipped something into it. How? The waitress? She had to find Nathan and Julie.

Confused and disoriented, she looked left and right. Oh God. Was whoever had drugged her out there? Waiting to strike? She was completely helpless. She couldn't fight off a fly right now.

Stick to the crowd. Make a scene. Draw plenty of attention to yourself.

David's words simmered in her consciousness. Someone bumped into her, and she panicked, shoving away. She yelled hoarsely and fell to her knees. She crawled and pushed herself up, fighting to stay conscious.

Where were Julie and Nathan?

The room was a blur and going darker by the minute. She ran into a hard back, bounced off and went down again.

"Angelina?"

The voice boomed in her ear, and she went weak with relief. Strong hands hoisted her up, and she latched onto Nathan's arms with fervent desperation.

Nathan and Julie's worried faces swam into view. Her knees buckled again, and Nathan caught her. He swept her into his arms and hurriedly shouldered his way off the dance floor.

The room passed in an indecipherable haze. Her head lolled back, and she lay limp and unresisting against his chest.

What if it had been someone else? Another man? She would have been powerless. A tear slipped down her cheek.

Nathan burst out of the club into the cooler night air. He stopped at his truck and stared urgently down at her.

"Angelina, can you hear me? What happened? What's wrong?"

"Someone . . . someone drugged me," she slurred.

More tears slid helplessly down her cheeks. Then everything went black.

CHAPTER 16

$\mathcal{N}$athan stared down at Angelina's unconscious form in shock. "Son of a bitch! Julie, get my keys out of my pocket. You'll have to drive. Get us to the damn hospital."

Julie fumbled with his jeans and yanked out the keys. She unlocked the passenger side first so he could climb in with Angelina, then she hurried around to the driver's side.

"Is she going to be okay?" Julie asked in a quivery voice as she pulled out of the parking lot.

Nathan smoothed a hand over Angelina's cheek and then her neck, almost afraid he wouldn't find a pulse. When it beat strong and steady against his fingertips, he breathed a sigh of relief.

"This could have been you, goddamn it," he seethed. "Never again, Julie. You don't ever go in a place like that without me. You got that?"

It was a testament to how frightened she was that she didn't argue. She nodded and didn't give him any grief over his dictate.

"Will she be okay?" Julie asked again.

She took a corner too fast and fishtailed as she overcorrected.

"Slow down, honey," Nathan said in a soothing voice. "She'll be fine I think. Her pulse is strong. I don't know what she was given."

Julie shuddered. "You think it was one of those date rape drugs? God, Nathan, what if she hadn't found us?"

"Shhh honey, don't torture yourself. The important thing is she kept her wits and did the smart thing. We'll take care of her."

"We should call Micah," Julie said anxiously. "He'd want to know even if he's avoiding her."

"Of course he wants to know. He's hooked. He just doesn't know it yet."

She shot him a curious look. "Sort of like you when you kept ignoring me?"

He made a low sound of amusement. "There wasn't ever a time you didn't have me hooked."

She smiled, her entire face lighting up. Hell. Did she still harbor doubts as to whether or not the sun rose and set at her feet?

"When this is over, you and I are going to have a long talk," he said. "With you underneath me. Naked."

If possible her smile became even more brilliant. Then her gaze dropped to Angelina, and her eyes dimmed.

"Who could have done this to her, Nathan?"

"I don't know," he admitted. "Micah is going to be furious."

Micah strode into the emergency room so tense he was about to explode. He stopped at the front desk and uttered two words.

"Angelina Moyano."

The clerk looked startled, but she clicked around on her

computer. "She's still here in the ER. There's someone back with her already, though. You'll have to wait out here."

"The hell I will," he muttered.

He walked toward the door leading to the exam rooms, ignoring the clerk's cries for him to stop. He nearly bumped into a nurse.

"Angelina Moyano?"

"Room eight," the nurse said as she continued on her way.

Micah hurried down the hall and stopped outside the room. The door was slightly ajar, and he could see Nathan sprawled in one of the chairs.

He shoved open the door, his gaze searching for Angelina. He ignored Julie and Nathan and went straight to the bed where Angelina lay.

Her eyes were closed, but she looked anything but at peace. Her forehead was wrinkled and a frown turned down the corners of her mouth. Her fingers clutched at the thin sheet as if she was seeking protection. She looked afraid and so very vulnerable.

He laid his hand over her forehead and gently threaded his fingers through the strands of hair falling over her face. He stroked gently, trying to ease the lines of strain furrowed into her skin.

Something inside of him unlocked. Dark and primitive. Possessiveness roared through his system like an out-of-control train.

Mine.

The word rolled over his tongue, begging for release. It shook him to his core. She wasn't his. She couldn't be his, but on some level he recognized her.

His.

No one else would have her.

He shook his head, dragging himself from the brink of utter insanity. He was losing his mind and self all at the same time.

Instead he concentrated on her fragile vulnerability. She needed him right now.

"I'm here, Angel girl," he whispered. "You're safe."

He leaned down to brush his lips across her brow. She emitted a tiny sigh and seemed to relax, but she didn't awaken.

Micah turned to Nathan, his gut so tied in knots he felt like puking. "Who drugged her?" he bit out.

"I have no idea," Nathan said wearily. "One minute she was fine. Julie and I left her to dance, and the next thing I know she's falling down at my feet."

Micah swore viciously. "What has the doctor said?"

"They're doing lab work. We'll know more when they get the results back, but from all appearances he said it looks like a date rape drug."

"Son of a fucking bitch."

It was all he could do not to put his fist through the wall. He collected himself and glanced over at Julie, who sat on the other side of Angelina's bed, her face pale and creased with worry.

"You okay, doll?" Micah asked gently.

She gave a short nod, but her eyes filled with tears. And on Julie, tears were not a good thing.

Alarmed, Nathan snatched her out of her chair and settled her on his lap.

"What's wrong, honey?"

"It's my fault," Julie said in a miserable tone. "I talked her into going out with us. This never would have happened if I hadn't strong-armed her into going."

Nathan pressed his lips to her temple. "Stop talking crazy, Julie. You did a good thing by asking her to come with us. She needs friends right now."

His words hit Micah right in the chest. Nathan was right about that much. Angelina was alone in a new city, no friends, and Micah had begrudged her his because he was too much of a goddamn coward to face his past.

"You did a very good thing, Julie," Micah said quietly. "Nathan's right. She does need friends, and you guys are the absolute best."

Julie smiled tremulously at him. The door opened, and Faith and Gray shoved in, followed closely by Connor.

"How is she?" Faith asked anxiously.

"Still out like a light," Julie said.

"If anyone asks, I'm her sister," Faith said. "The only way they'd let us back was if we were family."

Nathan and Micah both stared at her like she'd lost her mind. Julie snickered openly, and Gray just looked at the ceiling, his lips twitching suspiciously.

"Um, Faith. What side of the family exactly does Angelina spring from?" Julie asked with barely veiled amusement.

Faith flushed. "It was all I could think of on short notice. Don't tease me. I'll say she was adopted like I was."

Gray squeezed her shoulders while Connor walked to the other side of Angelina's bed, a deep frown on his face.

"What the hell happened?" he demanded.

Micah stared at his friend through narrowed eyes. He didn't want Connor near her. Didn't want him to touch her. His fingers curled into tight fists when Connor gently touched Angelina's cheek.

"Date rape drug," Julie said in a weary voice. "Someone slipped it into her drink."

The door opened again, and this time Damon and Serena appeared.

"How many damn people did you call?" Nathan grumbled at Julie.

The room was getting crowded. They'd be lucky if they didn't all get kicked out, and they probably would the next time a nurse made a pass through the room.

"This could have been any one of you," Gray said in a low voice, his stare encompassing first Faith and then passing on to Julie and finally Serena. "I shudder to think of what could have happened on your last girls' night out."

Nathan went pale. "Hell, he's right. I walked into Cattleman's and all three of you were flat on your backs on the floor giggling like fools. Anyone could have drugged your drinks and you would have never known."

The girls all exchanged uneasy glances. Damon's face had drawn into a thundercloud.

"They would have had protection if a certain someone hadn't blown off the driver for the night. It won't happen again, Serena mine."

"Shit," Julie breathed. "This is seriously going to cramp our fun."

"We just want you to be more careful," Gray said diplomatically. "No more going out alone and getting shit-faced. At least one of you is going to have to stay sober and look out for the others."

The girls all nodded.

"How long has she been out?" Serena murmured as she moved closer to the bed. "Will she be all right?"

"Doctor says so," Nathan replied. "He wants to watch her. Wait for her to wake up and monitor her for a while."

"You don't have to stay," Micah said, turning to include the entire room. "I'm going to stay with her. You should all go home and get some rest." He looked at Julie. "Especially you, doll."

"We'd rather stay until she comes around," Faith said stubbornly. "She shouldn't be here alone."

"She won't be alone," Micah said patiently. "I'm not leaving her."

"She should have friends around her," Connor said in a low voice.

Micah turned to see him still standing at Angelina's bedside. It pissed him off that Connor was passing judgment and it pissed him off even more that Connor was right. Micah hadn't been a source of support for Angelina. Ever.

That was all going to change starting now.

He could start by sharing his friends with her. It was obvious they all cared about her. Without saying anything else, he pulled up the remaining chair and situated it next to the bed so he could be close to her.

To his surprise, everyone hung out through the night. At various intervals the nurses made noises about shooing them all out, but gave up when the men growled their displeasure.

They took turns dozing. Julie stayed in Nathan's lap, and Gray took the vacated seat, pulling Faith down to sit across his thighs. Connor remained standing at the foot of Angelina's bed, his back resting against the wall. Evidently conceding to the inevitable, one of the nurses pushed another chair inside the overcrowded room, and Damon took it, and as the others had done with their women, he pulled Serena down on his lap.

Gray had taken care of calling the police, but until Angelina woke up and could answer questions, there was little they could do. Micah knew deep down that the chances of catching whoever had drugged her were very slim.

It was already well into the next morning when Angelina stirred and let out a low moan. Micah picked up his head from where it lay beside her on the bed and immediately reached for her hand.

"Angel?"

Her eyes fluttered, and she stared back at him, her gaze unfocused.

"Micah?" she whispered.

"Yes, Angel girl, it's me. How are you feeling?"

She swallowed, then licked her lips. "Water," she said hoarsely.

He turned, but Connor was already there, shoving a cup with a straw at him. Micah took it and put it carefully to her mouth.

"Take it easy. Not too much," he cautioned.

She sucked hungrily at the liquid and then he eased the cup away. She laid her head back, and suddenly her eyes widened in alarm. Panic raced across her face.

"What happened to me? Oh God, Micah, what happened? I don't remember."

The fear in her voice made him ache.

"Nothing happened, Angel. You're safe. I swear you're safe and nobody got to you."

Confusion muddled her features. She glanced around the room, her gaze lighting on its occupants. Recognition flashed in her eyes. Then she found Nathan and Julie, and relief flooded her face.

"All I remember is coming out of the bathroom. I couldn't remember if I found you," she choked out.

Nathan leaned forward, and Julie moved off his lap. "You found me, Angelina. You did exactly what you should have. You stayed conscious long enough to tell me what happened, and Julie and I brought you here."

Angelina reached out to catch Julie's hand. "Thank you."

Julie squeezed back "You scared me shitless, and I don't scare easily."

Again Angelina's gaze wandered over the room. "What are you all doing here?" she asked in bewilderment.

"We were worried about you, sweetie," Connor said as he leaned down to brush a strand of hair from her brow.

Micah tensed at the display of tenderness from his friend.

"Can you tell us what happened?" Gray asked. "We've notified the police, but there's little they can do until they've spoken to you. They'll question people from the club. Maybe someone saw whoever drugged your drink. Did you leave it or look away at any time?"

She shook her head adamantly, struggling to sit up in bed. Micah caught her shoulders and helped her into a sitting position. He maneuvered his way onto the bed beside her when she wavered. He slipped an arm around her to support her, and she leaned willingly into his side.

"No, I'd never do that. David and Micah told me constantly to never accept a drink from anyone no matter what. Order my own. Never leave it and come back to it. Never get distracted and look away. I never let it out of my sight," she said fiercely. "I drank it then went to the bathroom. I started feeling sick immediately and knew I had to get back to Nathan and Julie. I stuck to the crowd just like David always said. I was afraid whoever had drugged me was out there waiting for his opportunity."

Micah's grip tightened around her shoulders, and he swore under his breath. What if she hadn't been with Nathan and Julie? If she'd been alone, she would have been helpless and she could have been raped or killed, maybe both.

"Smart girl," Damon murmured. "You saved yourself with your quick thinking."

"Damn right she did," Micah growled. He picked up her hand and pressed a kiss to her palm. "You did good, Angel girl. David would be proud."

Tears filled her eyes as she looked up at him.

"Shit," Gray muttered. "That means that either the waitress drugged her or she allowed someone else to."

"Or someone at the bar distracted her while she was setting up her drinks and slipped the drug in while she wasn't looking," Nathan said.

"How the hell would anyone but the waitress have known which drink was hers? Unless it was random? Which makes no sense to me," Connor said.

"That's a good question," Micah murmured.

"I just ordered club soda," Angelina said helplessly. "I never drink alcohol."

The men all frowned, and Damon, who'd remained fairly quiet through it all, said, "Maybe it was a practical joke aimed at a potential designated driver?"

"But why?" Faith burst out. "None of this makes any sense."

"There are predators of all kinds out there, baby," Gray said. "That's why we want you girls to be more careful."

Angelina's fingers trembled in Micah's grasp. He tightened his grip on her hand and squeezed reassuringly.

"You're safe now, Angel girl. Do you understand me? I won't let anyone hurt you."

She tilted her chin so she could look at him. Her gaze skirted across his face as if she was judging his sincerity. He couldn't blame her for doubting him. But he wouldn't give her the chance to doubt him again.

A knock sounded at the door, and a police officer stuck his head in the door. "Ms. Moyano? My name is Officer Daniels. Do you feel up to answering a few questions?"

CHAPTER 17

When Angelina awoke, sunlight streamed through the slats of the blinds on her window. Still sluggish, she turned to look at the clock. Ten A.M.

She closed her eyes again and turned her head to burrow back into the pillow. At least she was home in her own bed, even if it had only been hers for a short time. Still, it beat the ER.

She'd been adamant about staying in her own place after she'd been released from the hospital. To her surprise, Micah had insisted on spending the night on her couch. When she'd told him there was no need, he'd scowled and then continued on as if he hadn't heard her.

He'd tucked her in with an admonishment to holler if she needed anything, and then he'd disappeared from her bedroom. And she'd slept, dreaming of being in his bed, in his arms.

The police had questioned her and had promised to do what they could, but she'd seen the looks that passed between Officer

Daniels and the others. It would be nearly impossible to find out what had happened unless the waitress could provide information.

She swallowed, wincing at the discomfort. Her mouth was dry like she'd eaten cotton, and thirst drove her to get out of bed.

She traveled through the living room, curious as to whether Micah was still there. A needle of disappointment pricked her when she didn't see him. When she got to the kitchen, she filled a glass with tap water and drained it in several gulps. As she set it back down on the counter, she noticed the piece of paper lying several inches away.

Angel,
  Gone back to my apartment, but I'll be back in a little while to check on you. I'll bring you something to eat.
  Micah

Warmth crept up her body, and she smiled at the knowledge that he'd be returning.

She leaned against the counter and folded her arms over her chest when a chill raised goose bumps on her skin. Friday night hovered around her in bits and pieces. She remembered nothing of the time between her leaving the bathroom and waking into the emergency room.

Though she'd been assured that nothing had happened to her, a thread of panic still lingered on the periphery of her mind.

She swallowed back the knot of fear. It was a fluke. An act of random maliciousness. She'd been in the wrong place at the wrong time, and some sick fuck had thought she'd be an easy conquest.

She felt a grim satisfaction at having thwarted whoever the hell it was.

Lead still traveled sluggishly in her veins, and it took effort to stay upright. A day in bed sounded like heaven. She wanted to lie down and wait for Micah to come back.

She walked out of the kitchen and glanced down the foyer to the front door. She saw another piece of paper on the floor and stopped in her tracks.

Someone had slipped a note under her door.

Probably Micah.

A little hesitantly, she went over to pick it up. Maybe something had come up and he wasn't coming back after all. She opened the note to scan the contents and froze.

Nausea welled in her stomach and exploded into her throat. She swayed on suddenly weak legs.

Oh God.

Next time you won't escape me.

The note drifted to the floor, and she clutched her stomach in an effort to prevent the overwhelming urge to vomit.

He was here. In Houston. How had he found her? *Why* had he found her?

An anguished moan escaped her stiff lips. She wanted to scream. Panic assaulted her and she rushed to the door, checking the locks. She fastened the chain and leaned heavily against the door as if she could keep the world out.

Oh God. What was she going to do?

It was the same handwriting. She knew it well. The creep had been sending her letters for a year.

He'd drugged her. He'd followed her to the club, and he'd drugged her, planning to take her then. That he'd been so close to her, that he knew where she lived . . . Fear paralyzed her.

She stared down at the note that she'd touched. Stupid. It was evidence and she'd put her fingerprints all over it. But how was she to have known that he'd followed her here? How could he have known where she went?

Micah. She had to get to Micah. But she didn't want to leave her apartment. *He* had been here. Right outside her door. He could be there now, waiting and watching.

Now she damned her decision to wait to get a phone until she'd saved enough money for the deposit. She had no way to reach out to anyone without leaving the apartment.

Wait. She could just wait. Micah said he'd be back. But what if he was too late?

Forcing herself to move, she stumbled into the kitchen and got a large plastic bag. Using a pair of tongs, she carefully picked up the note and slid it inside the plastic.

She had to get to Micah's apartment. It was just a simple walk down the sidewalk. The next building over. Thirty seconds tops.

A weapon. She'd be stupid to step outside her door without a weapon.

She yanked open the drawer where the knives were kept and selected the biggest and sharpest one she could find.

Feeling marginally better about her chances of making it past a possible assailant, she collected the bag, shoved it inside her shirt and walked back to the door.

Rising up on tiptoe, she looked out the peephole, but all she saw was dimmed sunlight and a fuzzy view of the parking lot.

Her heart pounding like a jackhammer, she removed the chain and unbolted the lock. She opened the door a crack and peered out, blinking at the sudden wash of sunshine.

She took a deep breath, gathering her courage around her. With a mental count to three, she bolted out of the apartment, her bare

feet hitting the warm cement of the walkway that would take her to
Micah's building.

Micah checked his watch again and tried to control the frustration
simmering through his veins. He was impatient to get back to
Angelina—he didn't want her to wake up alone in her apartment—
but when Gray had called wanting to come over to discuss Angelina's drugging, Micah hadn't wanted to chance Angelina overhearing
and it upsetting her again. So he'd gone back to his apartment to
wait. Only Gray hadn't shown up alone. Connor had come with
him, and despite the fact that he considered Connor one of his best
friends, right now he just wanted Connor removed from the situation with Angelina.

"You and I both know I have a healthy respect for the department. Hell, half of them are your friends, and they went to the wall
for Faith when Samuels kidnapped her. But I also know how over-
worked and underpaid and understaffed they are, and there's no way
they're going to give what happened to Angelina any more manpower. They'll question the waitress, and unless she comes up big for
them, they'll move on to more demanding investigations."

Micah gritted his teeth at Gray's cold logic. Micah had been
there, as had Gray. They both knew how it worked, but it didn't
mean he liked it. He wanted to find the son of a bitch who'd done
this to Angelina and nail him to the wall.

"Connor and I are going to poke around and see if we can come up
with anything. The club has security cameras. Maybe they got something. PD won't have time to sift through all that garbage, but we do."

Micah turned to Connor, only to see the same grim determination on his face. Before he could think better of it, he said, "What's
the deal with you and Angelina?"

Connor blinked in surprise and then his eyes went cold. When he didn't respond, Micah just got more pissed.

"Answer me. What's with all the sweetie bullshit, and why do you care so goddamn much what happens to her?"

Connor surveyed him calmly, but his eyes glittered with anger. "Maybe because you don't."

"That's bullshit!" Micah roared. "She's David's sister. Of course I care what happens to her."

"Take it easy," Gray murmured as he glanced warily between Micah and Connor.

"You know, I don't even know the man, but I'm really sick of hearing about David," Connor said bluntly. "He's dead. Angelina's not. She's her own person. Not just David's sister. Her worth isn't measured by her relationship to your best friend. You've done her a great disservice, and you keep on doing it every time you try to bind her identity to David's."

Through the haze of anger surrounding Micah like a storm cloud came the knowledge that Connor was exactly right, and it pissed him off the more that Connor had seen it so clearly, and that he thought to protect Angelina from him.

"Son of a bitch, I hate it when you're right, goddamn it," Micah muttered. "You're such a smug bastard sometimes."

Connor relaxed, and some of the tightness eased from around his eyes and lips.

"Christ but she has me in knots," Micah said honestly. "I say I don't know what she wants from me, but the fact is, I think I do, and that scares the shit out of me. I'm not ready—"

He broke off, embarrassed by the flood of emotion straining to break free.

Connor shoved his hands in his pockets and seemed to take pity on Micah's floundering.

"Look man, she reminds me . . . she reminds me of Faith."

Gray jerked his gaze to Connor. "What do you mean by that?"

"When Pop and I went to get Faith, after the last time her mom ended up in the hospital with an overdose. Faith was such a mess. She looked so young and vulnerable. We just wanted to protect her. Angelina reminds me so much of her. She seems . . . lost. And look, I'm not trying to tighten the screws or anything, but you've been a dick to her. She needs help. She needs people to care about her. Just like Faith did."

"Right or not, you're pissing me the fuck off," Micah snarled.

Connor's lips twisted in amusement. "She's gorgeous, Micah. Extremely hot, and I'd have to be missing my balls not to at least have a few hot fantasies when I look at her. But she's yours whether you acknowledge that or not, and I've never poached on a friend's territory. I don't aim to start now."

"She's not . . . goddamn it," Micah muttered.

Gray and Connor just looked at him with a mixture of amusement and sympathy.

"Look I really need to get back over—"

Micah was interrupted when his front door flew open. All three men lunged to their feet. To Micah's utter shock, Angelina flew into the living room, her eyes wild, stark terror outlined on her face. She was still wearing his T-shirt—the one he'd helped her into right before tucking her into bed—and she was barefoot. But what really drew him up short was the fact she held a wicked-looking kitchen knife in her right hand. Her fingers were curled so tight around the handle that her knuckles were white.

"What the fuck?" Connor murmured.

"Angelina, honey, put the knife down," Gray said in a firm voice.

Hell, she didn't even register them talking to her. Micah took a step forward and then another.

"Angel, girl," he said in a soothing voice. "What's the matter, baby? Did you have a bad dream?"

She blinked, and then with a cry she dropped the knife and flew into his arms. He caught her against him as she all but climbed up his body in her haste to get close to him. Her heart beat frantically against his chest, and she trembled and fluttered like an injured bird.

Gray quickly retrieved the knife and moved it way away from Angelina.

"Angel, tell me what's wrong," Micah said as he ran a hand through her long hair.

"He was here," she said in a muffled voice. "At my apartment."

He pulled her face away from his neck so he could better hear her.

"Who was here?" he demanded.

He, Connor and Gray all looked up again when the front door slammed loudly. Nathan stood in the entryway to the living room, his face drawn into a mask of fury.

"We have a problem," Nathan bit out.

CHAPTER 18

"Not now, Nathan," Micah said. "Whatever it is, it can wait."

He backed toward the couch, Angelina still wrapped around him like plastic wrap.

"No, it can't wait," Nathan argued. He thrust a piece of paper out in front of him, his brows drawn together in an angry line. "Next time you won't save her," he read aloud.

Angelina gripped Micah tighter, and she shuddered violently.

"What the hell are you talking about?" Micah demanded. "Where did you get that?"

"It was on the windshield of my truck."

Micah's confusion mounted, and then Angelina's words came back to him.

He was here at my apartment.

Holy fuck. It couldn't be. He couldn't wrap his brain around the implications.

Gently he pulled Angelina away from his neck so he could look into her eyes. "What scared you, baby? What made you run over here with that knife? Did someone try to hurt you?"

His voice dropped to a dangerous level. He tried to keep it even and light so as not to frighten her, but he was vibrating with fury.

With shaking hands, she reached underneath her shirt and pulled out a plastic Ziploc bag. There was a piece of paper inside.

"I touched it. I'm sorry. I wasn't thinking," she said in a small voice. "I'm hoping I didn't ruin any evidence."

Nathan glanced down at the note in his hand and swore. "I didn't even think about that. I thought it was just an advertising flier."

Gray held up his hand. "Okay let's slow down here so the rest of us can catch up. What does your note say, Angelina?"

Micah gently took the bag from her and laid it on the couch next to them.

"It said next time you won't escape," she whispered.

Four distinct curses rang out over the room.

"Holy fuck," Nathan breathed. "The son of a bitch targeted her."

"How?" Connor demanded. "She hasn't been here long enough for someone to have laid that kind of groundwork."

Angelina's fingers formed tight fists, the skin stretching thin over her knuckles.

"Angel?" Micah asked gently. "What are you thinking?"

She trembled again, and it was all he could do not to pull her back into his arms. But he needed answers if he was going to keep her safe.

She looked up at him, fear and trepidation in her eyes.

"I thought I'd escaped. I was so careful. I laid a false trail. I ditched my car and bought another one under a false name. I told no one where I was going. I was careful not to leave a paper trail of any kind. I didn't use credit cards, and I always worked for cash so I wouldn't have to give my social security number.

"I don't know how he found me," she said helplessly.

They all stared at her in astonishment. Micah opened and quickly closed his mouth, because what he had to say wasn't pretty. Gray shook his head, and Connor's brow was wrinkled up in confusion. Only Nathan found his tongue.

"Are you trying to say that the bastard who drugged you has been stalking you before you came here?"

"I'm lost," Connor muttered.

"You aren't the only one," Micah said. His eyes narrowed as he stared at Angelina's pale features. "Back up and start from the very beginning. Don't leave *anything* out."

She swallowed and tried to move off his lap, but he caught her waist and pulled her firmly against him. Cupping her chin, he tilted her face up until she met his gaze.

"I'm not leaving you again, Angel girl. Now tell me everything."

So much was reflected in her eyes. Fear mixed with relief. Hope and disbelief. He realized the thing he was most looking for was trust. She'd looked at him before with such faith. He wanted that again, wanted to go back to the time when she trusted him and David to make everything right in her world.

"He started sending me notes—things—a year ago," she said in a quivery voice.

Stunned exclamations met her statement on all sides. All the breath left Micah in a painful wheeze. He forced himself to remain silent as he waited for her to continue.

"At first it was harmless stuff. Kind of cute actually. I thought he was just a secret admirer. Someone too shy to confront me. He sent a few notes. Flowers. Chocolate and roses on Valentine's Day."

"Jesus!" Micah exclaimed. "Tell me you didn't eat chocolate from some stranger."

She looked affronted. "Of course not. I'm not stupid. It all seemed so harmless. Annoying after a while, but harmless."

She drew in a breath. "And then it changed. It was like I did something to make him angry. The tone of the notes changed. At first they weren't outright threats, but they gave me the creeps. It escalated from there. I found my tires slashed. He'd leave messages for me no matter where I went. And then he made outright threats."

"Why the hell didn't you go to the police?" Micah demanded. "For God's sake, you're David's sister."

She looked at him with hurt in her eyes. "I did go."

"And?"

Her lips tightened. "As I told you, they weren't exactly lining up to do anything for the sister of a man they thought had betrayed you. You didn't stick around for me, so why should they? The only one who took me seriously was Chad Devereaux."

A mixture of anger and sorrow hit Micah in the chest. Anger at himself and his department. Sorrow that she'd suffered because of his desertion.

"Chad did what he could, but we didn't have much to work with. He checked in on me for a while. Did regular patrols by my house. The notes and the 'gifts' stopped. I hoped he'd gotten tired of playing his game, but in reality he was waiting and growing angrier and more desperate. He broke into my house and destroyed every-thing."

She shivered, and Micah tightened his hold on her.

"It was awful. There was such rage behind his actions. I knew that if I'd been there when he broke in, he would have killed me. I couldn't stay there any longer. I packed light, liquidated my assets and left town, laying a false trail north.

"I went all the way to Chicago because I wanted it to look like I'd relocated there. I started a bank account, established a residence, and then I bought a car under an assumed name and drove here. Until the time I went to the ER, I didn't use my real name except with you all. But he'd already found me. Somehow he tracked me here," she whispered. "The first day I went to work in the café, when I got off that afternoon, I was missing some photos from my car. I honestly thought I had moved them or packed them somewhere, but now I'm not so sure. It could have been him."

Micah could remain silent no longer. "Why the hell didn't you tell me all this sooner?"

A shuttered look fell over her face. "Would you have been any happier to see me? I thought I'd dealt with the problem. I thought I'd left it behind. I didn't come here because I wanted you to solve my problems, and I think if you stop running long enough you'll know why I came."

Gray softly cleared his throat, and color worked into Angelina's cheeks as she turned in his direction. It was as if she'd forgotten all about the others. And hell, so had he.

"Angelina, you just said you'd always planned to come here. Did you tell anyone that?" Gray asked. "Think hard about this."

She pursed her lips in concentration and slowly shook her head. "There was no one to tell."

Micah dragged a hand through his hair and met the stares of his friends. Anger was alive in their eyes, and the message was clear. They considered Angelina theirs just as they did Faith, Serena and Julie. No way they were going to allow some psycho asshole to hurt her.

"I feel the need to point out that it's entirely possible that this isn't the same whack job," Connor said.

Angelina shook her head. "It's him. I'd recognize the handwriting anywhere, and he always uses that same paper. It's stationery. Plain, but the texture is different than regular paper."

"Did you save all the other stuff or did you turn it over to the police?" Micah asked.

"I wasn't going to turn over my only evidence to them when they weren't ever going to take me seriously."

"Did you bring it with you?"

"It's under my bed," she said. "Do you want me to get it?"

"I'll get it," Connor said. "You just stay put where it's safe."

Micah nodded his agreement. If it was up to him—and he was going to make damn sure it was—she wasn't leaving his side until they nailed the fucker responsible for terrorizing her.

When Connor left the apartment, Micah pulled Angelina down to his chest again and stroked her hair in a soothing pattern.

"I should get back to the house," Gray said uneasily. "Faith is alone."

Nathan balled up his fists, a mixture of rage and fear tightening his features. "Julie's alone at her place too. If this joker knew enough to pin a note on my truck, he'll know about Julie too."

Angelina sat up, her eyes so sad that it took Micah's breath away. "I'm sorry," she said, turning to Gray and Nathan. "I never thought in a million years he'd come here or I wouldn't have brought this to you, I swear it."

Gray stopped by the couch on his way to the door. He reached out and briefly touched her cheek. "Don't be taking blame that's not yours to take. Our girls are tough. We just want to make sure they know what's going on so they can be careful."

She nodded miserably, and Nathan and Gray hurried out the door, leaving her alone with Micah.

Restlessly she stirred in Micah's arms. She shoved and scooted as she tried to get up, but Micah held firm.

"Angel," he said in a soft voice. "Stop pushing me away. I already feel you putting up the walls and distancing yourself."

"Just let me up. I need to breathe," she begged.

Reluctantly he let her go, and as he'd anticipated, she put the entire room between them as she paced a tight line in front of the television.

Connor walked back in, holding a box. He set it down on the coffee table in front of Micah then took a seat in the chair next to the couch.

Angelina wouldn't even look at Micah when he opened the box. She turned away, tense and worried, her arms wrapped protectively around her slim figure.

He tried to tune her out, tried to think and act like a cop even if it had been several years. He tried to look at the stack of letters objectively, but as he read, rage took hold.

As she'd said, they started innocently enough, but he still found them creepy from the onset. And then it was as if a switch had been flipped. They went from seemingly harmless to an explosion of rage and violence.

A chill slithered down his spine as he read the countless promises, the threats. No longer was the man trying to be subtle. He outlined in stark clarity just what it was he'd do to her once he had her in his hands.

Jesus. It was a miracle he hadn't gotten to her before she left Miami. Only because of her sheer intelligence and determination had he not kidnapped her from the club. Thank God for Nathan.

"What do we do?" Connor asked when Micah put the last of the notes back into the box.

Micah blew out his breath in an effort to control the wash of emotion that threatened to overtake him. He was angry—oh yes, he was pissed beyond belief—but he was also scared.

Before he could answer or even think of what the hell to say, Angelina turned, her eyes no longer reflecting fear or upset. No, determination burned deep and red-hot.

"The logical thing for me to do is leave," she said evenly.

CHAPTER 19

Neither Micah nor Connor had any liking for her statement. Both got this pinched look on their faces, and Micah reddened, looking like he was about to erupt.

"Don't be stupid," he growled.

Angelina sighed. "I was stupid to come here, Micah. I thought I was playing it smart. Had a plan in place. Was meticulous in its execution. I'd hoped I could come here, start a new life and forget the past. *That* was stupid. Leaving is smart."

Micah gaped incredulously at her. Connor frowned and eased up from his chair.

"Think I'll just go into the kitchen and let you two hash this out."

Micah waited until Connor had left the room and then rose from the couch, crossed the room and took her shoulders in his hands.

"You aren't leaving, Angel. Where the hell would you go?"

"Back to Chicago first. After that? Anywhere I want."

He looked up at the ceiling, his cheeks puffing out with his breath.

She reached up and loosened his hands on her shoulders then stepped back, eager to put distance between them. He unnerved her when he got this close.

"Think about it, Micah. I've put a lot of people in danger here. Your friends. Their wives and girlfriends. I like Faith, Serena and Julie. They don't deserve to have this brought to their front door. I've only been here a few days. Just a blip on the radar. I'll be forgotten in a week and everyone can get on with their lives. It just makes sense."

He stared disbelievingly at her. "You really believe all that bullshit, don't you?"

Her eyes narrowed and she frowned. "Look, I'm not being a martyr here, Micah. It's stupid to involve all of you in this. It's not your problem. It never was. I'm not an idiot. I've been taking care of myself for a long time. Did he scare me? Hell yes. I was terrified. But that doesn't mean I'm going to be an easy target for him. I'm not a victim. I never will be. But I'm not stupid either. And I won't allow your friends to get involved in this."

"They're your friends too," Micah said.

She shook her head and sighed. "They're loyal to you, Micah. They love you. They feel a certain responsibility to me because of my association with you."

"Bull."

"Let's not argue," she pleaded. "I need help planning a way to get out of town unnoticed. The sooner the better. He wouldn't expect me to put together a plan this fast. If I could leave tonight, I'd get a jump on him while he's still so pissed about missing me at the club."

Micah closed the distance between them again. "You don't get it, do you? You aren't leaving, Angel. I bailed on you once. It won't happen again."

"Guilt is bullshit," she snapped. "I don't need it. Don't want it."

"Fuck guilt. Guilt isn't what I'm feeling right now. I'm so pissed I can't see straight. You think I'm thinking about David right now? Or Hannah? Or the fact that I walked out on you when you needed me the most? Hell no. I'm thinking about what would happen if that bastard got his hands on you. I'm thinking about how the fuck I'm going to keep you safe. I'm thinking about how I can keep you close and not take you over."

Her belly fluttered in awareness and a tingle snaked its way up her spine. He looked so furious, so intense. So focused on her. She shivered as goose bumps raced across her arms, her breasts, beading her nipples into tight little knots.

"You're so sure that I'm a mindless puppet who'd be content to let you pull my strings, that I'd be some brainless rag doll. No wonder you don't want me, Micah. I wouldn't want me either if I thought those things."

"I don't think that," he growled.

Her mouth twisted. "I'm capable of making my own decisions. David didn't raise me to be a fool. I know precisely what I'd be walking into with you, and yet you're so determined to be noble and save me from myself. Personally I think it's all bullshit. You're not saving anyone but yourself. You're scared of the way I make you feel because you don't want to feel anything. Okay, fine, but quit being a coward and pretending this is all about me and what I'm not getting. Man up and tell me you don't want me, but quit making excuses."

For a moment she thought she'd pushed him too far. He stepped forward and she retreated. They repeated the process until her back met the wall and there was nowhere else to go.

He pressed against her, his body melding with hers.

"Oh, I want you," he said in a hoarse, raspy voice. "I want you so goddamn much I ache. But I can't give you what you deserve, Angel. All I can offer you is sex. Fucking. I can't be any more honest than that. You deserve more than that from a man—any man. I want you. No doubt. But I can only give you so much."

"If that's all you have to give then that's what I'll take," she said calmly.

Micah swore and looked away. "Goddamn it, Angel. Tell me no. Send me packing. Tell me you never want to see me again. Find a man who can give you everything, body and soul. *Tell me no.*"

She reached up to touch his lips. "I'll never tell you no, Micah. You think I don't know you, that I don't understand you, that I can't handle what you'll throw at me. You're wrong."

He placed his hands on either side of her neck, his thumbs brushing her cheeks, his fingers thrust into her hair.

"Be sure, Angel girl. Be very sure this is what you want. I'll own you. There's no part of you that won't belong to me."

Her heart did a crazy flip and damn near burst out of her chest.

"Don't you know, Micah? I've always belonged to you."

His pupils flared, and a predatory light gleamed in his dark eyes.

"You go nowhere and I mean *nowhere* without me until we nail this bastard," he said. "There'll be no more talk of you leaving. You're mine and I protect what's mine."

She swallowed and nodded, her eyes never leaving his.

"We can't stay here, but until I work something out, you'll stick with me at all times."

"Okay," she said huskily.

There was savage triumph in every line of his face, the look of a predator who'd captured his prey. She might not mean anything to him on an emotional level . . . yet, but he wanted her, and pure male satisfaction greeted his conquest.

She belonged. Her own savage satisfaction gripped her, spreading like wildfire through her soul. Wholly and utterly to him. She didn't fool herself into believing it was forever. He'd already set a time limit. They'd be forced into close proximity until her stalker was apprehended, and he was as willing to take advantage of the situation as she was. But he was already deciding to walk away when it was all said and done.

Determined not to dwell on things she couldn't change, she opted instead to focus on the here and now and the fact that Micah was hers, even if only for a little while.

CHAPTER 20

*A*ngelina stood in the corner of the big meeting room at Malone and Sons, where there were more people packed in than sardines in a can. The flurry of activity bewildered her. She'd expected Micah to turn over the letters to the police and then they'd wait to see where the investigation went, but this?

Micah, Connor, Nathan and Gray were sitting at one of the long tables, heads bent in conversation with four police officers. Even Damon was present, though he stood to the side, his hands in the pockets of his expensive slacks. Though his pose might seem bored, his eyes were tuned in to every nuance of the conversation going on.

Pop Malone sat at the head of the table, and every once in a while he waded into the conversation with his gruff, raspy voice.

There were three other men, not in uniform, who Angelina could only surmise were either off-duty cops or just friends of the group.

They were going through the notes, using gloves, discussing and analyzing the stalker like a bug under a microscope.

It wasn't that police work was something new to her. She'd witnessed David and Micah and any number of other Miami cops deep into their cases. At any given time, Hannah had made dinner for a dozen cops when they were over discussing a particularly hard case.

But Angelina herself had never been the focus of any of it. Stalkers didn't rate up there with rapists and murderers, and other than getting a restraining order, provided the identity was known, there wasn't often a lot that could be done.

She wondered where Faith, Julie and Serena were. As fiercely protective as all the guys were, she couldn't imagine they'd been left alone somewhere.

It was as though she'd been forgotten in the intensity of the meeting. She didn't like standing on the edge, didn't like the feeling of helplessness that gripped her. She didn't like the idea of these people, Micah's friends, *her* friends, putting themselves at risk for her.

It wasn't until now that she'd realized how much she missed being part of the camaraderie and absolute loyalty of the police force David had belonged to. Until they'd turned away, thinking the worst of her brother.

"You want something to drink, sweetie?"

She blinked and looked up to see Connor standing in front of her. Her gaze went to the table, to see that the overall meeting was apparently over and now everyone had split into smaller groups, their heads bent in conversation.

"I'd love something with caffeine," she admitted.

He curled his hand around the back of her neck and squeezed and massaged gently.

"You look tired. You just got out of the hospital. You need to be resting."

"I'm not sure I'll ever rest again," she said honestly.

"We're going to take care of you," he promised. "Micah's not going to let this asshole get to you."

She wanted to believe it, but Micah was only one man. He wasn't invincible. If intentions were all it took, then nothing would ever hurt her. Micah was fierce in his intent to protect her.

"Stay right here. I'll get you a Coke."

She smiled faintly. "I'm not going anywhere."

If she stood any longer, she was going to collapse. Her legs felt all rubbery, and her knees trembled. Since there wasn't a free chair in the room, she simply slid her back down the wall behind her until her butt hit the floor.

In the next instant, Micah crouched down in front of her, his worried gaze seeking hers.

"Hey, Angel girl, are you okay?" he asked softly.

When Connor arrived, Micah reached up to get the Coke he extended. He popped the tab and put the cold can in her hand.

She sipped gratefully at it. The adrenaline was definitely wearing off, and she was crashing hard.

"What's the plan?" she asked after taking several gulps.

"I'll tell you everything later. Right now I need to get you home. You're dead on your feet."

She shivered when he trailed a finger over her cheek. No matter how fatigued she was, her body jumped to life whenever he touched her. He was a craving, dark and erotic, one she had absolutely no control over.

His nostrils flared, and his features went tight. He felt it too, this intense connection that sizzled between them. Right now she could see the war he waged with himself. He was so readable. He wanted her. He wanted to take her and use her, but he also wanted to care for her. He thought her too weak and tired for what he wanted.

Didn't he know that he was all she needed?

"Take me home," she whispered.

He pulled her to her feet and tucked her securely against his side. Damon stopped them when they got to the door.

"I have an idea," he said in a quiet voice.

"I'm listening," Micah said.

"You and Angelina should stay at The House."

Micah looked at Damon like he'd lost his mind.

"I'm not stashing her in a fucking sex club."

"That's just it," Damon said patiently. "It's probably the last place this asshole would look. Cover your tracks, take Angelina to The House. It has all the amenities. Kitchen, bathroom. You could have your choice of the upstairs bedrooms. I can close it to the public for as long as you need a place to stay. The security is impeccable, but I'm open to having your men do whatever updating or beefing up you feel is necessary."

Micah rubbed his chin thoughtfully and then glanced down at Angelina. She could feel the tension in his body, coiled like a snake.

"It's a good idea," Micah admitted. "You've got enough surveillance there that no one could breathe on the place and get away with it."

Damon nodded. "Take her there tonight. I can have Serena bring you both clothing and all the necessities tomorrow morning. The kitchen is stocked. I have a full staff, so you don't have to worry about cooking or housekeeping."

Micah shook his head. "I want everyone out. If I'm taking her there, it'll be just her and me."

"If that's what you prefer. I'll put my staff on vacation for as long as necessary."

Micah put his hand on Damon's shoulder. "Thank you. I appreciate this."

"We both do," Angelina said.

Damon smiled at her, his brown eyes warm with affection.

"I consider Micah a very dear friend, even if he doesn't allow me to make that claim very readily. I consider you a friend as well, Angelina. If there is anything either of you need, you have only to call."

"Come on, Angel," Micah said gently when she wobbled on her feet. "Let's go get whatever we'll need for tonight, and then we'll see about losing any potential followers on our way to The House."

"Do you really think he's watching?" she asked in a troubled voice.

"I won't lie. It's a possibility. He was certainly watching the apartment complex. He knew just when you were alone, and he knew enough about Nathan's association with you, and where Nathan lived, to warn him off."

She shuddered and burrowed closer to his body. He squeezed her shoulder reassuringly.

"We'll get him, Angel. You have a lot of people working this case."

She looked up at him. "I know you will. I trust you, Micah."

"Let me tell the others what we're doing and then we'll get out of here."

She nodded, and he left her briefly to go talk to the others.

"Are you going to be all right?" Damon asked.

"I don't know," she said truthfully. "I'm scared. More now than I was in Miami. There it was just me. Here there are more people involved. I don't want anyone hurt."

"You just worry about staying safe. Let us worry about ourselves."

"Where are Serena and the others?" she asked.

Damon smiled, his teeth flashing white. "They're unhappy with me at present, but I have them sequestered at my home with a very surly bodyguard who poses as a chauffeur."

She had to suppress the urge to giggle. "I'm glad they're safe."

"As I said, don't worry about them or us. We take care of our own. We'll find this guy." He gestured over his shoulder. "They have the manpower. I have unlimited capital. It's a good combination. He won't be able to hide forever."

Angelina winced. "I feel like I already owe you all so much."

Damon shrugged. "There is no debt. There is no price I wouldn't pay to keep the ones I love safe. Serena is everything to me. Micah is one of my closest friends. And you are someone who needs the shelter of friendship most of all."

She shook her head. "Unbelievable. I never dreamed people like you existed. All of you." She waved her hand in a helpless circle. It honestly baffled her that all these people were willing to go to the wall for *her.*

"You ready?" Micah asked as he slipped up next to her again.

She nodded.

He brought her palm up to his lips and kissed it lightly. "Then let's go."

CHAPTER 21

*W*hen they pulled into the parking lot at The House, it was already empty. Lights glowed from the interior, a fact she was grateful for. She didn't think she'd be comfortable going into any dark place at the moment.

Micah got out and she followed suit. His hand went to her back, and her skin danced in reaction as he hurried her toward the door.

She was riding high on stress-induced adrenaline coupled with intense arousal. She was exhausted and revved up all at the same time, and she knew she would never rest until she found release. And yet she couldn't ask. Couldn't demand. She was his to command, not the other way around.

They walked inside, and Micah hesitated in the hallway.

"Want something to eat or drink?"

She nodded and he turned her toward the kitchen at the far end of the facility. It was warm and inviting, like the rest of The House.

Rich browns, soothing yellows. It amused her that a place devoted to such decadence had all the comforts of an inviting home.

She caught Micah's gaze and shivered under the blatant awareness that flashed in his eyes. His nostrils flared slightly, and the tension rolling through his body was a tangible, breathing entity.

She met his stare levelly, allowing every ounce of her need to reach across the distance. He set the glass of juice he'd poured for her on the counter and stepped forward, his eyes glittering.

"Turn around," he ordered.

Her nipples hardened. Her clit pulsed and swelled, and her breath caught painfully in her throat. She forced herself to breathe out as she slowly turned, presenting her back to him.

His hands closed over her shoulders. One hand worked up, tangling in her hair then sliding the heavy veil over her left shoulder, baring the curve of her neck.

Warm breath blew sensuously over her bare skin and then his teeth nipped and grazed at the slim column. Her knees threatened to buckle when he laved his tongue up the side to her earlobe and over the frantic pulse point, but he caught her firmly and pushed her forward toward the table.

Urgency invaded his movements. He bumped her into the table, bending her over when her stomach met the edge. His fingers caught clumsily at her pants, pulling, reaching around to release her fly.

As he yanked her jeans down over the curve of her behind, his other hand pressed firmly in the center of her back, holding her down.

Cool air blew over her ass, raising chill bumps. He left the jeans at the bend of her knees. One hand still held her down, but the other left her, and she heard the rustle of his own pants.

His legs bumped into the backs of hers, and his body pressed into hers, hard and fast. The back of his hand brushed urgently against her buttocks as he positioned his cock.

Before she could take a breath, he was on her, in her, so deep she cried out in shock.

He leaned in, his body covering hers, his hips slamming against her ass, the resounding smack echoing sharply through the kitchen.

After the initial frenzy, he slowed, withdrawing then pumping forward with methodical, forceful thrusts. Each time he withdrew, he paused until she let out a small whimper and then he powered forward, driving deep.

"Hands up," he said harshly.

She placed her hands above her head, palms down on the flat surface of the table. Her entire body shook with the force of his next thrust. She closed her eyes. She was close. So close to bursting and he hadn't even touched her intimately.

He was only intent on his pleasure. His taking was selfish and primitive, and she knew in a flash of understanding why. He was reinforcing his earlier statement.

All I can offer you is fucking.

She relaxed, giving herself over to him. Surrender. Acceptance. No way would he find any resistance. Pleasure washed over her in waves. He reached deep, his cock stretching her, filling her.

His body pressed dominantly over hers, his hips arching into her ass. His hand tangled in her hair, pulling as he strained to go even deeper.

No, he wasn't concerned with her pleasure at the moment. She could feel the torment radiating from him. He acted. Did the only thing he knew to do to try and rid himself of the same vicious need that riddled her. Only she knew it would never go away. Never die.

Her fingers flexed and then curled into tight balls. Her head came up as he pulled relentlessly at her hair. She gasped as her orgasm built. The pressure was achingly fierce. His balls slapped against her mound with every lunge.

"Micah!"

"Mine," he hissed.

She let out a small whisper of pain as he pulled harder at her hair, but it was forgotten as the storm gathered. Lightning surged, gathering in her pussy, exploding outward and surging into her belly.

As soon as she cried out again, he ripped himself from her spasming pussy. He yanked at her hair, pulling her from the table.

"On your knees," he ordered.

Clumsily, she slid down his body, her muscles weak from her orgasm. She caught herself by grasping his knees. Even as she settled herself, he strengthened his grip at the back of her neck and tilted her head up.

He grasped his turgid erection with his free hand and forced his way past her lips. She barely had time to gasp a breath before he filled her. Her cheeks puffed outward, and she forced herself to relax so she could accommodate him fully.

He tilted her back so that she was at an angle. He went with her so his angle of entry was cleaner. The position enabled him to have complete control.

He withdrew, paused, then sank deep again.

As he held himself there, he stared down, his jaw twitching. "Most normal men would take care with you right now," he said harshly. "Treat you with kid gloves, like a fragile piece of glass. But you don't want that, do you, Angel? Even now you're wanting more. You're daring me to push you."

She stared calmly at him, refusing to flinch or pull away. She needed air, but she also trusted him never to take it too far.

He eased back, his cock sliding over her tongue. A small surge of fluid spilled into her mouth. He was close. His entire body trembled. His knees shook against her hands, and she gripped him harder.

"Put your hands on my hips."

She rose up further on her knees and pushed his jeans farther down until her hands met bare flesh. His cock jutted from the fly, hard and thick.

"Keep your hands there while I fuck your mouth. Don't move. Just hang on."

Again his hand tightened in the tangle of her hair, and he gave one sharp yank to position her the way he wanted her.

"Open," he ordered.

She let her lips fall open and he was already there, pushing insistently. He pulled her forward to meet his thrust, until the coarse hair at his groin tickled her nose. It took every ounce of restraint she had not to fight, to struggle. In a way it was what he wanted her to do. She knew it.

He wanted to prove it was too much. He wanted her to say stop and to walk away. He had no idea just how strong her conviction was.

A sound of impatience escaped in a snarl. Her eyes flew open to stare up at him. There was a savagery that should have frightened her, but she knew he wasn't angry with her. No, it was self-directed. He hated that he wanted her every bit as much as she wanted him. He hated that she wasn't going to tell him no. He hated that she would take whatever he dished out and beg for more.

"Damn you," he hissed.

He threw back his head, closing his eyes. His thrusts became desperate, almost brutal. His groin slapped against her mouth as she swallowed him whole.

The hand holding the back of her neck became gentle, almost

coaxing. Her cheeks bulged with exertion as he tunneled deeper into her throat. Then he gripped her neck harder, forcing her onto his cock.

Fluid filled her mouth, warm and sticky. She swallowed around his cock, and he moaned and jerked erratically. More came and she swallowed reflexively, her throat working around the head of his cock.

He retreated momentarily, grasped the base of his cock and tilted her open mouth higher. He worked his hand back and forth over the thick shaft as more semen dripped from the tip and into her mouth.

He continued to stroke. "Keep your mouth open. That's it, Angel girl."

Two, three more gentle splatters fell onto her tongue and then his grasp loosened. Slowly he eased away from her, and he pulled at his jeans, working them back over his hips.

She knelt there, heaving for breath as she swallowed the last of his release. Her hands fell to the tops of her legs and she glanced down at her jeans that were trapped mid-thigh.

She glanced back up at Micah, seeking permission to rise, to reclothe herself.

After he'd straightened himself, he reached down, holding his hands out to her. She slid her fingers into his grasp and allowed him to pull her to her feet.

Gently, he pulled her jeans up until they were around her waist again. He refastened the fly, his gaze wandering lazily over her face. When he was done, he raised his thumb to her mouth and rubbed the pad over her bottom lip, capturing a drop of his cum.

"Lick it," he said huskily.

She sucked slowly at the tip, running her tongue over the slip of moisture.

"You make me crazy, Angel girl."

She laughed, surprised at the cracked way it came out. "What do you think you do to me?"

"Go pick out our room," he said. "Strip. I want you naked and in bed when I get there. I'll bring up a tray so you can eat before we go to sleep."

CHAPTER 22

"*I* hate this," Julie grumbled.

"I don't like it any more than you do," Faith said from her perch on the couch.

Serena turned from her position by the window. "How long are they going to be? Damon didn't answer his cell phone and we haven't heard from them in hours."

"They're probably figuring out a plan to keep us under lock and key for the next year," Julie said glumly.

"You should move away from the window, Mrs. Roche," Sam said from the doorway.

Serena sighed and walked over to the couch to sit by Faith.

Julie scowled. Damon's hulking chauffeur had been tasked with babysitting the three of them for the day. What the hell kind of chauffeur was built like a tank?

The sound of the front door opening had all three women on

their feet. Damon strode into the living room, Nathan and Gray on his heels.

"How is Angelina?" Julie asked anxiously. The men's expressions were so grim that fear scuttled around her stomach.

"She's safe," Damon answered. Even as he spoke, he reached for Serena, and she went to him, melting into his embrace. "She's with Micah."

"You ready to go home?" Gray said to Faith.

She nodded readily and took the hand he extended to her.

"We'll stay in touch. You all do the same," Gray said as they headed for the door.

Julie glanced at Nathan, who stood silently to the side. The intensity in his gaze caused her to shiver. He looked positively . . . scary.

"You have a choice," Nathan said as he stalked into her space. "My place or yours."

Too unsettled to think straight, she merely stared up at him, her brows furrowed.

"We can stay at your place or my place, but you don't stay alone, so make your choice."

She reached out to touch his chest, seeking reassurance. "Should I be worried?"

He caught her wrist, and surprisingly, his fingers trembled against her skin. He brought her hand to his lips and gently kissed her closed fist.

"I don't want you to worry, honey, because I'm going to take care of you. Which means you aren't staying alone. He saw us, Julie. He had to have seen us that night. He got to me. He can get to you."

She swallowed nervously. "We can stay wherever you feel is best."

He relaxed. Had he expected her to argue? Was she that confrontational? Sure, she liked her independence, but that didn't make her a moron. She wasn't going to sacrifice her safety or his over pride.

"I think we should stay at your place. He may not know where you live, but he sure as hell knows where I do."

"Okay," she said softly.

"Come on."

He tugged lightly, pulling her into his embrace. For a moment he held her, and only the erratic rise and fall of his chest against hers signaled his unease. He kissed the top of her head and smoothed his hand over her hair.

"Let's go home."

She nodded and followed him toward the door.

All the way to her apartment she watched him intently. He held her hand between them and rubbed his thumb over her knuckles in a deceptively calm manner. He was wound tighter than a rubber band, and she wasn't sure if it was the danger he thought she was in or if it was something else entirely.

Paranoia crept into her mind despite her best effort to keep it at bay

He's not going to dump you, dumbass. Men don't move in with you temporarily if they're ready to move on.

Unless of course it was a man with an overdeveloped sense of responsibility. No doubt Nathan and all his buddies were extremely protective when it came to women. So was he protecting her because she was a woman or because she was *his* woman?

Shut up, Julie. Don't ruin this.

When they got to her apartment, Nathan made her stay behind him until he made sure no boogeymen were prepared to jump out of her closets. She might have found it endearing and amusing if she weren't so edgy.

He moved around her apartment like he was comfortable and at home. Lord knew he'd spent enough time there even if they'd never made the leap to official cohabitation. She frowned. Maybe she should have asked?

Screw this. She was a mess. She was tired and she wasn't going to analyze stupid girly feelings when she was feeling particularly hormonal. Someone ought to market stupid pills. They'd make a damn fortune.

Nathan followed her into her bedroom, and before she could head to the bathroom to do her thing, he pulled her back and hauled her into his arms.

His mouth crashed down on hers. He stole her breath and devoured her lips in a greedy, passionate kiss. His hands fumbled carelessly at her clothes, ripping without care.

"Lose the pants," he rasped between kisses.

Even as she hopped on one foot to get rid of her pants, he pulled frantically at her shirt. He forced her hands away from her jeans long enough to raise her arms over her head so he could get her shirt off. Then when she resumed shucking, he tore at her bra, ripping the lacy cups.

Even then the material didn't come completely away, but her breasts spilled free and he cupped them roughly in his palms.

With one foot, she kicked the pants several feet away just as his mouth closed over a nipple.

Her breath escaped in a hiss as pleasure exploded through her mind.

"God I love your breasts."

"I love that you love my breasts," she gasped out.

She clutched his head, holding him tighter.

"You've got too many damn clothes on," she complained.

"Easily fixed."

He picked her up, his mouth still sucking her nipple, and walked to the bed, where he dumped her onto the mattress. As she lay there, he loomed over her, his hands going to his pants.

God, she loved it when he stripped in front of her. She rose to one elbow, watching appreciatively as he yanked off his shirt. His muscles rippled as he moved his arms. His chest flexed and bowed and his six-pack quivered.

Finally his pants came off, and he stood in front of her, his huge erection fisted in his hand. His eyes glittered with promise as he stalked toward her.

She gulped and edged backward.

He merely smiled and crawled on to the bed. His hand closed around her ankle, and he yanked her back toward him.

"I believe I promised you we'd have a talk," he murmured when she was completely underneath him. "And I'm pretty sure I said it would take place with you naked. Underneath me."

"Well here I am," she said breathlessly.

He cupped her cheek in his palm and stroked over her skin, gently pushing her hair behind her ear. His intense gaze roamed over her face as if he was searching. For what?

"Do you have any idea what you do to me?"

Before she could answer—and really, what could she possibly say to that?—he lowered his mouth to hers in a surprisingly tender kiss.

Heat blistered over her skin, but the warmth went deeper, beyond her heart and straight into her soul.

"I love you," she whispered against his lips.

He drew away, still stroking her cheek with careful fingers. "I love you," he said seriously. "Do you know that, Julie? Do you believe that?"

He kissed her again, sweeping the words away before she could speak.

"I wonder sometimes if you aren't waiting for the other shoe to drop. Like maybe you don't think I'm in this for the long haul."

She let her hands wander up his arms, to the thick column of his neck and then down to his chest. One thing she wouldn't do is lie. Not to Nathan. He was the one man she could be herself with, and that meant letting him see straight into her heart.

"Sometimes," she admitted. "I don't doubt you, Nathan. I'm just scared. I know I can be difficult, and I worry that one day you'll decide I'm not worth it."

He parted her thighs with one insistent hand and found her heat with his fingers. She arched helplessly into him, her mouth falling open in a tortured moan.

He stroked. Petted. Slid his fingers insider her and then eased up to her clit, spreading her moisture over the straining bundle of nerves.

"For such a smart woman, sometimes you can be so dense," he muttered.

Her eyes narrowed just as he added a third finger and stroked the walls of her pussy.

"Ah hell. How am I supposed to argue with you when you're doing that?"

He found her lips again, silencing her with his mouth. And then his tongue. Like rough velvet, his tongue stroked over hers, warm, spreading his taste, and God, he tasted so damn good. He smelled good. He felt good.

"I think the idea is that you're not supposed to argue."

"Me not argue? Like that's ever going to happen."

He smiled and withdrew his hands. She wiggled in protest, wanting them back.

"I have something better," he murmured.

He shifted his body, pushing her thighs farther apart. He positioned his cock at her entrance and pushed in the tiniest bit.

"You're such a damn tease!"

He chuckled and inched forward, barely stretching her. She wrapped her legs around him and arched up, trying to make him slide deeper.

Finally he accommodated her and thrust all the way in with one forceful push.

She cried out. No matter how often he made love to her, she still felt the shock of that first penetration all the way to her toes. He was big and thick and she pulsed around him like warm honey. He just made her go all gooey, and she loved and hated him for that.

Still buried deep inside her, he put his arms down on either side of her head and levered himself up enough so that he wasn't crushing her. He looked down at her, his green eyes so serious that for a moment she was worried. Until she remembered that he was as deep inside her as he could be. Who the hell broke off a relationship while they were buried to the balls?

"We need to get something straight, Julie."

"Hell of a time for conversation," she muttered.

"Oh, I think it's a damn good time because you can't escape me. You can't run. You can't avoid me."

He flexed his hips, and she tightened her grip on his shoulders until her nails dug into his flesh.

"I love you, woman. And you damn well ought to know that."

"I do," she gasped. "Now fuck me please."

"I'm not leaving you. I don't want anyone else. You're it for me, Julie. *It*."

Her eyes widened and she went completely still beneath him.

"What are you saying, Nathan?"

He let out a string of curses. "Nothing I haven't said to you a million times already. I've told you with words, with actions. I tell you with my body every damn time we get together, but you're so determined only to see what you want to see. When are you going to get it into your head that unless you kick *me* to the curb, then this is forever?"

She honestly couldn't formulate a response to that. Her mouth hung open as she stared into his eyes. He was serious. There was no hint of deception in his gaze. Just earnest . . . love.

"I'm never kicking you to the curb, dumbass," she said in a low voice.

He withdrew and then rolled his hips forward, eliciting another gasp from her.

"Good. Now that we've got that out of the way, I vote we talk about making our relationship a little more permanent."

Fear, excitement, joy and trepidation all went a little nuts on her. But still she wasn't about to make any assumptions. And not only that, but what she was almost assuming scared the shit out of her.

"How permanent?" she asked cautiously.

He slid his hands down her body again, cupping her ass as he hauled her up. Now on his knees, he drove relentlessly into her, the force of his thrusts making her breasts jiggle uncontrollably.

"Shit, I love it when they do that," he muttered as he lowered his mouth to one straining peak.

He devoured her breasts, moving from one plump swell to the other. There wasn't a part of his body that wasn't touching hers. His hips met the backs of her thighs, and his balls slapped the crack of her ass. He rode her hard, and when he was hopelessly deep, he lowered himself back to her, gathering her tenderly in his arms.

"Very permanent," he said gruffly. "So permanent that you'll never doubt how much I love you and how much I want to be with you."

"I think I could go for that," she said softly.

He paused and looked deep into her eyes, and for the first time she saw vulnerability that took her breath away. He was worried. He was as scared as she was.

Feeling shattered, she reached up to touch his face. Her fingers smoothed over his forehead, down his cheeks and then over the roughness of his goatee.

"I want forever, Julie. Marriage. You tied to me, legally, emotionally. The whole nine yards."

Her heart fluttered in panic, but at the same time a tidal wave of sheer joy swamped her from head to toe.

"My ring on your finger," he whispered as he swept her lips into another kiss.

"I like jewelry," she murmured.

"And I like you. Naked."

She smiled and wrapped her arms around his neck. She followed suit with her legs, curling them around his waist.

"Ah damn I love it when you wrap yourself around me," he groaned. "You're so damn warm and soft. I love how you feel."

"I love the way you make me feel," she said seriously. "You make me feel beautiful, Nathan."

He scowled, his brows drawing together until he looked positively ferocious. "You are beautiful. You're fucking gorgeous. I swear to God I can't breathe around you sometimes."

"You have to stop or, swear to God, I'm going to cry."

"Ah hell, anything but that."

He gathered her tight, holding her so that no space separated them. Flesh against flesh, her breasts molded to his chest, her body curved around his.

His hips flexed, his body arched as he thrust into her, keeping a leisurely pace.

What she'd said was true. He made her feel so very beautiful. No man had ever made love to her the way Nathan did. Sure, they had hot, dirty sex, and she loved every minute of it, but just as many times he took things so slow and loved her so sweetly that it was all she could do not to burst.

Her chest ached. Her soul ached. She couldn't live without this man. She didn't want to.

Just jump.

Take the leap.

Fly.

And she did. Straight into his arms. He held her tight as she burst into a million tiny pieces. Love and warmth flooded her. She soared. She floated. He was there to catch her.

"I love you," she said brokenly as her orgasm splintered through her groin.

He buried his face in her neck, kissing the tender skin just below her ear. "Ah, I love you too, honey. So damn much. Hold on to me, baby. I'm coming."

She arched upward, gripping him tightly. Her nails dug into his back just the way he liked, and then she slid her hands down to his tight ass and cupped him as he pumped into her body.

His teeth sank into the column of her neck and an agonized groan burned over her skin. His entire body tensed over hers, and his warmth flooded her.

He collapsed onto her, driving them both into the mattress. She lay there, holding him, stroking his back up and down. He didn't stir right away and she was content to lie there, with him in her arms.

She kissed his muscular shoulder and then ran her hand over his bald head.

"Stay," she begged when he started to move away.

"Don't you know, honey? I'm never going anywhere."

He kissed her again and then rolled to his side, carrying her with him. He was still buried inside her, and their limbs were all tangled up like some crazy knot.

"I love you," he said gruffly. "That ain't going to change. Ever."

She smiled against his chest and for once didn't begrudge the shimmer of tears that welled in her eyes.

"You know, Tucker, I think I just might believe you."

CHAPTER 23

 $\mathcal{M}$ icah balanced the tray and headed up the stairs toward the private rooms. He'd mentioned sleep, but he knew he wouldn't sleep until he'd had Angelina again. Far from sated, his entire body ached with unfulfilled need.

When he pushed open the first door, he saw her draped naked across the bed, her long hair fanned out. Her arms were folded, her head resting at her wrists as she lay on her belly.

He hardened all over again.

She looked up when he entered, but she didn't move. She simply waited.

He set the tray aside, knowing the sandwiches would keep. In a matter of seconds, he had his jeans off, and he strode toward the bed, eyeing the delectable curve of her ass. He'd take her there later, when he had time to prepare her. For now, he wanted inside her so badly that the need consumed him.

He grasped her ankles and pulled her toward the edge of the bed.

When her ass was level with his cock, he cupped her full bottom and lifted and spread, baring her pussy to his advance.

With no work-up, no preamble, he shoved into her, sliding deep into her silken clasp.

He fell forward, his hands slapping the mattress on either side of her body. It wasn't a time for slow, easy loving. That would come later, when some of the edge was gone. She was a need that fired deep in his blood.

There was desperation to his movements. His hips pumped forward in quick, jerky motions. His hips slapped against her ass with little finesse. It reminded him of a crude, quick fuck. And it was.

No words, no gentle endearments. It shamed him even as pleasure sizzled through his groin and painfully through his dick.

He was getting off quick, and it didn't really matter if she did or not.

You're a bastard. You have no business touching her.

It didn't matter that he'd warned her. He'd been brutally honest with her. She knew what to expect and she'd accepted that. And still, guilt ate away at his gut.

He slammed into her, driving harder as he felt his orgasm flash over him. One . . . two more quick, brutal thrusts and he was spilling himself inside her.

As he eased away, his cum smeared over her skin, and it turned him on all over again.

He turned away in disgust, reaching for the tray. He'd turned into an animal. Always, always he'd put a woman's pleasure above his own. He loved and cherished women, and yet he treated Angelina with contempt almost. All because she claimed to care about him.

His hands shook when he set the tray down on the bed. Angelina slowly got up and walked into the bathroom. When she returned, no accusation reflected in her eyes. No animosity. He could swear they still brimmed with affection and trust.

She crawled onto the bed and sat cross-legged next to him. He handed her a plate but didn't look at her.

"Do you have the remote?" she asked.

He reached over to the nightstand to get the remote and handed it to her.

They ate in silence, the television covering the awkwardness. She ate the sandwich he'd fixed and periodically switched channels. After the thirteenth channel, he cast her a sideways look.

"I thought guys were the serial flippers?"

She grinned. "Can't help it. Short attention span. It used to bug the shit out of David. Hannah would leave the room when we started arguing."

For the first time since Angelina had burst into his well-ordered existence, he didn't experience a surge of pain when she talked about David and Hannah.

"She never did like arguing. She was a born peacemaker."

Angelina nodded. "And I was a born hothead. Not sure where I got it. David said our dad was a lot like Hannah. Quiet, reserved. I think David took after him. He was always so even keel. He used to tease me and tell me I got all the Latin genes."

She put her sandwich down and turned her soft dark eyes on him. "Do you ever see your folks, Micah?"

He recoiled and looked away. Where the hell had that come from? How much did she know about his family anyway? He never talked about them. As far as he was concerned they didn't exist. His family was David and Hannah, and they were dead.

"No," he said shortly.

"Why not?" she prompted. "It's been a long time. David said you hadn't seen them since you left home all those years ago."

"Then you have the answer to your question."

She sighed. "I thought maybe you'd gone to see them after David and Hannah died."

He turned back to her, his expression hard. "Why would I do that? They aren't my family, Angel. My family died."

She frowned unhappily. "What happened with them? Why do you hate them so much?"

His laugh cracked and sounded pretty pathetic. "I don't hate them. To hate someone you have to feel. I don't think about them at all. They donated genetic material to me. That's the extent of the credit I give them in my life."

"Wow," she breathed out.

"There won't ever be any Hallmark make-up moments with them. They stopped existing the moment I walked out of the door when I was eighteen. I'm happy with the arrangement, and I don't really give a shit whether they are or not."

"What did they do?" she asked softly.

He shook his head. "That's been years ago, Angel. No sense dragging it back up. It just doesn't matter anymore."

She turned her attention back to the TV and continued flipping the channels until he was ready to snatch the damn remote from her hand and knock her in the head with it.

"You done?" he muttered as he reached for her plate.

"Mmm hmm."

He gathered the dishes and the tray and trekked downstairs to return everything to the kitchen. When he got back upstairs, Angelina had burrowed under the covers, the remote still firmly in her grasp.

He stripped down to his underwear and stood by the side of the bed.

"If you promise not to knee me in the balls, I'll ditch the underwear too."

She looked up and laughed. "Have problems with women being too active in their sleep?"

He grunted as he slipped out of his underwear and climbed into bed.

"You try getting your balls rearranged in the middle of the night. Not a nice way to wake up."

She giggled and quickly burrowed into his side. She made a sweet sound of contentment and lifted the remote to turn off the TV. Thank God.

"Micah?"

"Mmm hmm."

"Did you, David and Hannah all sleep together? I mean in the same bed?"

He paused. Where the fuck had that come from?

"Angel, honey, you lived with us. Surely you ought to know the answer to that."

"I never ventured into your part of the house. I was never sure how much you were comfortable with me knowing."

Micah frowned. "Hannah never talked to you? I mean I thought women dished about pretty much everything."

"Hannah wasn't like that. You know how private she was."

"We had two bedrooms but more often than not, we shared the same one. Sometimes if one of us wanted some private time with Hannah, the other would bunk in the other bedroom for the night."

"I always thought yours and David's relationship was pretty special. You were there before Hannah, I mean with David."

Micah nodded. "I met David right after I left home. Your father had just died and he was taking care of you."

"Yeah, I remember," she said softly.

"I met Hannah after we got out of the academy. Since David and I were so close, we all naturally spent a lot of time together. I suspected they had feelings for each other, but both were too honorable to act on them. They were both afraid of hurting me."

He smiled at the sudden flash of memories.

"It takes a pretty special man to do what you did."

He shrugged. "It just seemed natural. I never gave it any thought. It never occurred to me to be jealous. If it had been any other man, I would have killed him, but it was David and I knew David would never do anything to betray our friendship."

He hadn't realized he was stroking her arm. She was nestled in his arms and his fingers wandered up and down her skin as he remembered the good times. It was nice to be able to think of them without the flood of grief that always came.

"I'm not trying to replace her," Angelina whispered. "I know how much you loved her."

Micah pulled her in close and kissed the top of her head. "I know, Angel girl. I know."

CHAPTER 24

ngelina stirred and stretched against the warmth of Micah's body. Lazy contentment invaded her limbs, and for a moment she lay there, enjoying the comfort of his arms.

Remembering the events of the night before and the fact she hadn't had a shower made her roll away and head for the bathroom. She left Micah sound asleep, his other arm thrown carelessly across his pillow.

Moments later she stepped under the hot spray of the shower and closed her eyes in pure ecstasy. Hot water was the cure-all. Wars could be prevented if everyone started the day with a steaming hot shower.

She stood there, letting the water stream over her face, washing away worry, strain, fear and hopelessness. It was a new day.

Eyes still closed, face turned up into the spray, she reached blindly for the bottle of shampoo. A hand gripped her wrist, and she pulled her head back and opened her eyes.

Micah, naked, droplets of water beading on his chest, stepped into the shower with her. He gently lowered her arm back to her waist and retrieved the shampoo himself.

He stepped in behind her and squeezed shampoo into his hand.

"Lean your head back," he said huskily.

He lathered the shampoo over her hair, working it into her scalp. When he was done, he pressed forward, forcing her underneath the showerhead again.

With the water beating down, rinsing the soap from her hair, he hiked her right leg upward, her knee rubbing against the shower wall.

He positioned his cock at her pussy and thrust forward. The force sent her into the wall, her hands flying up to brace herself.

He gripped her waist and held her tight as his hips slapped against her ass.

Pleasure rippled through her groin. Her pussy fluttered in response and gripped his cock as he went deeper. Water rained fast and furious. It felt hotter than before, and steam rose as their breathing sped up.

It was an ambush plain and simple. A quick, hard fuck and she loved every second of it. It was raw, primitive, a man reaching out to his woman, his possession. It was a reminder that she had no power except what he gave her. He took, she gave, and she gloried in her offering.

Trapped between the hard wall and his equally hard body, she took the punishing drive of his pelvis.

"I want your ass, Angel," he growled in her ear. "I'm tempted to see if you can take me right now, right here, just like this."

A shudder rolled down her body, and she closed her eyes as she balanced precariously on the edge of orgasm.

His movements gentled. He bit into her shoulder, a hard bite, and then he licked the spot before nipping again. Then he sucked hard, his intent to mark her, a visible reminder of his presence. As if she could ever forget.

He stroked in and out. She writhed helplessly against him, wanting more, wanting it harder, just a little push over the edge.

"Tell me what you want," he ordered against her ear.

He nipped at her earlobe then sucked it between his teeth.

"Tell me, Angel. You don't come until you tell me."

"Fuck me," she gasped. "Make it hurt. Hard, Micah. Please."

He slammed into her, driving her mercilessly into the wall. Her cheek banged against the slick surface heated by the water.

One more. Just once more.

He withdrew, reached down and spread her buttocks, pushing upward so that she was open and vulnerable. Then he ripped into her again and she fell over. Down, hard. Pleasure, mindless, numbing pleasure rolled over and over, expanding until she quivered, held tight between the world of pain and endless, sweet sensation.

He pulled out, and she registered that he hadn't come yet. She tried to drop to her knees, anticipating that he'd want to come in her mouth, but he caught her, holding her up.

"Easy, Angel girl," he murmured.

When he was sure she could stand, he reached for the soap and a washcloth. To her surprise, he gently soaped her body, taking extra care around her pussy that still pulsed from her orgasm. Each touch was agony and he didn't linger.

He followed the path of the washcloth with his mouth, his lips and tongue heating a path much hotter than the water. He kissed her skin so tenderly that her heart ached. How could he say he didn't care, that he didn't want to care when his every action contradicted his words?

Even when he tried to punish her, when he pushed, expecting

her to balk, there was such torment in his eyes that she knew it wasn't what he wanted to do but what he thought he should do.

And now his every touch, his every kiss, was an apology.

She closed her eyes and luxuriated in the tender care he lavished on her body.

When finally he was done, he reached up to turn the water off. She swayed as he let her go, and he put a hand on her arm to steady her.

"Wait here while I get a towel," he said.

A moment later he returned and extended his hand to help her from the shower. As soon as she stepped out, he enfolded her in the large towel.

She went willingly into his arms and buried her head against his chest as he rubbed at her skin.

He slid a finger underneath her chin and gently tilted her head up until she looked at him. Their gazes connected, and she saw so much in his eyes that she knew he wasn't aware of. He tried to keep himself closed off, but what she saw now took her breath away. It gave her hope. It made her believe.

His mouth lowered to hers in the most tender of kisses. Their lips made soft sounds as they moved together. Warm, so sweet. No one had ever kissed her like this. There was so much emotion, so much feeling. Did he feel it too? Would he retreat?

He pulled away, his breathing ragged and his eyes glittering with more than simple lust. He wanted her, but in that moment, Angelina knew he realized he also needed her. Would he admit it?

"Want to go for a drive this morning? Wouldn't hurt to get out for a while. Could head down to the coast as long as we're careful and pay attention to our surroundings."

"That would be fantastic. I haven't been to the beach since I left Miami."

"The beaches aren't as pretty here," Micah warned.

"I don't care. Just being able to breathe the salt air again will be heaven."

She went back into his arms and squeezed tight.

"Thank you."

He hugged her back and kissed the top of her head.

"Go get dressed and we'll head up. I need to make a few calls and let everyone know where we're going. I want to keep watch and see if we're followed."

She sucked in her breath. "Is it safe?"

"Don't worry. I'll be armed and we're going to stay in very public places at all times. If we're followed, then we know we're not safe here at The House. I'm hoping he's still waiting for you to show at your apartment or at your job. If he makes a move there, we'll bust him."

"Okay."

He kissed her again. "Now go get dressed so we can get out of here."

CHAPTER 25

$\mathcal{M}$icah watched Angelina arch her face into the sun and breathe deep of the sea air. The stiff breeze blowing off the water sent her hair rippling in a wave behind her.

He didn't move, didn't say anything. He didn't want her to move, because he was content to watch her turn into the sun like a cat seeking the warmth.

She was beautiful. Why had he never noticed before? He'd been married, not dead. Yeah, Hannah had been the only woman he was focused on, but that didn't mean he didn't appreciate the rest of the opposite sex. Angelina had never registered on his radar. She'd been David's little sister. Family.

"It's such a beautiful day."

Micah smiled at her rapt expression.

"Nothing can ruin this. I won't allow it. We won't even think about the asshole stalker. Agree?"

Well, he certainly encouraged her not to think about the guy after her. He'd prefer for her to relax and enjoy herself, but that didn't mean that he wouldn't be spending every minute of the day looking over their shoulders.

But he smiled and nodded, enjoying her enthusiasm.

She walked over and sat beside him, snuggling into his side as they overlooked the seawall. He wrapped his arms around her and enjoyed the feel of a warm, soft woman against him. He hugged women, his friends, but this was different. There was more than affection working.

"Tell me about Miami," he said as he stroked her hair.

"What do you want to know?"

"Did you finish school? You never told me."

"I did. I graduated a year ago. That's when the notes started actually. I'd gone out to celebrate on graduation night. Came home to a dozen roses and a sweet congratulatory note."

Micah frowned. "Wonder if it was someone at the university."

"Could be. I didn't date that many guys in school. I mean I kept it casual. Friends, movies, group dates, that sort of thing, so I doubt anyone could have gotten the wrong idea from me."

"So what did you study? Last I knew you were wanting to be an art major. David was less than enthused."

He felt her smile against his chest.

"I made him crazy with my hippie notions as he called it. Said I was too much like our flighty mother. He was always so sensitive about her. He was afraid I was too much like her."

"He never talked about her. Just your dad," Micah said.

"Yeah, I know."

She sounded a little sad, and he squeezed her a little tighter to him.

"She's not dead, you know."

Micah stiffened in surprise. "I was certain David said they were

both dead. Your mom first and then your dad right after David graduated high school."

She sighed against him. "Mom left when I was really young. I
don't remember her. I just get glimpses, you know? And even then
I'm not sure I'm remembering her. It could be someone else. David
never forgave her for breaking Dad's heart. According to David, she
was flighty and irresponsible. An artist with no ambition other than
wanting to travel to *en vogue* places and paint the clichéd scenes."

"Ah, so that explains the aversion to you being an art major."

She shrugged. "It was a passing fancy. I mean how many high
school kids really know what they want to be the minute they graduate? I took general studies my freshman year and then declared a
major my sophomore year."

"And? Dare I ask what you grew up to be?" he teased.

"A teacher," she said softly. "But I had to leave before I could go
to work."

"David always loved children. You share that with him."

She smiled. "I always saw David with an entire house full of kids.
One clinging to each leg, one in each arm and at least two running
behind him screaming 'Daddy' at the top of their lungs."

His stomach knotted. He'd wanted kids too. Hannah would
have been the perfect mother. He and David had worked out that
Hannah would stay at home with any children they had. They'd
even had plans drawn up to add on to the house when the time
came.

"I'm sorry," Angelina said as she reached up to touch his face. "I
didn't mean to bring up bad memories. I forget sometimes just how
tied you were to him and Hannah."

Micah shook his head. "You should be able to talk about your
brother without worrying what it's going to do to me. He was your
family. He loved you."

"Do you ever wonder why them and not us?"

His brows furrowed and he looked sharply at her. "What do you mean?"

"I don't know. I just wonder why some people die when they do. Why wasn't it me? I wasn't married. No connections to anyone. It would have been easier for it to be me. David would have mourned, but he would have had you and Hannah. Or do you wonder why not you instead of David? Or am I the only crazy one who asks those kinds of questions?"

"I think you can make yourself crazy going around in circles like that. Who knows why anyone dies? I've never believed in all that 'it's their time' bullshit. I believe in bad luck and even worse decisions. I've seen enough in my time as a cop to know that things are rarely as random as they appear. There's always a series of events that lead up to that one moment where all is lost."

"You sound so cynical," she said sadly. "I can't say I blame you. I lost a lot of my belief in good when they died. It was such a senseless tragedy. As you said, bad choices. A driver not paying attention and David and Hannah paid the price. We paid the price."

"How about we move on to happier things," Micah said as he touched her nose.

She smiled, though her face still looked sad.

"I wish I could go back and do things different, Angel girl," he said in a low voice. "You have no idea how much I wish it."

She cupped his cheeks in both hands and pulled him down in a kiss.

"You're here now. That's all that counts."

"So let me ask you something."

"Shoot," she said as she adjusted herself so she faced the ocean again.

"Do you ever think about trying to find your mom?"

She went still. "No. She left. She made her choice pretty clear. She didn't want me or David. Why would I want her now?"

"Because she's your only family," he said gently.

She glanced sharply at him. "Just like your parents are your only family."

He held up his hands in surrender. "You've made your point. Okay, both our parents are off-limits. I won't talk about yours and you don't remind me of mine."

"Deal," she muttered.

They sat not talking, the sounds of the sea in front of them, the traffic along the seawall boulevard behind them. It surprised him how content he was just to hold her. To feel her, to listen to her soft breathing.

They stayed until the sun slipped below the horizon and the sky was bathed in pink and golden hues. She stirred against him, and it was then he realized she'd fallen asleep.

"You ready to head back home?" he asked softly when she looked up at him with sleepy eyes.

She smiled and nodded. "Thank you for today, Micah. It was nice to get away for a while, to escape reality for a few hours."

Unable to resist the soft, tousled look she presented, he kissed her lips, then the corner of her mouth, then her jaw and down to her neck. He nuzzled her ear and then worked his way back over her cheek and up to her eyes. He pressed the lightest of kisses to each of her closed eyes and then dropped a playful peck on her nose.

"Come on, sunshine. Time to get you home and in bed."

She stretched and stood, taking his hand as he started for the truck.

CHAPTER 26

"*W*e have company coming over tonight," Micah said.

Angelina looked up from her perch on the couch. "We do? Who is it?"

Micah smiled. "It's a surprise. But we need to get you ready."

Her eyebrow went up, and her pulse leapt. In the weeks since they'd moved into The House, Micah had kept them secluded. They'd slipped into a comfortable relationship that extended beyond sex and his complete mastery over her body. She'd grown used to being with him, to having him to herself, a barrier to the outside world. Now their sanctuary was being breached, but she found herself excited and intrigued instead of resentful of the intrusion.

He walked over to her and held out his hand to help her up.

"First a shower. I'll wash your hair. Afterward I'll dry and brush it out for you. Have I ever told you how much I love your hair?"

She swallowed, her nervousness—no, anticipation—tightening her throat.

"There's no reason to be afraid," he murmured as he touched the pulse point at her throat.

"I'm not afraid," she said huskily.

"Good."

He pulled her with him up the stairs to the bedroom. As soon as they got past the door, he started undressing her. His movements were slow and measured. The calm and precision in which he touched her excited her.

He was exceedingly gentle, almost as if he were truly afraid of frightening her. This puzzled her because before he'd always been quick to demand, impatient and forceful. This . . . this was a side to him she hadn't seen but had always longed for. She'd seen how tender he was with Hannah. She knew he was capable of such caring and love. Could he be softening toward her?

The last of her clothes dropped to the floor, and he cupped her shoulders as he stared down at her.

"Go lie down on the bed. On your stomach. Get comfortable."

She was curious, but she didn't question him.

She settled onto the bed and rubbed her cheek on the soft comforter. A few moments later, the bed dipped and he crawled onto up next to her.

He placed his hand on the back of her knee and ran it up her leg and over the swell of her buttocks. He stopped there and gently kneaded the soft flesh.

His fingers dipped low, and he ran his thumb over the seam of her pussy, down to her clit. He toyed with it for a minute and then rubbed gently over her folds, pushing inward then withdrawing.

"Has anyone ever had your ass, Angel girl?"

She swallowed and shook her head.

"I don't want your first experience to be with another man. I want to ease you into it. I don't want to hurt you. A lot will happen tonight. I want you to be prepared."

She shivered at the promise in his voice.

He bent and kissed one cheek of her ass, then nibbled playfully at it. His thumb worked up from her pussy, over the tight opening. She flinched and tightened reflexively.

"Relax," he murmured.

She forced herself to go limp under his coaxing hands.

He kissed her other cheek and then slid his mouth up to the small of her back. All the while, his thumb worked back and forth over her anus. It slid easily, dipping into the opening, and then she realized he'd used lubricant on his fingers.

"You have a gorgeous ass. I get hard just watching you walk. You could hypnotize a guy with that sexy swing of yours."

She smiled and remained still, relaxing further under his sweet seduction.

"I'm going to push you tonight, Angel girl. I don't think it's anything you can't handle. You're a lot like me. More than anyone else I've known. We like the same things. We're into the same kinks. Now I want to see just how far I can push you."

Oh God. Chill bumps raced across her back, and he chuckled softly as he ran his tongue up her spine.

"You'll be powerless tonight. I expect you to obey. I want you to trust me, but at the same time, if it becomes too much, all you have to do is say stop."

"I do trust you, Micah."

"You're beautiful, Angel, and tonight I'm going to share that beauty. I'm going to watch other men possess that beauty. I'm going to offer what is mine because it's mine to give."

She let out a small moan as his thumb pressed deeper, slipping past the natural resistance of the opening.

"I'm too possessive to allow another man to be the first," he admitted. "I don't want to chance another man hurting or frightening you."

He kissed the area just above where his thumb probed, and then he slid his thumb in to the knuckle. Her fingers curled into the blanket and formed tight fists at her head.

The bed dipped again, and then his body covered hers like a warm, comforting blanket. His knee went between her thighs and spread them wider.

He kissed one shoulder and then the other. His hands caressed her arms, then slid over her back and down her waist.

"We're going to take this nice and slow, baby. Relax and trust me. It might hurt, but it won't last long. Once I'm in, the worst is over."

His voice soothed and lulled her. His touch incited deep longing.

His hand pressed into her buttocks and then she felt him position the blunt head of his cock at her opening. When the tip touched the sensitive flesh, her pussy tingled in reaction.

Again he kissed her back and then her neck.

"Relax," he whispered. "When I start to push in, I want you to push out against me."

She nodded her understanding and braced herself for what was coming.

"No, baby, don't tense up like that."

He moved his hand up to her hair, smoothing it away from her face. He stroked soothingly and then he kissed her ear.

"Relax. Trust me. I won't hurt you any more than I have to."

Taking a deep breath, she forced herself to go limp again.

He pressed inward, and her eyes flew open as she began stretching around the head of his cock.

"Push out. Meet me halfway," he whispered into her ear.

She pushed. He pushed. She stretched, and it felt like fire. She sucked in her breath and then held it, her heart pounding against the mattress.

"Breathe, Angel girl. Breathe and try to relax. I'm almost there. It won't hurt for much longer."

As soon as she expelled her breath, he gave a firm push and her body gave way. He slid into her body, and she cried out at the overwhelming barrage of sensation.

She struggled, unable to process whether it was pain or pleasure or some heady mixture of both.

"Shhh, baby, it's all right."

He kissed her neck and then her shoulder, and he held himself completely still against her as he gave her time to adjust to his size.

"God, you're big," she wailed.

He chuckled as he rested against her.

"It just feels that way because you've never taken anyone this way."

He withdrew a few inches and carefully pushed inward again. There was relief, and it felt good when he eased out, but then the fire was back when he thrust forward again.

The stark differences made her crazy. The sweet tenderness he exhibited warmed her all the way to her heart. The edgy pain woke the dark hunger deep inside her in places that only he'd awakened.

"Am I hurting you, baby?"

"No, yes, God I don't know," she gasped.

His teeth grazed her shoulder, and then he licked the spot before kissing her again. He rose up so his weight was almost completely off her.

He placed his hands on either side of her body and surged forward, deeper than before. The thick base of his cock stretched her impossibly and his balls rested against her pussy.

God, he was completely embedded in her. All the way to the balls. He stayed there, allowing her more time to adjust.

Then he began a slow, easy motion. In. Out. He was careful not to push too hard, be too forceful or go too fast.

She needed to touch herself. Needed him to touch her. She was desperate for clitoral stimulation. She whimpered and fidgeted underneath him.

He stopped immediately.

"Nooo, don't stop. Touch me. Micah, please, I'm dying here."

He pulled out, and she flinched at the shock.

"Get up on your knees," he said. "Back up to the edge of the bed."

Shakily, she rose up, planted her hands in the mattress and got to her knees. She moved back until his hand stopped her.

"Touch yourself," he said huskily. "While I fuck your ass."

The rawness of his command sent desire flooding through her body. Leaning forward, she tucked one arm underneath her and slid her fingers over her belly and lower to her pussy. She circled her clit once just as he positioned himself again.

This time he wasn't as easy. He slid forward, reopening her with one thrust.

She cried out as pleasure exploded through her groin.

"I won't last," she said desperately. Already she was on the verge of orgasm.

"You can control it," Micah soothed. "When you get close, stop touching yourself. Give yourself time to come down. You can come with me."

"Don't go easy, Micah. I don't need you to. Please. I need you to go hard."

In answer to her plea, he gripped her ass and used his thumbs to part the cheeks. The motion stretched her even tighter around his cock and they both moaned.

"Get ready then, baby. I'm going to ride you hard."

She closed her eyes and began stroking herself again just as he rammed into her. Hard, fast, deep.

He began slapping against her ass, his thrusts jostling her entire body.

It hurt, it burned, it was magnificent.

She reached for the pain, embraced it, reveled in its darkness.

"I can't stop," she panted. "I'm going to come."

"Me too, Angel girl. Come with me. Let's go together."

He increased his pace until he was pounding against her, hard and urgent.

Her mouth opened, but her scream was muffled by the comforter. Her entire body bowed, writhed, and she came completely apart. Spasm upon spasm rippled through her belly until the tension was more than she could bear.

She could no longer feel him in his frenzy. His hands gripped her ass, and she knew she'd wear his fingerprints for a long time to come.

Then he collapsed forward, driving them both onto the bed. His pelvis twitched against her as he flooded into her. He continued pumping against her in short, jerky motions until finally he stopped and his harsh breathing rasped against her ear.

"I think you killed me," he groaned.

"I think that's my line," she gasped.

He stirred against her. "Don't move."

"As if I could," she muttered.

He carefully lifted his weight off her and withdrew. Warm semen slipped down the inside of her leg.

Instead of going for a towel, he simply picked her up and carried her toward the bathroom. She cuddled against his chest, grateful he hadn't made her walk. Her legs had the consistency of putty at the moment. She'd be lucky not to fall on her face in the shower.

She needn't have worried. He took care of her completely, holding her against him while he washed every inch of her body. After he'd washed and rinsed her hair, he stepped out and dried her from head to toe.

"Come into the bedroom. I'll finish drying your hair and then I'll brush it for you."

She smiled and leaned into him for a moment. She wrapped her arms around him and hugged him tight.

He'd vowed not to give her any part of himself. Just fucking. All he could offer her was sex. He'd lied, and she wasn't even sure he'd realized it yet.

Micah took his time, first drying her hair and then combing through each strand. He was infinitely tender, his hands sorting through the heavy tresses. Every once in a while, he pressed his lips to the curve of her shoulder or the column of her neck.

When he finished, he patted her on the behind.

"Are you sore, baby?"

She shook her head.

"Good. I want to put a plug in so you'll be ready for tonight."

Her stomach fluttered in response, and she swallowed rapidly.

"Lie down on your stomach."

She rolled away from him and stretched out as she'd done before.

He moved from the bed, and she heard him rummaging in one of the drawers. He returned a moment later and ran his hand over her ass.

"Just relax, just like you did earlier. It might be uncomfortable at first."

She sucked in her breath but didn't hold it this time. Cool gel slipped between her cheeks, and his fingers carefully probed, spreading it inward.

His hand left her and was replaced by the blunt tip of the plug. Thick and plastic feeling, it was hard and unyielding, more rigid than his cock had been.

Her opening stretched and she willed herself not to tense. He pulled back, allowing the tip to retreat. He added more lubricant and then eased it forward again, stretching her more this time.

It was several minutes of patiently working the plug in before he finally sent it all the way. She flinched away when the broad base sunk into her ass, but he placed his hand on her back and rubbed soothingly.

"Take a deep breath. It's over."

She shuddered and went limp, closing her eyes as she processed the bombardment of sensations. Her ass pulsed and quivered around the plug. Edgy and restless, she couldn't remain still. Need curled in her groin, and she ached for release already.

"Turn over," he commanded in a quiet voice.

She maneuvered over, taking care with her throbbing ass.

"Spread your legs for me, baby. Let me see your pretty pussy."

She parted her thighs and watched as he took position beside her. Their eyes met. Their noses were just inches apart. She sighed softly just as his lips took possession of hers. His hand slid down her belly to her pussy. He rubbed his fingers over the folds, delving inward to find her clit.

She arched immediately into his touch. God, she was so close to orgasm already and all he'd done was put the plug in.

As his mouth made love to hers, he fingered her gently to orgasm, swallowing her cry of pleasure.

CHAPTER 27

$\mathcal{A}$ngelina lay on the couch in the main social room downstairs while Micah went to answer the door. He'd arranged her almost artfully. She was positioned on her side, her long hair over her breasts, but her nipples peeked from between the strands.

He hadn't told her much, just that some friends were coming over to watch the football game. But she knew what would happen.

Voices in the hallway had her breaths coming fast and erratic. A moment later, Micah appeared in the doorway followed by three men.

Holy hell.

She tried not to stare and instead studied their entrance from underneath her lashes.

They walked in but came to a complete stop when they saw her. They stared openly, their eyes glittering with appreciation. As her gaze traveled from one to another, she recognized one of the men. Cole. The man who'd flogged her that first night Micah had seen her at The House. The other two she didn't know, but she seemed to remember seeing them around the premises on the nights she'd come to play.

Micah walked over to stand by the couch. He reached down and tangled his hand in her hair, gently rubbing her head. Then he trailed his fingertips over her shoulder and down to cup her breast.

"This is Angelina. She belongs to me. Tonight she is yours to do with as you wish. There are conditions, however. You will show respect and care for her. If I tell you to stop, you stop. If she tells you to stop, you stop. You'll protect her by wearing condoms. This is nonnegotiable."

"She's gorgeous," one of the men said hoarsely.

"Yes, she is," Micah agreed. "She's new to anal sex. I'd ask that you treat her gently. Other then that, she enjoys pain. She craves it."

He put a finger under her chin and lifted until she looked up at him.

"Angelina, these are friends. You know Cole, I believe. Next to him is Rick. On the end is Chris. You'll obey them as you obey me. You'll see to their pleasure as you do to mine. Understand?"

She nodded.

"Come to me," he said.

She rose to stand beside him, conscious of the male stares from across the room. She wasn't shy, nor did she have any hang-ups about her body being on display. The stares warmed her skin, and she enjoyed the appreciation she saw reflected so clearly in their eyes.

They were handsome men. Rick was tall. Blond-haired, muscular, with a great tan. He wasn't GQ good-looking. Not polished or pretty. He looked like he worked outside a lot. Maybe construction. With his build, it was obvious he did a lot of physical work.

Chris was shorter and stocky. A football player's build. He had broad shoulders, legs like tree trunks and bulging biceps. If he didn't indulge in bodybuilding, then he was blessed with extraordinary genes.

Cole. Quiet, observing Cole. She always saw him watching. Rarely participating, and then only on a superficial level such as when he flogged her. But she never saw him having sex. She'd never even seen him without his clothes on. He was the last person she'd have expected to be here, but he watched her now with such quiet intensity that she shivered. Of the three men, he would be the one to push her the most.

Micah led her to the middle of the room, just to the side of where the couches and chairs were positioned in front of the big screen.

"Kneel here," he said.

She sank gracefully to her knees and then Micah turned away to the others.

"Ready for the game?" he asked.

They nodded and voiced their agreement, though their eyes never left her as they sprawled into chairs and onto the couch.

For a while they ignored her, but she caught the quick glances thrown her way. The game started, and they were quick to start throwing around ridiculous bets and bitch about bad calls.

"Angel," Micah called softly.

She raised her head until their gazes met. There was such pride and approval in his eyes.

"There's beer in the fridge. Bring it to us."

She rose gingerly, mindful of the plug rubbing against her tender flesh. Once in the kitchen, she opened the fridge and took out a six-pack of chilled beer. She was nervous because now she would be getting close to them, and she knew at some point they would want to touch her. They would want to do a lot more. It excited her, but she also didn't want to disappoint Micah.

She walked back into the living room and stopped in front of

Chris. His pupils flared and his gaze tracked downward to her breasts
that bobbed in front of him.

He took one of the beers she handed him and let his fingers
linger over hers.

"Thanks," he said in a low voice.

She almost smiled. He was cute. It was almost like he was afraid
to touch her.

She went to Rick next, and he was bolder. He placed his hand
on her hip and slid it over her skin and up to cup her breast. His
thumb brushed across her nipple, bringing it to a sharp point.

"Bring them their beer and come back to me," he rasped.

She nodded and moved on to Micah. He didn't touch her, but he
didn't have to. He caressed her with his gaze. So warm and loving.

Lastly she stood in front of Cole. His blue eyes pierced her and
his gaze was hungry. Very hungry. Chill bumps dotted her skin and
her nipples puckered and jutted outward.

"You've been told to return to Rick," he said.

She ducked her head and moved quickly back to Rick. To her
surprise, he already had his pants undone, and his cock was fisted in
his hand. Her eyes widened. He was thick, hard and very large.

He stroked his hand up and down, exerting pressure on the head
with each motion.

"Kneel in front of me," he ordered.

He spread his knees and she went to hers.

"Suck it."

Her hair fell forward as she leaned over him. She reached to
grasp his cock, but he pushed her hand away.

"On my legs. Keep them there."

She braced herself on his legs. He curled his free hand around
her neck and guided her down to his fisted cock. Just before her lips

met the head, she hesitated. In response, he yanked her down, forcing her onto his erection.

She closed her eyes and let him have his way. She relaxed her
throat muscles and took him deep. He groaned and his fingers curled
tighter around her neck.

Not knowing if he wanted her to take the initiative, she remained still and waited. His hand was still curled around the base
of his cock, but now he removed it and forced her down until his
balls pressed against her chin.

"Holy shit, she's magnificent," he gritted out.

He pulled her head up, giving her a chance to take a breath.
Then he pushed her down, raising his hips to meet her.

"Fuck, I'm not going to last long with a mouth like yours," he
panted. "Keep your mouth open and don't move."

He began fucking her mouth with rapid, sharp thrusts. He wound
his hand into her hair and pulled her down over and over.

Suddenly he jerked her away and forced her lower. He grasped his
cock again and moved his free hand from her hair to grip her jaw. He
forced her mouth open and began rapidly stroking his cock.

He thrust his hips forward until the head of his dick bobbed just
centimeters from her open mouth. The first jet of semen hit the
inside of her cheek and splashed onto her tongue.

"Don't swallow," he directed. "Hold it all in your mouth."

He continued jerking and more cum filled her mouth. He tilted
her chin up and ran his hand up his erection, squeezing and milking
more of his release into her mouth.

When he was done, he gently stroked her jaw with his thumb.

"Now swallow," he said huskily. "Swallow it all."

She did as he ordered and ran her tongue over her lips to remove
the moisture from the corners of her mouth.

"That was fucking amazing, sweetheart."

She glanced over at Micah, who was watching the game. He played it cool, and for some reason that aroused her all the more. A glance in the other direction had her eyes wide again.

Chris had his dick out, stroking the stiff erection. When his hand went down, he cupped his balls and squeezed before stroking upward, rolling the foreskin over the swollen head.

"Over here," Chris directed. "Face the TV."

She pushed herself up, and Rick touched her cheek in a tender gesture as she moved away. She stood before Chris and then turned away as he'd ordered.

"Put your hands on your knees and bend just a bit," he husked.

Trembling, she leaned forward and rested her palms on the tops of her thighs. Chris's fingers glanced over her skin and carefully pulled at the plug. It came free and she closed her eyes as a soft moan escaped her lips.

She heard the crinkle of a condom wrapper and then Chris placed his hand on her waist. He pulled her down, almost roughly. Using one hand to guide his cock, he used the other to spread and position her. As soon as she felt the tip nudge at her pussy entrance, he pulled her down hard.

She cried out as she took him as deep as she could. Her ass ground against his groin.

"Jesus, she's tight," he breathed.

He wrapped both big hands around her waist and picked her up before slamming her back down on his cock. She closed her eyes and arched her neck. Her hair dangled down, sliding across his chest.

He buried his face in the heavy veil and began pumping into her with strength that surprised her despite her observations about his build.

He stretched her impossibly, to the point of pain. It was delicious.

He was incredibly thick, by far the thickest cock she'd ever tried to take. Each time he forced himself back into her, she felt a ripple of pain followed by edgy, sharp pleasure.

Then he picked her completely up, his cock coming free.

"Turn around. I want to taste those tits."

On shaky legs, she turned back around and straddled his huge thighs. She was spread so far across him that all he had to do was hold his cock in place while she came down on him again.

This time he raised his hips as he yanked her down, and she yelped as he slipped deeper.

He smiled, his white teeth flashing in front of her.

"You can't take all of me, baby? Not many women can. Before the night's over with, you will. You'll take me in every one of your holes."

He leaned up and captured a nipple between his teeth. He bit into her flesh, and even as she whimpered in pain, she was arching closer, wanting more.

"Oh hell yeah," he muttered. "I'm going to fucking take you home with me."

He wrapped both hands in her hair and yanked, forcing her head back and her breasts forward. He sucked at one and then went to the other.

"Ride me. Put your hands on my shoulders and ride me."

She curled her fingers into his skin, gripping, her nails digging deep. He didn't seem to mind at all. His groans mixed with her cries. He bit, sucked, and ravaged her nipples. She rode him, rising up and slamming down as the pressure built higher and higher.

He was right. She couldn't take all of him, but it was close.

"Relax," he crooned. "Come on, baby. One more inch and you've got me to the balls."

"I can't," she gasped. "You're too big."

He wrapped his arms around her and stood suddenly, carrying her with him. She gasped in surprise at his strength and the fact that he was still buried deep in her pussy.

He dropped to his knees and fell forward, carrying her with him to the floor. He slipped free from her as he yanked impatiently at his pants. As soon as he was free, he was on her, spreading her wide.

Close, so close. His forehead was creased with tension, and her own orgasm lurked just out of reach.

He slammed into her, and she cried out.

"Take me. All of me," he hissed. "Take me."

He hammered into her again, and she felt herself give way around him, giving him that last inch. His balls wedged against her ass, and he gave a shout of satisfaction.

The world went blurry around her. There was no more pain, only intense, mind-numbing pleasure. Her orgasm crashed and kept on crashing as he rode her relentlessly, driving her into the floor.

She went slick around him.

"Oh hell yeah. Goddamn, she took all of me."

His entire body went tense over her. He strained as if trying to go even deeper. Then he dropped his forehead to her shoulder, and his chest heaved uncontrollably.

He turned his mouth into her neck and kissed her gently, a direct contradiction to the pounding force in which he'd taken her.

"That was amazing," he whispered.

She smiled faintly. If she'd been capable of saying anything, she'd have agreed that it had been pretty damn amazing.

Slowly he pushed himself off of her. He was careful when he withdrew not to hurt her. She was swollen and she clasped him tighter than she had before.

To her surprise, Micah was there to pick her up. He cradled her in his arms and walked back to the sofa to sit down. She snuggled into his arms as he petted and stroked her back, her arms and her legs.

He didn't say anything. He just held her as they watched the game, and every once in a while he pressed a kiss to her hair.

After a while, he whispered, "Rest, Angel girl. We're all hungry for you, and we're not going to be easily satisfied."

CHAPTER 28

$\mathcal{A}$ warm hand caressed her cheek, and her eyes fluttered open to see Cole standing over her. Her pulse fired and sped up, and her breathing shallowed. Micah's hand was still resting possessively on her hip, but Cole's eyes commanded her.

"It's halftime. You're up," Cole said in a quiet voice.

He held out his hand, and she slipped her fingers into his grasp. Micah helped her from his lap, and she rose to stand in front of Cole.

To her surprise, he pulled her to him, grasped her jaw and kissed her hard and deep.

He swallowed her gasp of surprise and moved his lips forcefully over hers. At first she remained still, allowing him to take, but he wasn't satisfied with complacency.

He tightened his grip on her jaw in a demand for response.

She opened to his advance, and his tongue slid sensuously over hers, licking, touching, probing. Tentatively she offered her tongue, sliding it over his bottom lip.

A low sound of approval rolled from his throat into her mouth. The pressure lessened on her jaw, and his fingers brushed across her cheek to her neck. Both of his hands tangled in her hair, a soft but urgent caress as he ravaged her mouth.

When he finally pulled away, his eyes were bright with passion. Her lips were swollen and tingling from the roughness and the sensuality of his kiss.

She wasn't quite sure how to react for a moment, and she looked back at Micah for some sort of read. He stared intently at her, desire and approval reflected in his dark eyes. It was that approval that gave her the courage to turn back to Cole.

It was then she realized that she'd in fact questioned Cole's command. She lowered her head, thought better of it and then raised her gaze to meet Cole's and whatever rebuke he might offer.

He smiled and he reached out to touch her cheek. "So expressive," he murmured. "Your thoughts are reflected in your every expression."

"I'm sorry."

"Don't be. You're beautiful to watch, and it's a credit to Micah that you look to him for permission. You remember well who you belong to."

His words made her ache. More than anything she wanted to belong to Micah. Not just on a temporary basis for some sexual fantasy they played. She wanted forever.

"And now you're sad," Cole murmured. "Why?"

Startled, she focused back on him. Her lips trembled, and she begged him with her eyes not to pursue it any further.

His gaze softened and then he turned and pulled her to the

middle of the room once more. There was an apparatus there they'd obviously brought in while she slept. It was much like the one she'd been tied to the first night she was flogged, but it was shorter. Much shorter.

Cole pushed her to her knees and motioned her forward underneath the beam.

"Arms up," he ordered.

She raised her wrists over her head, and he wrapped the strips of leather around them, binding them together and finally to the beam. She was forced up, her knees just grazing the floor as her upper body was stretched.

Then Cole gathered her hair in his hand and threaded it between her neck and her raised arm so that it hung over her shoulder and down her front, leaving her back bare.

She heard the snap of leather, knew that Cole was working the whip in his hand. He was good. Very good. She knew it firsthand.

"I'm going to mark you, Angelina. Not just a red welt here and there. It will hurt. It will be beautiful. You can stop me, but I don't think you will. I want to see just how far I can take you."

She closed her eyes and shivered, her stomach clenching in nervous apprehension.

The first lash caught her unaware. It was like a blowtorch across her back. Wicked. Hot. Fierce.

She bowed her body forward, seeking escape from the cruel sensation, but almost as quickly as she did, another lash fell, and she cried out.

Oddly, the sound wasn't harsh. It wasn't ugly. What she thought would sound like agony, came out as a breathy sigh of intense pleasure.

Rick and Chris gathered to her right, absorbed in the display before them.

A third lash fell, and this time the cry came out garbled and choked.

And then Micah was in front of her, his hands cupping her face as he pressed his cock to her mouth. He tapped her jaw, a simple command for her to open to him.

He was past her lips and deep in her throat in a second. He held her in place, a prisoner, for she couldn't rear back. The lash awaited her there. She couldn't move forward because she couldn't take him any deeper. She was their captive. Their pleasure.

Micah fucked her mouth with hard, deep strokes. He pistoned in and out as if he were fucking her pussy.

Another lash seared across her flesh, forcing her onto his erection. Micah caught her head and held himself deep, his hips humping forward almost spasmodically.

They fell into a rhythm. He thrust. Cole lashed. She made a choking sound around Micah's cock, and he gripped her tighter until he was fucking her fast and furious.

"Holy shit," Rick breathed out. "That's fucking hot."

"How the hell is she taking it?" Chris asked in awe.

Micah withdrew, put his hand on her forehead to tilt her head back, and then hot semen splashed onto her neck and slipped down her body and over her breasts.

She sucked in air through her nose as she breathed through the fiery pain that Cole had inflicted. She didn't dare relax, because she knew another would come.

Only when Chris shoved his way forward, his huge cock fisted in his hand, did Cole administer another searing lash. She arched forward just as Chris shoved his cock into her mouth.

Her lips stretched around the head, and her cheeks puffed outward as she sought to take him in. She was in for a rough ride. He was hard. He lacked the finesse of Micah, and it was obvious he was so turned on that he was nearly mindless in his actions.

He fucked her mouth brutally, his groans mixing with the slap of leather and her muted cries of pain.

Amazingly, her clit throbbed. Her breasts swelled, and her entire body was wound so tight that she knew she'd climax soon, and no one had so much as touched her pussy.

"Take me," Chris said hoarsely.

He tilted her head up, and he rose up on tiptoe to angle downward. She choked and coughed. He only fucked harder.

The lashes fell, fast and furious. She twisted and undulated her body. She sucked as he powered into her throat. She wanted to come. She was frantic. She danced, her body jumping and writhing. Mindless.

When Chris ripped himself out of her mouth, she whimpered in protest. His cum coated the front of her body, just as Micah's had. It ran in rivulets over her skin, warm, soft, evidence of their passion.

Rick angled in from the side, his hand pumping furiously at his cock. Chris was still coming when the first rope of Rick's release landed on her breast.

"Fuck," Rick gasped. "Fuck!"

Chris backed away, and Rick leaned forward as the last of his cum danced on her nipple and dripped to the floor.

She had no more strength in her arms. Her back was coated in fire. Her front was coated in warm, sticky semen.

"Your ass now, Angelina," Cole whispered next to her ear.

Her head dipped to the side, and she closed her eyes as she tried to catch her breath. Did he intend to fuck her ass?

She had her answer a moment later when a loud crack echoed through the room. She jerked forward and yelped in pain as the wood made contact with the globe of her ass.

Holy hell. It hurt.

Another shot and the wood landed against the opposite cheek. Burn. Pure fire. It was almost unbearable at first, before arousal bloomed. Sweet pleasure settled in like a haze.

A buzz began at the point of contact and spread outward, heated, prickling outward into a warm flush that invaded her veins like a drug. Sluggishly she processed the pain, but pleasure took over. Warm, sweet. Euphoric.

The blows landed hard. Each one was delivered with biting force. He alternated cheeks, and occasionally he'd stop and smooth his palm over her abused flesh.

His touch was nearly unbearable. It more than the wood aroused her hypersensitive skin. And then he bent low and kissed her simmering flesh.

Micah appeared in front of her, and she could barely focus on him as he untied her wrists. He helped her to her feet and then pulled her forward as two ropes fell from the ceiling. He quickly secured her wrists with the leather straps and then he motioned to Rick, who pushed a button on the wall.

The ropes began tightening as they retreated into recessed holes in the ceiling. Her arms stretched high over her head until she balanced on tiptoe.

She shivered when Micah wiped a cool rag over her breasts, removing the semen from her skin. With careful motions, he cleaned her belly and then leaned forward to press his lips to hers before backing away to leave her alone again.

Cole moved in behind her, his chest flush against her aching back. He reached underneath her right leg and hiked it up at an angle. His cock touched her pussy and then moved higher to her anal opening.

His lips met the curve of her neck in the gentlest of kisses as he pushed against her ass. She resisted at first, her entire body tensing. He nibbled delicately at her neck and then whispered against her ear. "Relax, Angelina. I'm not going to hurt you, baby. Let me in."

He was achingly gentle where before with the whip he'd been hard and brutal. If he'd punished her before, now he made love to her, his hands caressing the curves of her body, sliding over her belly and up to cup her breasts.

He thrust upward, and reflexively she tensed away again. This time Cole's hand tangled in her hair, and he yanked down, his lips pressed against the shell of her ear.

"Don't resist me."

Before she could acknowledge his command, he thrust again, and this time he slipped past her resistance and plunged deep.

His hand moved down to hook under her leg again, and he held it up as he thrust into her ass. In front of her, the game had begun again, and she could hear the others, on the couch behind her.

But Cole's attention was solely focused on her. His teeth grazed her neck, her shoulder and then he turned her face back to him so he could kiss the corner of her mouth.

After the initial thrust in which he asserted his control and his demand for her acquiescence, his thrusts gentled. He stood with her back nestled into his body, his arms wrapped protectively around her. His cock slid in and out of her body.

Slow. Tender. It was odd to her that they made love this way. Anal was supposed to be kinky, bold, somehow forbidden, and yet Cole made it seem so normal, a demonstration of his caring and regard for her.

She shook her head, confused by the sensations coursing through her body.

With one arm still propping her leg at an angle, he wrapped his other arm around her waist and slid his fingers down to her pussy.

As soon as he touched her clit, she sucked in her breath and tensed as sharp bursts of pleasure streaked through her belly.

Even then, he didn't hurry. He stroked in and out of her body with infinite patience, his every movement so gentle that her stomach clenched and her breath caught in her throat.

She quivered against him, her orgasm stoking and building, like breeze to flames.

"That's it," he murmured. "I want you to come for me, Angelina."

His finger rolled around her clit, pressing and rotating in just the right mixture to drive her crazy. She wanted him to come too. It was suddenly important that she please him in the same way he pleased her.

She twisted restlessly, her nipples beading and puckering. She went up on her toes, her feet flexing as her arms strained and pulled above her.

Then he began thrusting harder. Slow, but firmer, with more force, as if he knew she needed more to put her over.

His fingers slid lower, circling and rimming her entrance. He plunged a finger inside and then withdrew it, spreading her wetness over her folds and back up to her clit.

"Let me hear you," he whispered. "Don't hold back."

She let out a soft cry that elongated and became louder as his finger picked up speed. Pressure. So much tension. Her entire body was bowed, so tight she thought she might break.

He was pounding against her now, harder and faster, his balls slapping against her ass. And then he slid farther inside, deep, so deep. She gasped and fell apart, and he held himself there as he shook against her. He strained forward, pushing himself tight against her willing flesh.

Her sob echoed over the room and she fought for breath as pleasure overtook her, robbing her of sight, of her sense of time and place.

Her back throbbed. Her ass ached. And still he worked in and out, not yet soft after his release.

"You're beautiful," Cole said as he kissed her shoulder. "I've seen so many beautiful women come into The House. You're the first I've been with."

With that statement, he withdrew and moved away from her. Her knees buckled, but again Micah was there to catch her. The ropes descended from the ceiling, and the ache in her arms increased as she was able to lower them.

He gathered her in his arms and picked her up. When he walked past the couches, she looked inquisitively up at him.

He smiled and kissed her forehead. "We're going upstairs. I don't think anyone has any interest in the game anymore."

CHAPTER 29

Cole walked ahead of Angelina and Micah into the common room and flipped on the lights. Micah carried her over to one of the couches and set her down. He touched her cheek and said, "Cole and I have some setting up to do. You can entertain Chris and Rick until we're done."

Rick stood to the side and stripped out of his clothing as soon as Micah moved away. When he finished, he sat down on the end of the couch and reached for Angelina's hand. With his other hand, he stroked his cock to hardness then pulled her toward his lap. When she was close, he reached up and tangled his hand in her hair. He pulled her head down to his lap.

"Get her on her knees," Chris said. "I want to fuck her again while she gives you a blow job."

"You heard him," Rick said roughly. "Up on your knees. Stick that pretty ass in the air."

She complied with his order and then lowered her head. Rick

gripped the base of his cock low, his fingers wrapped around his balls. He pushed her down with his other hand while he fed his erection into her mouth.

The couch dipped as Chris got on his knees behind her.

"Did Cole stretch your ass out enough for me?" Chris taunted softly.

Despite the crudity of his words, he carefully prepped her, sliding lubricant over her opening. He worked patiently, easing one finger inside and then two. While she sucked Rick's cock, Chris gently fucked her ass with his fingers, adding more lubricant as he stretched her opening more.

"I won't lie to you, sweetheart. This is going to feel like your first time all over again. It'll hurt like hell when I first get in. I'm going to take it easy, but don't fight me. It'll go a lot better for you if you don't."

Rick stroked his hand through her hair, holding it back so he could watch his cock disappear into her mouth.

"Don't fight him," Rick advised with a grin. "He'll just enjoy it more, and he'll get rougher."

She nodded her acceptance just as Chris butted his cock head to her opening. She swallowed nervously, and Rick groaned.

"Ah, shit, that feels good."

He lifted his hips as he held her firmly in place.

"Tell me how you want this," Chris said. "I can go real slow and take forever to get inside you. Or I can make it quick. Micah said you like the pain. You want me to make it hurt?"

Oh God. She was going to come. She closed her eyes and inhaled through her nose.

Chris slapped her ass, rocking her against Rick.

"Answer me or I'll make the decision," he said sharply.

Rick released her hair so she could slip his dick from her mouth.

"Do it quick," she said hoarsely.

"Do you want it hard?" he asked. "Do you want it to hurt?"

She turned to look over her shoulder. "I don't get to make the choices," she said quietly. "I belong to Micah. He gave me to you for the night. If I disobey you, if I challenge you, if I tell you no, then I tell *him* all those things. I disrespect him. And I love him more than life."

Chris leaned over her, caught her jaw between his fingers and kissed her. He ran his tongue over the seam of her lips and then kissed her softly once more.

"Micah is a lucky son of a bitch. I'm so goddamn jealous of him right now it's all I can do not to gut the bastard."

She smiled and turned back to Rick, who curled a hand around her neck and yanked her to his own mouth. His kiss was carnal, almost brutal as he tasted her. He sucked at her bottom lip and then nipped until she tasted blood.

"Suck my dick," he rasped into her mouth. "He's going to fuck your ass until you make me come."

He forced her back to his lap and guided his length past her lips and deep into her throat. Chris parted her ass cheeks with this thumbs and fitted his cock to her opening. She didn't have time to tense, prepare or take a breath.

He rammed into her, knocking her forward. Rick was prepared. He cupped both hands over her head and held her so that she was forced all the way down onto his cock.

She would have screamed as pain lanced through her throbbing anus, but Rick's cock was buried so deep she couldn't even breathe around it.

"I have some bad news, baby," Chris said as she fought to maintain control. "I'm only halfway in."

She moaned just as he gripped her hips and hammered forward again.

This time she ripped her mouth from Rick's cock and cried out as Chris's balls came to rest against her pussy opening.

Oh God. She wiggled, she fought, she tossed her head even as she moaned at the burning pain consuming her.

Rick grabbed a handful of her hair and yanked her head back down, forcing his cock back into her mouth.

"Ah, fuck," Chris groaned as she bucked and fought. "Don't fight me, baby. Ah, shit."

His big hands circled her waist. He pulled back and she cried out as his thick erection rippled across her impossibly stretched tissues.

Rick made a garbled sound and raised his hips to fuck at her open mouth. His hands were all over her head, her hair, his fingers tangling, pulling as he pumped spasmodically.

Chris slammed into her again, and she went crazy.

"Holy shit," Chris gasped. "Hold her, Rick. Christ, this is amazing."

Chris grabbed her hips as she bucked beneath him. She wanted more, less. More pain, more pleasure. She needed release.

"Slow down, baby. Don't hurt yourself," Chris said, even as he thrust into her writhing body.

"Shut the hell up and fuck her," Rick growled.

And they did. Their hands gripped her, suddenly less tender and patient. They held her down and in place as they used her for their own pleasure.

Chris pumped against her ass, his balls slapping at her pussy with each thrust. Rick gripped her head, his fingers digging into her scalp as he arched into her over and over.

She felt alive. Powerful. Beautiful. She was driving them every bit as crazy as they were making her. Their sounds of pleasure and approval spurred her own desire, and it became a race to see if she could get them off before she exploded with her own orgasm.

The pain subsided completely, replaced by intense, unwavering pleasure. She whimpered and shoved back against Chris, wanting the edge back.

"You want it harder, baby?"

In response, she sucked Rick deeper into her mouth.

"Oh hell yeah, she does," Rick said. "Give it to her, Chris. Shit, I'm close."

Chris bent over her back, gripped her shoulders and began thrusting hard and deep. There was no pause, no reprieve. Her body shook with the power of his big body, and Rick held her down as he fucked deep into her throat.

She lost sense of reality. She floated, and for a moment, she feared losing consciousness. Her body was so tense she felt close to breaking. Tight. Strung out. And then Chris reached around, palmed her mound and slid his finger between her folds. As soon as he touched her clit, she burst like an overinflated balloon.

Her hoarse cry was muffled when spurt after spurt of hot semen flooded her mouth. Chris jerked against her and his harsh cry filled her ears. Incredibly as he continued fingering her, his thrusts growing more gentle, another orgasm rushed over her, not as intense as the first, but sharp and fast.

"Shit, she came again," Chris panted as he went still against her, his cock wedged deep in her ass.

She collapsed onto Rick, too spent to move her head as his cock slipped from her lips.

He stroked her hair tenderly, and then a cloth smoothed over her cheek and her lips.

"You want something to drink?" Risk asked huskily. He almost sounded embarrassed.

She nodded against his lap and he slid from underneath her to get up.

"I'm going to pull out now, baby," Chris said, his tone regretful.

She was too weak to tense, and it was probably good because even relaxed, his withdrawal hurt.

Rick came back and sat on the couch beside her. She was sprawled indelicately over the cushions, but in that moment, she just didn't care. She wanted Micah. She wanted his comfort. His love and his care.

"Here," Rick said as he carefully lifted her to a sitting position. He put the glass to her lips and tilted it so she could sip at the cool liquid. "I meant to pull out. I wasn't going to come in your mouth. That's kind of uncool. Sorry."

She smiled faintly and leaned her head against the back of the couch. "It was only uncool if you didn't enjoy it."

"Enjoy it? Hell, it was fucking amazing. This is the kind of shit guys fantasize about but know there's no way in hell it's ever going to happen. Do you have any sisters?"

She laughed. "No, sorry. I guess you'll have to hope Micah invites you over for football again."

"Football?" Chris asked as he sat beside her. "What football?"

"You two are good for my ego," she said.

She glanced up, automatically searching for Micah, and saw him standing across the room with Cole. They were both watching her. Had they watched the entire time?

When their gazes met, Micah started forward, a hungry gleam in his eyes. Her nipples automatically puckered, and Rick leaned in to suck one into his mouth. She gasped at the sensation, but her eyes never left Micah.

"Cole is ready for you," he said as he approached.

She glanced beyond him to where Cole stood, but Cole's expression gave nothing away.

Micah extended his hand, and she took it without hesitation.

CHAPTER 30

Micah led Angelina to a narrow, well-padded rectangular table where Cole waited. Chris and Rick pulled on their pants and stood at a short distance away.

Cole approached and stood just in front of her, his gaze devouring her. His eyes were so sexy. Deep, intense blue, sparking with so much fire that she felt the warmth to her toes.

He reached out to cup both breasts and run his thumbs over the taut nipples, stroking them to hard points. Unable to resist, she snuck a sideways glance at Micah, but he was gone.

"Look at me and only me," Cole said in a stern voice.

"I'm sorry," she said softly.

He touched her cheek and then pulled her toward him. He touched his lips to hers in one, chaste kiss.

"Come," he said.

He lifted her up and placed her on the table, and it was then she saw Micah lighting candles on the opposite side.

"Lie back and get comfortable," Cole urged.

She reclined, settling against the soft leather.

"Raise your arms over your head."

Again she did as he directed.

Chris and Rick each took a hand and wrapped soft leather ties around each wrist until she was tightly bound. Micah stepped to the end of the table, spread-eagled her legs and secured her ankles to the iron loops positioned on the sides. Then he put his hand on her leg and walked up the length of the table, his palm gliding over her skin.

When he got to her breasts, he bent down and licked one nipple. His tongue left a wet trail around the puckered flesh. He sucked, nipped and toyed with one and then the other. He was in turns exceedingly gentle and forceful, until she was ready to crawl out of her skin.

With light smooching sounds, he kissed his way to her neck and then her lips. He was warm and sweet against her tongue, and he tasted of comfort. Of love.

"Cole is quite handy with wax," Micah murmured. "Usually this is something I'd only entrust to myself, but he's good. Very good. I know you'll be in good hands. Do this for me, Angel girl. I want to watch while he drapes your body in wax. I want to watch you writhe in the sweetest of pains, gasp when fire spreads across your skin and to watch your eyes when the pain turns to pleasure."

She swallowed and nodded, not trusting herself to speak. Her entire body throbbed. She was sore. She was exhausted, and yet arousal stirred deep within. The promise of another high, one that would push her further than before.

"I don't want you to worry," Cole murmured next to her. "These candles have lower burning points so the wax isn't as hot. A little pain can be extremely pleasurable. I wouldn't risk causing you extreme pain by using unsafe candles."

As soon as she acknowledged his statement, the room went black around her. She gasped in surprise when a blindfold covered her eyes.

"Don't be afraid, Angel girl. I'll be right here the whole time."

Micah's voice broke through her sudden apprehension, and she latched onto his strength, braced her shoulders, and a secret smile lit her lips. She wasn't just doing this for Micah.

"Anticipation is half the pleasure," Cole said. "Not knowing when the wax will drip onto your skin will heighten the experience."

Every muscle in her body tensed as she waited. Breathless. Excited. Nervous as hell. Almost giddy.

And she waited. And waited.

Her breathing calmed. She tuned into the room around her, but there wasn't a single sound. Had they left her? Gradually she relaxed, her arms and legs going limp.

Hot wax splattered onto her arm. Just a drop, but it felt like liquid fire. She hissed in shock, more surprise than true pain, and her pulse raced to life.

A hand delved between her legs, thumbing up and down her folds, carefully parting them. Micah. She'd know his touch anywhere.

As his thumb made contact with her clit, hot wax spilled onto her belly just above her navel. She went rigid, her fingers curling into tight fists above her.

Micah's touch soothed the hurt, and the pain faded to sharp pleasure.

Another splash, this time hotter. She cried out, and Micah's fingers plunged inside her opening.

"You make a beautiful canvas, Angelina," Cole said in a husky voice.

Before she could process the barrage of heat and edgy euphoria, an entire trail of wax blazed up her midline to the valley between her breasts.

"Ahh!"

She arched upward, straining against her bonds. Hot. Wicked. Fucking incredible. She panted and sucked air like a dying fish. Never before had she experienced this much of a cessation between the line of too far and not enough.

Two mouths closed around her nipples, and she let out a low sob. Micah's hand between her legs, his thumb circling her clit with lazy precision, and now warm, wet mouths sucking at her breasts.

She whimpered, part in ecstasy, part in protest. She wanted more. Wanted the burn, the incredible sensation of her skin burning alive.

And then the rhythmic sucking ended as soon as it had begun. Her nipples, wet now, puckered and stood up as the air from one of the ceiling fans blew over the tips.

Wax dripped onto one of the nipples. She shrieked, the sound shrill to her ears. Oh God, it was too much. She twisted and bucked, trying to escape her bonds. Tears burned her eyes and she blinked furiously, wishing she could see, wishing she knew when to expect the next drop.

She cried out again when the other nipple was bathed in wax. Micah's thumb stilled, and she pleaded in a broken voice for him not to stop. How desperate she sounded, but she didn't care. She needed, oh how she needed, to be freed from this torment.

This time the wax poured into her navel, filling the shallow indention. She yelled hoarsely and flinched, sending some of the liquid spilling down her belly.

And then cooling air blew gently across her skin. She didn't know who did it, but his breath whispered over the wax, hardening it.

Her entire body was alive. Her skin crawled, itchy and unsatisfied. Her blindfold was ripped off, and she blinked away the moisture that still gathered at the corners of her eyes.

Cole stood over her, his eyes dark, brooding almost. He terrified and aroused her all at the same time. Then she saw Micah standing on her other side, and her stomach knotted into a ball.

His expression was fierce, his eyes glittering with a dangerous edge. He looked every inch the stalking predator. His nostrils flared, and his lips were pressed tight together as if he was holding a tenuous grip on his control.

There was want, need and blazing approval set in his dark eyes. His gaze scraped across her body, and she followed his path down, shocked to see the intricate design of wax decorating her skin.

What had seemed like a random smattering of wax had actually been a delicate-looking design of splatters from her navel up to her breastbone. Her nipples were covered, and tiny droplets circled the buds. Her navel was completely filled now with hard wax, and the only deviation from the pattern was the splatter down her belly where she'd flinched. It looked exotic in a crazy sort of way. With four sets of male eyes admiring her naked, wax-splattered body, she felt beautiful, desirable. Ultra feminine and powerful.

"And now we'll all have you, Angel girl," Micah said, his voice vibrating over her in a husky growl.

Her stomach jumped into her throat, and she eyed him nervously.

Chris and Rick untied her hands and carefully rubbed them until the circulation was restored. Cole and Micah helped her sit up, and she swung her legs over the side of the table. Micah stepped between her legs and simply picked her up, her legs circling his waist as she held on.

He walked her over to one of the cushy pallets in the corner of the room and dumped her onto it. The four men stood over her and stripped out of their remaining clothing. Her mouth went dry as she realized she was in for the fucking of her life.

Cole knelt on the pallet first. He moved over her, dragged her beneath him and fused his mouth to hers in a heated rush. His patience seemed at an end. He took her hungrily, his hands moving down to spread her thighs even as he drank deeply from her lips.

Arching over her, he wedged himself between her legs and thrust forward.

"Wrap your legs around me," he said into her mouth.

When she raised her legs, he slipped deeper, and she gasped. He wasn't gentle or easy. He fucked hard, his hips slapping harshly against her ass.

"You feel so good," he said hoarsely. "So tight. Hot."

He pinned her to the ground, held her in one spot and thrust repeatedly into her pussy. If she attempted any response, any movement, she was met with a swift reminder of his dominance. So she lay there, accepting, offering her submission as he used her body to slake his lust.

Suddenly he withdrew and rolled away, and just as soon, Rick was on her, spreading her as he positioned his cock. He pushed inside her, deep, just as urgent and impatient as Cole had been.

Rick said nothing. His eyes closed and his face was tense above her as he pumped against her fast, forceful. He panted, and he clenched his jaw as he slowed his thrusts, but with the decrease in speed, he became more forceful. And then he, like Cole, simply rolled away.

Her legs went limp, and she lay there as Chris took Rick's place.

He gathered her legs, wrapped them around his waist and then leaned down, pressing his body to hers. He seemed to know how tired she was and he carefully eased into her pussy, pausing at intervals to give her time to adjust.

When he was fully seated, he kissed her collarbone, hesitated for a moment and then began thrusting. None of them had come yet, so she could only imagine this was the buildup to something bigger. She lay there in Chris's arms, closed her eyes and gave herself to the mounting tension in her belly.

He moaned, a regretful sound that told her he didn't want to stop, but he pulled roughly away, leaving her as the others had done.

She looked for Micah, but he wasn't there. Wasn't he next? Cole returned to her and stretched out on the pallet beside her on his back. He reached for her and coaxed her upward with gentle hands.

"Straddle me, Angelina. Face away from me and put my cock in your ass."

Even as she rose, Rick and Chris took her hands to help her. Each took an arm as she stepped over Cole's body, and they supported her as she went to her knees, straddling his thighs.

Cole put a hand to the small of her back and held his cock with his other hand to help guide her down. She hesitated when the tip breached the tight ring, but both Rick and Chris pressed down on her shoulders, giving her no choice but to take Cole's erection.

Her body quivered, and her muscles bunched and rolled as she adjusted to the position. He seemed bigger this way. She was stretched so much tighter and there was more pressure. Pressure she couldn't escape.

"Now lie back," Cole murmured. "I've got you. I'll hold you. Just relax and lie back against me."

He leaned up as she reclined, and her back met his chest. He reached down to slide his hands underneath her legs, and he pulled up and spread her. And then she realized why.

Micah stepped between hers and Cole's legs and knelt on the pallet. Finally Micah. Her heart soared and she immediately relaxed, all the tension leaving her.

Cole nuzzled her neck. "You trust him so completely," he said in a low voice.

She didn't respond. She didn't have to. He was right.

Micah's hands slid warm and comforting along the tops of her thighs. He moved in closer, fitting his cock to her pussy.

"Have you ever taken two men at the same time, Angel girl?"

She swallowed and shook her head.

"It'll be tight. We'll fit. We'll stretch you, but it'll feel so good. Just relax and let us do all the work. All you have to do is lie back and enjoy it. Trust us."

She moaned as he stretched her the tiniest bit. The head of his penis rested just inside her entrance, made much smaller by Cole's presence in her ass.

With infinite care and patience, Micah worked his way in, stopping when she gasped, moving further in when she squirmed with impatience.

And then he lunged forward, forcing the last few inches into her pussy.

She bucked and wiggled uncontrollably. It took both men to hold her, and they caressed and soothed her, both murmuring praise and encouragement. They both remained still, allowing her time to adjust. Finally she calmed as their words and their caresses broke through the bombardment of sensation their dual penetration had caused.

"Angel girl," Micah said lovingly. He leaned down to kiss her even as Cole kissed the delicate column of her neck. Then Micah began to move, in and out, slowly at first, his cock dragging across super-sensitive, swollen tissues.

She clasped him so much tighter because of the added pressure of Cole's penetration.

And then Cole began to move. In unison with Micah. In and out. Cole held her hips in place as he and Micah fucked her openings.

Forgotten were Chris and Rick until they knelt on either side of her, rising up on their knees so their cocks were in line with her mouth.

Rick put a finger to her jaw and turned her in his direction even as he nudged his cock to her lips. She opened and he slid inside, deep, quick.

Mentally, she checked out. She could no longer process their actions, the sensation of being fucked by so many men at the same time. It was edgy, forbidden and so exciting that she shivered uncontrollably. If Rick hadn't held her head, his cock would have slipped from her mouth.

Then Chris pulled at her hair, directing her to him and his waiting cock.

"Lick it," he said, strain evident in his voice.

She held out her tongue and allowed him to guide the head over her tongue, in and then out again as it rasped over her taste buds.

Cole's fingers dug into her hips as he raised his hips, thrusting tightly into her ass. Before she turned her head back to Rick, she locked gazes for a brief moment with Micah. What she saw in his eyes took her breath away. Raw possession. Pride. And something else entirely. Something that made her chest ache and her pulse come alive. He cared about her.

She raised her hands and pressed them against Rick's and Chris's thighs to steady herself as Micah and Cole shook her body with the force of their thrusts. Encouraged by the fact that Rick and Chris didn't object, she ran her fingers up to grasp their cocks. Her fingers curled around the bases and both men let out harsh sounds of pleasure.

She fisted the cocks and stroked, rolling her hand up and down over the steel-like erections. No longer did she wait for their prompting. She alternated sucking their cocks, giving each equal attention.

"Shit," Rick muttered. "I'm not going to last."

"Me either," Chris hissed.

They pushed her hands away and fisted their own cocks. Chris forced her gaze forward so she watched Micah between her legs. He held her there as he and Rick jerked frantically at their erections.

Hot semen washed onto her cheeks and breasts. It splashed over the wax design on her skin and ran slowly down the valley of her breasts.

Rick tangled a hand in her hair and petted affectionately. He pulled away and then ran a gentle finger over the curve of her jaw.

Cole relaxed his grip on her hips and trailed his fingers over the line of her waist and around to cup her breasts. His thumbs rubbed over her semen-coated nipples, and he massaged the liquid into her skin outside the perimeter of the hardened wax. Then he lowered his hands down her midline, rubbing the sticky substance onto her belly.

His hips arched, driving himself deeper into her ass. Micah surged forward, wedging himself tighter into her pussy.

"I'm going to come, Angelina. Stay still. Let me hold you," Cole whispered harshly.

He tilted his ass up off the floor, bumping her higher and forcing Micah deeper. Micah thrust and forced her back down onto Cole's erection.

She allowed them complete control. Surprisingly, Chris and Rick each took one of her hands and held it, supporting her as Cole pounded into her from below.

Their hands snaked up her arms until they held her underneath her shoulders. Cole's hands circled her waist and he lunged upward one last time, his shout echoing over her ears.

She stared into Micah's eyes, and he looked back, so calm. He hadn't come yet, and now she realized that had been his intention.

As Cole caressed her hips and belly, Micah carefully withdrew and stepped back. Chris and Rick lifted her arms, helping her free of Cole's cock. Micah was waiting to pull her against his body, and he wrapped his arms around her, shielding her with his strength.

"You guys are welcome to crash here," Micah said in a low voice. "I'm going to take Angelina to our room and take care of her."

Chris touched her shoulder and pulled her carefully away from Micah. When she faced him, he framed her face in his hands and pressed his lips to her forehead.

"You are an amazing woman, Angelina. Thank you for tonight."

As Chris stepped away, Rick moved forward and slid one finger underneath her chin, tilting her mouth up to accept the soft brush of his lips.

"Rest, sweetheart. You took on four very demanding men. I've never seen anything like it. Thank you."

She smiled through her fatigue and then watched as Cole closed the distance between them. Instead of kissing her as the others had done, he pulled her into his arms and hugged her tightly.

"Tonight was very special to me, Angelina," he said in his quiet, steady voice. "More than you'll ever know, I think. Micah is very lucky to have you."

"I hope he thinks so," she whispered so only he could hear.

Cole pulled away and touched her cheek in a brief, affectionate gesture.

"Get some rest, okay? You're going to be sore tomorrow."

Micah pulled her back into his arms, and then he simply lifted her and walked toward the hallway and down to their bedroom.

He took her into the bathroom and set her down just long enough to spread a towel across the counter. Then he lifted her up to sit on the towel so the surface wouldn't be cold on her skin.

He started bathwater and added sweet-smelling soap. It foamed and formed a cloud of bubbles as the steam rose from the tub.

"Ready?"

He stood in front of her, his hands sliding up her arms. He touched her hair, playing with the strands as if he couldn't resist touching her.

He lifted her again and stepped over the edge of the bathtub, lowering her into the steaming water. Then he settled behind her and pulled her back against his chest.

The water lapped soothingly around them, and she relaxed in his embrace, closing her eyes as exhaustion claimed her.

"Wake up, sleepyhead," Micah said tenderly in her ear.

She stirred and frowned when water sloshed over her body. Where the hell was she? How long had she slept?

"You're all clean and hopefully relaxed and limber now. Time to get out and go to bed."

Bed she could certainly be down with. Parts of her body ached she hadn't even known she had. She stretched and arched her body. Micah cupped her breasts, and it was then she noticed all the wax was gone. How the hell had she slept through that?

Micah stood and stepped out. She watched in open appreciation as he toweled the water from his lean body. When he was done, he tossed his towel aside and pulled another from the rack.

He reached down to take her hand and pulled her to a standing position. She was quickly enfolded in warmth when he wrapped the towel around her.

"Come to bed, Angel girl. I want to hold you right now."

Still wrapped in the towel, she padded into the bedroom and looked longingly at the lush covers and plump pillows.

Micah unwrapped the towel and gave an extra rub to her hair before dropping the towel on the floor. She didn't need any extra urging. She crawled onto the mattress and promptly collapsed in the middle of the bed.

The lights went out, plunging the room into darkness. Then the bed dipped as Micah crawled in next to her. She turned, seeking him and his warmth. He rolled her underneath him, his body pressed flush against hers.

Arousal stirred within in her, and the realization came swift. No matter how tired, how depleted she might be, she'd never get enough of Micah.

He parted her thighs and slipped inside her with one gentle push. There wasn't an inch of her flesh not covered by his. He hovered protectively over her, a shield between her and the rest of the world.

His muscles rolled and flexed as he moved his hips, up and down. She lay there, content to let him dictate the pace, to make love to her.

Warmth invaded her veins. Sweet, indescribable pleasure flooded her mind, her heart. He rocked against her, his mouth finding her neck, her ear, her shoulder and then her jaw and finally her mouth.

Their tongues tangled and dueled. Warm, wet, incredibly sweet.

He took her slow, his cock sliding back and forth with such tenderness. He cupped her body to his, holding her tightly as his hips met hers.

Her orgasm lapped closer, like calm waves spreading across sun-warmed sand. There was nothing frightening, sharp or overwhelming about the rise of her desire. This wasn't about kinky sex, crazy lust or a race to completion. It was about her and Micah. Two people making love. Him taking care of her. Him keeping a promise.

She wound her arms around his neck and raised her mouth to his. She tensed in his grasp and kissed him hard, deep, passionate, even as she came apart.

Even in his release, his movements were tender and measured. He let his body cover and surround her and then rolled to the side, taking her with him. He slipped from her pussy, but he gathered her against his chest as he kissed her temple.

"Go to sleep, Angel girl. We were hard on you tonight."

She rubbed her face along his shoulder and sighed in contentment. Then she let her eyes close, and she surrendered to the velvet clasp of his protection.

CHAPTER 31

$\mathcal{M}$icah got out of the shower and wrapped a towel around his waist before ambling into the bedroom. Angelina was sprawled on her belly, her face buried in one of the pillows. He smiled and shook his head. Morning person she wasn't. He'd learned that in the time they'd been staying at The House together.

He dressed quietly so as not to awaken her. He had several phone calls to make, and he'd rather not make them in front of Angelina.

The fact that they'd not found a single lead in Angelina's case frustrated the hell out of him. He couldn't help but think this asshole was just waiting for them to relax. He was obviously patient. He'd been after her for a year, and he'd followed her through five states. Those weren't the actions of a man who gave up just because the going got tough.

Micah's life was on hold. Angelina's life was on hold, and so were all his friends'. Something had to give and give soon.

But when it's over, you lose Angelina.

He looked back at Angelina asleep on the bed and then walked out of the bedroom.

He'd told Angelina it was temporary. He didn't want or need another relationship. And yet they'd settled into this arrangement with ease. They were positively domestic if you didn't count the sexual kink.

If he was honest, and he was, he'd admit that he wanted to keep Angelina. On his own terms. He wanted to keep her on a shelf, away from his heart but close enough that he could take her out whenever he liked. And that made him the most selfish asshole alive.

The best thing he could do for her would be to let her go so she could have a decent life. A family. Babies. All the things he knew she wanted.

All the things you could have.

He shook his head and continued down the stairs. His cell phone rang as he hit the bottom step, and he pulled it out of his pocket.

"Hudson," he said without checking to see who it was.

"Micah, we've got a problem," Damon said grimly.

Micah didn't like the alarm or the anger in Damon's voice.

"What's up, man?"

"The bastard threatened Serena."

"What? How the hell did he get to her? When did this happen?"

"She went into her office early this morning. Sam drove her, walked her into the building. She came out without calling to let Sam know so she was alone for about two minutes. She never saw him coming. He got in behind her, put his hand over her mouth and said, 'You can't hide her from me forever.'"

"Son of a bitch," Micah bit out. "Is she okay? Did he hurt her?"

"She's shaken up. It scared her to death, and it pissed her off, but she's fine. Guy ran off as soon as he saw Sam coming."

"Did Sam get a look at him?"

"No. He was too concerned with Serena's well-being. By the time she told him what had happened, the guy was long gone."

"Fuck," Micah swore.

"We're at the police station now, but I thought you'd want to know."

"I'm coming that way," Micah said. "I'll see you in a few."

He switched his phone off then turned around to head back up the stairs. Angelina was still asleep when he entered the bedroom. He hated to wake her. She looked so peaceful and content. He didn't want to spoil that for her with news of her stalker.

He touched her shoulder and followed the smooth surface of her skin to the curve of her neck.

"Angel girl," he said in a low voice. "Wake up."

She scrunched up her nose and frowned. "Go away."

"Hey, wake up for me. I need to talk to you."

At that her eyes flew open and she pushed herself up on one elbow. "What's wrong?"

"He showed himself today."

He hated the way her eyes went wide with fear. Her hand flew to her throat, and her breathing sped up.

"Did they catch him?"

"Unfortunately not. He threatened Serena outside her office this morning."

"Oh my God! Is she all right? He didn't hurt her, did he?"

"Shh, baby. Serena is fine. Scared and shook up, but she's fine. He didn't hurt her. I'm going down to the police station now."

She flung the covers aside. "I'm not staying here by myself."

"Okay, but take your time. Get dressed and meet me downstairs. It's going to be fine, Angelina. I need you to believe that."

Her troubled gaze met his. "I brought him here, Micah. And now innocent people are paying the price. How am I supposed to feel about that?"

"You're innocent in this too, Angel. You don't deserve this. We'll find him."

He dropped a kiss on her hair and then turned to go. "I'll wait for you outside."

"This makes me nuts," Serena muttered. "Damon is beside himself. I won't be able to so much as take a piss by myself for the next year."

No one laughed. Angelina, Julie and Faith sat with Serena in one of the conference rooms at the police station while all the men did God knows what in the next room.

"I'm sorry this happened to you, Serena," Angelina said. "I never meant for anyone to become involved. I shouldn't have—"

Julie held her hand up. "Don't say it. Don't say you shouldn't have come and all that bullshit because I'll have to hurt you if you do."

Faith smiled then, but she reached over and took Angelina's hand in hers and squeezed. "She's right. Don't say it. It's completely wrong anyway. I'm glad you came. You're good for Micah."

Angelina sighed.

"Oh, come on, girl. It can't be that bad. You've been shacked up with the man for several weeks now. Surely the sex makes up for any cabin fever," Julie said.

"Sex is good. Great. No complaints."

"Huge *but* in there," Serena said.

"Yeah, huge," Faith agreed. "What's going on, Angelina? Is he still being a butthead?"

Angelina shifted forward in her chair and put her hands on her cheeks. "You guys don't need to hear me whine. We're here for Serena. Let's forget about Micah."

"We're waiting for the *but*," Julie drawled.

"Micah's great," Angelina said gloomily. "He's tender, very loving. Great in bed. Very generous lover. But . . ."

"Ah, here we go," Serena said.

"He's still holding a part of himself back. It's almost as if he's pretending to play house with me and loves it in theory but he only loves it because he knows it's not permanent."

"Whoa," Julie said. "My head is spinning after that explanation. Way too deep for my limited brain power."

"I wish I knew what to say," Faith said unhappily. "Gray resisted at first. He resisted hard. I just had to keep after him."

Julie nodded in agreement. "Nathan was a stubborn bastard as well. I sorta did give up on him. Well at first anyway. But I'm glad I didn't, so you definitely shouldn't give up on Micah if you love him."

"I'm afraid I was the difficult one in my relationship with Damon, and I can't tell you how glad I am that Damon didn't give up on me," Serena said softly. "He's the best thing that's ever happened to me, and I cringe every time I think of the way I tried to drive him away."

Angelina's lips curved into a rueful smile. "In other words, I should shut up and quit whining. Do what I need to do."

"Whining's good. We do whining," Julie said. "It's sort of required when dishing about men." She reinforced her statement by wrapping her arm around Angelina and squeezing. "You've got a lot on your plate, hon. Micah isn't going anywhere. Not yet. Take it one day at a time and focus on staying safe. I don't care what the man tells you or doesn't tell you, he's gaga over you. He probably doesn't even know it, and he'll probably want to cut out his tongue before admitting it. You just have to be the bigger person and wait for him to pull his head out of his ass."

"Very good advice," Serena said with a nod. "It was pretty much the same advice she and Faith gave me when I was busy fucking things up with Damon."

Faith and Julie both laughed, and Angelina smiled at the three of them.

"You're lucky to have such good friends in each other," Angelina said.

"Yes, they are extremely lucky to have me," Julie said smugly.

"Good grief," Faith said with a roll of her eyes. "What a huge ego."

"We're your friends too, Angelina," Serena said, her blue eyes somber. "You're not alone anymore. No matter what happens with Micah, we're your friends. Okay?"

Julie and Faith both nodded their agreement. Angelina smiled but couldn't speak around the knot in her throat.

"How much longer are we going to be here?" Julie muttered. "I'm going insane."

"Chad was faxing over his reports from Miami. Micah talked to him on the way here. Other then that, I don't know anything," Angelina said. "They've been at this for hours. He's smart. He's not making any mistakes. How can they catch him if he doesn't make mistakes?"

Faith sat down on the other side of Angelina and put her arm around Angelina's shoulders, sandwiching her between Faith and Julie.

"Gray said sooner or later they all fuck up. There's no such thing as the perfect crime or the perfect criminal. Eventually they either get desperate or stupid, and either one gets him caught."

"I hope you're right," Angelina said wearily. "I hate this. I hate it for all of us."

"Oh, I don't know. I'm kind of liking the twenty-four-hour bodyguard thing Nathan's got going on," Julie said with an appreciative grin. "He's made it his mission to make sure my body is guarded at all times."

Serena sighed in exasperation. "Like he needs an excuse? You two fuck like rabbits."

"Why, Serena. I'm shocked," Julie said in mock horror.

"The day something shocks you is the day I become a nun," Faith muttered.

Angelina giggled and then they all broke into laughter.

The door opened and Micah stuck his head in.

"Angel, you ready to get on out of here?"

She surged to her feet and crossed the room to stand in front of him.

"What's going on, Micah? Did you hear from Chad? What did the police here say?"

He put a finger over her lips and then tucked her hair behind her ear. "We can talk about it on the way home. It's been a long day. Everyone is tired and frustrated."

Her face fell. Obviously it wasn't good news.

He put a finger under her chin, tilted her neck back and lowered his mouth to hers. His kiss was sweet and comforting, and it infused her with courage.

"We'll get him, Angel."

He put a hand on her shoulder and squeezed and then he looked beyond her to the others.

"You girls okay? Need anything?"

"Our husbands?" Faith said in exasperation.

Micah smiled. "Coming down the hall now, if I'm hearing right." His gaze lingered on Serena. "You okay, doll?"

Angelina turned to see Serena smile at Micah.

"I'm fine. Really. Damon has taken the episode personally. I won't be able to leave the house without a full security detail until this guy is caught."

"That's not a bad idea," Micah said seriously.

He looked back at Angelina. "Ready, baby?"

CHAPTER 32

"*W*as Chad able to give you anything to go on?" Angelina asked as they headed upstairs after arriving back at The House.

She flipped on the lights in the bedroom and stood inside the doorway as Micah passed her.

"He faxed over all his notes from the reports you filed in Miami. He's doing some follow-up in the department records. Seeing if there have been any other reports of stalking in the Miami area that match your guy's MO. He's digging back five years, so it'll take some time. He'll get back to me as soon as he gets the information."

"And what about here?" she asked softly. "Are our guys coming up with anything?"

"They processed Serena for trace but didn't come up with anything. This guy is good. Damon has beefed up security again because PD can't afford to spare the kind of manpower necessary to monitor everyone involved."

Micah tossed his keys onto the nightstand and pulled Angelina into his arms. He rested his chin on top of her head and sighed.

"I know this is hard on you, Angel girl, but it'll be over soon. He'll screw up. He'll get impatient and then we'll nail his ass to the wall."

She nodded against his chest.

Micah pulled her away and grasped her shoulders, his gaze intense as he stared down at her.

"I need you to think, Angel. I know we've been over this, but you have to be missing something, somewhere. I want you to start from the beginning. I want a list of people you talked to even on a casual basis back in Miami. Someone had to know you were leaving. Where you were going. He found you much too quickly."

Angelina put her hands to her eyes and rubbed tiredly. A pulse beat painfully at her temples, and an ache centered her forehead and drew her features in tight.

"I don't know," she said helplessly. "I know I never told anyone what my plans were. Not even Mama Rose. I secretly made my arrangements and then I left."

Micah went rigid at the mention of Mama Rose, and in her exhaustion she had just let it slip out. Her heart sank as she saw the total shock and outrage reflected in his features.

"What the hell do you know about Mama Rose?" he asked in a soft dangerous voice.

He backed away, arms crossed over her chest, his eyes glittering with anger.

"It was you, wasn't it?" he asked before she could respond. "Goddamn it, Angelina, it was you! You were there each time. How the hell did you even know?"

His voice cracked through the room like a shot. He stalked

forward, his entire body bristling. Anger rolled off him in waves. There was such fury in his eyes.

"You had no right. *No right!*" he seethed.

"Micah, please," she begged softly.

If only she could take it back. She hadn't ever intended him to know that it had been her in that Miami club, to know that it had been her lovingly kissing his bare flesh with the whip. She'd known it then as well as now that he would never want what he perceived as a weakness to be revealed to anyone. It was private. It was him grieving. It was him baring his soul.

"Get out."

He turned his back and his hand went to his hair in agitation. "I don't give a damn where you go, but get the hell away from me. I'm tired of being manipulated by you."

Every ounce of blood drained from her face. She followed him across the room and put her hand on his arm, only wanting to comfort, to apologize, to somehow make it right.

He flinched away and then rounded again. "Out." He flung his hand toward the door to emphasize his demand.

Numb to her toes, she slowly walked out of the bedroom, grabbing her purse as she went. Next she found herself standing outside beside her car, with no memory of coming down the stairs. The cool autumn air blew across the tears on her cheeks and caused her to shiver involuntarily.

She fumbled with the door and got inside the car. For a moment she sat there, her hands on the steering wheel, her forehead resting on the backs of her hands.

Get out.

His harsh words echoed through her mind, and she winced at the anger, the loathing in his voice.

Knowing she had to get away before she completely lost her composure, she cranked the engine and drove down the winding drive-way. She pulled onto the highway and accelerated until The House disappeared in her rearview mirror.

She clutched the steering wheel like a lifeline. Where could she go? The smart thing to do would be to keep driving. Lose herself in another city where hopefully the maniac wouldn't find her. But she also knew she was in no shape to do that tonight.

She had to be smart and not make mistakes that could cost her her life. Which left the question open of where to go right now.

He was out there. Waiting. He'd gotten to Serena with surprising ease. Angelina was alone. An easy target.

Her head throbbed, and her nose felt swollen to twice its normal size thanks to the tears she was fighting. Staying alone anywhere would be suicidal and just plain stupid. Maybe she could go camp out in the police station until morning.

She shook her head. Nathan was staying at Julie's, and she had no idea where Julie lived. Ditto for Faith and Serena. Which left Connor. She'd feel a lot better about asking him for help over one of the girls. She'd already put them in enough danger. As much as she hated the idea of going back to a place she knew the stalker had been, she didn't have a choice.

The drive was a blank in her mind. She navigated in a daze. By the time she pulled into the apartment complex, she was wound so tight she thought she might burst. She parked beside Connor's truck and glanced nervously around. Not seeing anyone, she took a deep breath and bolted from the car.

She ran up the walkway to Connor's door and banged her fist on the wood. Her other hand went to the doorbell, and she punched the button repeatedly.

Jittering impatiently as she waited, she stared from side to side, looking for anyone lurking in the shadows.

The door flew open and Connor stood there in gym shorts, no shirt and no shoes, a dark scowl on his face.

"What the—" He broke off when he saw her.

He reached for her wrist and yanked her inside the apartment. He released her long enough to shut and lock the door and then he turned back to her, gripping her shoulders.

"Are you all right? What happened? Where the hell is Micah?"

Despite the firm grip her teeth had on her bottom lips, tears welled in her eyes.

Connor herded her into the living room and pushed her down onto one of the leather sofas.

"Talk to me, sweetie," he said in a gentle voice.

Some of his calm invaded her, and she took several steadying breaths. Despite his calm, she noticed that he gripped his cell phone as if he were ready to place a call the instant she told him what was wrong.

"Nothing's happened," she said. "Micah is fine. He's pissed but he's fine."

Connor relaxed just a bit, but his brows drew together in confusion. "Where is he? Why the hell are you out by yourself?"

She closed her eyes. "He told me to get out so I left. If I wasn't so tired, I would have just kept on driving. It's what I should have done."

Connor's mouth worked up and down, and his right eye twitched. He raised a hand to his head and ran it raggedly over his hair. Finally he found his voice, only to spit out a string of expletives.

"What the ever-loving fuck? He told you to get out when some crazed asshole is stalking you?"

Her lips turned down into a sad frown. "He had good reason."

For a minute she thought Connor was going to explode. He was absolutely furious.

"There is *no* reason he should have thrown you out. I don't care what you did to piss him off."

"He was right," she said in a small voice. "I've manipulated him at every turn, but I didn't mean . . ." She closed her eyes and bowed her head. "I never meant to hurt him."

"Christ," Connor muttered.

He moved beside her on the couch and pulled her into his arms.

"Do I even want to know what the hell you supposedly did that warranted him tossing you out to face some crazed lunatic on your own? Because I can't think of any goddamn reason to justify it."

"I can't tell you," she said against his chest. "He's pissed enough that *I* know."

Connor pulled her away and stared fiercely back at her. "You don't owe him a goddamn thing. Not now."

Connor's cell phone rang, and he yanked his gaze to the coffee table, where he'd placed it.

He scowled. "It's Micah."

She pulled away and hugged herself protectively.

Connor shook his head and reached for the phone.

"What the fuck do you want?" he snarled into the phone.

"Have you seen Angelina?"

It was said so loud that Angelina could hear every word. He sounded so furious.

"Yeah, I've seen her. I'm looking at her now."

"Sit on her until I get there."

Connor pulled the phone away in surprise. "Asshole hung up on me."

She nodded miserably, knowing that round two with Micah was coming.

She stiffened her spine. Some of her shock melted away, replaced

by her own anger. No way in hell she was going to apologize for loving someone.

Micah roared into the apartment complex parking lot and whipped
into the space next to Angelina's car. His anger over her revelation
had quickly fled and been replaced by gut-wrenching fear the minute
he realized she'd left.

He wanted to shake her until her teeth rattled and then he
wanted to spank her ass.

He holstered his pistol in his shoulder harness and stepped out
of the truck. He hadn't worn a weapon since he'd left Miami and yet
it still felt like second nature. An extension of himself. Some things
never changed.

He hurried to Connor's door and rapped sharply. The door
opened immediately, and Connor stood there looking for the world
like he wanted to beat Micah's ass.

Micah sighed and brushed past his friend. "Where is she?"

"I put her to bed. She probably cried herself to sleep."

Micah winced. Talk about playing dirty.

"What the fuck were you doing, Micah?" Connor asked in a
dangerously low voice. "Have you lost your goddamn mind? I don't
give a shit what she did to piss you off. You're a fucking bastard for
tossing her out when some asshole is after her."

Micah mentally counted to ten. He had no desire to get into a
damn fight with Connor over a misunderstanding. He sat down on
the couch and rubbed the back of his neck. Hell, how had it come
to this? Not an hour ago, he'd planned a night of making love to
Angelina. Now everything had gone to hell, and he wasn't sure how
to fix it.

"Look, man, I'm guilty of getting pissed. I'm guilty of losing my temper and I'm guilty of hurting her feelings, but goddamn it, I did not kick her out of the house. I told her to get out. I meant of the *room*. I was pissed. Hell yes. She has the uncanny knack of making me insane. I swear to God no one else can make me react like her. But I'd never do anything to put her in danger."

The corner of Connor's mouth lifted. "What did she do to piss you off so bad?"

Relief made him fold inward. Angelina hadn't told Connor everything. Of course she wouldn't. She was intensely loyal. Head-strong, courageous and loyal to her bones.

"No offense, man, but that's between me and Angelina."

Connor shrugged. "Look, it's no secret I feel protective of Angelina, and when she showed up on my doorstep it was hard not to want to kick your ass. You have no idea how close you came to losing her," he said seriously. "She said she started to just drive and keep on driving, but she was tired and distraught and had the common sense to know she needed a safe place to stay."

Micah's knees went weak. God. He rubbed his forehead and then gripped the bridge of his nose between his fingers.

"Son of a bitch. Swear to God I'm going to spank her ass," he muttered.

Connor chuckled. "I'd pay money to see that."

"She doesn't need to be here. It's not safe."

"Agreed. She's in my bedroom."

Micah's jaw tightened. He was just enough of a Neanderthal that it set him off to even think of her all snuggled up in another man's bed, whether the man was there or not.

"Relax, man. I didn't have any other place to put her." Connor watched him shrewdly through narrowed eyes. "You've got it bad for her."

Micah's mouth opened in a snarl. But then he snapped it shut again. He wasn't even going to dignify that with a response. If he did, Connor would just be convinced he was right.

Keeping a tight leash on his irritation, he got up and headed for Connor's bedroom. It was dark, but there was just enough light coming from the cracked bathroom door that he could make out her outline.

He closed in, reaching for the lamp beside the bed. Soft light poured over her features. She flinched and screwed up her eyes but didn't wake up. She looked . . . vulnerable. His gut twisted into a giant knot when he saw the redness under her eyes. Connor was right. She'd been crying.

He cursed softly under his breath and then leaned down to kiss her cheek.

"Angel girl," he whispered. "Wake up. Time to go home."

She roused, blinking sleepily as she stared up at him. He knew the moment recognition set in because her eyes lost their sheen. Her lips trembled, and so help him God, if she started crying again, he was a goner.

So he did the only thing he knew to do. He kissed her.

He caught her gasp of surprise and swallowed it up. Not giving her any time to protest, he licked over her lips and then plunged inside. Warm and moist and so damn sweet.

She wrenched away and scooted backward across the bed, her eyes shooting daggers at him. And she definitely wasn't crying.

"Go to hell, Micah."

She hissed and spit like an angry kitten. A broad smile attacked his face at the image, which only served to piss her off more.

"You think it's funny?"

He molded his features into a solemn expression and regarded her as earnestly as he could.

"I don't find you running around the streets of Houston when a madman is on the loose funny at all."

"You told me to get out," she accused.

Micah sighed. "Angel girl, I was pissed off. I wanted you to get out. Of the room, not the house! I needed a few minutes to breathe because I didn't want to tear a strip off your hide in my temper. I don't remember you being this sensitive before."

She gaped incredulously at him, and then before he could defend himself, she smacked him with a pillow. Hard. "It's my fault because I'm sensitive?"

He reached over to snatch the pillow before she could launch it again. He snagged her wrist and held it in front of her and then slid on the bed next to her.

"Look, Angel. I've got a temper. I lost it. You dropped a bomb. I didn't react well. I can't apologize for reacting the way I did, but I can guarantee you it will happen again. You seem to have the knack of getting under my skin like no one else."

"What the hell kind of apology is that?" she demanded.

Again he sighed. They were getting nowhere and he wanted to get her back to The House pronto. Ignoring the small fist beating his chest, he simply swept her up in his arms and strode toward the living room.

"Let me down," she said behind gritted teeth.

Micah nodded to Connor as they past. "Get the door for me?"

Connor's lips were twisted in amusement, but to his credit, he didn't say anything. He opened the door for them and waved at Angelina.

"See you later, sweetie."

"Traitor!" she hissed.

Micah dumped her into his truck and then pointed a finger at her. "You don't move. I swear to God, Angelina, if you so much as try to get out of this truck, I'll tan your ass like there's no tomorrow, and furthermore I'll enjoy it."

She stared rigidly ahead as he slammed the door. He hurried around to the driver's side and slid in beside her.

Not wanting to waste any more time in plain sight, he started the engine and pulled out of the lot.

"I won't apologize," she said stiffly. "I know you're pissed, and maybe you have the right, but I refuse to apologize for caring about you."

His chest caved in just a little bit at the ferocity of her words.

"Damn but you know how to take the wind out of someone's sails," he grumbled. "It's damn hard to stay pissed at you when you come at me like that."

She frowned harder at him.

"I'm not nearly as pissed at you over Mama Rose—but don't think we won't talk about it again—as I am over you leaving alone. Damn it, Angel, he could have gotten to you and there isn't a damn thing I could have done about it!"

"You told me to leave."

"Hell, I tell you a lot of things and you don't ever seem to think you have to listen. Why on earth would you pick now to become all obedient on me?"

Her lips twitched suspiciously and she looked away to hide her smile.

He reached over to take her hand. "I never meant for you to take it so literally, but you know what? Even if I had meant it, you should have told me to go to hell just like you're telling me now and you should have locked yourself in another room for three days and withheld sex if you really wanted to punish me."

Her shoulders shook. She dragged a hand through her long, unruly hair and looked at him with a grimace. "So you're saying I over-reacted."

He shrugged. "We were both upset. I'm just saying you should have stood your ground. You've never had that problem before."

"I've never cared about someone this much before."

His chest tightened, his throat closed off, and he gripped the steering wheel all the more tightly.

"Don't care about me, Angel," he said hoarsely. "Save your love for someone else."

"It doesn't work that way," she said calmly.

Micah shook his head as if he could shake off her words. He didn't want this. Didn't want to become emotionally involved, and he didn't want to hurt her. He'd been honest with her. Brutally so. Sex was all he could offer her. Sex and his domination. How the hell was that a substitute for love? He'd had love once, and he damn well knew sex was a piss-poor substitute.

He was still inwardly seething when they pulled up to The House. Angelina started to open her door, but he stopped her by grabbing her wrist.

"Don't get any ideas of running and hiding from me now, Angel girl. It's time to pay the piper."

CHAPTER 33

$\mathcal{A}$ngelina stared at him with a mixture of nervousness and heightened awareness. Arousal flooded her veins at the authority in his voice, and yet she felt compelled to argue.

"This was all your fault, Hudson. Not mine. If anyone needs punishing, it's you."

He had no liking for the reminder of him being underneath her whip. His eyes narrowed dangerously and he rubbed a thumb sensuously over the pulse at her wrist.

"Who said anything about punishment?" he said silkily. "Maybe I enjoy watching you writhe under the heat of a whip, how you flinch away and then beg for more with your next breath."

She swallowed as heat rose from her belly to her throat. There was no denying his effect on her. Already she felt the touch of leather on her skin. The pain and exquisite pleasure all rolled into one.

"Hell, if I wanted to punish you, I'd lock you in your room and withhold sex from you. Something tells me I might survive it longer than you," he said in amusement.

She yanked her wrist from his grasp and glared at him. He met her gaze and then said in a low voice, "Inside, Angel girl. It's time to take what's mine."

On shaking legs, she walked into The House ahead of Micah. How quickly she'd gone from upset to anger and now to aching arousal. He brought out the best and worst in her, but then she'd always known loving him wouldn't be easy.

She chanced a look over her shoulder as they entered, and the answering arousal she saw in his eyes sent a shiver straight up her spine. He wouldn't be easy tonight, and maybe a part of her longed for him to give her every ounce of his passion, his need. She wanted him to take her to her very limits. It both frightened and excited her.

"Upstairs," he directed.

The walk seemed endless, each step more difficult than the last. For all her dread, anticipation licked over her skin like fire over dry wood.

His hand closed around her arm when they stood at the top of the stairs, and he turned her in the direction of the common room. It was dark when they entered, and he flipped the lights, flooding the room.

It looked different without people having sex. It looked almost normal except for the miscellaneous pieces of furniture positioned around the room. A spanking stool. Would he use it? No, what he intended went beyond a simple spanking she was sure.

Sure enough he motioned her toward the beam where he'd flogged her that first night. She stood silently under it, waiting his command.

His gaze slid over her, his eyes gleaming with approval.

"Take off your clothes, Angel. Slowly. Pants first. Then your shirt. Leave your underwear on for now."

She fumbled with the snap of her jeans. Despite her attempt to be graceful and seductive, she knew she appeared clumsy. Remembering his dictate, she peeled the denim slowly down her hips. Picking up one leg, she pulled her foot out, and then she did the other. She felt surprisingly vulnerable and she had yet to take off her shirt.

There wasn't much to her underwear. Sheer lace, soft and silky, with thin strings over the curve of her hips connected to a small triangle at the juncture of her legs.

Her bra matched, a simple push-up to display her small breasts to their best advantage. Even being the breast man she knew him to be, Micah didn't seem disappointed in her assets.

Chill bumps spread across her chest and belly when she tossed the shirt aside.

"Arms up," he commanded.

She raised her arms over her head, each feeling like it had a hundred-pound weight attached.

He pulled her wrists and looped the leather ties around them then pulled tight to secure the loops to the beam. She had to go up on the balls of her feet as her body stretched. Her back bowed under the strain, pushing her breasts until they threatened to spill out of her bra.

Micah stepped around, his hand sliding over her belly and up to cup her breast through the material of her bra. He pushed, plumping the swell until her nipple peeked over the lace.

Electricity sizzled through her body when he brushed his thumb over the taut peak. Once, twice and then again, until it puckered and strained outward as if begging for more.

He bent his dark head to her breast and nipped sharply at the bud, seizing it between his teeth. He bit down hard and simultaneous streaks of pleasure and pain pushed her forward, arching desperately into him.

He went to his knees in front of her, his big hands gliding down her sides. His lips skimmed over her taut belly and he ended in a kiss just above the lace band of her panties.

There was no way she'd ever be able to explain to another person how she felt bending to his control. She was helpless before him, her body his to do with what he wanted. He liked inflicting pain, liked exerting his will, but she loved receiving it just as much. They were two halves to a whole, their passions the same. They were aroused by the same kinks, the same dark thrills.

She craved more. He was a drug, and he held her in his thrall.

Her underwear slipped down her legs, and he gently lifted each foot until she was free of the material. Then he ran his hands back up her legs as if he were worshipping her with every caress. No, he wasn't punishing her. Micah did nothing in anger. He simply wanted to see her bound before him while he exerted his mastery over her body. His pleasure. Hers. They were irrevocably entwined.

He lifted her legs, supporting her as she hung by the leather ties around her wrists. Even as he lifted, he spread her, baring her pussy to his avid gaze.

"You have the prettiest pussy," he murmured, his mouth just a breath away from her most intimate flesh. "So small and feminine. I love to watch my dick open you up, see you stretched so tight around me that I wonder if you can take all of me."

He looped her legs over his shoulders, and slid one hand to the soft folds between them. He ran a finger down her slit and back up again. At the top, he delved inward, finding the hood of flesh that

sheltered her clit. He traced the edge, flaring it outward before finally touching the pulsing button.

She closed her eyes and threw back her head, her hands straining
at her bonds. And then his mouth found her. Hot, damp and urgent.
He tongued her, licking lower down to her entrance and then back
up again to swirl around her clit.

Using his fingers, he parted her flesh and began lapping, his
rough tongue setting fire to her insides. Over and over again he
licked, teasing and torturous.

He found her opening and teased the rim. Circling, his tongue
flicked with the lightest of brushes. And then he latched on, sucking
hard as if he wanted to taste everything she had to offer.

It was simply too much. She exploded into his mouth and he
never let up. Her anguished cry echoed across the room. Her legs
trembled and quaked against his head, and still he wouldn't let up.

Slowly and tenderly, her worked her down from her orgasm, licking and soothing her pulsing flesh. When he finally released her, she
sagged like a deflated balloon.

Her pulse raced, and she heaved for air as he collected one of the
many whips from the wall. This was no silken flogger meant to titil-
late more than bring pain.

He doubled it over then brushed it under her chin, forcing her to
meet his gaze.

"Do you want a safe word, Angelina? Do you want to be able to
quit?"

She shook her head. "I trust you."

"Then you're a fool," he bit out.

"You'll know when to stop," she said resolutely, so much conviction shining in her voice that she throbbed. "You'll know when I
can't take any more."

His eyes flickered, and his mouth drew into a grim line. With those words she had ceded complete and utter power to him. He was solely responsible for her well-being.

"So be it."

He walked soundlessly behind her, and she closed her eyes, waiting for that first lash. It was always the worst. Unexpected and shocking. Afterward she'd know what to expect.

The whip sliced through the air, and only a faint whistle alerted her a split second before fire blistered across her back.

She clamped her lips shut against the cry that threatened to burst out. Heat raced across her flesh, leaving a sharp ache in its wake. After the initial bloom of pain, pleasure blossomed and radiated through her abdomen.

Her nipples tightened and her pussy pulsed in anticipation. This was her sweet. Her sugar rush to end all rushes. Pain was a high for her that could never be explained. Only experienced.

The second lash came harder, surprising her with its intensity. She gasped and then held on to the sensation, not wanting it to fade away.

When he took too long to administer the third lash, she moaned her disappointment. His hand tangled in her hair and he yanked her head back, his lips pressing against her temple.

"I'm in charge here, Angel. Not you. I call the shots. This isn't about your pleasure or pain. It's mine. You're mine. You just have to stand here and take it."

He released her hair then backed away again. She swallowed rapidly, trying to quell the rise of anticipation that threatened to overwhelm her.

Breathe. She had to remember to breathe.

Her body jerked, the leather straps digging into her wrists as she reacted to the third lash. Tears swamped her eyes, and she breathed raggedly through her open mouth. Oh God. Red. So much red. It gathered in her periphery and the room swirled around her.

Four. Five. Six. The lashes fell, the sound sharp. She twisted and writhed, but she endured without a sound.

Seven. Eight. Nine.

A low hum settled in her ears and she floated, no longer feeling the strain on her wrists. She was enveloped by warmth, soft and comforting. She smiled even as she closed her eyes in anticipation of the next lash.

This. This is what she craved. The high after the pain. The edge and then toppling over. It was dreamy, smooth, more exotic than anything else she'd ever experienced.

He walked around the front and she opened her eyes. He was nude, his cock stiff and distended. Beautiful. So beautiful. His body was sculpted and molded as if someone had lovingly crafted him by hand. His hair hung wild to his shoulders, unruly, like him. Savage.

She saw a kindred soul when she looked into his eyes. Could he see one in hers? Did he recognize her?

The whip came up and flicked across her belly, not as hard as he'd struck her back, but the shock sent her flinching away. Before she could process the sensation, he flipped his wrist and the whip stung across her right breast, perilously close to her nipple. Then her left breast.

She found herself pushing forward, wanting the contact, her nipples surging, tightening, wanting to feel the kiss of the whip.

He feathered welts in a distinct pattern across her chest and abdomen but always missing her nipples. She panted and then sucked air through her nose. She needed. God, she needed.

The whip went silent, and in the next moment excruciating pain and the most indescribable pleasure assaulted her. Her nipples felt pierced by hot needles. Her eyes flew open and she looked down to see a clamp with vicious little teeth attached to each stiff, distended nipple.

Her entire body burned, an inferno that raged across her welted skin. Arousal was savage within her. If she hadn't been bound, she would have taken Micah before he could ever take her. It was a need so fierce she felt she might die from it.

As if sensing how close she was to absolute overload, he dropped the whip, stalked forward and threw her legs over his forearms, standing to his full height.

She was spread and draped helplessly over him, and he wasted no time possessing her. He yanked her onto his cock, plunging through her swollen tissues like a hot knife through butter. She enveloped him, swallowed him, welcomed him with every particle of her being.

Over and over his hips slapped against her ass. He fucked her savagely, his features drawn tight in agony. He was hard, brutal even, and still she wanted more.

Power rolled through his big body and bled into each thrust. His cock battered her, ramming without mercy. He yanked her forward even as he stepped into every thrust.

Her arms pulled and stretched. Her muscles burned. Her abused flesh protested his every movement.

Without warning, he dropped her limbs, her feet hitting the floor. She stumbled, her hands flexing as her bonds held her upright.

His hand curled around his engorged cock, nearly purple the skin was stretched so tight at the head. He yanked, aiming at her body.

He directed his release onto her skin. It splattered her breasts and rolled between them down to her belly. It splashed onto her thighs and trickled farther downward.

His. He marked her in the most primitive way he could. She loved the feel of his liquid heat sliding down her skin. She felt empowered. She felt beautiful. She felt like she belonged.

He reached up to untie her hands and she collapsed downward. Instead of catching her, he urged her down to her knees and placed a hand to her forehead to tilt her head back.

With his other hand he guided his still erect cock into her mouth.

"Suck me," he said huskily.

His taste exploded into her mouth, and she ran her tongue along his length, cleaning every drop of fluid from his skin. He rocked back and forth, stroking her cheek with gentle fingers.

After several moments, he pulled free and let his softening erection drop. There wasn't a spot on her body that didn't throb, and she couldn't control the wince when he helped her to her feet.

He released the clamps from her nipples, and she cried out in agony as feeling rushed hot and wicked back into the tips. He lowered his head and licked gently at each one until the pain lessened to a dull throbbing. Then he raised his head again and kissed her lightly on the lips.

"Let me draw you a bath, Angel girl. You can soak while I fix us dinner."

The gentleness was back in his voice, and his eyes glowed with . . . She swallowed, not wanting to speculate on what he might be feeling. She'd have liked to say *love*, but he'd never made any pretense of the fact that he was done with love.

CHAPTER 34

Angelina curled up on the leather couch in one of the sitting rooms of The House and stared out of the window at the lush landscape. They were up on a hill, and the terrain sloped gently down until it met the high iron fence that separated the property from the highway.

Her body still throbbed, but she savored the sensation. She felt utterly content this morning, as if all was right in the world, which was a pretty stupid sentiment given there was some creep out there watching and waiting. It was a testament to how Micah made her feel, though. Safe and cherished. Protected, and yet he didn't treat her gently. No, he was content to push her to near the breaking point. As she'd known he wouldn't, however, he hadn't pushed too far. He'd taken her to the brink and gently pulled her back.

His voice came over the intercom system. "Angelina, come down here."

There was strength in the command. He expected her to obey.

He'd been in Damon's office most of the morning making phone calls and getting updates.

They still hadn't talked about Mama Rose or his reaction to finding out she was the woman behind the mask who'd flogged him in the Miami club. Maybe they would talk now?

She rose, her stomach in knots. He'd been so angry the night before, but then he'd been angrier because she left.

When she got to Damon's office, the door was open and she stepped inside. Micah was sitting behind the desk, leaned back in the chair as he waited for her. To her surprise, Cole was sitting in one of the chairs by the window just to the right of the desk. When had he arrived? Micah must have let him in when she was upstairs dressing.

Her gaze drifted to the left, and she came to an abrupt halt. Her mouth fell open as she stared at the equipment just a few feet away. Specially designed stocks. The highly polished wood told her the stocks were new, and the fur lining the hand and neck holds told her they'd been designed with some comfort in mind, but holy hell. She didn't need an overly active imagination to figure out their uses.

"Take off your clothes, Angel," Micah said.

Though she complied immediately with his quietly voiced command, her fingers shook nervously as she pulled at her jeans. Adrenaline jumped through her veins, leaving her flushed—and excited.

She paused at her panties and bra and looked to him for direction. He nodded. "Those too, Angel girl. We want to see you naked."

Her eyes slanted sideways to look at Cole in her periphery. He was sitting forward in his chair, his gaze lean and hungry.

She slipped out of her underwear and then reached behind her to unclasp the bra. The cups fell forward, and she slowly pulled the straps down her arms and let the bra fall to the floor.

"Come here, Angelina," Cole said.

She quickly glanced at Micah, and he nodded his permission. She walked over to where Cole sat. As she neared, he leaned back and reached to pull her between his thighs.

His hand slid over her hip and to her back. With gentle force he pushed until she leaned forward, her breast just an inch from his mouth. His lips closed ever so gently over the budding crown of her nipple. He didn't pull hard or bite. He sucked lightly, his tongue lapping at the point.

She drew in her breath and put her hands on his shoulders to brace herself as he continued to feed gently at her breast. It was slow and sensuous and erotic as hell.

"You taste so good," he murmured as he pulled away to stare into her eyes. Then he lowered his head once more, to take her other nipple into his mouth. He lapped and kissed, worked the soft flesh between his teeth, but he never exerted any pressure. She moaned and arched into him, seeking more.

The sharp slap on her ass with his open palm startled her.

She looked down into his eyes to see a reprimand glittering in his pale blue orbs.

"What do you think we're going to do to you today, Angelina?"

She swallowed. "Whatever you'd like."

He smiled. "Good answer. That's very true. Micah is being very generous with you. I think he knows how much I desire you. He and I have much in common I've found. Though it's not in my nature to share a woman—I tend to be very possessive—I find that being allowed to fuck another man's woman is very satisfying. Very, very satisfying."

He pulled her down onto his lap and cupped her cheek. He was such a contradiction. His actions and words were firm, but every time he touched her, he did so with exquisite care.

"Do you like it when he watches, Angelina?" Cole whispered. "Are you turned on when he gives you to another man, or do you secretly wish he would keep you all to himself?"

"I like to please him," she replied in an equally soft voice. "I understand him. He understands me. We aren't threatened by each other's kinks."

She turned to look at Micah, seeking confirmation. He stared at her, a warm smile on his face. Open desire reflected in his eyes, but there was also pride.

"Do you see how he looks at you?" Cole asked. His voice lowered as he said the next. "He knows how lucky he is even if he won't admit it."

Her breath caught and hung, her lungs squeezing. Cole's hands smoothed over her belly, rounding the curve of her hips and then sliding up her spine to her nape. He gripped the slim column and massaged before forcing her to his mouth again for a long, breathless kiss.

Then he stood, carrying her with him. For a moment he held her in his arms, and then he let her slide down his body until her feet met the floor.

"Come," he directed as he started toward the stocks.

Micah continued to watch from the desk, his gaze following her progress across the room. Cole pulled the top up and then gestured for her to get on her knees.

Warily she lowered herself to the floor and eased her head through the opening.

"Hands too," Cole said.

She placed her wrists in the small cutouts lined with the fake fur. It was soft and nonabrasive against her skin. For that she was grateful. Who knew how long they intended to leave her here?

She gulped when the stocks closed around her neck and hands. She was well and truly trapped until they decided to free her.

"Now that is a pretty sight," Micah growled.

"Indeed," Cole murmured. "What would make it prettier is if her ass was a nice shade of red."

Micah stood and walked around the desk. She glanced up to see him removing his belt. Oh God. Then he disappeared from her view while Cole moved around in front of her.

He reached for his fly, unfastened his jeans and pulled out his cock. Then he got to his knees in front of her.

"Just relax, Angelina. I'm going to fuck your pretty mouth while he marks your ass."

He put his hand on her forehead and pushed upward so that her mouth was at the angle he wanted, and then he guided his cock past her lips.

"You expect me to be gentle. I won't be. Not today."

She closed her eyes and forced herself to give over completely to their authority. She was theirs. Their toy, the receptacle for their pleasure. They would take what they wanted whether she gave it or not.

A loud crack shot over her ears and fire exploded over her ass. She jerked forward, and Cole thrust hard to meet her forward motion.

"Better hope I come quick," Cole said as he gathered her hair in his hand. "Micah won't stop with the belt until I've come all over your mouth."

Micah wasn't easy. God, he wasn't easy. The pliant leather bit into her flesh, sending a heated buzz sizzling over her ass. She opened her mouth and allowed Cole to fuck her, blanking out, tuning only into the slap of the belt against her ass.

He knew how hard to push. He knew she didn't want it easy. He, unlike the others, was comfortable with her, knew her limits. He wasn't afraid to test them. She belonged to him. He didn't have to worry about stepping over the line like Cole did.

She twisted restlessly, arching, seeking the heat. Micah wasn't gentle, but then neither was Cole. Cole fucked into her throat with ruthless precision. He timed each thrust with the methodical lashes Micah rained down on her ass.

"Suck me, Angelina," Cole said harshly. "Use that tongue. Close your lips around me."

With a groan she forced herself back to awareness. She tightened her mouth around his cock and sucked as he thrust deep. When he paused, she ran her tongue around the flared ridge.

"That's better," he murmured. "This is about us today, Angelina. Your only job is to see to our pleasure."

"Make him come, Angel," Micah said from behind her. "Your ass is only going to get redder. And then I'm going to fuck it."

She sucked in air through flared nostrils as her excitement mounted. Their words were crude, raw, nothing loving or tender about them, and she loved it. Loved the power they had to make her crazy.

"Oh yeah," Cole said as she swallowed against him. "Fuck yeah."

His hips slapped against her cheeks. The sharp crack of leather rang out. Harder. Faster. Both men worked her over from opposite ends, one with his cock, the other with his belt.

Finally Cole locked her against his body, holding her head tightly as he ejaculated deep in her throat. Warmth flooded her tongue, some of it escaping and running from the corner of her mouth. She swallowed the rest, sucking eagerly as he gave her more.

Before he even withdrew, Micah's hands parted her ass cheeks, spreading her as his cock bumped impatiently against her anus. In one forceful lunge, he was buried to the balls in her ass.

She shouted around Cole's cock, and he stroked her cheek with gentle fingers, almost as if he were offering comfort and support as Micah ruthlessly opened her up.

Micah had always been so gentle when he'd taken her ass. Slow and leisurely. Now he took her without mercy, his cock sawing in and out of her ass with frantic, rapid pumps.

Touch me. Oh God, please touch me.

Cole withdrew, but he stayed close, his fingers idly caressing her cheek as Micah fucked her ass. He made no effort to wipe the cum from her mouth, and she could feel his gaze on her, looking at the evidence of his possession.

After a moment, he held his cock up again. It was semi-erect and his fluids mixed with her saliva gleamed on his skin.

"Lick it clean," he ordered huskily as he wiped the tip over her mouth.

She opened to him and carefully licked and sucked, covering every inch of his dick. He thrust slowly, allowing himself to linger as she laved the broad head.

Then he pulled away and stood. He stepped from her view, but she knew he watched as Micah fucked her.

Micah's fingers curled into her hips. He slid his hands up to her waist and held tight as he slammed his hips against her ass. Over and over. It was a test of her endurance because he had incredible staying power.

She closed her eyes and waited. She wanted to beg him to touch her. Just once. It was all she needed, but she wouldn't fail him in front of Cole.

His movements became more urgent. His hands tightened around her and he pumped frantically into her. Then suddenly he yanked out.

"Spread her," Micah said hoarsely.

Cole's hands cupped her ass and, to her shock, spread her cheeks, holding her open. Micah moaned low in his throat and then she felt the hot wash of his semen spill into her ass. It splattered onto her back, slipping down her crack, but most was directed directly into her opening.

Wow. Her entire body trembled. She closed her eyes to ward off her impending orgasm, but it was completely out of her control. As soon as Micah dipped his cock back into her ass, sealing the fluid inside, she came apart.

Her knees shook and she bucked as he fucked her with long, deep strokes. Her nerve endings shrieked, and pleasure spilled sweet and unrelenting into her veins. The wave traveled her entire body, until the world blurred around her.

Her head fell forward, her jaw clenched so tight her teeth ached. Micah went still against her, and she felt the heaving of his belly as he leaned into her. He was still buried in her ass, and he remained there a long moment. Then he kissed her back. Just one gentle brush. And he withdrew.

"Are you hungry?" Micah asked Cole in a casual voice.

"I could eat."

What? They were talking about food at a time like this? Her entire body was in shutdown mode. She'd shed her skin at least twice already.

"I have leftover pizza in the fridge."

Their voices grew dimmer, and she realized they'd left her. Cum dripped from her chin and seeped down the inside of her thigh. Her pussy throbbed and pulsed from her orgasm. But she was powerless to move.

With a resigned sigh, she closed her eyes and waited for them to return.

* * *

She felt the vibration of their footsteps before she heard them enter the room. Her head came up, and her senses came alive. Amazing that as soon as Micah returned, her body responded. Fatigue was gone, and in its place arousal hummed through her body.

Without a word, with no warning at all, a thick cock slid into her ass. She gasped in surprise. Cole. He stroked in and out, silent, almost brooding. Then he simply pulled out and moved away.

Micah carefully removed her from the stocks and helped her to her feet. As she turned, she saw they were both naked and incredibly aroused. It was all she could do not to reach out and fondle Micah's jutting erection.

Cole lay down on the floor and stretched his big body out. He already wore a condom, and his erection bobbed above his body, heavy and hard.

"Come sit on my cock, baby. I want your ass."

Micah caressed the curve of her ass as she walked by. She stood between Cole's bent knees and he motioned for her to turn around. It was an exact replication of what he and Micah had done the night Cole and the other two men had taken her.

She eased down, trusting Cole's hands to guide her. He grasped the base of his cock with one hand and her waist with the other.

Her opening flared and stretched around him as he eased inside. Inch by inch, he crept forward until her ass met his pelvis.

"Lie back. Just like you did the other night," Cole murmured. "I'll hold you."

She reclined into his body, allowing him to cradle her. As before, he curled his hands underneath her legs then lifted and spread her, baring her pussy to Micah.

Micah stepped between her legs, his eyes alive with savage lust. He curled one hand around her knee and grasped his dick with the other.

"No mercy this time, Angel girl," he warned.

Oh shit. She squirmed, and Cole issued a sharp slap to her hip. Micah positioned himself to her small opening and lunged forward. Cole gripped the backs of her legs and his breath hissed over her ears.

"Shit," he gasped out. "Fuck, this is tight."

The two cocks, separated only by the thin membrane, rubbed over each other. Neither man seemed to care. Micah dictated the pace, and it was hard, rough and fast. Cole didn't do much moving. He was locked deep in her ass, and Micah provided the friction.

Micah fucked her savagely. She didn't even understand how he could move with her squeezed so tight around him. His possession was a mixture of pain and almost unbearable pleasure.

He yanked out, rippling across her swollen tissues. She yelped, but he didn't give her any time to process the sensation. He stepped over her body, straddling both her and Cole as he lowered his straining erection to her mouth.

"Suck it," he said hoarsely.

As Cole began to move in her ass, Micah plunged into her mouth, leaving her taste on her tongue. For several long seconds, he rubbed over her tongue, dipping deep into her mouth. He thrust hard one last time and hit the back of her throat. He stayed there, his hands tangled in her hair. Then, as he'd done before, he ripped out and moved down her body again.

He yanked her knees apart and tucked his cock into her pussy. He thrust, but this time he only got part of the way in. Easing back for more leverage, he surged forward again, this time finding his depth.

She yelled, uncaring of the repercussions. It was simply too much for her to bear. Her body splintered, fractured into a million tiny pieces. They gathered into a tight ball, so tight she was sure she couldn't stand it another second. Then with the force of a hurricane, she exploded outward, the pieces flying.

Both men growled and held her tightly as she fought them. She was mindless in her release. The room blurred as wave upon wave of the most intense orgasmic pleasure of her life seized her and wouldn't let go.

She emitted a final gasp and then her head went back as she lost consciousness.

Micah threw back his head and with a hoarse shout surged into her tight clasp, his release jetting into her body. God almighty she was incredible. Never, never before had he experienced such a rush.

His hands gentled around her legs, and he let his head fall forward again. Her head lolled to the side and rested against Cole's shoulder. Her eyes were closed, and it took a moment for Micah to realize she had passed out.

"I'll be damned," he murmured.

Cole groaned and shifted underneath Angelina. Micah felt the twitch and swiftly withdrew from Angelina's pussy.

"We fucked her unconscious," Micah said.

Cole nuzzled the exposed curve of her neck and kissed her gently, his eyes glowing with contentment.

"Yeah, I noticed. Talk about an ego boost."

Micah laughed and reached down to pick Angelina up. Cole's cock came free, and Cole lay there on the floor, his arm flung over his eyes.

"I think she killed me, man. I swear to God I've never had a woman like this before in my life."

Micah looked down at the woman in his arms. "Neither have I," he said softly. "Neither have I."

Angelina stirred, her eyes almost too heavy to open. Her body was bathed in lethargy, and she almost decided it wasn't worth the effort to wake up, but then she felt Micah beside her.

"You're back," he said softly as he claimed her lips.

She opened her eyes to see him lying next to her on their bed. They were face-to-face and his arm was thrown possessively over her hip.

"Where's that other guy?" she asked drowsily.

Micah laughed. "Cole's gone. While I don't mind sharing my woman in certain circumstances, no one else is allowed in the bedroom. This is our place. Here you're mine. Just mine and I don't have to share you with anyone."

She shivered at the possession in his voice. She snuggled closer, melting into his embrace. Here . . . here everything was right. Perfect. Nothing could intrude. The rest of the world didn't exist. He was right. This was their place. Their haven from reality.

He took her hand and slowly guided it down her body, low to the juncture of her legs.

"Touch yourself," he said huskily. "I want to watch you make yourself come."

She stretched sleepily but rolled onto her back so he could see her hand as she slid it into the curls between her legs.

Already she was aroused, and she knew it wouldn't take long. Her clit ached, and she was wet.

Micah rose up on one elbow to watch her, his eyes warm as his gaze lingered on her body.

She slipped her fingers through the folds, fingering her entrance.

She ran a finger around the circle and then went back to her clit, stroking with one finger. She pressed inward, finding just the right amount of pressure.

Almost there. Almost . . . She had braced herself for the inevitable swell when Micah grasped her wrist and pulled her hand away. Her eyes flew open, and she wasn't able to stifle the sound of her protest.

He brought her fingers to his mouth, and he sucked each one, licking her moisture from the tips. Then he kissed her palm and slowly brought her hand back down to her pussy. He motioned for her to continue, and she went back eagerly, wanting to maintain the edge on her orgasm.

To her frustration, she had to work up again. Her hips rolled impatiently, her fingers worked frantically. Her breathing sped up. Perspiration beaded her forehead. Almost. Almost. She was poised on the precipice, looking over, ready to fall.

Again he gripped her wrist, a faintly amused glint in his eyes when she gripped her fingers into a tight ball against his hand.

He was going to drive her crazy.

"Please," she whispered.

His gaze softened, and he let her hand go.

Her fingers glided through her wetness. She closed her eyes, tilted her head back and rolled her hips in rhythm with her fingers. Building, swelling, tighter.

She strained upward, bucking as her fingers danced over her clit. She was distantly aware of Micah moving, of the bed dipping, but her only concern was that he might stop her again, so she rushed on, determined not to be denied this time.

She ground her teeth together, and suddenly Micah yanked her to the edge of the bed. He brushed aside her hand and swept down, sucking her clit into his mouth.

His tongue flicked repeatedly over the quivering button, and just as quickly, she broke.

He lapped her up like a starving man, his mouth working over her screaming tissues, working her into a frenzy. She arched, bucked, her ass coming off the mattress as she forced herself onto his tongue.

He cupped her ass, raising her higher, helping her as he devoured every inch of her pussy. She shuddered uncontrollably as wave upon wave of intense pleasure blew over her like a thunderstorm.

"Micah," she whispered. Her anchor.

He eased her back down onto the bed and then pulled her forward until she slid off the edge and into his waiting arms. She rested her head on his shoulder as he held her tightly, his arms wrapped around her body.

He kissed her neck as soft as a whisper and stroked her hair with gentle fingers. She stirred and pulled slightly away so she could look at him.

She kissed him, long and lingering, enjoying the smoothness of his mouth, his tongue, like velvet.

"You taste just like a man should taste," she said with a sigh.

He chuckled. "And how does a man taste exactly?"

"Strong. Like he'd never allow anyone to hurt me."

He leaned in and kissed her again, hard and breathless. "Take that to the bank, Angel girl."

CHAPTER 35

$\mathcal{A}$ngelina studied Micah over her glass of tea as they sat in the kitchen eating lunch. As angry as he'd been over her revelation, now it was like he was pretending it never happened. He'd certainly asserted his dominance. He and Cole had fucked her mercilessly in every way imaginable. Was that what it was all about? Trying to wipe away the fact that for a brief moment he'd been under her control, at her mercy?

She understood the male psyche was a fragile thing. It didn't take much to bruise an ego. And for a man like Micah who was always in control and liked the women in his relationships to be completely submissive, it would be a definite sore point that something he deemed as a weakness had come to light.

She sighed. If only she could make him see that it didn't make him weak. Only human.

"What are you looking at, Angel?"

She blinked and focused in to see him staring at her. She hesitated a moment and then took a deep breath.

"Do you trust me, Micah?"

His eyes narrowed. "Of course I trust you. What the hell kind of question is that?"

"I want you to prove it," she said softly. "Tonight . . . tonight is mine. One night where I call the shots."

He shook his head. "That was not our agreement."

"Stop being a coward," she said bluntly. "Surely you're man enough to grant a woman her fantasy."

He raised an eyebrow. "Just what is your fantasy, Angel girl?"

"You'll just have to see, won't you? Do you agree? One night? Or are you scared?"

His eyes flashed and his lips tightened. "One night. Then this bullshit is over. Unless of course you've decided this isn't working for you after all."

There was a challenge in his tone as well, an ultimatum almost.

"One night is all I need."

She hoped.

Angelina stood in the common room of The House and waited for Micah to appear. She was nervous, yes, but anticipation tightened every nerve ending. This was her chance to show Micah that trusting himself to another person didn't mean a loss of control. Then maybe he'd understand why she'd done what she did at Mama Rose's.

Micah shuffled in a few seconds later, hands shoved into his pockets, his expression locked in stone. He walked over to her and stood watching her for a moment.

"Okay, I'm here."

"Strip," she said.

His lips curled up in a half smile. "You have to know I'd get naked for you anytime, Angel girl. No need to go to this extreme."

She watched him silently, waiting for him to comply. With no modesty, he quickly undressed and tossed his clothing aside. Then he stood to his full height, his stance challenging.

God, he was beautiful. All male. So solid. Strong.

"Over there," she said gesturing to a taller beam than the one she'd been tied to. "Arms up."

Again he complied, his expression almost one of boredom. But then he wouldn't show anticipation. No, that would make him weak and it would make her right.

She had to use a chair to stand on in order to secure his wrists above his head. When she was done, she stood back and soaked in the image of this gorgeous man suddenly vulnerable before her.

He still looked dangerous. Caged, but still dangerous, like if she came to close, he'd pounce and devour. He wasn't happy with the situation in the least, but he was keeping his word.

"You're so beautiful," she whispered as she came closer. She put out her hand to touch his chest and ran her fingers along the lines and contours, down to his flat abdomen and lower until her fingers tangled in the wiry hair between his legs.

She found his cock, long and at rest. The moment she touched him, it came alive in her palm, twitching and expanding in size.

Mesmerized, she stroked and petted over his hips, around to his firm buttocks and then up over the small of his back to the broad expanse of his shoulders. Here the muscles coiled and bulged tightly in response to his arms being stretched over his head.

Unable to resist, she pressed her lips to the center of his back and let them rest there for a long moment. He trembled beneath her lips despite his obvious effort to remain unaffected.

Finally she drew away and retrieved the whip she'd selected. She faced him, holding the leather in her hands.

"You like inflicting pain. I know it's a turn-on for you. But you enjoy receiving it as well. Is it a weakness that I like the same pain, Micah? Am I weak and pathetic for acknowledging my desires?"

He shook his head. "Of course not. A woman who knows what she wants, who's honest with herself and her partner, is a woman to be desired above all others."

"Then why doesn't the same apply to you?" she asked. "Why are you ashamed to admit your desires? Why do you think allowing me or anyone else to give you what you want makes you weak?"

He closed his eyes and turned his head away. When he looked back at her again, anger and frustration bubbled in his eyes.

"It's not the same. I'm supposed to be the strong one. I'm supposed to take care of Hannah—you."

Not responding, she circled him, remembering the last time she'd held the whip in her hands as she gazed at his tanned back. She remembered his soft plea not to go easy. He hadn't known it was her, but he'd needed what she could give him. Now she would show him again.

She flicked her wrist, expertly sending the whip over his back. The crack was loud, echoing over the silence. He flinched as the red welt appeared as a diagonal slash across his flesh.

"Tell me how to please you," she murmured as she stood to the side. "You see, Micah, you can still be in control. Tell me what you want. What you need."

"Harder," he said on a groan. "Cover my back. Leave your mark, Angel. Make it burn."

She moved again and added an identical stripe just two inches lower than the last. His hands clenched and unclenched above him. The muscles in his arms bulged and rippled.

She worked down, leaving a row of neatly placed welts. She started light and added intensity with each additional lash. When she reached his ass, she worked back up, crossing the earlier marks until all lines were crossed, each one redder than the last.

"Harder," he hissed.

Her brow furrowed in concentration because despite his command, she wouldn't shred his skin. Tiny droplets of blood welled, beading the thin lines, but she held back. Never would she hurt him. Never would she go too far.

By the time she'd covered his back in an intricate design of crisscrossing marks, he was panting, his breaths coming long and hard. Sweat dripped from his face, and he hung his head as exhaustion crept over him.

She dropped the whip and walked around to face him. His head was lowered, but his eyes glowed with arousal, with excitement.

Her gaze went to his groin, and his cock pushed impatiently outward, stiff and erect. She fell to her knees and fisted it in her hands.

"Oh God, Angel," he whispered when her mouth closed around him. "Don't, baby. I'm too big, too hard this way. You can't take me."

Oh yes, he was aroused, and she was determined she'd take everything he had to give and more.

She relaxed her entire body, gripped his hips and eased him forward until he touched the back of her throat. She sucked in air through her nose and then forced him deeper, taking him all the way to the balls.

She fought the reflex to gag and focused her entire concentration on his pleasure. She eased back, letting him slide over her tongue until the head balanced delicately there. Holding him tight in her hand, she swirled her tongue around the flared edges, exploring the differing textures. Rough, smooth, puckered and silky.

He moaned softly when she took him all the way again. For a long moment she held them there, deep against her throat, until she was forced to relent and ease away again.

This time when she grasped him in her hand, she pulled her mouth away and tilted his cock up so she had access to the underside. She ran her tongue along the thick vein, following it down to his puckered sac.

She licked, kissed and nibbled, letting his balls roll over her tongue. She sucked one into her mouth, and he gave a hoarse shout. She cupped him, fondled him and made sweet love to him with her mouth.

A tiny spurt of fluid spilled onto her cheek where his cock lay as she played with his sac. Knowing he was close, she rocked back on her heels and guided him back into her mouth.

She took him hard and fast, working him with her hand, swallowing him with her mouth. She tightened her grip and clamped down around him as she sucked.

A hot spurt hit the back of her throat. Then another and still it kept coming. She swallowed and continued sucking him, taking him deep, allowing him to pour himself into her mouth.

When the last spilled onto her tongue, she eased up, lapping gently at him, her hand soothing now instead of hard. She cupped his balls and massaged as she finally allowed him to slide from the clasp of her lips.

He was spent. Exhausted. His entire body trembled and a sheen of sweat lay over his skin. She hurried to retrieve the chair, and then climbed up to untie his wrists. He swayed and took a step back, but she was there, tucking herself against his waist and wrapping his arm around her shoulders.

"Come with me," she said quietly. "I'm not finished."

"I hope to hell you are," he said hoarsely. "I can't take any more."

She smiled and guided him quietly down the hall and into the bedroom. He started for the bed, but she pulled him in the direction of the bathroom.

He went willingly, and she left him long enough to start the shower. Hot and full of steam just the way he liked.

Despite his lethargy, one of his eyebrows went up when she started to pull off her clothes. She ignored him and pushed him toward the shower.

The spray hit them both, and he groaned as the water sluiced over his raw back. For a moment he leaned against the wall of the shower, his forehead resting on his arm. He closed his eyes and let the water wash over him.

She took a washcloth and lathered it well with the bar of soap. Then she began to wash him. Sudsy foam made a trail up his body, only to be washed away as soon as it appeared. She lovingly touched every single part of his skin. She bathed his wounds, caressed his hurts and followed each touch with a gentle kiss.

Her heart welled with love for him. Seeing him vulnerable had shaken her to the core. He was so strong and yet he had needs just as she did. She wanted to tell him he didn't always have to be the strong one. He could lean on her when he needed to.

After washing and rinsing his hair, she turned the shower off and started to get out. He caught her arm. "But what about you, Angel?"

She smiled and shook her head. "Tonight was all about you, Micah."

When he reached for the towel she held, she again shook her head and proceeded to dry his body, taking extra care not to abrade his tender back. She wiped all the way down to his feet and back up again. Then she had him sit on the toilet seat so she could dry his hair.

Through it all he watched her with a bemused expression, as if he couldn't quite figure out what he thought of it all.

Tossing aside the towel, she held out her hand to Micah. For a minute he stared at her and then her hand, before finally sliding his palm over hers and gripping her fingers.

She led him into the bedroom and urged him onto the bed. After toweling her hair one more time to get rid of the wet, she crawled in beside him and pulled the covers over them both. His warmth reached out to her and she snuggled close, pulling him into her arms until his head rested on her breasts.

At this moment, everything was right in her world. Nothing could intrude. Nothing could ruin this moment.

They lay there in silence for a long time. She thought he'd fallen asleep, when he shifted onto his back and pulled her up so she was cradled in the crook of his arm.

"Tell me about Mama Rose, Angel. Why were you there? You were no novice with the whip."

Her chest heaved with a sigh and she laid her palm over his chest. "I was there for you, Micah. Only you. I practiced because I'd never hurt you with my inexperience. I worked for hours with Mama Rose and one of the other girls there, but you were the only one I ever whipped. You were the only one I ever went there for."

He swallowed and was silent for a long moment. She waited for the questions, but they didn't come. She waited for the anger or outrage, but he lay still beside her as if processing what she'd divulged.

"Once a year," she murmured. "It was the one time I could see you and be with you. I wanted to be close to you, but you weren't ready. Your grief was still so deep. Maybe I shouldn't have done it, but the thought of someone else giving you release from your pain was more than I could bear. I wanted to be the one to take care of you."

A light quiver worked through his body and she felt him inhale sharply.

"That's what I was missing with Hannah," he said in a low, pained voice.

She ran her fingers down the midline of his chest and back up again, her movements slow and soothing. She didn't ask him what he meant. Just waited for him to continue.

"I was always the strong one. It's what I wanted. It's what she wanted. She had me and David to protect her, to take care of her."

"But no one ever took care of you," she said softly.

"No," he agreed. "I didn't think I wanted it. But now . . ."

She raised her head to stare down at him, her hair falling over his chest, still damp. "Now?" she whispered.

"You make me want. You make me want things I've never wanted. How is that possible? The idea of sharing myself so deeply with another person. Of trusting them to see me . . ."

"Vulnerable?"

He nodded, his Adam's apple bobbing as he swallowed.

"I'm vulnerable too, Micah. Always with you. Only with you. Is it so wrong for you to be vulnerable to someone who cares so much about you?"

"Yes," he said painfully. "I don't want to ever give someone that kind of power to destroy me."

She leaned down to kiss him. His hands gripped her shoulders and he pulled her closer, his mouth melting over hers in a warm, sweet rush.

It was she who took control of the kiss. She touched his cheek, in a loving gesture, stroking as her tongue swept over his, light and soothing. She inhaled deeply, holding his scent, letting it wash through her quivering nostrils.

Though he wouldn't say it, wouldn't admit it, his actions screamed louder than the boldest of words. He cared. Maybe too much. Maybe not enough. But when he touched her, all she felt was the most exquisite rush of love. It filled her with hope, made her heart ache.

She rotated, sliding her leg over his body, her lips never leaving his. Only when she'd straddled him did she break away.

She slid back until his cock jutted upward against her belly. She stroked lightly, running her fingers up and down the steel length. Then she rose up and tucked it into place. Slowly, reverently, she lowered herself onto his erection.

Their harsh breathing filled the air. She trembled. He shook. He reached for her waist, holding tight. She fell forward, bracing her hands against his chest.

When she was seated fully, she traced a path down his chest with her fingers, touching, loving. So soft, as if she could instill a hundred years' worth of love in just a few moments' time. She rolled her hips, making sweet, slow love to him.

Through half-lidded eyes, he watched her, a glow emanating from his dark depths. Yes, he could say what he want, he could hide behind his fears, but his eyes didn't lie.

She reached for his hands, pulled them together over her belly and then slid them up her body until she clasped them over her heart.

"I love you, Micah," she whispered. "You may not want it. You may not need it. But you'll always have it. It doesn't come with any strings or expectations. It's given freely."

With an agonized groan, he rose up, gathering her in his arms. He buried his face in her neck as he shuddered his release deep into her body.

She wrapped her arms around him and held him tight to her. She soothed her hands over his skin and just held him as he held on to her.

"Don't love me, Angel."

She smiled against his hair. "That's one thing you can't control, Micah."

CHAPTER 36

$\mathcal{M}$icah sat on the edge of the bed watching Angelina sleep. She was sprawled indelicately across the mattress, the sheets tangled at her feet. Her hair spread in a disheveled veil across her pillow, and she looked completely at peace.

When had she managed to creep past his defenses? He almost snorted. What defenses? He didn't seem to have any where she was concerned.

She loved him. It awed him and scared him shitless. He hadn't wanted her to love him—she deserved so much better than him—but he wasn't going to lie to himself. Her love restored life to parts of him that had died with Hannah.

An ache started low in his gut when he thought of Hannah. So young and beautiful. So full of life. His only comfort was that she hadn't gone alone. David had been there with her, had gone with her. And Micah had been the one left alone.

And you left Angelina alone.

The thought was a fist to the gut. He'd spent so much time alternately grieving for and being angry at Hannah because she'd left him. And then he'd done the same thing to Angelina. Hannah hadn't had a choice, but he had.

His cell phone rang, and he reached to grab it off the nightstand so it wouldn't wake Angelina. He moved away from the bed as he flipped it open.

"Hello," he said in a low voice.

"Micah, this is Chad. Look I have some stuff you need to see. Is there somewhere we can meet?"

Micah shook his head in confusion. "Where are you?"

"In a cab. I flew into Bush half an hour ago. I think I have our guy."

Adrenaline surged in Micah's veins. "You know who it is?"

"Yeah, I think so. Now we just have to find him. I brought all the information I could dig up on him with me. Can we hook up somewhere?"

"Yeah, sure. Look, give the cabdriver this address. Have him bring you here." Micah relayed the address to The House. "Thanks a lot, Chad. I owe you one, buddy."

"No problem. David was my friend too. I looked out for Angelina the best I could after he died."

"Yeah, I know," Micah said quietly.

He hung up and went back to the bed where Angelina was now propped up, her eyes sleepy and her hair falling in waves over her shoulders.

"Who was that?" she said in a drowsy voice.

"Chad. He's on his way here. He thinks he knows who our guy is."

Her eyes widened. "That's great! I mean, I guess it is. Will you be able to find him?"

"Just having a lead on his identity will give us plenty to work with. We can track him then. Learn his habits, his quirks, find out if he has any connections here. If he's used any credit cards. Yeah, we'll get him, baby. Don't worry."

He leaned forward and kissed her forehead. "You should probably get dressed. He'll be here in half an hour."

He got up and walked toward the door. "I'll wait downstairs for you. Come down when you're ready."

She nodded and he went down the stairs to wait for Chad.

Angelina took her time showering and getting dressed. She was in a mellow mood today and her clothing would reflect it. She chose her most worn pair of jeans—her most comfortable—and a cotton T-shirt that had been washed until it was faded and soft. Not bothering with shoes, she padded down the stairs.

She heard voices from the front sitting room, so she ventured in there. Micah and Chad were sitting across from each other and both looked up when she entered.

Micah stood, as did Chad, and she went to stand next to Micah. It was automatic, and he pulled her into his side, a gesture that comforted her.

"Hi, Chad," she said softly.

He smiled warmly at her. "Hey, kiddo. You doing okay?"

She nodded. "Micah said you've found him?"

"Yeah, we were just getting to that."

Chad pulled out a folder and handed it to Micah. What happened next was a blur. One moment Micah was flipping open the folder, and the next Chad whipped out his pistol and hit Micah in the back of the head.

Micah went down, blood spilling from the wound on his head.

Angelina's knees buckled, and she dropped down next to Micah, her hands going to his shoulders.

"Oh my God, what are you doing?" she screamed up at Chad.

Chad pointed the gun at Micah, his eyes so cold she shivered.

"Get up, Angelina. Do it now."

"What is wrong with you? I need to call an ambulance. Are you crazy?"

The realization was slow to come, but when it did, it hit her like a sledgehammer. Her gaze flicked to the open folder lying next to Micah on the floor. It held empty sheets of paper. There was nothing there. It was all a trick.

She stared in horror at Chad. Nausea bubbled in her stomach. "It was you," she whispered. "You're the creep who's been stalking me."

"Not stalking. I never stalked you."

"What the hell would you call it then?" she spit out. "You made my life hell. I lived in constant fear. I had to pack up and move in the middle of the night."

"You should have come to me," he said calmly. "I took good care of you. For a little while you leaned on me. You should have seen that I was perfect for you."

Oh, sweet Jesus. He was insane. Out of his ever-loving mind, and now Micah lay on the floor with a head injury.

"Get out of the way, Angelina. I don't want to accidentally shoot you when I shoot him."

Terror blew through her chest, robbing her of breath. He was utterly serious. There was no emotion, no reaction in his eyes. He would calmly kill Micah without a second thought. Unless she could stop him.

She rose to her feet, careful to keep her body in between Chad and Micah. Her knees shook, her palms were sweaty, and if she so much as breathed wrong, she was going to puke.

"Please don't kill him, Chad," she said in her softest voice. "I'll go with you. I'll be whatever you want me to be. We can be together. I won't fight you. But don't kill him."

His eyes narrowed suspiciously as he stared at her, but the gun never moved. "I'm supposed to trust you? After you betrayed me by sleeping with him? You've been holed up here acting as his sex toy for weeks now."

"I didn't know it was you. You should have realized what a crush I had on you. Why do you think I went to you for help? But you ignored me. You treated me like a kid sister. Like David's sister. What was I supposed to think?"

"Why do you care what happens to him then?"

Angelina glanced down at Micah and prayed he was still alive, that she could buy him enough time.

"He was David's best friend. And if you kill him, you'll go to prison for murder. How can we be together then? You'll leave me just like Micah left me, like David and Hannah left me. I'm tired of being left behind, Chad. If you care for me like you say you do, then you won't leave me either."

His eyes flickered and he slowly lowered the gun. She held her breath as tension knotted her belly. Then he gestured toward the door.

"Let's go."

"I need my stuff. My clothes. It's all upstairs."

Suspicion glittered in his eyes again, and his lip curled upward in a snarl.

"Forget it. I'll provide you what you need. For now we're getting out of here."

Swallowing back the stark terror that swelled in her throat, she took a step forward and made herself not look back at Micah. It would enrage Chad, and she needed him calm if she ever hoped to escape him.

He took her arm roughly with his free hand and kept the gun pointed at her side as they walked out of The House.

Sunlight accosted her vision and she winced, blinking away the brightness. She stumbled when he yanked her forward. How could this be such an utterly gorgeous day when her entire world had gone to hell in a matter of seconds?

"Get in," he ordered.

She stood inside the open car door and everything inside her balked at getting into this vehicle.

Like the cop he was, he put his hand on her head and shoved her down into the car just like she was some criminal he was arresting.

The magnitude of her situation slammed into her brain with the force of a hurricane. She was being kidnapped by a lunatic cop. Crazy or not, he was a good cop. He'd be hard to find. He knew how cops thought.

She clamped her lips shut to quell the desperate moan that threatened to escape.

Think, Angelina. Keep your cool.

Chad slid in beside her, and to her relief his gun was at least holstered. To her dismay he clapped one cuff around her wrist and proceeded to secure the other cuff to his.

"Just in case you get any stupid ideas," he said as he yanked her arm forward so he could start the engine.

"Where are we going?" she asked with fake calm.

He drove onto the highway, ignoring her question. There was sick determination on his face, and she knew no one was going to find them. If she was going to get out of this alive, she was going to have to do it herself.

Real calm descended over her. Her mind quit screaming. Her gut, which was knotted in worry over Micah, loosened, and she began to think. Really think.

Images from when David had taught her self-defense at the gym came to mind. He stood over her, making her repeat her moves until she was sore and exhausted.

You can beat anyone if you use your head. Intelligence always beats brawn. No matter how small you are or how big the guy, you can find a way to win, Angelina. You just have to outwit him.

Chad drove on, obeying all the speed limits. He was careful not to bring attention to them. He made all the correct stops. In fact he looked decidedly casual, one arm on the steering wheel in a nonchalant manner. He firmly believed he was invincible. He'd won. He'd gotten the girl.

Or so he thinks.

Somehow, someway, she was would escape. She only prayed she would get an early opportunity, before she had to endure whatever he had in mind for her.

CHAPTER 37

$\mathcal{M}$icah stirred and was immediately assaulted by a rush of pain so intense that he gagged, which only made the pain in his head all the more vicious.

He tried to force himself up, but his arms and legs wouldn't cooperate. Beside him, his cell phone lay on the floor, and he stared curiously at it as it wavered in out and out of his vision, so blurred he had to blink to try to bring it back into focus.

And then it came back, sharp, like a lightning bolt. Knowledge exploded through his head and he panted against the pain.

Angelina. Chad. Oh God.

He was an idiot. He'd trusted the wrong person and now Angelina would pay the price.

He closed his eyes and swallowed, forcing himself to focus, to shake off the nausea and the pain. He wiped at his head, and his fingers came away red and sticky with his blood.

With shaking hands he grabbed at his cell phone, swearing when the buttons wouldn't work right. He punched the speed dial for Connor because he knew he couldn't navigate through his address book for another number.

"Hey, man," Connor said, and Micah winced as the too loud voice seemed to crack his skull all over again.

"Chad Devereaux," Micah rasped. "He has Angelina. Came here. It was him all along."

"Whoa, back up. First, are you all right? You sound hurt. What the hell happened?"

"Get here," Micah gritted out. "Need you to call it in. Get everyone looking. Find what you can on him."

"On it," Connor said and the line went dead.

Micah dropped the phone and tilted his head back, closing his eyes as an agony of a different kind flooded him.

Bits and pieces of the exchange between Angelina and Chad came back to him. He'd drifted in and out of consciousness, but he'd heard her agree to go with Chad if Chad wouldn't shoot him.

Fear and rage slashed viciously through his chest. Fear for her. Rage at Chad.

She'd given herself to a man who'd tormented her for a year—to save Micah.

I love you, Micah. You may not want it. You may not need it. But you'll always have it. It doesn't come with any strings or expectations. It's given freely.

Her words hit him like a ton of bricks. She loved him and she'd just sacrificed everything for him.

He'd been so afraid to love again, to open himself up to the kind of pain that came with losing someone. He'd loved Hannah deeply, the kind of love he thought he'd only feel once in his life. And he'd lost her. He hadn't wanted to love Angelina. Hadn't wanted to form an emotional attachment to her. He'd lost her anyway.

Shut the fuck up. You haven't lost her yet. You'll get her back.

He sagged against the couch and then tried to elbow his way up by putting his arms on the cushions and levering. It took longer than he'd have liked, and he felt like a goddamn wimp, but he finally managed to get himself off the floor.

I'm coming, Angel girl. Don't give up. I'm coming for you.

Angelina looked up wearily when Chad pulled onto yet another bumpy backwoods road. They'd been driving forever. She'd tried to keep up, to notice road signs, landmarks, but all she knew was that they'd driven north of Houston, and he'd taken her on a veritable maze of unmarked, shabby roads. On purpose she was sure. He wasn't a man who left anything to chance.

The road narrowed and the surrounding woods grew thicker, until they were following what looked to be an old ATV trail. At the end, they came upon an old frame house that looked like the woods had tried to swallow it up.

Gnarly bushes grew up the sides. Two trees stretched their massive branches over the roof, dipping low as if they'd punch a hole right through it.

The house looked intimidating. It looked isolated. Like it hadn't been lived in for years.

"How did you find this place?" she asked helplessly.

"Spent a lot of time looking for just the right spot after you left Miami. I knew you'd wind up in Houston sooner or later. You were so transparent. Like a bitch in heat after Hudson. I just had to wait for you to appear."

She closed her eyes. All that work for nothing. Her predictability and her love for Micah had been her ultimate downfall.

"What are you going to do to me?" she asked calmly. As calmly as she could when she was afraid she'd die. He'd picked the perfect spot. Who would ever find them here? Who would hear her screams? Or a gunshot?

He ignored her question and opened his door. None too gently, he hauled her across the seat, forcing her out his side. Still attached to him by the cuffs, she had no choice but to scramble out or have her arm ripped off. She winced when her bare feet hit the ground and immediately picked up at least three stickers.

He grabbed her arm and propelled her forward, onto the sagging porch and then inside. There was no electricity, probably no running water. The house had been abandoned for years.

Once inside, he fumbled with the cuffs and removed them, but he took his gun out of his holster and kept it up and ready.

"Don't be stupid. I'll shoot you before you ever get three steps. You made me a promise. Now let's see you deliver."

"What do you want me to deliver, Chad? I told you I'd come. I did. I told you I wouldn't fight. I haven't. Now you tell me. What am I supposed to do? What do you want? Did you bring me out here to kill me? Why not just shoot me back there with Micah?"

He curled his hand around her shirt and yanked her to him. He held the gun to her cheek with his other hand, and his breath blew hot over her face as he seethed.

"Don't push me, Angelina. I'm already pissed at you. You've fucked with me for over a year, teasing, making promises you had no intention of keeping. You're mine now. I've run out of patience."

She gaped at him. The crazy asshole honestly believed she'd somehow led him on some merry chase. He'd made her life hell, forced her to leave Miami and spend many exhausting hours running. He'd drugged her, terrorized her friends and now he'd hurt Micah and kidnapped her.

She wanted to knock the ever-loving shit out of him, but she forced herself to calm. She didn't have the advantage . . . yet. No matter what it took, she had to play it smart and wait for her chance.

"I'm sorry."

It nearly choked her to say the words and actually sound sincere. But they seemed to have the effect she was going for. He loosened his hold on her and pushed her away.

He circled the room, lighting candles. It was obvious he'd spent time here and arranged everything just so. Was this his attempt at seduction? Nausea rose in her throat. How could she endure him touching her?

He returned to her a moment later, a box in his hand. He shoved it at her, and to her astonishment it was a home pregnancy test.

"What is this for?"

"Get in the bathroom and take it. Now. I have to know. I want to know what I'm dealing with. If you're coming to me with someone else's baby."

"Chad, this is ridiculous. I use birth control."

It was the wrong thing to say. His face darkened into a savage mask at her reminder that she'd had sex with another man.

"I won't have it. I won't have Hudson's bastard. Your babies will be mine. Just like you're mine. Now get into the bathroom."

She stumbled when he pushed her forward. God, this was crazy. More crazy was the worry of what would happen if she *was* indeed pregnant. Frantically she searched her memory for her last period. She couldn't think. How long had she been here? Had she taken all her pills? Had she missed any? Would Chad go over the edge if she was pregnant?

He stood in the doorway and lit two candles on the small counter. Coupled with the thin stream of sunshine from the hallway, the light was enough for her to see.

"Are you going to watch?" she demanded. "Don't I deserve some privacy?"

"Don't talk to me about what you deserve," he hissed. "Take the damn test. I'm not letting you out of my sight."

Refusing to let him see her humiliation, she fumbled with her jeans and tried her best to shield what body parts she could. He yanked the box from the counter and tore it open. He thrust the stick at her, and she took it, praying she could pee on command.

After several long moments, she managed enough to comply with the test instructions. When she set the test on the counter so she could clean up and get her pants back up, he took it, curling his hand around the plastic tube.

"It takes five minutes," she mumbled.

"Get back in the other room," he ordered.

She went ahead of him, back into the living room. Despite the warmth of the late afternoon, a chill whispered over her skin. She was scared. More scared than she'd ever been in her life. How did you reason with someone who had clearly lost whatever grip on reality he once had?

"Why didn't you just tell me?" she asked.

It felt clichéd, the whole thing of trying to get her captor to talk, but her mind had shut down, and she needed time to figure a way out of this mess.

"Tell you what?" he snapped.

"Your feelings. That you wanted me. You never said a word. I trusted you, Chad. I went to you for help when I started getting all those creepy notes. I thought you cared, but it was you all along."

He seemed put off by her bluntness, as if she made a very valid point and he was at a loss as to how to respond.

Then his eyes narrowed and rage boiled off him in waves.

"I went to David."

"What? Chad, he's been dead for three years."

"Before. I went to him before. A long time before. When you were sixteen. I told him I wanted you. I asked for his blessing. He told me if I ever came near you he'd kill me with his bare hands."

His hands shook, and she watched nervously as his fingers tightened around the gun in response.

"He had the nerve to act like I was some piece of shit not good enough for you. He freaked. Completely lost his cool."

"I was sixteen," she said gently. "Of course he freaked. What would you do if some guy so much older started paying attention to your sixteen-year-old sister?"

"He said *never*," Chad snarled. "I've always loved you. Always. I waited. Waited until you were twenty. I did the right thing. Instead of going to you, trying to sneak around him, I approached him like a man. Told him my intentions. Told him I wanted you."

Angelina caught her breath. He was well and truly obsessed. He saw himself as the victim. To him he had done nothing wrong.

He glanced down at the test in his hand, and Angelina caught her breath when he threw it across the room, splintering it on the wall.

"You bitch! You fucking whore. You did this on purpose. You did it thinking if you got knocked up I wouldn't want you. You don't think I'm good enough either, do you?"

Oh God. Her knees gave out, and she went to the floor holding her stomach with both arms. Pregnant. Tears welled in her eyes. He'd never let it live. And she'd never let him touch her.

This changed everything. She not only had herself to protect, she had to protect her baby.

He lunged at her, grabbed her hair and yanked her painfully toward him. Spit hit her face as he raged at her.

"I'll get rid of it. Just like I got rid of David. I won't let you get away with this. You're mine."

She went cold. "What did you say?"

He dropped her hair and backhanded her across the mouth. The taste of blood exploded onto her tongue, and she reeled away, holding her split lip.

She scrambled up, fury raging through her veins like acid. Burning. Eating.

"What the hell did you do to David?" she hissed.

"I got rid of him and that bitch lover of his. He had a hell of a lot of nerve thinking I wasn't good enough for you when he was shacked up with Micah and his wife. You needed to be removed from that situation. They weren't a good example for you."

Tears of rage scalded her cheeks. "They died in a car accident."

"Stupid bitch. Who do you think caused the accident?"

She forgot all about caution. About preservation. About patience and waiting for the right moment. She lunged at him and drove her knee directly into his balls.

He dropped to his knees, the gun clattering across the floor as he dropped it. Both hands went to his groin and he doubled over in pain.

She made a fist and punched him in the eye, and when his head reared back, she jabbed him right in the throat.

He went down hard, and she didn't waste any time bolting for the door.

He grabbed her ankle and yanked. She hit the floor with enough force to knock the breath out of her. He rolled her over, and she came up fighting.

She landed another punch to his face before he grabbed her wrists and yanked her arms over her head. No way. No fucking way she was going down this easy.

She arched her back and slammed her knee into his crotch again. He managed to dodge this time, but she still hit him where it hurt.

"Bitch! Goddamn you. You promised not to fight me."

"Sue me, asshole."

When he leaned down to kiss her, she reared back and then head butted him right in the nose. Blood spurted like a geyser, splattering her shirt. He loosened his hold enough for her to wrench free, and she rolled, kicking and punching for all she was worth.

She bounded to her feet, but he gained his as well. He lunged and she dodged, but he caught her waist and they both went to the floor, her taking the brunt of his weight.

Fear for her baby outweighed everything else. She had to end this quick or he'd kill her baby.

Be smart. Use your head. You can beat your opponent no matter how big or mean he is.

She relaxed and went completely still. In his surprise, Chad loosened his grip, and his eyes narrowed in suspicion. She waited until he reached for her shirt and then she jabbed her fingers into his unprotected eyes.

He roared in pain and rage. She shoved with all her strength and he fell away. The gun. It was lying just a few feet away.

She dove for it, her hands stuttering over the barrel.

Chad landed on her, driving the breath from her. She felt a pop in her ribs and pain exploded through her chest. They wrestled, rolling as she gripped the pistol. His hands gripped hers cruelly, squeezing until she thought her bones would surely break, but she wouldn't let go.

They grappled for control, their bodies tangling as they rolled over and over. She was fighting for her life and that of her child. She fought for David and Hannah. And for all that she and Micah had lost.

A loud explosion rattled her ears, and pain seared through her shoulder. She was knocked backward several feet and fire licked up her arm, searing, hot, excruciating. God help her, he'd shot her.

He climbed over her, straddling her body as her blood flowed onto the floor. She saw the intent in his eyes and knew that unless she found a way to survive, his face would be the last she saw.

Whispering an urgent prayer to God, to David and Hannah, who watched over her, she made one last stand.

Maybe Chad thought she was done. Maybe he didn't think she was a threat any longer. It was his mistake. Ignoring the agony any movement of her arm caused, she wrenched the pistol from his grip with both hands. Before he could react, she cracked the butt over his face, shattering his nose that was already damaged from her head butt.

He fell backward, landing on the floor with a thump. She lay there a long second, heaving for breath. She was light-headed and the room spun crazily around her. Gasping for breath, she struggled up, only to see Chad out cold in front of her.

The cuffs. She couldn't chance him waking up. Couldn't chance him following her. She wouldn't be able to hold him off again.

Silver glinted in the candlelight and she saw the cuffs across the room, thrown carelessly aside when he'd freed her before.

She crawled over and grabbed them, her hands shaking violently.

Simply cuffing him wouldn't do. She had to incapacitate him. She quickly cuffed one wrist and then rolled him so that he lay on his belly. She yanked both arms around and then secured the other wrist.

Rope. She'd seen rope when they walked in. But where? She searched the living room frantically and then remembered it was out on the front porch. Hoping it was sturdy and not rotted and frayed, she stumbled out to get it, ignoring the blood that dripped from her bullet wound.

Calling on strength she didn't know she had, she looped the rope around his ankles and then pulled until his legs were bent back, and his body was bowed, belly out. She tied the rope as tightly to the cuffs as she could, winding and winding again until he was bent at an impossible angle, his arms and legs tied together behind him.

Keys. Where had he put the keys? First things first. She had to stop the bleeding. She ran to the kitchen and rummaged through the drawers until she found some old rags. As best she could with one hand, she fashioned a tight bandage, but blood was soaking through them already.

She tucked the gun into the waist of her jeans and went in search of the keys. Frustration ate at her when she came up with nothing. She searched his pockets, the living room, even the bathroom. He hadn't left them in the car. She knew that much.

A groan rose from across the room, and she panicked. She pulled the gun and eased over, pointing the barrel down at him as he moaned again and tried to move.

Rage. Such red-hot fury descended. Her hand shook and her finger curled around the trigger. She could shoot him. Right here, right now. No one would blame her. No one would ever know it hadn't been done in the heat of the fight. She could shoot him and then untie him and leave him to die. He deserved to die like a gut-shot animal. Slow and painful.

Do it. Just do it.

The voice whispered over her ears. She was tempted, so tempted. He'd taken everything from her. From Micah. He'd tried to kill her baby. He didn't deserve to live.

Tears filled her eyes and she wiped at them, leaving sticky blood.

She lowered the gun and turned away. No. David had taught her to value life. He'd never want her to kill another human being for him.

She left the house, stumbling down the steps, the gun once more tucked into her jeans. Cell phone. Chad's cell phone. He'd left it on the seat of the car.

She wrenched the door open and looked again for the keys, though she'd seen him bring them inside. She grabbed the phone and slammed the door shut.

From inside the house, she heard Chad curse and then yell at her. He called her a litany of names and vowed to kill her if he ever got his hands on her again.

She needed no urging; she turned and ran down the road they'd driven in on.

CHAPTER 38

$\mathcal{M}$icah paced the interior of the meeting room at HPD. He was about to go out of his mind. Nathan, Gray, Connor and even Damon had gathered along with several detectives. They had crawled over Chad's entire life, tracked his movements by credit card receipts, knew where he'd stayed in Houston and when he'd taken leave from Miami PD.

Micah blamed himself. The taste of guilt was sour and overwhelming. How could he not have seen what a nutcase his friend was? Hell, they'd worked together for years. Nothing had ever made him suspect Chad was off his rocker.

He'd made it entirely too easy for Chad to get to Angelina. He'd failed to protect her then just as he'd failed her now.

His cell phone rang and he flipped it open in his hand. He froze as he stared at the incoming number.

"It's him," he barked.

Silence fell, and one of the detectives motioned him over to the table.

"Put it on speaker," he mouthed to Micah.

Micah pushed the button and snarled into the phone. "Where is she, you son of a bitch?"

There was a moment's hesitation and then Angelina's voice quivered across the room. "Micah?"

Fear exploded over him. He snatched up the phone even though it was still on speaker. He needed to be closer to her voice.

"Angel? Angel, baby. I'm here. Where are you? Are you all right?"

Her breath came out in a low sob, and she sounded winded and scared out of her mind.

"I don't know where I am. I need help, but I don't know where I am."

The desperation in her voice scared him shitless.

"Okay, baby, calm down a minute. Where is Chad? Is he there?"

"I left him in the house," she said faintly. "I handcuffed him and tied his legs and arms so he couldn't come after me."

Stunned expressions met her statement. The detective's mouth dropped open. "Holy shit."

Micah ignored him, his only focus on Angelina. "Good girl. You got away from him. Now tell me where you are so I can come get you."

Another sob poured through the phone. "I don't know. I've been walking forever, but I don't see any signs and it'll be dark soon. He . . . he shot me."

All the blood drained from his face. He collapsed into a chair still holding the phone to his ear. Oh God.

"How bad?" he asked, trying to stay calm when his heart was ready to pound out his chest.

"My arm. Or my shoulder. I'm not sure. Hurts. I've lost a lot of blood."

Her voice sounded weaker.

"Angel, Angel, baby, listen to me. I want you to find a place to sit down. I need you to save your strength so you can help us find you."

There was wind noise and a light whimper and then silence.

"Angel. Angel! Stay with me. I need you to stay with me," he pleaded.

"Who is the cell provider?" the lead detective whispered loudly. "We can try to lock onto her location. I need that cell number."

Micah held up one finger. His first priority was making sure Angelina was still on the line.

"Angel, talk to me."

"I'm here," she said faintly.

"I'm going to need just a second. I'm not going anywhere. I promise."

"Okay," she whispered.

He held the phone away and related the number to the detective.

"Keep her talking," he said to Micah. "Have her tell us as much about her location as possible."

"Angel, do you know what direction he took you?"

"North," she said after a brief hesitation. "Last highway I took note of was 146. After that he took back roads. Dirt farm roads, only they weren't marked. He took me to an abandoned house at the end of one of the roads. The woods are thick here."

"Okay, Angel, don't worry. We're working on it," he said soothingly. "Have you stopped the bleeding? How bad is it?"

"I'm pregnant," she blurted. "He made me take a pregnancy test." Tears were thick in her voice. "He was so furious. I knew I had to protect my baby."

Micah laid the phone on the table and covered his face with his hands. Someone put a hand on his shoulder, but he didn't look up.

"Angelina, can you hear me?" the detective said in a loud voice.

"I hear you," she said in barely a whisper.

"My name is Detective Sanchez. I'm here with Micah. We're going to find you. I need you to believe that. You and your baby are going to be okay."

"I can get a helicopter in the air," Damon said. "Two, three, whatever we need. We can use the last known highway as a jumping-off point."

"I won't turn it down," Sanchez said. "I have Carol working on getting a trace on the cell signal. If we can just get a tower, it will narrow the search field."

"Micah?"

Micah raised his head. "I'm here, baby. Right here. We're coming for you."

"I should keep moving," she said.

"No!" Micah protested. "Save your strength. We'll come to you."

"I need to stay awake. I feel so sleepy now. I'm cold. I'm afraid to close my eyes."

Oh God. Tears knotted Micah's throat. "Keep moving then, Angel girl. But go slow. Don't hurt yourself."

The wind noise stopped and the line went eerily silent.

"Angel?"

Silence greeted his demand.

"Angel? Goddamn it!"

He looked down to see the call had disconnected. He punched

the send button to reconnect the call, but it went straight to voice mail.

"Son of a bitch!"

"We'll find her, Micah."

Micah looked up to see Connor standing over the table, his hands braced on the surface as he leaned forward.

Nathan, Gray and Damon stood to the side, their expressions grim but resolute.

"We can spread out. It's only been a few hours. He couldn't have gone too far," Gray said.

"I'll notify the sheriff's department in Liberty County and have them out looking," Sanchez said. Then he looked at Damon. "How fast can you get the choppers in the air?"

In response, Damon flipped his phone open and started barking orders and directions.

Micah stood, gripping the phone, his thumb hitting the send button again. Connor put a hand out to stop him as he went to leave the room.

Micah shrugged him off. "Don't," he bit out. "Don't even say it. That's my child out there. Angelina. I'm going."

"I'll drive," Connor said. "You're in no shape to."

Before Micah could protest, Connor shook his head. "You need to keep trying to get her back on the phone. I'll drive."

Micah nodded, ignoring the jackhammer going off in his head. "Let's go then."

CHAPTER 39

$\mathcal{M}$icah wavered in and out of consciousness. His head felt like someone had popped it like a grape. But he forced himself to remain as focused as possible. Angelina was out there. Hurt, scared and alone.

"It's been hours," Micah said hoarsely. "Why the hell haven't we found her? Why can't I get her on the phone?"

Connor gripped the steering wheel as he turned onto another dirt road that led to nowhere.

"Keep trying, man. Signal sucks ass out here. If we're moving and she's moving, sooner or later you'll get her."

"If she's still moving. She's been shot. God knows what else."

Micah ran a hand through his hair, wincing when his fingers glanced over the knot behind his ear.

Where was she?

Damon had three of his company helicopters in the air, a medic and search personnel on each. They had narrowed the search radius thanks to the trace on Angelina's one call, but there was still a wide area to canvas.

Micah punched the send button again even as he scanned the road ahead. It took a second for him to realize that the call hadn't gone immediately to voice mail. He yanked the phone to his ear, his pulse accelerating when he heard it ringing.

Come on. Come on. Answer. Come on, baby.

It stopped ringing, and he heard distortion.

"Angelina!" he shouted. "Can you hear me? Are you there?"

"Micah."

Her voice, whispery soft, thin and strained, came over the line. He nearly wept in relief.

"Baby, talk to me. Have you gotten any bead on your location yet? How are you doing?"

He forced himself to curtail the questions before he overwhelmed her. Connor glanced sideways at Micah, his hands gripping the steering wheel tighter.

"I'm tired."

"I know, Angel girl. I know. As soon as we find you, I promise you can sleep for a week. Now talk to me about what's around you."

"It's not so heavy now," she said. "I'm next to an open field, but there's no houses. No cars. Am I going in circles?"

Micah closed his eyes and pinched the bridge of his nose between his fingers.

"Ask her about helicopters," Connor said.

"Angel, have you heard any helicopters? Close by?"

There was a hesitation.

"I thought I heard one a while ago, but it didn't seem close."

"I want you to stay on the phone with me, okay? Just keep talking and keep walking."

"Micah, I see a sign up ahead!"

His heart started hammering double time.

"Take your time. Don't rush. When you get close enough to see, tell me what it says."

Connor picked up his phone, ready to call the information in to Damon so he could relay it to the helicopters and the others on the ground.

All Micah could hear was her harsh breathing blowing through the phone. He was afraid to ask her about the bleeding, and as much as he wanted to, he didn't dare bring up the baby. He'd lived with a knot the size of a football in his gut ever since she'd dropped the bomb about Chad forcing her to take a pregnancy test.

"Moss Hill. It says Moss Hill."

Micah turned to Connor, a question in his eyes. "She said Moss Hill. Where the hell is that?"

Connor held up a finger as he quickly related over the phone the information Angelina had given them.

"Micah, there's a car coming," Angelina said. "They'll see me. They have to see me."

"No! Angel, stay off the road."

He heard her voice, faint as if she'd pulled the phone away from her ear. The sound of a vehicle, distant at first and then louder, spilled through the phone.

He curled his hand around the cell phone and cursed long and hard.

There was muffled conversation. A man's voice and then Angelina's, but he couldn't make out what was being said.

Finally Angelina came back on the line.

"Micah?"

"I'm here, baby. Talk to me. Tell me what's going on."

"This man said he'd help me."

"Put him on," Micah demanded.

"Uh, hello?"

The man sounded older and worried.

"My name is Micah Hudson. I'm looking for Angelina, the woman you stopped to help. I need you to tell me your exact location."

"She's hurt pretty bad, mister. I think I should take her on to the hospital. There's a lot of blood."

Micah blew out his breath to try to assuage the sickness swelling in his stomach.

"No," he said calmly. "Tell me where you are. We have helicopters close. We can get her to the hospital much faster and every second counts. Get her inside your vehicle and keep her warm until we get there."

Angelina lay across the seat in the extended cab of the truck, shivering as the heater piped in warm air. It wasn't actually cold. Far from it—the man who'd stopped for her was standing outside the truck to escape the heat, although he popped his head in regularly.

She thought it likely he was worried she was going to die on him.

At times she was worried too.

She drifted in and out, but she wasn't sure if it was an actual loss of consciousness or if she just fell asleep and woke at varying intervals.

The pain had numbed, and all she felt was a bone-deep chill. That loss of pain worried her. Her body should be screaming, but it seemed she became less aware of her injuries and her surroundings with each passing minute.

Micah was coming for her. She'd be okay.

She blinked against the sudden tears and then closed her eyes as the tears slipped down her cheeks, warming her chilled skin. Micah had lost so much because of her. Because of one man's obsession.

Looking back, there didn't seem to be much difference between Chad's preoccupation with her and her own fixation on Micah.

No doubt in Chad's fractured mind he wasn't capable of doing her harm either, and all he did he did out of love.

Nausea boiled like acid in her stomach.

"Miss? Are you still awake?"

The stranger's worried voice seeped into the cab.

"There's a helicopter landing. I think they've come for you. Thing's landing in the road. Damndest thing I ever saw. Someone's coming up the other way too. Guess the rescue is finally here."

She closed her eyes in relief and shivered despite the stifling heat inside the truck. Again she drifted. What seemed only a few seconds later, she heard the door wrench open. A breeze ruffled her hair and then a hand touched her cheek, smoothing tenderly over the skin.

She roused, her eyes fluttering open. Micah's face was close to hers, concern burning brightly in his eyes.

"Hi," he said softly.

She tried to smile, but it just took too much effort. Instead, she let go and stopped fighting the darkness that threatened. Micah was here now. He wouldn't let anything happen to her.

Micah watched her eyes close and a surge of panic nearly crippled him. He jammed his fingers to her neck, seeking a pulse. When he felt the faint pitter-patter, he nearly melted in relief.

He leaned out of the truck and waved frantically at the medic getting out of the helicopter. As he stared back at Angelina, he took in for the first time just how bad it seemed.

Her shirt was bathed in blood, though most looked to be dried. That was a good thing, right? Her mouth was swollen, and he ran a thumb over the raw-looking cut. Bastard had hit her. Hard.

He tried to pull her shirt away from her shoulder so he could see her wound, but it stuck to her skin via the dried blood, and the last thing he wanted to do was cause it to start bleeding again.

"What have we got?" the medic shouted behind him.

Micah moved back out of his way, though he hovered just a footstep away.

"She told me he shot her in the shoulder. Looks like he roughed her up pretty good."

"We need to get her out of the truck and over to the chopper," the medic said. "I'm light on equipment. This isn't my usual ride, but Mr. Roche needed me fast so I grabbed my jump bag and hopped aboard."

"I appreciate you coming so quickly," Micah said. "I'll help you get her to the chopper."

"I'll hook under her shoulders and pull. You get her feet when you can and make sure you don't jostle her. Since I'm not sure what we're dealing with, I don't want to chance aggravating any injuries we don't know about."

Micah nodded and then he swallowed. "Look, you need to know . . . She's pregnant."

The medic grimaced. "How far along, do you know?"

Micah mentally calculated the possibilities. It had to have been that first time. The night at The House when he'd all but raped her. He wanted to puke. "Can't be more than a few weeks at most."

"Okay, I'll be sure to put it in my report so the hospital knows. Let's get her out of here."

The medic reached under her shoulders and gently pulled her out. Micah moved forward and hooked his arms under her knees, and the two maneuvered her out of the truck.

Connor was standing by the old man who'd stopped for Angelina, and the two were deep in conversation.

"Is there room for me to ride along?" Micah hollered as they neared the waiting helicopter.

"It'll be tight but you should fit."

"Let me tell my buddy I'm going. Don't leave without me. I'll be right back."

The medic nodded as he and Micah placed Angelina flat on her back on the floor of the helicopter. The medic hopped in beside her and reached for his bag as Micah turned back toward Connor.

He jogged over to where Connor stood talking to the man, both silhouetted in the beam of Connor's headlights.

"I'm riding along with her," he told Connor. Then he turned to the old man. "I can't thank you enough, sir."

The man nodded and ducked a little self-consciously. "I couldn't very well drive on with that little girl needing help so badly. I hope she turns out okay."

Micah extended his hand to shake the man's, then he nodded at Connor and started to leave.

"What hospital?" Connor asked.

"I'm not even sure. Holler at Damon. He'll know."

"Okay, meet you there."

Micah nodded and ran back over to the helicopter. The pilot motioned for him to get up front. Reluctantly, Micah left Angelina in the care of the medic and climbed aboard.

Angelina woke to instant disorientation. White. Everything was white and harsh. It hurt her eyes and she quickly snapped them shut again.

The second thing she registered was the smell. And then pain. Dull, not completely overwhelming, but nagging, distant.

Relief. If she hurt, she couldn't very well be dead. Now that she was certain she was alive, the pain could go away, thank you very much.

She opened her mouth to ask that the pain go away, but her voice didn't cooperate. She coughed. Big mistake. A groan escaped. A pitiful-sounding groan, but at least she hadn't lost all her vocal capabilities.

"Angel? Baby, you awake?"

She chanced another peek, cracking one eye open, and saw Micah standing over her bed, his eyes so worried she wanted to reassure him.

"Light," she croaked. "Hurts."

"Sorry," he said contritely.

She closed her eyes again until he returned, touching her cheek tentatively with his hand.

"You can open now."

She opened her eyes and found the dark much more comforting. His outline became discernible when he flicked on the bathroom light. She blinked at the sudden burst, but then he closed the door so that only a faint glimmer shone through.

"Where am I?" she asked hoarsely when he returned to the bed.

He sat down in a chair by her head and cupped her cheek with a gentle hand.

"You're in the hospital. Do you remember any of it? They had you in the ER for quite a while. The bullet wound wasn't serious so they moved you to the floor. You cracked some ribs, though, and they want to watch you for a few days."

She licked her dry lips. "The baby?"

She couldn't look at him when she asked the question. The pregnancy had been a huge shock to her. She could only imagine what the news had done to him.

He nudged her chin, still stroking her cheekbone with one finger.

"The baby is fine for now. They did lab work to confirm the pregnancy, and they said your HCG levels were normal."

Fear sliced through her chest. "For now?"

"Shh, sorry. Bad choice of words. You're pregnant. I just meant that we have to play it by ear. You went through a hell of a lot."

You could still miscarry.

She heard the words as surely as if he'd said them.

She sagged into her pillow, pain pounding a little more fiercely through her shoulder. She took a deep breath and immediately regretted it. Fire swelled through her rib cage. Tears slid down her cheeks as she panted.

Micah swore and pulled his hand away from her face. "Let me get the nurse. She can give you something for pain."

He punched the call button, and when he didn't get an immediate response, he abruptly got up and strode out the door. A few minutes later, he returned with a nurse in tow.

Angelina gratefully extended her good arm with the IV line in her hand for the nurse to give her the injection. When she was done, the nurse patted her softly on the arm.

"Try to get some rest, hon. I'll be back to check on you later."

"I have so many questions," Angelina murmured when the nurse had gone. "So much to say."

Micah bent and kissed her forehead. His breath stuttered unevenly over her skin as if he held to his control by a thin thread.

"We'll talk later, Angel girl. We have all the time in the world. Right now you need to rest and get better."

"Stay with me," she said.

The drug worked through her veins, leaving in its wake sweet relief and marked lethargy.

"I'm not going anywhere."

"Hold me?"

"I wish I could, baby. I don't want to hurt you."

"Won't hurt. There's room. I can move over a little."

"No! No," he said in a softer voice. "Stay where you are. I'll manage."

She held her breath as he gingerly settled himself next to her, but she shouldn't have worried. He took such care that she barely felt him when he edged close.

Awkwardly, he put his arm over her waist, lower than her injured ribs.

"This okay?" he asked.

She nodded against his chest and nuzzled her cheek against his shirt. It didn't hurt to dream a little longer. Dreams were a safe harbor against hurt and grief. For just a little while she could escape, because when she woke up, she had to let Micah go.

CHAPTER 40

Micah lay next to Angelina, listening to her breathe. She'd drifted off almost as soon as he'd climbed into bed with her, and he didn't dare move now for fear of disturbing her. Plus he liked holding her. He needed to hold her. He'd come so close to losing her.

He carefully moved his hand from her back, sliding over her hips and then low on her belly. He cupped the area just above her pelvis where the baby—his baby—was nestled.

That knowledge blew him away. His baby. A life created by him and Angelina. Part of him was shamed that the baby had been created in a moment of blind lust, at a time when he'd lost complete control. He would have rather the conception happened when he'd tenderly made love to Angelina. But their relationship wasn't tender. It wasn't easy. It was volatile. She gave and he took. But that was going to end. Starting now.

A soft knock sounded at the door, and he stiffened. Then it cracked open and Connor stuck his head in.

"Uh, I can come back," he said.

"No, it's okay. She's sleeping. Just keep it down," Micah said.

Connor walked in, followed by Nathan. They stopped at the foot of the bed and stared down at Angelina sleeping in Micah's arms.

"How is she doing?" Nathan asked.

"She woke up for just a few minutes and the nurse gave her pain medication. She's been out ever since. Doc said the shot was just a flesh wound and she'll be okay."

"And the baby?" Connor asked softly.

"According to lab work, everything's normal."

"Hey, that's great, man. You gonna kick my ass if I congratulate you?" Nathan asked.

Micah smiled. "No, not at all. I think I'll be happy about it once it's all said and done and I know for sure Angelina's going to be all right. She's my priority right now."

"They found Devereaux," Connor said. "Just like Angelina said. Tied up in the abandoned house he took her to. She worked him over pretty good. He looked like shit."

"Good. I wish she'd killed the bastard," Micah gritted out. "I was such a goddamn fool for trusting him. I brought him right to her front door. Hell, I practically gift wrapped and delivered her up on a silver platter."

"Don't beat yourself up, man," Nathan said. "He wasn't going to stop until he had her. She took care of herself. You should be proud of her for that. Think I'll have her teach Julie a thing or two about self-defense."

Connor snorted. "Men are already afraid of Julie."

Nathan grinned. "That's good. Then I don't have to worry about beating their asses for getting too close to her. Now I can lead a peaceful existence."

"Not if you keep her around for a long time," Connor said.

Nathan smiled. "As a matter of fact, I'm going to pick up the ring tomorrow."

"Hey that's great, man," Micah said sincerely. "Julie's a great girl. You know I love her to death."

He hadn't seen Nathan so happy since he'd hooked up with Julie. He remembered how happy he'd been with Hannah. He wanted that again. He wanted what his friend had. It hit him like a ton of bricks. Longing. Envy. He wanted what Angelina had so sweetly offered him. Her love. Her trust. And he never wanted to let go.

He'd wanted some kind of guarantee that he'd never hurt again like he'd hurt when Hannah died. But what he'd experienced in the hours following Angelina's abduction was a hell like no other. There had never been any hope when he'd learned of Hannah's death. It was quick, merciful. He'd spent the longest day of his life not knowing if Angelina was alive or dead or if he'd ever see her again.

Now that he had her back, he only wanted one more day. One at a time. To make the best of each and every one.

"You okay, man?" Connor asked.

"I've been such a dumbass."

He pressed his lips to Angelina's temple and breathed in the scent of her hair.

How much had he hurt her with his adamancy? He'd told her he'd take whatever she had to offer but told her in no uncertain terms not to expect a damn thing from him. He winced as his own words played over and over in his memory.

"You finally figure it all out?" Nathan asked.

Micah turned to look at his friend. "Figure what out?"

"What the rest of us have known from the day Angelina walked back into your life."

"I didn't love her then," Micah admitted. "She blindsided me."

"Don't they always," Nathan drawled. "Julie ring any bells?

Woman was as subtle as a freight train, but hey, us guys live in stupidity, or so I'm told."

Connor pinned him with an even stare. "So what are you going to do about it?"

"Whatever it takes. She's pregnant with my baby. Even if she wasn't, I'd never let her go. I want us to be a family. She's my second chance, one I tried to throw away so many times it's a wonder she never gave up on me."

"We wouldn't be men if we didn't do stupid shit women don't understand," Nathan said. "'It's genetic' is a perfectly good excuse."

Micah cracked a grin. Angelina stirred beside him and he looked down, his finger over his lips. But all she did was snuggle a little closer to his chest and go still again.

Not caring that he had an audience, he ran the tip of his finger over her jaw and to her chin.

"We're going to skate on out of here," Connor said. "We just wanted to check in on Angelina. Let us know if there's anything you need, okay?"

"Thanks for the update. I'm glad they found the son of a bitch," Micah said. "If you see Sanchez, let him know how much I appreciate all his efforts."

"Think he's planning to come by later to see if Angelina's up to talking," Nathan said.

Micah nodded and gathered Angelina close once more. His two friends waved and headed back out of the door, leaving them alone.

He stared back down at her face, her lashes resting delicately against her cheeks, the dark smudges beneath her eyes, like bruises.

This . . . this was what love looked like. Vulnerable yet strong. Constant, unwavering. She'd fought her way back to him, protecting not only herself, but her unborn child and him. She'd put herself between him and Chad, a fact that laid him low every single time he remembered lying helpless on the floor while she bargained for his life.

He was absolutely, completely unworthy of her loyalty. The magnitude of injustice he'd heaped on her was enough to make him sick. He'd treated her like some sexual conquest, a toy to slake his lust while he kept his heart guarded and safe.

She was beautiful inside and out. She was strong, resilient, and he couldn't imagine anyone else having his children.

God, children.

He closed his eyes and blew out his breath. The knowledge that she carried his child blew his mind. Not even with Hannah would he have experienced such indescribable satisfaction that the life he and a woman had created was theirs and solely theirs. A child shared between him and a woman he loved. With Hannah, that child would have been shared with David, his but not his. It was an agreement that caused no regrets, but now the knowledge that he had to share nothing with another man was a revelation that opened the door on possessiveness he'd never known he could feel.

He could never share Angelina or their child with another man. It made him crazy to even think about it. She was his and only his.

He bent and whispered against her soft skin. "I never want you to know another day without my love, Angel girl."

CHAPTER 41

"$\mathcal{D}$etective Sanchez is here to see you. Do you feel up to talking to him?"

Angelina lay quietly on the bed, absorbing the dark around her. Her shoulder and ribs throbbed, but she'd refused any more pain medication, even though the nurse had assured her that it wouldn't harm her pregnancy. Angelina didn't want to take any chances, though.

She glanced up at Micah, who stood over her bed, concern etched deeply in the lines of his face.

"I'll speak to him," she said softly, knowing she could no longer delay the inevitable.

For two days she'd refused any visitors and stayed in her room with only Micah for company, but even so, she'd been moodily quiet and reserved, only answering direct questions from Micah and refusing to discuss what had happened.

Micah likely thought she was still processing the fright she'd received, but in fact she was collecting herself. Preparing herself for the future she had decided on. And dreading the moment when she had to tell Micah that Chad had been responsible for David and Hannah's deaths.

Micah watched her uncertainly, as if he wasn't sure what to say to her or how to say it. He hesitated a moment then reached for her hand and squeezed it. He opened his mouth as if to speak but then shut it again. Then he turned and went back to the door.

A few moments later he returned with Detective Sanchez.

"Turn the light on," she told Micah in a quiet voice. There was no reason to conduct the interview in the dark.

She turned her face away and into her pillow when the room exploded with light. It took several long moments before she could focus on the detective without squinting.

"Thank you for seeing me, Miss Moyano," Sanchez began formally.

"Please, call me Angelina."

He nodded. "Angelina. I'm hoping you can answer some questions for me. We have Devereaux in custody, but he's not saying anything. He lawyered up as soon as he hit the door, and he hasn't opened his mouth since."

Angelina sighed. "I'll answer your questions to the best of my ability."

For an hour she recounted the exact sequence of events, from the time Chad took her from The House to the moment the helicopter took her to the hospital. She left nothing out, not even the part when she'd stood over him with the gun wanting so desperately to shoot him.

Micah and Sanchez exchanged glances at the sudden tension in her voice. She went completely stiff, and she struggled even now with the surge of anger that assaulted her.

"Why did you want to kill him?" Sanchez asked gently. "Is there something else?"

"Did he hurt you?" Micah interjected fiercely. "More than what you've told us?"

Angelina looked away. "No. I told you everything he did."

"Angelina look at me," Micah said. "What aren't you telling us?"

She raised her gaze to meet Sanchez's, and she took a deep breath. Tears filled her eyes. The detective leaned forward and touched her hand.

"He killed David and Hannah."

Micah went completely silent and Sanchez's brow wrinkled in confusion.

"What did you say?" Micah asked in a dangerously quiet voice.

Sanchez looked at Micah and shook his head sharply. Then the detective turned back to Angelina and his expression softened.

"Now tell me what you mean. Who are David and Hannah?"

She avoided Micah's gaze and focused on the detective. "David was my brother and Micah's best friend. Hannah was Micah's wife. They were killed in a car accident three years ago. Or what we thought was an accident."

"And what makes you say that Chad killed them?"

"He confessed. It was why I flew into such a rage and attacked him in the house. It was how I got away from him."

An inarticulate sound of rage came from Micah's direction, and Sanchez ignored him. He stared hard at Angelina. "Did he tell you why? Did he give you details?"

Angelina closed her eyes as hot tears slipped down her cheeks. "He killed David because of me. I don't think he cared anything about Hannah. He was obsessed with me even then. I never knew. David never told me Chad had approached him about me. Chad spoke to him when I was sixteen years old, and apparently David hit the roof. Told Chad if he ever caught him near me he'd kill him. Chad waited and approached David again when I was twenty. Apparently David must have told him to buzz off again, and it sent Chad over the edge. He said he caused the accident that killed David and Hannah. All because he saw David as a barrier to him getting to me."

Micah got up so abruptly he knocked over the chair. Without a single word, he left the room, letting the door swing open behind him.

Angelina turned on her side, curling into as tight a ball as she could. She'd seen the anger and the torment in Micah's eyes. The pain and betrayal. He'd lost everything because of her. Because of a man's obsession with her.

Sanchez touched her arm in a gesture of comfort, but she flinched away.

"Please," she begged. "I've told you everything. Just go away. I want to be alone."

More tears spilled down her cheeks and she buried her face in the pillow. Her shoulders shook, causing excruciating pain to the bullet wound. Sharp pain stabbed at her ribs, but she ignored the physical discomfort.

She honestly didn't know if Sanchez left or not. She ignored everything but the unrelenting pain in her chest.

I'm so sorry, David.

God, it wasn't fair. One man had cost her everything. Worse, Micah, completely innocent in the whole thing, had lost the two people he loved most. David and Hannah had lost their lives and their future together.

She hunched her body in misery, ignoring the pain slicing through her shoulder and ribs.

"Hey," Connor said softly next to her ear. "Sweetie, what's wrong?"

She turned and all but flung herself into his arms. He caught her awkwardly and was forced to sit on the bed next to her so he could ease her back down on the pillows.

"You're going to hurt yourself. You should be more careful," he admonished even as he stroked her hair in a soothing motion. "Where's Micah? Sanchez came out and said you were upset as hell."

"He walked out," she said, her voice muffled by Connor's shirt.

"Any particular reason why?" Connor asked mildly.

"Oh, Connor, if only I didn't have to tell him. I didn't want to hurt him, but he had to find out."

"You're not making a lick of sense, sweetie, but I'll sit here and listen if you want to talk."

Despite her vow not to ask for any more pain medication, after two days of battling pain, she was at the end of her limit.

"I hurt," she croaked out. "Can you call for pain medication? I'll tell you all about it and then maybe I can forget for just a little while."

Micah walked blindly through the hospital corridors, no clear direction in mind. He needed air. He needed to be alone before he completely lost his composure.

Tears blinded him, and he steeled his jaw, furious at his display of emotion.

Where the fuck were the exits?

He rounded the corner and encountered another maze of hallways. He strode to the far end, only to dead-end at the chapel.

At least it would be quiet and maybe he'd be alone.

He entered the small area of respite and slid into the last pew in a row of four. It was blanketed in quiet, and more importantly, he was the only occupant.

Long-held tears slid down his cheeks. He braced himself on the back of the pew in front of him and leaned forward, burying his face in his arms.

For too long he'd held back any emotion when it came to Hannah. He'd always assumed he was the unlucky victim of a random tragedy. He saw them all the time when he was a cop. Too many times he'd been the one to tell a husband or a wife, a mother or a father, that a loved one was gone. And then it had been him.

Never had he imagined that an act of rage had been responsible for taking away the people he loved. And God, Hannah, completely innocent. A victim. She'd been in the wrong place at the wrong time. If she hadn't been with David that day, she'd still be alive.

Fury blew through his consciousness, a bleak, destructive storm. That bastard had taken David and Hannah from him, and he'd damned near taken Angelina.

So many lives devastated because of Chad's sick fixation on Angelina. Angelina, who had just been a teenager, innocent. There was no way she should have attracted the attentions of a man old enough to know better. A man who'd sworn to uphold the law and protect the innocent.

Micah raised his head and stared down at the simple cross that hung high on the far wall, overlooking the pews. It was a symbolic gesture, but it left Micah cold.

"Why?" he asked in a cracked voice.

The cross blurred in his vision, and he closed his eyes in an effort to hold back the tears. His chest was heavy and ached so damn much that breathing was hard.

Promise me, man. If anything ever happens to me, promise me you'll take care of Angelina. She's something special, Micah. Heart way too big for her own good. I worry because she doesn't see everyone for who they are. She's too busy looking for the good. I've tried to get her to adopt some cynicism, but the truth of the matter is, she wouldn't be the same girl if she did.

A long-ago conversation, one he hadn't remembered until now, floated through his mind with such clarity that it was like David was sitting next to him in the pew.

He hadn't given Angelina any thought after the funerals. He'd made a cursory effort to support Angelina in her grief, but he'd been too wrapped up in his own to do her any justice. He'd left Miami within the month, just as soon as David's affairs had been settled and Angelina was provided for. Financially. He damn sure hadn't stuck around to make sure she had the emotional support she needed.

He should have been there when she started getting the creepy notes. He should have been heading the investigation. He should have been protecting her. He never should have left her to fend for herself.

I failed her, man. I'm so sorry. I'm so damn sorry.

He closed his eyes again.

I'm sorry, Hannah. I loved you so much. We were happy. I wanted forever. I should have seen it. I should have protected you better.

An image of Hannah's smiling face wavered in his memory. Laughing, so happy. So gentle and loving. Yes, he'd loved her with everything he had. Angelina deserved that same love, that same depth.

Hannah was gone. It hurt to say it. It hurt to think about it. Maybe the hurt would never fully go away, but Angelina understood. She'd always understood.

Angelina was here. She loved him. He loved her. He wanted a life. With her. He wanted a family, one they'd build together. Love, laughter, children's smiles, Angelina's love. He wanted that.

He bowed his head and whispered a simple prayer, one he hadn't said since he was a boy struggling to survive in a house where there was no love or understanding.

He asked for forgiveness. He asked for peace for Hannah and David. He asked for peace for himself and Angelina. And he asked for one more chance to make things right.

CHAPTER 42

*A*ngelina woke to a darkened room once more. Connor was gone and Micah was slumped in a chair beside her bed. He was asleep and he looked uncomfortable as hell.

The remnants of the medication still lurked in her system, and she enjoyed the sweet respite from the pain. She needed strength for the things she needed to say.

"Micah," she said in a soft voice.

He roused immediately and sat forward.

"Are you all right? Need more pain medication? I wish you hadn't waited so long to ask for it this last time. If you need it, you should take it."

"I'm okay. I need to talk to you. Turn the light on please."

He got up and went to flip the switch on the wall. They both winced at the sudden burst of light. He looked haggard, his face raw and his eyes haunted.

When he started to sit down on the bed next to her, she shook her head and warned him off with her hand.

"Please. I have a lot to say, and I can't do it if you're touching me."

His brows furrowed in confusion, but he took his seat again in the chair next to the bed.

"I need you to listen to everything I have to say and not interrupt. This is hard enough and I need to just get it out."

"All right," he said quietly.

"After I get out of the hospital I'm going to move back to Miami. When I'm able. Connor said I could stay in my apartment as long as I needed to."

Micah surged forward, his face stormy.

Before he could respond, she shook her head. "You promised."

"Goddamn it, Angel."

He was furious, but she was determined to have her say.

"I've done a lot of thinking, Micah. A whole lot of soul searching, and what I've found makes me ashamed."

Micah dragged a hand through his hair and pulled it tight at the base of his skull. He looked like he was going to explode, but he remained silent. It was probably killing him.

"I was so determined to show you how perfect we could be together. I loved you. I thought that was enough. I guess being naïve, I thought I could make you love me. Chad was convinced he and I belonged together. He was obsessed, but in his mind he was only doing what he thought was right. He thought if he could just make me see how much he loved me that somehow I could love him back."

Micah made a strangled sound. His eyes glittered with rage, and she realized he knew where she was going with this. She held up her hand, determined to ward off the meltdown.

"I was as wrong as Chad was," she said quietly. "I had no right to intervene in your life. I had no right to intrude in your private grief when you went to Mama Rose's. I certainly had no right to barge into your life here and insert myself into your group of friends and remind you of everything you'd tried to forget. I judged you, I was angry at you for wanting to forget, when it was your right to do so."

She took a deep breath and plunged ahead.

"When it was just me I had to think about, I was okay with the possibility of rejection. I was okay with putting my life on hold and taking risks. Young and in love and all that. Whole life ahead of me. Nothing to lose. That's all changed now. I have a baby to think of. I can no longer make decisions based on what affects *me*. I have to make them with my child in mind. She deserves that much.

"So I'm going back to Miami. I have a house there. I can use my degree and teach. I have to do this for our child, Micah. You can't give me or her what we need the most, and I'm not willing to settle for less. Not anymore."

"Are you finished yet?" Micah demanded.

His entire body vibrated with anger. She wasn't up to a lengthy diatribe. He'd bitch, yell, make ludicrous demands. Especially now that she was pregnant. Probably *only* because she was pregnant. He'd certainly never made it a secret that it was over with once her stalker had been captured.

"It's over, Micah," she said evenly. "You told me to expect sex and nothing more. This was a temporary situation. I told you I'd take whatever you could give, but I've changed my mind. That's my prerogative just like it was yours to make conditions. I'll never try to keep you from your child, but you need to understand that I'm no longer willing to be the one making concessions."

As she said the last, her finger found the nurse call button. It was a cowardly thing to do, but she was hanging on by the thinnest thread. Pain, physical and mental, coursed through her chest and knotted in her throat.

"If you have any affection for me at all, Micah, please don't make this difficult. I'm tired. I hurt. I'd like you to leave."

Micah stared at her, his lips pressed together so tightly they were thin, white lines. The door opened, and the nurse bustled in, an inquiring look on her face.

"Are you ready for more pain medication? I'm glad you changed your mind. Pain isn't good for you or the baby."

Without a word, Micah got up, and as he'd done before, he left the room without looking back.

Tears brimmed in Angelina's eyes as she watched the door swing closed.

Mistaking her upset for discomfort, the nurse placed her cool hand on Angelina's forehead. She wiped her hand into Angelina's hair in a gesture of comfort as she readied the syringe to inject medication into the IV.

"You'll feel better in just a few minutes," the nurse soothed.

She wouldn't feel better, but she'd made the right decision.

Micah stood outside Angelina's hospital room waiting for the nurse to wheel her out into the hall. He'd respected Angelina's wishes. He hadn't been back to her room, and he'd damn well given her plenty of time to think.

Well, he was done with all that now. Oh, he understood why she'd said all she did. It was nothing less than he deserved, and in an absurd way, he was proud of her for making a stand for their child. She'd make one hell of a mother. But hell would freeze over before he'd leave her to be a single mother and care for their child alone. And duty had nothing to do with it.

He paced back and forth until finally the door opened and the nurse pushed Angelina out into the hall. She visibly flinched when she saw him, but she didn't say anything. She just waited, her dark eyes looking so soulful that his chest tightened.

"Thank you," Micah said as he took the handles of the wheel-chair. "I'll take it from here."

The nurse handed him Angelina's discharge papers and then smiled cheerfully at Angelina as Micah rolled her away.

He took her down in the elevator and out to the front, where his truck waited. She didn't say anything, but then neither did he.

He helped her into the passenger seat, and after making sure she was settled and buckled in, he walked around to the driver's side and slid in.

She kept glancing sideways at him. He hadn't told her he was coming to get her from the hospital. If he had, she probably wouldn't have been there when he arrived.

"Where are we going?" she asked in a nervous voice.

"Your apartment," he said in an effort to dispel her trepidation.

She relaxed against the seat and turned to stare out the window. Did she honestly think he was going to deposit her at her apartment and walk away while she prepared to walk out of his life?

Of course he hadn't given her any reason to think differently. That would change quickly enough.

He pulled into the apartment parking lot in front of her building and turned off the truck.

"Stay there. You need to take it easy," he said as he opened his door.

It was a gorgeous fall day. Bright blue skies and no hazy smog hanging over the city. Beautiful day, and his entire life was falling apart. It seemed apropos.

He walked around and opened the door for Angelina. Hugging

her arm to her injured shoulder, she wiggled across the seat. He reached up and carefully eased her into his arms so he wouldn't jar her ribs.

"I can walk," she said in a stuttering breath.

Her body trembled against his, and as much as he wanted to keep her in his arms, he didn't want to push too soon. Not yet.

He set her down and waited for her to get her feet underneath her. He kept his hand at her elbow to steady her, and they walked toward her door.

"Let me have the keys," he said.

She handed them to him, and for a moment, his hand curled around hers. She looked tired. Fragile. Lost. He wanted to pull her into his arms and go to bed for a week. Just him and her. No outside world. No worry. No pain. No past.

He pulled away and unlocked her door, shoving it open. She walked in ahead of him and when they stepped into the living room, it erupted in chaos.

"Surprise!"

The voices echoed across the room as people jumped up. Okay, the girls jumped up. The guys sort of stood there looking faintly amused as Julie, Serena and Faith ran over to greet Angelina.

Angelina took a step back, her expression horrified. Tears welled in her eyes and her face crumpled. With a choked sound, she turned and ran into the bedroom, shutting the door behind her.

The girls stood looking mystified at Angelina's abrupt departure.

"I told you this wasn't a good idea," Connor muttered as he walked up beside Faith. "She's just getting out of the hospital after a hellish experience. The last thing she's up for is a damn welcome home party."

Micah sighed as he scanned the room. "Look, guys. I really

appreciate this. More than you know. I love all of you. I know I can be a dick, and I know I've kept some pretty heavy-duty shit from you. I don't deserve your friendship, but I'm damn grateful for it. But I'd really, really appreciate it if y'all could give me some time here. I'm fighting for my life. For a woman who means everything to me."

"I'm sorry, Micah," Faith said in a stricken voice. "I thought . . . I don't know what I thought."

She looked so distressed that Micah immediately pulled her into a hug and kissed her forehead.

"Don't be sorry, doll. You have a heart of gold, and the thing is, Angelina needs your kind of friendship. She's not upset at you. She's upset with me and rightfully so. She thinks she's moving back to Miami."

"And you're going to let her?" Julie challenged, her lips turned down into a ferocious frown.

"No, I'm not," he said quietly.

"Good," Serena said. "She loves you, you know."

"I know. I love her too. I just have to convince her of that fact."

"Okay, so let's get out of here and leave them to it," Connor said impatiently.

Nathan pushed off the wall and walked up beside Julie. "Connor has an excellent idea. Why don't you take me home and convince me you can't live without me."

Julie snorted. "Like I want you to have the big head?"

They all filed past Micah, each of the girls stopping to give him a fierce hug. He didn't deserve their loyalty, but it felt damn good to have it. It made him feel good that part of it extended to Angelina and had nothing to do with him. She'd won them over, no thanks to any effort on his part to include her in his life.

After seeing them out, he shut the door and turned in the direction of the bedroom Angelina had disappeared into.

If there was ever a time he needed wisdom, needed just the right words to say, it was now. This was . . . this was everything. His future, his happiness, his chance to have it all again. He couldn't afford to fuck it up.

He paused outside her door, closed his eyes and took a deep breath. Then he slowly pushed it open and stepped inside.

She was sitting on the bed, her head down, and she was crying.

Ah hell. It took everything he had not to go over and scoop her up in his arms, but he was determined to have this conversation with her without resorting to physical manipulation. Their chemistry was off the charts, and that wasn't what he wanted deciding their future. He wanted her heart, not just her body.

"Angel baby," he said softly.

She looked up and quickly rubbed her eyes with the back of her hand.

"I'm sorry. I was so rude."

He shook his head as he crossed the room to sit on the end of the bed. There was a respectable distance between them, and he didn't want to be any farther away from her than was necessary.

"No, you weren't rude. You just came home from the hospital. You're entitled to be freaked out by a half dozen people waiting for you in your apartment."

"It's not that," she said quietly. "I'm going to miss them. I really like them."

"And me, Angel? Will you miss me if you go back to Miami?"

She looked away.

"Look at me please," he said. "It's time I got a chance to talk. I listened to what you had to say. I gave you space. Now it's time for you to listen to me."

She raised her gaze to him, her lips trembling. "Okay."

Suddenly nervous, he stood and began to pace back and forth in front of her.

"I loved Hannah. You know that. David and I both loved her. I thought I'd spend the rest of my life with her. That was always my plan.

"When I lost her, a part of me shut down. All I could think about was getting away from a place where I saw her at every turn. I left Miami because I wanted to start a new life in a place where no one knew me and I wasn't faced with unhappy memories on a daily basis."

"I understand," she said in a quiet voice.

"I didn't think about you, Angel. I don't say that to hurt you. To me you were still the sixteen-year-old sister of my best friend. To think about you meant I had to think about David and I wanted my past behind me.

"And then you walked back into my life, only you weren't a teenager. You weren't a schoolgirl, nor were you my best friend's little sister. You were a gorgeous woman with a sexuality to match my own. But you were also the embodiment of everything I wanted to forget.

"I looked at you and I ached. I wanted you, but I also wanted you to go away. I didn't want to let you into my life because I didn't want to love again. I didn't want to risk losing someone I cared about. It was a lot easier to approach sex in a casual, fun way. No strings. No love. No relationships. I wasn't celibate in the three years since Hannah's death. Far from it. But I never gave away any part of myself in the process. Until you."

A tear slipped down her cheek as she stared up at him.

"You were right, Angel. I didn't want to want you. God, I fought it. I told myself all kinds of lies when it came to you. I told myself it was just sex. I told myself I could let you go when it was all said and done. I resented you for inserting yourself so fully into my life, and then one day I realized I couldn't imagine my life without you.

"And then when Chad took you, I was so damn scared. I was scared I'd lose you. I was scared he'd hurt you. I was scared I'd never get to tell you how much I goddamn love you. I was scared I'd never get to tell you how sorry I am for leaving you alone after David died and how sorry I am for pushing you away when all you did was love me."

No longer able to keep his distance from her, he sat on the bed and turned so he faced her. His hands covered hers and he pulled them to his chest.

"I don't want to live without you, Angel. I want it all. I want you. I want our baby. I want us to be a family. I want you to love me as much as I love you, and I want to spend the rest of my life proving that love to you."

A sob escaped and more tears trickled down her cheeks. She made no move to wipe them away. She shook almost violently, and he couldn't tell if it was from upset or a true chill, but he pulled her into his arms anyway.

His shoulders shook as he gripped her almost desperately against his heart. His breaths came out in a short staccato that had him feeling light-headed.

He kissed her hair over and over, and he prayed. Prayed she'd give him another chance.

Knowing he had more he needed to say, he carefully pulled her away, and his own eyes stung as he saw how ravaged her face was.

"I know I have a lot to prove to you, Angel. I know you're probably thinking a lot of crazy things right now. Like whether I'm saying all this because I feel guilty about Chad. Or whether I'm only saying it because of the baby. I can't convince you of my sincerity in an hour or even a day. What I want, what I need, is for you to give us a chance. Stay with me here in Houston. Let's take it one day at a time. I want it all, baby. I want you to marry me. I want us to have lots of babies. But I won't pressure you. I want you to be with me because you absolutely *know* that I love you more than life. When you know that, that's when I want you to commit to being with me forever. But until then, I just want a chance. I want you to stay with me so I can take care of you and our baby. And one day I want you to marry me. When you're ready and when you trust me fully."

"Oh, Micah," she said in a tear-choked voice. "I love you so much. Are you sure you're ready for this? Are you sure you want me to stay here?"

"I want it more than I want to live. Give us that chance, Angel. Just say yes you'll stay. We can work everything else out in time."

She went into his arms, wrapping herself so sweetly around his body that he closed his eyes at the exquisite joy of just holding her again.

"I love you. I want this to work. I want us to work, but I want you to be sure, Micah."

"I want us both to be sure," he said solemnly as he pulled her away to stare down into her eyes. "I'm not going to change my mind, and in time you'll know that, I promise. Until then, just promise me you'll keep loving me and take it one day at a time."

She smiled, her eyes all watery and red, her nose swollen and her lips ravaged from her nervous chewing on them, and she'd never looked so beautiful to him than right now.

"Okay," she whispered. "I'll stay." She looked down and smoothed a hand over her stomach. "We'll stay."

He closed his eyes, and for a moment he simply couldn't breathe around the knot of emotion welling in his throat. He tried to speak, tried to tell her how damn much he loved her, but nothing would come out. God, he loved her.

He put his hand over hers at her stomach. "Are you happy about the baby, Angel?"

She smiled again. "I love her already. She'll be just like me and drive her daddy crazy."

"God help me." Then he smiled, and it felt so goddamn good he wanted to cry like a damn girl. "You're so sure it's a daughter."

She shrugged. "Just a feeling. It could be a boy who'll be death on women just like his daddy."

"I just want to be death on one woman," he said softly. "I plan to love his or her mama so well that she never doubts even for a minute how much she means to him."

"Can we go to bed now?" she asked as she leaned back into his arms. "Could you just hold me for a while?"

He brushed his lips over her temple in a tender gesture and stroked his fingers through her hair.

"I never intend to let you go, Angel girl."